All About Love

All About Love

Stephanie Laurens

W F HOWES LTD

This large print edition published in 2010 by
W F Howes Ltd
Unit 4, Rearsby Business Park, Gaddesby Lane,
Rearsby, Leicester LE7 4YH

1 3 5 7 9 10 8 6 4 2

First published in the United Kingdom in 2007
by Piatkus Books

A CIP catalogue record for this book is available
from the British Library

ISBN 978-1-40743-526-8

Typeset by Palimpsest Book Production Limited,
Falkirk, Stirlingshire
Printed and bound in Great Britain
by MPG Books Ltd, Bodmin, Cornwall

FSC
Mixed Sources
Product group from well-managed
forests, controlled sources and
recycled wood or fiber
SA-COC-1565
www.fsc.org
© 1996 Forest Stewardship Council

The Bar Cynster Family Tree

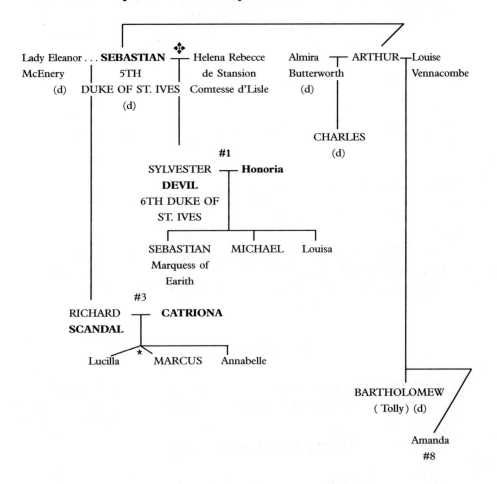

Lady Eleanor . . . **SEBASTIAN** ⚜ Helena Rebecce   Almira ┬ ARTHUR ┬ Louise
McEnery │ 5TH   de Stansion   Butterworth │   Vennacombe
(d)   DUKE OF ST. IVES   Comtesse d'Lisle (d)
            (d)

                                          CHARLES
                        #1   (d)
               SYLVESTER ── **Honoria**
                DEVIL
               6TH DUKE OF
                ST. IVES

        SEBASTIAN   MICHAEL   Louisa
        Marquess of
          Earith

        #3
RICHARD ── **CATRIONA**
SCANDAL

    Lucilla ★ MARCUS Annabelle

                              BARTHOLOMEW
                               (Tolly) (d)

                                    Amanda
                                     #8

THE CYNSTER NOVELS

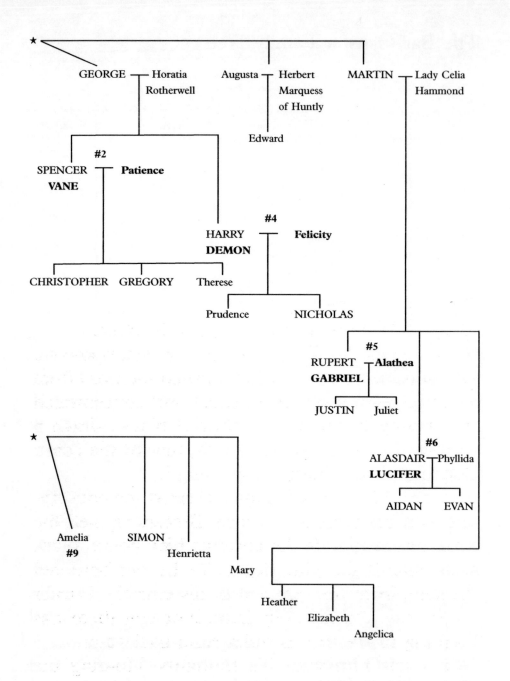

MALE CYNSTERS in capitals ★denotes twins

CHAPTER 1

June 1820
Devon

Abstinence.

It didn't even *sound* comfortable.

Alasdair Reginald Cynster, widely known, with good reason, as Lucifer, pushed the word from his mind with a disgusted snort and concentrated on turning his pair of highbred blacks down a narrow lane. The lane led south, toward the coast; Colyton, his destination, lay along it.

Around him, early summer clasped the countryside in a benevolent embrace. Breezes rippled the corn; swallows rode the currents high above, black darts against the blue sky. Thick hedges bordered the lane; from the box seat of his curricle, Lucifer could only just see over them. Not that there was anything to see in this quiet rural backwater.

That left him with his thoughts. Holding the blacks to a slow but steady pace along the winding lane, he considered the unwelcome proposition of having to survive without the type of feminine company to which he was accustomed. It wasn't a pleasant prospect, but he'd rather suffer that torture than risk succumbing to the Cynster curse.

It wasn't a curse to be trifled with – it had already claimed five of his nearest male relatives, all the other members of the notorious group that had, for so many years, lorded it over the ton. The Bar Cynster had cut swaths through the ranks of London's ladies, leaving them languishing, exhausted in their wake. They'd been daring, devilish, invincible – until, one by one, the curse had caught them. Now he was the last one free – unshackled, unwed, and unrepentant. He had nothing against marriage per se, but the unfortunate fact – the crux of the curse – was that Cynsters did not simply marry. They married ladies they loved.

The very concept made him shudder. Its implied vulnerability was something he would never willingly accept.

Yesterday, his brother, Gabriel, had done just that.

And that was one of the two principal reasons he was here, going to ground in deepest Devon.

He and Gabriel had been close all their lives; only eleven months separated them. Other than Gabriel, the one person he knew better than anyone in the world was their childhood playmate Alathea Morwellan. Now Alathea Cynster. Gabriel had married her yesterday, and in so doing had opened Lucifer's eyes to how potent the curse was, how irresistible it could be. Love had bloomed in the most unlikely ground. The curse had struck boldly, ruthlessly, powerfully, and had conquered against all odds.

He sincerely wished Gabriel and Alathea joy, but he had no intention of following their lead.

Not now. Very possibly not ever.

What need had he of marriage? What would he gain that he didn't already have? Women – ladies – were all very well; he enjoyed dallying with them, enjoyed the subtleties of conquering the more resistant, encouraging them into his bed. He enjoyed teaching them all he knew of shared pleasure. That, however, was the extent of his interest. He was involved in other spheres, and he liked his freedom, liked being answerable to no one. He preferred his life as it was and had no wish to change it.

He was determined to avoid the curse – he could manage very well without love.

So he'd slipped away from Gabriel and Alathea's wedding breakfast and left London. With Gabriel married, he'd succeeded to the title of principal matrimonial target for the ladies of the ton; consequently, he'd dismissed all invitations to the summer's country house parties. He'd driven to Quiverstone Manor, his parents' estate in Somerset. Leaving his groom, Dodswell, a local, there to visit with his sister, he'd left Quiverstone early this morning and headed south through the countryside.

On his left, three cottages came into view, huddled around a junction with an even narrower lane that ambled down beside a ridge. Slowing, he passed the cottages and rounded the ridge – the village of Colyton opened out before him. Reining in, he looked about.

And inwardly grimaced. He'd been right. From the looks of Colyton, his chances of finding any local lady with whom to dally – a married one who met his exacting standards and with whom he could ease the persistent itch all Cynsters were prey to – were nil.

Abstinence it would be.

The village, neat and tidy in the bright sunshine, looked like an artist's vision of the rustic ideal, steeped in peace and harmony. Ahead to the right, the common sloped upward; a church stood on the crest, a solid Norman structure flanked by a well-tended graveyard. Beyond the graveyard, another lane ran down, presumably joining the main lane farther on. The main lane itself curved to the left, bordered by a line of cottages facing the common; the sign of an inn jutted over the lane just before it swung out of sight. Nearer to hand was a duck pond on the common; the blacks stamped and shook their heads at the quacking.

Quieting them, Lucifer looked to the left, to the first house of the village standing back in its gardens. A name was carved on the portico. He squinted. *Colyton Manor*. His destination.

The Manor was a handsome house of pale sandstone, two stories and attics in the Georgian style with rows of long pedimented windows flanking the portico and front door. The house faced the lane, set back behind a waist-high stone wall and a large garden filled with flowering plants and roses. A circular fountain stood at the garden's center, interrupting the path joining the front door and a gate to the lane. Beyond the garden, a stand of trees screened the Manor from the village beyond.

A gravel drive skirted the nearer side of the house, eventually leading to a stable set back against more trees. The drive was separated from a shrubbery by an expanse of lawn punctuated here and there by ancient shade trees. Somewhat overgrown, the shrubbery extended almost to where the curricle stood; a glimpse of water beyond suggested an ornamental lake.

Colyton Manor looked what it was, a prosperous gentleman's residence. It was the home of Horatio Welham – the reason Lucifer had chosen Colyton as his temporary bolt-hole.

Horatio's letter had reached him three days ago. An old friend and his mentor in all matters pertaining to collecting, Horatio had invited him to visit at Colyton at his earliest convenience. With the grande dames turning their sights on him, convenient had been immediately – he'd grasped the excuse to disappear from the social whirl.

At one time he had haunted Horatio's house in the Lake District, but although he and Horatio had remained as close as ever, over the three years since Horatio had moved to Devon, they'd met only at collectors' gatherings around the country and in London; this was his first visit to Colyton.

The blacks shook their heads; their harness clinked. Straightening, gathering the reins, Lucifer was conscious of a welling impatience – to see Horatio again, to clasp his hand, to spend time in his erudite company. Coloring that anticipation was Horatio's reason for asking him to visit – a request for his opinion on an item that, in Horatio's words, might tempt even him to extend his collection beyond his preferred categories of silver and jewelry. He'd spent the drive from Somerset speculating on what the item was, but had reached no conclusion.

He'd learn soon enough. Clicking the reins, he set the blacks in motion. Turning smartly in between the tall gateposts, he drew the curricle up by the side of the house with the usual crunching and stamping of hooves.

No one came running.

He listened – and heard nothing but the sounds of birds and insects.

Then he remembered it was Sunday; Horatio and all his household would be at church. Glancing up the common, he verified that the church door stood ajar. He looked at the Manor's front door – it, too, stood partially open. Someone, it appeared, was home.

Tying off the reins, he jumped down and strode along the gravel path to the portico. Ablaze with summer blooms, the garden caught and held his gaze. The sight teased some long-buried memory.

Pausing before the portico, he struggled to pin it down.

This was Martha's garden.

Martha was Horatio's late wife; she'd been the anchor around which the Lake District household had revolved. Martha had loved gardening, striving through all weathers to create glorious displays – just like this. Lucifer studied the plantings. The layout was similar to the garden in the Lake District. But Martha had been dead for three years.

Outside of his mother and aunts, Lucifer had felt closer to Martha than any other older woman – she'd occupied a special place in his life. He'd often listened to her lectures, whereas to his mother he'd been deaf. Martha had not been related – it had always been easier to hear the truth from her lips. It was Martha's death that had lessened his enthusiasm for visiting Horatio at home. Too many memories; too acute a sense of shared loss.

Seeing Martha's garden here felt odd, like a hand on his sleeve when there was no one there. He frowned – he could almost hear Martha whispering in her soft, gentle voice.

Abruptly turning, he entered the portico. The front door was half open; he pushed it wide. The hall was empty.

'Hello! Is anyone about?'

No response. All he could hear was the summer buzz outside. He stepped over the threshold and paused. The house was cool, quiet, still . . . waiting. Frowning more definitely, he strode forward, bootheels clacking on black-and-white tiles. He headed for the first door on the right. It stood open, pushed wide.

He smelled blood before he reached the door. After Waterloo, it was one scent he'd never mistake. The hairs at his nape lifted; he slowed.

At his back, the sun glowed bright and warm – the cold quiet of the house intensified. It drew him on.

He halted in the doorway, his gaze drawn down to the body sprawled a few feet inside the room.

His skin turned cold. After an instant's hiatus, he forced his gaze to travel the old, lined face, the straggly white hair covered by a tasseled cap. In a long white nightshirt with a knitted shawl wound around heavy shoulders, twisted onto his back with one arm outflung, bare feet poking out toward the door, the dead man looked as if he might be asleep, here in his drawing room surrounded by his antique tomes.

But he wasn't asleep – he hadn't even collapsed. Blood still seeped from a small cut on his left side, directly beneath his heart.

Lucifer dragged in a breath. '*Horatio!*'

On his knees, he searched for a pulse at wrist and throat, and found none. Hand on Horatio's chest, he felt a lingering warmth; slight color still graced the old man's cheeks. Mind reeling, Lucifer sat back on his heels.

Horatio had been murdered – minutes ago.

He felt numb, detached; some part of his brain continued cataloguing facts, like the experienced cavalry officer he'd once been.

The single killing stroke had been an upward thrust into the heart – like a bayonet wound. Not much blood, just a little . . . oddly little. Frowning, he checked. There was more blood beneath the body. Horatio had been turned onto his back later – originally he'd fallen facedown. Catching a glimpse of gilt under the shawl, Lucifer searched with fingers that shook – and drew out a long, thin letter knife.

His fingers curled around the ornate hilt. He scanned the immediate area but could see no sign of any struggle. The rug wasn't rumpled; the table between the body and the rug appeared correctly aligned in its normal place.

The numbness was wearing off. Emotions welled; Lucifer's senses flickered, then flared to life.

He was cursing beneath his breath; he felt like he'd been kicked in the gut. After the serenity outside, finding Horatio like this seemed obscene – a nightmare he knew there'd be no waking from. Deadening loss engulfed him; his earlier anticipation lay like bitter ashes on his tongue. Pressing his lips tight, he drew in a deep breath—

He wasn't alone.

In the instant he sensed it, he heard a sound. Then came a clunk and a scuffle behind him.

He sprang to his feet, gripping the letter knife—

A heavy weight crashed down on his skull.

It hurt like hell.

He lay slumped on the floor. He must have gone down like a sack of bricks, but he couldn't remember the impact. He had no idea whether he'd lost consciousness and only just regained it, or whether he'd only just reached the floor. Exerting every last ounce of his will, he cracked open his lids. Horatio's face swam into – and out of – focus. Closing his eyes, he bit back a groan. With luck, the murderer would think he was insensate. He almost was. The black tide of unconsciousness surged and dragged, trying to suck him under. Grimly, he resisted its pull.

The letter knife was still in his fist, but his right arm was trapped beneath his body. He couldn't move. His body felt like a lead weight he was trapped within; he couldn't defend himself. He should have checked the room first, but the sight of Horatio, lying there still bleeding . . . *damn*!

He waited, oddly detached, wondering if the murderer would stop to finish him off or just flee. He hadn't heard anyone leave, but he wasn't sure he could hear at all.

How long had he been lying there?

From behind the door, Phyllida Tallent stared wide-eyed at the gentleman now stretched lifeless beside Horatio Welham's body. A squeak of dismay escaped her – the ridiculous sound prodded her into action. Dragging in a breath, she stepped forward, bent, and wrapped both hands around the pole of the halberd now lying across the fallen man.

Bracing, she counted to three, then hauled. The heavy head of the halberd rose. She staggered, boots shuffling as she fought to swing the unwieldy weapon aside.

She hadn't meant it to fall.

Having only just walked in and discovered Horatio's body, she hadn't been thinking at all clearly when the stranger's footsteps had sounded on the gravel outside. She'd panicked, thinking him the murderer returning to remove the body. With all the village in church, she couldn't imagine who else it could have been.

He'd called a 'Hello,' but so might a murderer checking to see if anyone else had come upon the scene. She'd frantically searched for a hiding place, but the long drawing room was lined with bookcases – the only gap that would have hidden her from the door had been too far away for her to reach in time. Desperate, she'd secreted herself in the only available spot – in the shadows behind the open door, between the frame and the last bookshelf, squeezing in alongside the halberd.

The hiding place had served, but once she'd realized from his actions and his muttered expletives that this man was no murderer, and after she'd debated the wisdom of showing herself – the daughter of the local magistrate and quite old enough to know better than to slip into other

11

peoples' houses dressed in breeches to search for still other peoples' misplaced personal belongings – once she'd got past all that and realized that this was murder and she'd gone to step forward to make herself known, her shoulder had nudged the halberd.

Its descent had been inexorable.

She'd grabbed it and fought vainly to halt it or deflect it; in the end, all she'd been able to do was twist it enough so that the heavy blade had not struck the man's head. If it had, he'd have died. As it was, the hemisphere at the side of the iron axe-head had connected with a sickening thud.

With the halberd finally angled to the side, she lowered it to the floor. Only then did she realize she'd been repeating a breathless litany: *Oh, God! Oh, God! Oh, God!*

Wiping her palms on her breeches, sick to her stomach, she looked at her innocent victim. The sound of the halberd connecting with his skull echoed in her ears. It hadn't helped that he'd chosen that precise moment to leap to his feet. He'd come up propelled like a spring, only to meet the halberd going down.

He'd hit the floor with a sickening thud, too. He hadn't moved since.

Steeling herself, she stepped over the pole. 'Oh, God – *please* don't let me have killed him!' Horatio had been murdered, and now she'd murdered a stranger. What was her world coming to?

Panic gnawing at her nerves, she sank to her

knees; the gentleman lay slumped forward, facing Horatio . . .

Lucifer sensed a presence approaching. He couldn't hear, he couldn't see, but he knew when they knelt at his back. The murderer. He had to assume that. If only he could gather enough strength, even to lift his lids. He tried, but nothing happened. Unconsciousness welled, lapping about him – he refused to let go and sink under. There was a roaring in his head. Even through it he knew when the murderer reached out. The roaring in his head escalated—

Fingers – *small* fingers – touched his cheek gently, hesitantly.

The touch blazed across his brain.

Not the murderer. Relief swept through him, and relentlessly carried him into the black.

Phyllida traced the fallen man's cheek, mesmerized by the stark beauty of his face. He looked like a fallen angel – such classically pure lines could not possibly be found on mortal men. His brow was wide, his nose patrician, his thick hair very dark, sable black. His eyes were large under arched black brows. His lids didn't flicker; her stomach clenched tight. Then she saw his lips, lean and mobile, ease, softening as if he'd exhaled.

'Please, please, don't die!'

Frantically, she searched for a pulse at his throat, ruining his cravat in the process. She nearly fainted with relief when she found the throbbing beat, steady and strong. *'Thank God!'* She sagged.

Without thinking, she carefully rearranged his cravat, smoothing the folds – he was so beautiful and she hadn't killed him.

Wheels crunched heavily on the gravel drive.

Phyllida jerked upright. Her eyes flew wide. The murderer?

Her panicky wits calmed enough for her to distinguish voices as the conveyance rolled on around the house. Not the murderer – the Manor staff. She looked at the unconscious stranger.

For the first time in her life, she found it difficult to think. Her heart was still racing; she felt light-headed. Dragging in a breath, she fought to concentrate. Horatio was dead; she couldn't change that. Indeed, she knew nothing of any relevance. His friend was unconscious and would remain so for some time – she should make sure he was well tended. That was the least she should do.

But here she was in Horatio's drawing room, in breeches, instead of being laid down on her bed at the Grange with a sick headache. And she couldn't explain why, not without revealing her reason for being here – those misplaced personal belongings. Worse, they weren't hers. She didn't actually know why they were so important, why their revelation was to be avoided at all costs, which made it all the more incumbent on her not to reveal their existence. Aside from anything else, she'd been sworn to secrecy.

Damn! She was going to be discovered any

minute. Mrs Hemmings, the Manor housekeeper, would even now be entering the kitchen.

Think!

What if, instead of waiting here and landing herself in a morass of impossible explanations, she left, cut home through the wood, changed, and returned? She could easily think of an errand. She could be back in ten minutes. Then she could make sure Horatio's body had been discovered, and oversee the tending of the stranger.

That was a sensible plan.

Phyllida clambered to her feet. Her legs wobbled; she still felt woozy. She was about to turn away when the hat on the table beyond Horatio's body caught her eye.

Had the stranger carried a hat when he'd entered? She hadn't noticed it, but he was so large, he could have reached forward and put it on the table without her seeing.

Gentlemen's hats often had their owners' names embroidered on the inside band. Stepping around Horatio's body, Phyllida reached for the brown hat—

'I'll just go up and check on the master. Keep an eye on that pot, will you?'

Phyllida forgot about the hat. She shot through the hall, out of the front door, then raced across the side lawn and dove into the shrubbery.

'Juggs, open this door.'

The words, uttered in a tone Lucifer usually

associated with his mother, jerked him back to consciousness.

'Nah – can't do that,' a heavy male voice answered. 'Mightn't be wise.'

'Wise?' The woman's tone had risen. After a pause, during which Lucifer could almost hear her rein in her temper, she asked, 'Has he regained consciousness at all since you picked him up from the Manor?'

So he was no longer at the Manor. Where the hell was he?

'Nah! Out like a light, he is.'

He wasn't, but he might as well have been. Beyond hearing, his senses weren't functioning well – he couldn't feel much beyond the massive ache in his head. He was lying on his side on some very hard surface. The air was cool and held a hint of musty dust. He couldn't lift his lids – even that much movement was still beyond him.

He was helpless.

'How do you know he's still alive?' The woman's imperious tone left little doubt she was a lady.

'Alive? 'Course he's alive – why wouldn't he be? Just swooned, that's all.'

'Swooned? Juggs, you're an innkeeper. For how long do swooned men stay swooned, especially if they're jolted about in a cart in the fresh air?'

Juggs snorted. 'He's a swell – who knows how long they stay swooned for? Right liverish lot, they are.'

16

'They found him slumped by Mr Welham's body. What if he hasn't swooned but sustained some injury?'

'How could he have sus – got any injury?'

'Maybe he fought with the murderer, trying to save Mr Welham.'

'Nah! That way, we'd have his nibs here and someone else the murderer – that'd make two people coming in separate from outside in one day with no one seeing either of 'em, and that just plain doesn't happen.'

The lady lost all patience. 'Juggs – *open this door*! What if the gentleman dies, all because you decided he'd swooned when that wasn't so at all? We have to check.'

'He's *swooned*, I tell you – not a mark on him that Thompson or I could see.'

Lucifer gathered every last shred of his strength. If he wanted help, he was going to have to assist the lady; he didn't want her going away defeated, leaving him with the uncaring innkeeper. He lifted one hand – his arm shook . . . he forced the hand to his head. He heard a groan, then realized it was his.

'There! *See?*' The lady sounded triumphant. 'It's his head that hurts – the *back* of his head. Why, if he'd simply swooned? Quickly, Juggs – open the door! There's something very wrong here.'

Lucifer let his hand fall. If he could have, he would have roared at Juggs to open the damned door. Of course there was something wrong – the

17

murderer had coshed him. What on earth did they think had happened?

'Maybe he hit his head when he fell,' Juggs grumbled.

Why the hell did they imagine he'd fallen? But the jingle of keys pushed the thought from Lucifer's mind. The lady had won; she was coming to his aid. A lock clanked, then a heavy door scraped. Quick footsteps briskly crossed stone, heading his way.

A small hand touched his shoulder. A warm, feminine-soft presence leaned near.

'Everything will be all right in a moment.' Her tone was low and soothing. 'Just let me check your head.'

She was hovering over him; his senses had returned enough to tell him she wasn't as old as he'd thought. The realization gave him the strength to lift his lids, albeit only a fraction.

She saw and smiled encouragingly, brushing back the lock of hair that had fallen across his brow.

The pain in his head evaporated. Opening his eyes further, Lucifer drank in the details of her face. She was not a girl, but she would still qualify as a young lady. Somewhere in her early twenties, yet her face held more character, more strength and blatant determination than was common for her years. He noted it, but it was not that that held him, that captured his awareness to the exclusion of the debilitating pain in his head.

Her brown eyes were large, wide, and filled with concern – with an open empathy that reached past his cynical shields and touched him. Those lovely eyes were framed by a wide forehead and delicately arched brows, by dark hair, almost as dark as his, cut short to curve about her head like a sleek helmet. Her nose was straight, her chin tapered, her lips . . .

The sudden surge of sensual thoughts and impulses for once didn't sit well: Horatio was dead. He let his lids fall.

'You'll feel much better directly,' she promised, 'once we move you to a more comfortable bed.'

Behind her, Juggs snorted. 'Aye – he's that sort of gentleman, I'd wager. A murderer and the other, too.'

Lucifer ignored Juggs. The lady knew he was no murderer, and she now had the upper hand. Her fingers slid through his hair, carefully feeling around his wound. He tensed, then bit back a groan when she gingerly probed.

'See?' She pressed aside his hair so the air touched his wound. 'He's been hit on the back of the head with something – some weapon.'

Juggs harrumphed. 'P'rhaps he hit his head on that table in the Manor drawing room when he swooned.'

'Juggs! You know as well as I do this wound is too severe for that.'

Eyes closed, Lucifer breathed shallowly. Pain was rolling over him in sickening waves. In desperation, he conjured the image of the lady's face, struggled to concentrate on that and hold the pain at bay. Her throat had been slender, graceful. That augered well for the rest of her. She'd mentioned a bed – He broke off that train of thought, once again disconcerted by its direction.

''Ere, let me see,' Juggs grudgingly said.

A heavy hand touched Lucifer's skull – his head exploded with pain.

'Papa, this man is seriously injured.'

His guardian angel's voice drew Lucifer back to the living. He had no idea how much time had elapsed since last he'd been with them.

'He's been hit very violently on the back of the head. Juggs has seen the wound, too.'

'Hmm.' Heavier footsteps approached. 'That right, Juggs?'

A new voice, deep, cultured, but tinged with the local county accent – Lucifer wondered just who 'Papa' was.

'Aye. Looks like he's been coshed good and proper.' Juggs – the clod – was still with them.

'The wound's on the back of his skull, you say?'

'Yes – here.' Lucifer felt the lady's fingers part his hair. 'But don't touch.' 'Papa' thankfully didn't. 'It seems very sensitive – he regained consciousness for a moment, but fainted when Juggs touched his head.'

'Hardly surprising. That's quite a blow he's taken. Administered with that old halberd of

Horatio's by the look of it. Hemmings said he found it beside this gentleman. Given the thing's weight, it's a wonder he isn't dead.'

Letting his hair fall, the lady stated, 'So it's obvious he's not the murderer.'

'Not with that wound and the halberd lying beside him. Looks like the murderer hid behind the door and coshed him when he discovered the body. Mrs Hemmings swears the thing couldn't have fallen on its own. Seems clear enough. So we'll just have to wait and see what this gentleman can tell us once he regains his senses.'

Precious little, Lucifer mentally answered.

'Well, he's not going to get better lying in this cell.' The lady's voice had developed a decisive note.

'Indeed not. Can't understand what Bristleford was about, thinking this fellow was the murderer who'd swooned at the sight of blood.'

Swooned at the sight of blood? If he'd been able, Lucifer would have snorted derisively, but he still couldn't speak or move. The pain in his head was just waiting for a chance to bludgeon him into unconsciousness. The most he could do was lie still and listen, and learn all he could. While the lady held sway, he was safe – she seemed to have taken his best interests to heart.

'I thought Bristleford said he had the knife in 'is fist.'

That came from Juggs, of course.

'Papa' snorted. 'Self-defense. Had a moment's

warning the murderer was behind him and grabbed the only weapon to hand. Not much use against a halberd, unfortunately. No – it was obvious someone had found the body and turned it over. Can't see the murderer bothering – it wasn't as if Horatio would have been carrying any valuables in his nightshirt.'

'So this man is innocent,' the lady reiterated. 'We really should move him to the Grange.'

'I'll ride back and send the carriage,' 'Papa' replied.

'I'll wait here. Tell Gladys to pile as many cushions and pillows as she can into the carriage, and . . .'

The lady's words faded as she moved away; Lucifer stopped trying to listen. She'd said she'd stay by him. It sounded like the Grange was 'Papa's' residence, so presumably she lived there, too. He hoped she did. He wanted to see more of her once the pain had gone. The pain in his head, and the pain around his heart.

Horatio had been a very dear friend – how dear he hadn't realized until now, now that he was gone. He touched on his grief, but was too weak to deal with it. Shifting his mind away, he tried to find some way past the pain, but it seemed to feed on the effort.

So he simply lay there and waited.

He heard the lady return; others were with her. What followed wasn't pleasant. Luckily, he wasn't far removed from unconsciousness; he was only dimly aware of being lifted. He expected to feel the jolting of a carriage; if he did, the sensation didn't make it past the pain.

Then he was on a bed, being undressed. His senses flickered weakly, registering that there were two women present; from their hands and voices, they were both older than his guardian angel. He would have helped them if he could, but even that was beyond him. They fussed and insisted on pulling a nightshirt over his head, being inordinately careful of his injured skull.

They made him comfortable in soft pillows and sweet-smelling sheets, then they left him in blessed peace.

Phyllida looked in on her patient as soon as Gladys, their housekeeper, reported that he was settled.

Miss Sweet, her old governess, sat tatting in a chair by the window. 'He's resting quietly,' Sweetie mouthed.

Phyllida nodded and went to the bed. They'd left him sprawled on his stomach to spare his sore head. He was much larger than she'd realized – the broad expanse of his shoulders and chest, the long lines of his back, the even longer length of his legs – his body dominated the bed. He wasn't, perhaps, the largest man she'd seen, but she suspected he should have been the most vital. Instead, a sullen heaviness invested his limbs, a weighted tension quite unlike relaxation.

She peered at his face; the section she could see was pale, still starkly handsome but stony, lacking all sense of life. The lips that should have held the hint of a wicked smile were compressed to a thin line.

Sweetie was wrong – he was unconscious, not truly resting at all.

Phyllida straightened. Guilt swept her. It had been her fault he'd been hit. She glided back to Sweetie. 'I'm going to the Manor – I'll be back in an hour.'

Sweetie smiled and nodded. With one last glance at the bed, Phyllida left the room.

'I really couldn't say, sir.'

Phyllida entered the Manor's front hall to find Bristleford, Horatio's butler, being interrogated by Mr Lucius Appleby directly before the closed drawing room door. They both turned. Appleby bowed. 'Miss Tallent.'

Phyllida returned his nod. 'Good afternoon, sir.' Many local ladies considered Appleby's fair good looks attractive, but she found him too cold for her taste.

'Sir Cedric asked me to inquire as to the details of Mr Welham's death,' Appleby explained, clearly conscious of the need to excuse his intrusion. He was secretary to Sir Cedric Fortemain, a local landowner; no one would be surprised at Sir Cedric's interest. 'Bristleford was just telling me that Sir Jasper has declared himself satisfied that the gentleman discovered by the body is not the murderer.'

'That's correct. The murderer is as yet unknown.' Unwilling to encourage further discussion, Phyllida turned to Bristleford. 'I've asked John Ostler to tend the gentleman's horses.' His *magnificent* horses – even to her untutored eye, the pair were expensive beauties. Her twin brother, Jonas, would be over to see them just as soon as he learned of their existence. 'We'll put them in the stables here – the stables at the Grange are full now my aunt Huddlesford and my cousins have arrived.'

They'd arrived that afternoon, just as she'd been rushing off to rescue the unknown gentleman; because of her useless cousins, she'd been too late to save him from Juggs's clutches.

Bristleford frowned. 'If you think that's best . . .'

'I do. It seems obvious the gentleman was coming here to visit – presumably he was a friend of Mr Welham's.'

'I don't know, miss. The Hemmingses and I haven't been with the master long enough to know all his friends.'

'Quite. No doubt Covey will know.' Covey was Horatio's valet and had been with him for many years. 'I take it he's not back yet?'

'No, miss. He'll be devastated.'

Phyllida nodded. 'I just looked in to pick up the gentleman's hat.'

'Hat?' Bristleford stared. 'There was no hat, miss.'

Phyllida blinked. 'Are you sure?'

'Nothing in the drawing room or out here.'

Bristleford looked around. 'Perhaps in his carriage?'

Phyllida fabricated a smile. 'No, no – I just assumed he must have had a hat. No cane, either?'

Bristleford shook his head.

'Well, then, I'll be off.' With a nod for Appleby, who returned it politely, Phyllida walked out of the house.

She paused beneath the portico, looking out over Horatio's gorgeous garden. A chill washed down her spine.

There had been a hat – a brown one. If it didn't belong to the gentleman and hadn't been there when the Hemmingses and Bristleford discovered the body . . .

The chill intensified. Lifting her head, Phyllida glanced about, then walked quickly to the gate and hurried home.

The pain in his head grew worse.

Lucifer tossed and turned, struggling to escape the needles driving into his brain. Hands tried to restrain him; gentle voices tried to soothe him. He realized they wanted him to lie still – he tried, but the pain wouldn't let him.

Then his guardian angel returned. He heard her voice at the edge of his awareness; for her, he found strength and lay still. She bathed his face, neck, and the backs of his shoulders with lavender water, then placed cool cloths over his wound. The pain ebbed, and he sighed.

She left, and he grew restless again. But before the pain could peak, she returned and changed the cloths, then sat beside the bed, one cool hand on the back of his wrist.

He relaxed. Eventually, he slept.

When he awoke, she was gone.

It was dark; the house was quiet, slumbering. Lucifer lifted his head – the pain stopped him. Gritting his teeth, he shifted onto his side; raising his head just a fraction, he looked around. An older woman in a mobcap sat slumped in an armchair by the window. Focusing his hearing, he could detect gentle snores.

The fact that he could reassured him. Setting his temple back down on the pillow, he took stock. While still painful when he moved, his head was otherwise much better. He could think without agony. He stretched, flexing his limbs, careful not to shift his head. Relaxing again, he did the same with his senses; all seemed in working order. He might not yet be hale, but he was whole.

That established, he reconnoitered his surroundings. Bit by bit, the immediate past cleared and his memories fell into coherent order. He was in a chamber comfortably furnished in a manner befitting a gentleman's residence. Recollecting that 'Papa' had been called upon to pass judgment over his involvement in Horatio's death, 'Papa' might well be the local magistrate. If so, he'd made contact with the one gentleman above all others he needed to know. As soon as he was well enough to lift his head, he intended finding Horatio's killer.

His thoughts paused . . . he pushed them in a different direction. His guardian angel wasn't here – doubtless she was asleep in her bed . . .

Not that direction.

Inwardly, he sighed. Then, closing his eyes, sinking into the bed, he opened his mind and let his grief take him.

Let sorrow for the good times he would not now share with Horatio rise and spill over – let grief for the passing of one who had, in one way, been a kind of father, well and pour through him. No more the joy of shared discoveries, the eager quest for information, the shared hunt to pin down some elusive provenance.

The memories lived, but Horatio was gone. A formative chapter in his life had ended. It was difficult to accept that he'd reached the last page and now had to close the book.

Grief ebbed and left him empty. He'd seen death too many times for the shock to hold him for long. He came from a warrior caste; unjust death was the trigger for one of his most primal responses. Revenge – not for personal satisfaction, but in the name of justice.

Horatio's death would not go unavenged.

He lay in the soft sheets while grief transmuted to anger, eventually coalescing into icy resolution.

His emotions hardened, he mentally returned to the scene, replaying every step, every recollection, until he came to the touch . . .

Fingers that small belonged to a child or a woman. Given the fascination behind the touch – one he recognized instinctively – he would wager his entire collection that a woman had been there. A woman who was not the murderer. Horatio might have been old, but he hadn't been so infirm that a woman could have stabbed him so neatly. Few women would have the strength, or the knowledge.

So – Horatio had been murdered. Then *he* had entered and the murderer had coshed him with the halberd. Then the woman had entered and found him.

No – that couldn't be right. Horatio's body had been turned onto its back *before* he'd arrived; he agreed with 'Papa' – it hadn't been the murderer who'd done that. The woman must have, then she'd hidden when he appeared.

She must have seen the murderer strike him, then leave. Why hadn't she raised the alarm? Some man called Hemmings had done that.

Something more than the obvious was afoot. He revisited the facts, but couldn't shake that conclusion.

A board in the hallway creaked. Lucifer listened. A minute later, the door to his room opened.

He remained relaxed on his side, lids lowered so he appeared asleep, but he could see through his lashes. He heard a soft click as the door shut, then footsteps padded across the floorboards; a pool of candlelight approached.

His guardian angel came into view. She was in her nightgown.

She halted six feet away, studying his face. One hand held the candlestick; the other rested between her breasts, anchoring her shawl. It was the first time he'd seen all of her; he didn't try to stop himself looking, noting, assessing. Her face was as he recalled, wide eyes, tapered chin, and sleek dark hair giving an impression of intelligence and feminine resolve. She was of average height, slender but not thin. Her breasts were full and high, nipples just discernible beneath the shawl's fringe. He couldn't judge her waist under the nightgown, but her hips were neatly rounded, her thighs sleek.

Her feet were bare. His gaze locked on them, tantalizingly revealed, then concealed beneath her nightgown. Small, naked, intensely feminine feet. Slowly, he dragged his gaze back up to her face.

While he'd studied her, she'd been studying him. Her dark eyes roamed his face, taking in, it seemed, every line. Then she turned away.

Lucifer bit back an urge to call to her. He wanted to thank her – she'd been a madonna of kindness and caring – but if he made a sound, he'd scare her out of her wits. He watched her stop by the sleeping woman; setting her candlestick down, she lifted a blanket, shook it out, then tucked it around the other woman. As she turned away, candle once more in hand, the soft light lit her smile.

She started for the door, but, as if she'd heard his silent plea, she halted before she passed the bed. She looked his way, then, hesitantly, drew nearer. And nearer.

Holding the candle aside so his face was screened by her body, she rested against the bed a foot away and studied his face anew. He fought to keep his lids steady; he could only just see her face. Her eyes were fathomless, her expression unreadable.

Then she released her grip on her shawl. Slowly, she reached out. With her fingertips she lightly traced his cheek.

Lucifer felt like he'd been branded – and he recognized the brand. He surged up on one elbow, seizing her wrist, transfixing her with a glare.

She gasped; the sound echoed through the room. The candlelight wavered wildly, then steadied. Eyes dilated, she stared at him.

He tightened his grip and held her gaze. *'It was you.'*

CHAPTER 2

Phyllida stared into eyes so vibrant a dark blue they were nearly black. She'd seen them earlier, but they'd been hazed with pain, unfocused; they'd been startling enough then. Now, focused mercilessly on hers, clear and brilliant as a dark sapphire, they stole her breath away.

She felt like she'd been the one hit by the halberd.

'You were there.' His gaze held her trapped. '*You* were the first to reach me after the murderer hit me. You touched my face, just as you did then.'

She kept her expression blank. Thoughts popped up, then sank, flotsam thrown up by her whirling mind. His fingers clamping about her wrist had shocked her; they'd locked before she could react. She twisted her arm, trying to ease from his hold; he tightened his grip enough for her to sense his strength and the futility of struggling.

She felt light-headed. She'd forgotten to breathe.

Dragging her gaze from his, she did. Staring at his lips, she wondered what to say. How could he know just from a touch? He had to be guessing.

Draped in shadow, his face was even more

compelling than she recalled. The impact of him – his conscious physical presence – was potent; he appeared altogether more dangerous, and he'd appeared dangerous enough before. He was decently covered in one of her father's nightshirts, but the collar was open, exposing a V of chest – dark hair curled invitingly in the gap.

The realization that she was standing by a gentleman's bed staring at his chest, in the small hours, in her nightgown, slammed into her. Heat prickled across her skin. Gladys was near, but . . .

She glanced across the room. As if sensing her hope that Gladys wouldn't wake and hear him, he eased onto his back, pulling her across him.

Phyllida bit back another gasp. 'Be careful of your head,' she hissed.

His eyes gleamed. 'I'll be careful.'

His voice was deep; it almost purred. He kept extending his arm, the one shackling her wrist. She had to lean across him, balancing the candlestick in her other hand. Inexorably, he drew her on.

She swallowed as her breasts neared his chest. Heart thudding, she scrambled onto the bed.

He smiled in triumph. 'Now you can tell me what you were doing so secretively in Horatio's drawing room.'

The command was blatant. Phyllida lifted her chin. At twenty-four, she wasn't about to be bullied. 'I don't know what you mean.' She tried to slide her wrist free, to no avail. Kneeling beside him on the bed, one hand locked in his, the candlestick in the other, was not a position of strength. She felt like a supplicant.

His expression hardened. 'You were there. Tell me why.'

She looked down her nose at him. 'I fear you're still delirious.'

'I wasn't delirious before.'

'You kept talking about the devil. Then, when we assured you you wouldn't die, you asked for the archangel.'

His lips thinned. 'My brother's known as Gabriel, and my eldest cousin is Devil.'

She stared at him. Devil. Gabriel. What was *his* name? 'Oh. Well, this idea you have is nonsense. I know nothing about Horatio's murder.'

She met his gaze on the last, and fell into the blue. It was the most peculiar sensation; the nerves under her skin, all over her, tingled. Warmth spread through her. The sense of being held captive grew. The odd notion that her nightgown was transparent she dismissed as ridiculous.

'You weren't in Horatio's drawing room when I was lying on the floor?'

The words were soft, subtly challenging; an undercurrent of danger rippled beneath. Held trapped by his gaze, by his hold on her wrist, Phyllida pressed her lips tight and shook her head. She couldn't tell him – not yet. Not until she'd spoken with Mary Anne and been released from her oath.

'So these fingers' – deftly, he altered his grip so

his fingers wrapped around hers – 'weren't the ones that touched my cheek as I lay beside Horatio?'

He raised her hand, then looked at it; she looked, too. Long, tanned fingers surrounded hers. His hand swallowed hers in a warm clasp. That clasp firmed; slowly, he lifted her fingers to his face. 'Like this.' He touched her fingertips to his cheek, then drew her hand down.

His stubble had grown, prickling against the pads of her fingers; the sensation only emphasized the fact that the sculpted lines were not rock but living flesh. Fascinated anew, Phyllida watched her fingers trace, drifting down, following her gaze to the tempting line of his lips . . . then she realized he'd slackened his grasp. Her fingers were tracing on their own.

She snatched her hand away, but he was quicker. His fingers shackled her wrist again.

'You were there.' His tone was grimly determined; conviction resonated through it.

Phyllida looked into his deep blue eyes; every instinct she possessed urged her to flee. She tugged. 'Let me go.'

One black brow rose. He considered – heart thumping, she wondered what alternatives he was weighing. Then his lips eased; the intensity of his gaze didn't. 'Very well – for now.'

She tried to draw her hand free but he didn't release it. Instead, he raised her fingers – this time, to his lips. His gaze remained locked on her face; she prayed her reaction – panic melded with insidious excitement – didn't show.

His lips brushed her knuckles – she lost her breath. His lips were cool yet her skin burned where they'd touched. Eyes wide, she felt her senses sway. Before she could drag in a steadying breath, he turned her hand and pressed a burning kiss into her palm.

She snatched her hand back – he let her go, but reluctantly. Backing off the bed, she stood; her gown fell to decently cover her legs. From not breathing at all, she was now breathing too rapidly.

Satisfaction gleamed in his eyes.

Lifting her head, she gathered her shawl, hesitated, then haughtily nodded. 'I'll check on you later in the morning.'

She turned to the door. A wave of peculiar heat washed over her. Without risking a backward glance, she escaped.

Lucifer watched the door close. He'd let her go. That hadn't been what he'd wanted to do. But there was no need to rush, and matters might have rushed rather more than was wise if he'd kept her kneeling on his bed.

He inhaled deeply and could smell her still, sweet feminine flesh warm from her bed. Her nightgown had been totally opaque, but the material had lovingly outlined every curve it touched. Once she'd released the ends of her shawl, his distraction had been complete.

If the older woman hadn't been in the room . . .

A minute passed; then he shook aside his thoughts. Tactically, it hadn't been wise to so blatantly display his intent. Luckily, his guardian angel seemed committed to taking care of him, despite the threat she now clearly perceived.

Her last words had been more declaration than statement, uttered as much for her benefit as for his. If she'd found him struck down in Horatio's drawing room but had been forced, for whatever reason, to leave him there, her stance was understandable. She felt guilty. No matter how difficult he proved, she would try to do the right thing.

In that respect, he already felt certain of her – she was a woman who would strive to do what she deemed right.

He stretched, easing muscles that had tensed; then he shifted onto his side, the better to spare his head. It still ached, but, true to form, while she'd been in the room, he hadn't been aware of it.

All he'd been aware of was her.

Even before she'd touched his face.

But the knowledge that it was she who had knelt beside him in Horatio's drawing room and traced his cheek with that hesitant, wondering touch had powerfully focused the attraction he'd been doing his best to decently ignore. The revelation meant he no longer needed to feign indifference; his attraction, her fascination, and her consequent skittishness were going to prove exceedingly helpful.

She knew something – he'd read that much in her wide dark eyes. They were easy to read; her face was not. Her expression had remained open but uninformative, her emotions screened. Even when he'd kissed her hand, only her eyes had flared. She seemed contained; judging by all he'd seen, she was used to being in control, in command.

Whatever the case, she wasn't about to disappear; he'd have time to pursue his questions, and her. None knew better than he how to persuade women to do what he wanted, to give him what he wanted – that was, after all, his specialty. And after he'd learned what she knew of Horatio's murder . . .

He drifted into sleep and dreamed.

At eleven o'clock the next morning, Phyllida marched into the bedchamber at the end of the west wing. She held the door wide so Sweetie, followed by Gladys carrying a laden tray, could enter.

'Good morning.' She addressed the room in general, as if the large body lying in the bed hadn't immediately captured her entire attention.

As per her instructions, Sweetie had fluttered down to find her the instant their patient awoke. Phyllida knew he was awake – she could feel that midnight-blue gaze on her face, and on the rest of her, now unexceptionably garbed in a morning gown of sprigged muslin. It was infinitely easier to assert control while properly dressed.

'Good morning. Ladies.' The deep, reverberating words were accompanied by a graceful nod. Phyllida resisted the urge to frown. That direct 'Good morning' had been for her; the 'Ladies' and the nod had been for the others.

Wrapping her habitual calm, collected demeanor

38

about her, she followed Gladys to the bed, ignoring the heat still lingering in the center of her palm. Just as she was going to ignore him. She was determined not to succumb to the foolish fascination that had overcome her last night.

'We've brought you some broth, which is just what you need to set you up again.' She let her glance slide over him, a confident smile on her lips; she made sure not to meet his eyes.

'Indeed?'

Sweetie and Gladys preened; a swift glance showed he was smiling at them. 'Indeed,' she averred, with rather more steel. 'How is your head?'

'Considerably improved.' He glanced at her. 'Thanks to you.'

'Indeed, yes!' Sweetie twittered. 'So very right of dear Phyllida to insist you be brought here. Why, you were quite out of your senses, dear.'

'So I understand. I do hope that, in my delirium, I said nothing to distress you.'

'Of course not, dear – do set your mind at ease on that score. Gladys here and I have *brothers,* so you may be sure you surprised us not at all. Now, let me help you . . .'

He struggled to sit up; Sweetie grasped his arm and tugged. Phyllida plumped his pillows, careful not to touch his shoulders. Once he was settled, Gladys deposited the tray on his knees.

'Thank you.'

The smile that went with that left both Gladys and Sweetie happily dazed; Phyllida mentally frowned. The man was past dangerous. His next words confirmed it.

'This is excellent broth. Did you make it?'

Gladys confessed; pink with pleasure, she excused herself to return to her duties, pausing at the last to assure him that, should he require anything further, he only had to ask.

Phyllida inwardly sniffed. She stepped back from the bed, biding her time, letting him eat. He did so smoothly, steadily – she could detect not the smallest tremor in his hands. Strong, long-fingered, inherently graceful, they plied the spoon and broke the bread.

'Good heavens!' Sweetie fluttered. 'We forgot the butter. I'll fetch some right away.' She rushed out the door.

Phyllida found herself staring at the closing door before she had time to protest. Being alone with a gentleman in his bedchamber was unquestionably improper. Still, what harm could befall her? He was more or less tied to the bed. And she was quite capable of keeping him in his place, disturbing blue gaze or no. There wasn't a man in the district she couldn't manage, and despite his elegant facade, he was just a man. Folding her arms, she faced the bed. 'I daresay you have a number of questions—'

'Oh, I do.'

She inclined her head, avoiding his eyes. 'I'll attempt to answer them while you eat. You need to build your strength.' He nodded in acquiescence;

she continued. 'You are presently at the Grange, my father's house. It lies south of the village. You were found at the Manor, which as you probably recall lies on the village's north boundary.'

'That much I remember.'

'My father is Sir Jasper Tallent—'

'Is he the local magistrate?'

She frowned. 'Yes.'

'Has he any idea who killed Horatio?'

Phyllida pressed her lips together, then relented. 'No.'

'Do you?'

She'd looked at him before she'd thought; his gaze locked with hers. Phyllida looked into eyes diabolically blue, took in the hard lines of his face, the unwavering determination, the hard mask that concealed his intention not at all. 'No.'

He held her gaze for a moment longer, then inclined his head. 'Perhaps not.'

She almost sighed with relief.

He looked down at his soup. 'You do, however, know something.'

His conviction rang absolute. Phyllida nearly threw her hands in the air – there was clearly no point in arguing. She gripped her elbows and looked past the bed at the window. After a moment, she said, 'I daresay you're ravenous, but at this stage, you would be unwise to bite off more than you can chew. Your constitution may be excellent, but the blow you suffered was severe – you'll need time to recover full use of your faculties.'

From the corner of her eye she saw his lips twitch, felt his gaze drift assessingly over her. She mentally replayed her words and felt pleased with them. A subtle warning and a clear statement she would not bow to *force majeure*. With most men, just the question of what she really meant would be enough to keep them puzzled and no more threat to her.

'My faculties,' he murmured, 'are returning in leaps and bounds.'

Suggestive and openly threatening, the shocking warmth in his voice slid over her skin, a wanton, explicit caress.

Without thought, she sucked in a breath and whirled to face him, as if he were a predator. She was suddenly sure he was. 'You'll need to be careful.'

She kept her expression blank, her tone direct.

He opened his eyes wide; innocence wasn't what she saw in them. 'Shouldn't you check my wound?'

'Your wound needs nothing more than time to heal.' No power on earth would get her closer to the bed – closer to him. Phyllida frowned, and held tight to her role. *She* was in charge, not he. 'Papa would like you to join us for afternoon tea, if you're able.'

His smile made her nerves tingle. 'I'm able.'

'Good.' She turned to the door. 'I'll have your bags brought up – as a precaution, we left them downstairs.'

'Precaution?'

'Why, yes.' Reaching the door, she looked back.

'We kept your clothes from you in case you turned difficult over remaining abed.'

His lips curved; his eyes glinted. The combination looked positively wicked. 'Lying abed is one of my favorite pastimes. However, if I'd wanted to get up, the mere absence of clothes wouldn't have deterred me.' His gaze slid over her; his voice deepened. 'Not in the least.'

Gripping the doorknob, Phyllida met his gaze blankly and prayed she wasn't blushing. 'I'll let Papa know you'll be joining us later. Your name?'

His untrustworthy smile deepened. 'Lucifer.'

Phyllida stared at him; even with the width of the room separating them, all her instincts were screaming, warning her not to call his bluff. Any of his bluffs.

Some part of her knew he wasn't the sort who bluffed.

It went seriously against her grain to let him trifle with her and escape retribution, but arguing would simply be playing into his hands. She forced herself to incline her head and evenly state, 'Sweetie – Miss Sweet – will return shortly. She'll take away your tray.'

On that note, she opened the door; with a regal nod, she left.

Later, after he'd bathed and dressed, Lucifer sat on the window seat in his bedchamber and looked north, over a dense wood. Through the shifting canopies he could occasionally glimpse the gray slate roof of the Manor.

Gaze fixed, he thought of Horatio, and of Martha, and of what he should do next, how best to move forward. Horatio's death was an accepted fact in his mind, but the tale had only just begun.

It was quiet beyond the open window. The snoozy quality of a summer's afternoon blanketed the village, yet somewhere in that peace a murderer waited, and watched and worried. Horatio's death had not been neat. Not only had he, Lucifer, stumbled on the scene far too soon, but so, too, had Phyllida Tallent.

Lucifer pondered that last, and all that it might mean.

A knock interrupted his reverie. He faced the door, keen to see if intuition proved correct. 'Come in.'

Phyllida entered; he smiled in private triumph. Retreating earlier and leaving the field to him must have been difficult; despite her wariness, he'd predicted she wouldn't stay away. She glanced around the room, then discovered him. She hesitated, then, leaving the door wide, crossed toward him. Frowning, she studied his face, his eyes. He let her draw near before smoothly rising – no sudden movements.

Her lovely eyes widened. She immediately halted. 'Ah . . .' From four feet away, she stared up at him, her expression a telltale blank. Her gaze drifted, passing over him, then she wrenched it back to his face. And caught him returning the favor. Her eyes snapped even as her expression smoothed to impassivity. 'Are you sure you've recovered enough to join us downstairs?'

He continued to smile, relishing her resistance. 'I'm quite recovered enough to brave a drawing room.' The frown in her eyes deepened; he added, 'My head only aches – it no longer throbs.'

'Well . . .' She searched his eyes once more. 'I'm afraid my aunt and cousins have arrived for the summer, and, of course, they're agog to meet you. You must promise you won't overtax yourself.'

Fussing was not something he readily endured, yet the idea that she'd elected herself his keeper, and was determined to do her duty despite the urgings of her common sense to keep a safer distance between them, was oddly satisfying. Oddly endearing. He smiled charmingly, too wise to smirk. 'If I weaken and need support, you'll be the first to know.'

She glared, but the concern in her dark eyes was very real. As was her suspicion.

'Very well.' She lifted her head. 'And now, if you please, your real name?'

Lucifer looked down at her; he made no attempt to disguise the tenor of his smile. 'I told you. Lucifer.'

She met his gaze directly. 'No one is called Lucifer.'

'I am.' He stepped forward; she backed.

'That's ludicrous. That cannot be your real name.'

He continued his advance; she continued to fall back.

'It's the name I'm known by. There are many who would tell you it suits me.' He held her gaze and continued his prowling stroll. 'If you ask anyone in the ton for Lucifer, they'll instantly send you to me.'

Her eyes had grown wider – their expression informed him she'd never encountered a man such as he. She was both fascinated and defensive – and, he suspected, disapproving. Desire flared; he tamped it down, kept that truth from his eyes. That he delighted in transforming disapproving ladies into wanton whores was a truth she didn't need to know.

He took the last step that backed her over the room's threshold. Glancing about, she discovered herself in the corridor. She stiffened; the look she threw him as she stepped aside was distinctly irate. And not a little surprised. He hid a grin. It seemed likely that no one had ever managed her as he just had. He'd herded her out of the room – no hands, no voice – simply him. And there was hay yet to be made on this fine summer's day.

Closing the door, he looked down at her. 'You shouldn't be alone with me. Especially not in a bedroom.'

She held his gaze; he struggled to keep his eyes on hers rather than focus on her swelling breasts, rising as she drew in a long, rigidly controlled breath. Lips compressed, she held it in, along with her temper.

Not at all innocently, he raised a brow at her.

Her eyes spat sparks. So fleeting was the sight, he could almost think he'd imagined it; his body's reaction confirmed he hadn't. In the next instant, her eyes once more dark pools of calm composure, her expression, as it so often was, deceptively serene, she inclined her head and turned down the corridor.

'Thank you for the warning.' Her words drifted back to him. 'You may tell Papa your name directly. If you'll follow me?' Head high, she moved toward the stairs.

Lucifer watched her hips sway, unconsciously seductive, the delectable hemispheres of her derriere and the graceful lines of her legs occasionally outlined by her gown. Lips lifting, he stepped out in her wake, very ready to oblige.

The room she led him to gave onto the back lawn and onto the terrace along the side of the house. The long windows were open, letting the balmy breeze bring the summer day inside. A family group was gathered about the tea trolley, stationed in front of a *chaise*. A middle-aged lady with a hard expression wielded the teapot; beside her, a dandy, her son by his features, lounged petulantly. On her other side, a younger gentleman slouched – another son, this one sulky. No wonder the lady looked so worn down.

Two other gentlemen stood beside the *chaise*. The younger, an insouciant male version of Phyllida, grinned engagingly. The older man, large and dressed in country tweeds, studied Lucifer from under shaggy brows.

Preceding Lucifer into the room, Phyllida waved to this gentleman. 'Papa?'

Lucifer joined her as she halted before her father. She slanted him a glance. 'Allow me to present . . .'

He smiled, then turned to her father and held out his hand. 'Alasdair Cynster, sir. But most call me Lucifer.'

'Lucifer, heh?' Sir Jasper shook hands without any evidence of disquiet. 'What names you youngsters do take. Now! How're you feeling?'

'Much better, thanks to your daughter's care.'

Sir Jasper smiled on Phyllida, who had turned to the tea trolley. 'Aye, well, that was a nasty blow, no doubt of that. Now let me make you known to m'sister-in-law; then we'll take our tea and you can tell me all you know about this distressing business.'

His sister-in-law, Lady Huddlesford, summoned a smile and held out her hand. 'I'm delighted to meet you, Mr Cynster.'

Lucifer politely shook hands. Sir Jasper gestured to the dandy. 'M'nephew, Percy Tallent.'

Percy, it transpired, was her ladyship's son by her first marriage to Sir Jasper's late brother. One minute of affected conversation and Lucifer had Percy pegged – he was on a repairing lease. Nothing else could account for his presence in rural Devon. His sullen half brother, Frederick Huddlesford, openly stared at Lucifer's well-cut coat, hard pressed, it seemed, to marshal the words for even a simple greeting.

With a nod, Lucifer turned to the young man so like Phyllida, who promptly grinned and stuck out his hand. 'Jonas. Phyllida's little brother.'

Clasping the proffered hand, Lucifer smiled and raised his brows. Loose-limbed, with the same careless grace that characterized his sister, Jonas stood a good six inches taller than she. Lucifer glanced at her as she straightened from the tea trolley. For all his transparent, good-natured insousiance, Jonas didn't appear younger than she.

Phyllida caught his glance; her chin rose. 'We're twins, but I'm the elder.'

'Ah. I see. Always the leader.'

Her brows rose haughtily. Jonas chuckled.

So did Sir Jasper. 'Quite, quite. Phyllida keeps us all in line – don't know what we'd do without her. Now' – he waved to a grouping of chairs at the end of the room – 'let's move down there and you can tell me what you can about this terrible business.'

As he turned, Lucifer felt Phyllida's gaze on his face.

'Indeed, Papa. I do think Mr Cynster should sit down. I'll bring you your cups.'

Sir Jasper nodded. Lucifer followed him down the room. They settled in wing chairs angled to each other, a small table between. The length of the room assured them of privacy; the others watched them go, their curiosity palpable, then reluctantly returned to their own company.

As he gingerly rested his head back on the chair's cushion, Lucifer considered Sir Jasper. His host was a type he knew well. Men like him were the backbone of county England. Bluffly good-natured, genial if unimaginative, they were, nevertheless, no one's fools. They could be counted on to hold the line, to do whatever needed to be done to keep their community stable, yet they had no taste for power; it was appreciation of their comfort plus trenchant common sense that drove them.

Lucifer glanced at Phyllida, busy at the tea trolley. Like father, like daughter? He suspected so, at least in part.

'So' – Sir Jasper stretched out his legs – 'are you familiar with Devon?'

Lucifer went to shake his head, but stopped. 'No. My family home lies north of here, to the east of the Quantocks.'

'Somerset, heh? So you're a west countryman?'

'At heart, but I've lived in London for the last decade.'

Phyllida arrived with cups on saucers; she handed one to each of them, then whisked back up the room. Sir Jasper sipped; Lucifer did, too, conscious of reawakening hunger. An instant later, Phyllida reappeared with a cake plate piled high. She offered it around, then subsided onto a love seat beside her father's chair, and patently settled to listen.

Lucifer glanced at Sir Jasper. His host was aware

50

of his daughter's presence, and clearly saw nothing odd in her being privy to his investigations. His flippant remark about her being a born leader was not, it seemed, far from the mark.

Hands folded in her lap, she sat quiet and contained. Lucifer studied her as he consumed a piece of cake. She wouldn't see twenty again, but how much older was she? Her cool composure he suspected was misleading. Jonas's age was easier to estimate; his body was still all long bones and spare frame. He was in his early-to-mid twenties, at least four years younger than Lucifer's twenty-nine.

Which made Phyllida the same.

And a puzzle. There was no ring on her finger, nor had there ever been one. He'd noted that last night; even in extremis, his rakish instincts hadn't failed him. She was twenty-three, twenty-four, and still unwed. Definitely a puzzle.

She was aware of his scrutiny, but not a smidgen of that awareness showed. The urge to shake her – to see her lose that cool control – flared. Lucifer looked down, set aside his cake plate, and picked up his cup.

Sir Jasper did the same. 'Now, to business. Let's start with your arrival. What brought you to the Manor yesterday morning?'

'I received a letter from Horatio Welham.' Lucifer settled his head back on the cushion. 'It was delivered in London on Thursday. Horatio invited me to visit the Manor at my earliest convenience.'

51

'So you were previously acquainted with Welham?'

'I've known Horatio for over nine years. I first met him when I was twenty, while staying with friends in the Lake District. Horatio introduced me to serious collecting. He was my mentor in that field and became a close, very trusted friend. Over the years, I frequently visited Horatio and his wife, Martha, at their house by Lake Windemere.'

'Lake District, was it? Always wondered where Horatio hailed from. He never said and one didn't like to pry.'

Lucifer hesitated, then said, 'Horatio was deeply attached to Martha. When she died three years ago, he couldn't face living alone in the house they'd shared for so long. He sold up and moved south. Devon appealed because of the milder climate – he used to say he chose to move here because of his old bones and because he liked this village. He said it was small and comfortable.' *With no managing local mesdames.* Lucifer glanced at Phyllida – how had Horatio viewed her?

Her eyes had grown dark. 'No wonder he never spoke of his past. He must have been deeply in love with his Martha.'

Lucifer inclined his head, then looked at Sir Jasper.

'Would any of Welham's servants know you?'

'I don't know who he kept on. Is Covey still with him?'

'Yes, indeed.'

52

'Then he knows me, certainly.' Lucifer frowned. 'If Covey's here, why did the servants suspect me of killing Horatio? Covey knows how long I've known Horatio and the nature of our relationship.'

'Covey wasn't here,' Phyllida said. 'He visits an old aunt in Musbury, a village nearby, every Sunday. By the time he returned, you were here at the Grange.'

'Covey would be very cut up by Horatio's death.' Phyllida nodded.

Sir Jasper sighed. 'No getting any sense out of him yesterday – I did try. Daresay he's still feeling it today.'

'Covey was devoted to Horatio over all the years I knew them.'

Sir Jasper threw Lucifer a shrewd glance. 'Quite – no reason to suppose Covey knows anything about his master's death.' He sat back. 'Now, let's see. This is your first visit to Colyton?'

'Yes. Until now, matters never fell out suitably for a visit. Horatio and I discussed it, but . . . We met at least every three months, sometimes more frequently, in London and at collectors' gatherings around the country.'

'So you're a collector, too?'

'I specialize in silver and jewelry. Horatio, on the other hand, was an acknowledged expert on antique books and a highly regarded authority in a number of other areas, too. He was an inspired teacher. It was an honor to have learned from him.'

'Were there others who learned from him?'

'A few, but none who remained so closely in touch. The others took up collecting in Horatio's own spheres, and so became competitors of sorts.'

'Could one of them have killed him?'

Lucifer shook his head. 'I can't imagine it.'

'Other collectors? Jealous ones, perhaps?'

Lucifer waved a negative. 'Collectors might metaphorically kill for certain items, but few actually do. For most collectors, half the joy is displaying your acquisitions to other collectors. Horatio was highly respected and well liked among the fraternity; his collections were well known. Any item of his unexpectedly surfacing in someone else's collection would draw immediate attention. As a motive for murder, a known collector wanting to gain a particular piece is unlikely. We can, however, check for missing items, although it will take time. Horatio kept meticulous records.'

Sir Jasper was frowning. 'We knew Welham was a collector and dealer, but I, for one, had no notion he was so highly regarded.' He glanced at Phyllida.

She shook her head. 'We all knew he had visitors from outside – beyond the local area – but no one here knows much about antiques. We had no idea Horatio held such a prominent place in that sphere.'

'I think,' Lucifer said, 'that that was part of the attraction of Colyton. Horatio liked being "one of the locals."'

Sir Jasper nodded. 'Now you mention it, he

became "one of us" very quickly. Hard to believe it's only been three years. He bought the Manor and rebuilt and refurbished it. He put in that garden – his pride, it was. Used to potter in it for hours – his success turned some of the local ladies green. He always did all he could – went to church every Sunday, helped out in many ways.' Sir Jasper paused, then quietly concluded, 'He'll be missed.'

They sat silently for a moment, then Lucifer asked, 'If he always went to church, why was he at home yesterday? I hadn't sent word I was coming.'

'He was ill,' Phyllida said. 'A bad cold. He insisted the others go as usual, and that Covey was not to disappoint his aunt. Mrs Hemmings said she left him reading upstairs.'

'So' – Sir Jasper shifted in his chair – 'let's recount what happened as we know it. You arrived on a social visit—'

'That's not quite true – or not all of the truth. I left Horatio's letter in Somerset, so you'll have to bear with my paraphrasing, but he specifically asked me to visit because he wanted my opinion on some item he'd discovered. He was obviously excited by it – the impression I received was that it was a wholly unexpected find. The inference was that he personally felt sure the item was authentic, but wanted a second opinion.'

'Any idea what this item was?'

'No. The only thing I can be sure of is that it wasn't silver or jewelry.'

'But those are your specialties.'

'Yes, but Horatio wrote that if the item was authentic, it might even tempt me to expand my collection beyond silver and jewelry.'

'So it was a desirable piece?'

'My interpretation was that it was desirable and valuable. The fact that Horatio asked me to appraise something not in my area of expertise, when he could easily have invited the opinion of any of the established collectors of whatever type of collectible it is, suggests that the item was one of those finds that no sane collector tells anyone he has until he's established ownership and perhaps arranged greater security. Horatio might have been old, but he was still very sharp.'

'But he told you – why not others?'

Lucifer met Phyllida's dark gaze. 'Because for various reasons, among them our long friendship, Horatio knew he'd be safe telling me. Indeed, I might be the only one he mentioned the item to at all.'

'Would Covey know of it?'

'Unless his duties have changed, I doubt it. Covey helped Horatio with arrangements and correspondence but was never involved with the actual dealing or assessing.'

Sir Jasper mulled over their words. 'So you came here to meet with Horatio and view this new item of his.' He looked at Lucifer, who nodded. 'You drove into the village . . . ?'

Lucifer leaned back, his gaze fixed above Phyllida's head. 'I passed no one on the road, nor

did I see anyone about. I turned into the drive . . .'
Simply and succinctly, he described his movements.
'And then someone hit me over the head and I
collapsed beside Horatio.'

'You were hit with an old halberd,' Sir Jasper
said. 'Nasty weapon – you're lucky not to have
died.'

Lucifer lowered his gaze to Phyllida's calm face.
'Indeed.'

'This letter knife Horatio was stabbed with – do
you recall it?'

'It was his – Louis Quinze – he'd had it for
years.'

'Hmm – so that's not this special item.' Sir Jasper
kept his gaze on his boots. 'So as things stand,
you have no idea who might have killed Welham?'

Phyllida stared into deep blue eyes and prayed
her welling panic didn't show. It hadn't occurred
to her, not until he started recounting his movements, that, in truth, Lucifer held her in the palm
of his hand. If he told her father that someone
had been there after the murderer had struck, and
that he was convinced – no, he *knew* – that that
person was she . . .

Her father would instantly know she'd lied – not
by act but by omission. He'd realize her un-
characteristic surrender to a headache last Sunday
morning had been a ruse, that it would be easy
for her to cut through the wood and reach the
Manor without being seen. That she'd known no
one else should have been in the house.

What he wouldn't understand was why – why she'd done it and then so deceitfully kept silent. And that was the one thing she couldn't tell him, couldn't yet explain – not until she was released from her oath.

The dark blue gaze never wavered. 'No.'

She breathed shallowly and waited, knowing he knew, knowing he was debating whether or not to expose her. To her father, one of the few people whose good opinion mattered to her.

Time slowed. As if from a distance, she heard her father ask the fateful question, the one she'd realized he would eventually ask. 'And there's nothing else bearing on this matter you can tell me?'

Lucifer's eyes held hers steadily. Giddiness threatened.

It suddenly occurred to her to consider the next step: What if he didn't tell?

'No.'

She blinked.

He held her gaze for an instant longer, then glanced at her father. 'I have no notion who killed Horatio, but, with your permission, I intend to find out.'

'Indeed, indeed.' Her father nodded. 'Commendable goal.' He looked up, and frowned.

'Good gracious, Jasper!' Lady Huddlesford swept forward. 'You've been interrogating Mr Cynster for quite long enough. His poor head must be aching.'

Lucifer rose, as did Sir Jasper.

'Nonsense, Margaret, we have to sort this matter out.'

'Indeed! I haven't been so shocked in years. The very thought of a London cutthroat slipping into the village and stabbing Mr Welham is more than enough to overset me.'

'There's no reason to think it was someone from London.'

Lady Huddlesford stared at her brother-in-law. 'Really, Jasper! This is such a sleepy little place – everyone knows everyone. Of *course* it must be someone from outside.'

Phyllida sensed her father's resistance. He doggedly held to the logical approach, which meant that at any second he was going to turn to her and ask if she knew of anyone local with a reason to wish Horatio dead.

She didn't, but her answer might come close to being a lie. An outright lie. She avoided prevarication on principle, except in pursuit of the greater good. As her gaze touched Mr Cynster – Lucifer – she acidly wished she'd made no exception. Just look where it had landed her.

First swamped by guilt. Now chin-deep in his debt.

Percy sauntered up to them. Phyllida glanced his way, then let her gaze drift to Lucifer. Percy was unwise to stand beside him; the comparison left Percy looking like a pasty-faced, effeminate weakling. Percy was pasty-faced, but otherwise presentable – it was the competition that served him so ill.

Her aunt continued to proclaim the impossibility of the murderer being local. Phyllida grasped the moment when she paused for breath. 'I must call on Mrs Hemmings, Papa, to make sure she has all she needs for the wake. I also need to stop at the church and speak with Mr Filing.'

Her nemesis spoke. 'Perhaps I could accompany you, Miss Tallent?'

'Ah . . .' Transfixed by blue eyes that warned her there was no alternative to his company, Phyllida bit back a refusal, couched as a polite reminder about his head.

His lips curved; his gaze remained steady. 'I know I promised not to overtax myself, but as I'll be in your company, there's surely no risk.'

He'd kept her secret; now she had to pay the price. She inclined her head. 'If you wish. A walk in the fresh air might ease your head.'

'An excellent notion.' As Lucifer straightened from bowing to her aunt, her father caught his eye. 'Give you a chance to get the lay of the land, heh?'

'Indeed.' The reprobate turned to her, a definite glint in his eyes. He smiled and gestured elegantly. 'Lead on, my dear Miss Tallent.'

CHAPTER 3

She took him to the Manor by way of the lane through the village; it was too dangerous to walk through the woods with a predator, especially one in whose power she now was. Her father, of course, had no idea – he was impressed with the fiend, she could tell.

As she walked through the sunshine with him prowling beside her, she grudgingly admitted that if he hadn't been such a threat to her, she might have been impressed, too. He felt just as he ought to about Horatio. But being managed was a novel experience for her, one she didn't like. However, he hadn't done the unforgivable and given her the ultimate ultimatum – that either she tell him the whole truth, or he would tell her father she'd been in Horatio's drawing room. She was therefore willing to humor him.

She glanced at him. His dark hair shone mahogany brown in the sun. 'You forgot your hat.'

'I rarely wear one.'

So much for that. She walked on. The village proper lay just ahead.

Lucifer looked at her; her bonnet shielded her

face from his view. 'I think' – he waited until she glanced up at him – 'that, given we've formed an alliance of sorts, you'd better tell me what happened after I was discovered.'

She studied his eyes, then faced forward. 'You were discovered by Hemmings, Horatio's gardener. Mrs Hemmings, the housekeeper, went upstairs, imagining Horatio to be there. Hemmings went into the drawing room to lay the fire. He raised the alarm and Bristleford, Horatio's butler, sent for Juggs and Thompson.'

'To take me, as the murderer, into custody?'

Her bonnet bobbed. 'Bristleford was overset – he thought you were the murderer. There's a cell beneath the inn where prisoners are held awaiting transportation to the assizes. Thompson's the blacksmith – they used his dray to shift you.'

'And where were you?'

She glanced swiftly at him, then away. A full minute passed before she said, 'I was laid upon my bed with a sick headache – that was why I hadn't gone to church.'

When she said no more, he prompted her. 'You appeared in the cell insisting I wasn't the murderer.'

'I didn't know whether you remembered.'

'I remember. How did you come to be there?'

'I often borrowed books of poetry from Horatio. I recovered from my headache and thought I'd fetch a new volume. But just as I reached our front door, Aunt Huddlesford's carriage drew up.

I'd forgotten she was arriving that morning, but all the arrangements were already in place – or so I thought.'

The irritation in that last reached Lucifer clearly. 'But . . . ?'

'Percy and Frederick – I wasn't expecting them. They don't usually favor us with their gracious presence.'

'I'd wager Percy's on a repairing lease.'

'Very likely, but their arrival meant that I had to wait until our staff returned from church to give orders for extra rooms, and entertain them and Aunt Huddlesford until Papa and Jonas appeared.'

'And when that happened?'

'I left as soon as I could, but when I reached the Manor, you'd already been taken away.'

'Is this the inn?' Lucifer stopped; Phyllida did, too. The building beside them was a half-timbered structure, worn and a little shabby but still serviceable.

'Yes – the Red Bells.'

'And Juggs is the innkeeper.'

She started walking again. 'He gets paid for holding prisoners, so you shouldn't judge him too harshly.'

He swallowed his response to that. 'What happened next?'

'I made sure they'd sent for Papa, then I came to the Bells.' She glanced at his face. 'How much do you remember?'

'Not all of it, but enough. You stayed until your father arrived, and then he rode home and was to send the carriage. The next thing I remember clearly was . . .' – he studied her eyes while he replayed his memories – 'waking up in the witching hour.'

'Yes, well, that's really all there was to it.' Looking ahead, she paced on. 'You were restless, but your skull was intact – it was all just the pain.'

Lucifer glanced at her. Why hadn't she taken the opportunity to tell him of her vigil by his bed? He'd put her in a position of being grateful to him; why hadn't she evened the score?

They strolled past a succession of neat cottages and on around the curving lane. The Manor came into sight.

'Very well,' he said. 'I now know your story. I also know that you were in Horatio's drawing room before I entered, and that you were there after I was hit.'

'You know nothing of the sort.'

He looked smugly superior – she was watching from the corner of her eye.

'You can't possibly tell it was me from a mere touch.' The glance she flung at him was both irate and uncertain.

'I can. I did. I know it was you.'

'You can't be sure.'

'Hmm . . . perhaps not. Why not touch me again, just to see if I'm certain?'

64

She stopped and faced him, latent sparks in her eyes –

'Hoi! Miss Phyllida!'

They swung around. A heavy man in a leather apron and vest was lumbering down the common toward them.

'The blacksmith?'

'Yes – Thompson.'

Thompson approached. His gaze on Lucifer, he nodded respectfully. 'Sir.' He nodded at Phyllida, then looked back at Lucifer. 'I just wanted to apologize, like, for any bruises you mighta taken when we dumped you in my dray. 'Course, we thought you was the murderer and you weren't easy to lift, but I wouldn't want no hard feelings.'

Lucifer smiled. 'None taken. I don't bruise easily.'

'Well.' Thompson blew out a relieved breath and grinned back. 'That's all right, then. Not but what it was no fit welcome to the village, 'specially not with a bash on the head an' all.'

Phyllida inwardly squirmed. She glanced up the lane toward the Manor.

'Has Sir Jasper got any clues as to this murderer, then, sir?'

Her 'No' clashed with Lucifer's 'None' – Phyllida nearly outwardly squirmed when she realized the question had not been addressed to her.

With a subtly amused glance, Lucifer added, 'Sir Jasper's investigations are proceeding.'

'Aye, well . . .'

Phyllida waited while Thompson pointed out the forge on the far side of the common and assured Lucifer that he could count on him for any assistance, either in laying the murderer by the heels or with his horses.

With a final nod, Thompson took himself off back over the common.

She stepped out again; Lucifer prowled by her side, his stride an exercise in effortless grace. He murmured, 'It seems a peaceful little place.'

'Usually.' She glanced up and found him scanning the common and the church on the crest.

They avoided the duck pond and its vocal inhabitants and reached the Manor's gate. She opened it and stepped through; Lucifer had to duck the trailing fingers of wisteria hanging from the framing arch. She led the way around the small fountain. Gaining the porch, she realized he'd fallen behind. Looking back, she saw him studying a bed of burgeoning peonies. His gaze moved on to a bed of roses and lavender; then he glanced up, saw her waiting, and lengthened his stride.

He joined her on the porch, but glanced back at the garden.

'What is it?'

He looked at her, his expression closed, his eyes screened. 'Who did the garden?'

'Papa told you – Horatio. Well' – she glanced at the beds – 'Hemmings helped, of course, but Horatio's was always the guiding hand.' She studied his face. 'Why?'

He looked at the garden. 'When they lived in the Lake District, Martha did the garden – it was hers, totally. I would have sworn Horatio wouldn't have known a hollyhock from a nettle.'

Phyllida considered the garden with new eyes. 'All the time he was here he was most particular about the garden.'

After a moment, Lucifer turned; she noted his closed face. Swinging around, she led the way inside.

The house was silent; they walked quietly forward, halting level with the open drawing room door. Horatio's coffin rested on the table just beyond the spot where they – yes, *they* – had found his body. For a moment, they both simply looked, then Phyllida led the way in.

A yard from the coffin, she stopped. It suddenly required effort to breathe. Long fingers touched hers; instinctively, she clung. His hand closed about hers, warm and alive. He stepped forward to stand beside her. She felt his gaze on her face. Without looking at him, she nodded. Side by side, they stepped to the polished wooden box.

For long moments, they stood gazing down. Phyllida drew comfort from the peaceful expression that had settled on Horatio's face. It had been there when she'd found him, as if his departure from this world, although violent and unexpected, had been a release. Perhaps there truly was a Heaven.

She'd liked him, approved of him, and was sad

that he was gone. She could say good-bye and let him go, but the manner of his going was not something she could let be. He'd been murdered in the village she'd virtually managed for twelve years; that she'd been the one to find him, already gone and beyond her help, had only increased her outrage.

It was as if something she'd worked for all her life – the peace and serenity of Colyton – had been violated, tainted.

The memory returned to her, crystal-clear, that moment when she'd found Horatio dead. She felt again her shock, the chill touch of fear, the paralyzing fright when she'd realized she'd heard no one leaving . . .

Lifting her head, she stared down the room. She'd only just remembered.

She'd come to the drawing room from the back of the hall; before that, she'd been in the kitchen. Even from there, if anyone had left the house, she would have heard them cross the hall or cross the gravel. No one had. She'd idled in the hall, then decided on searching the drawing room.

How long had all that taken? How long had Horatio been dead before she'd found him?

What if the murderer hadn't left but had still been in the drawing room when she'd entered?

She focused on the gap between two bookcases, almost at the end of the room. It was the only hiding place the murderer could have used.

He *must* have been there. That was the only explanation for the disappearing hat. There was certain to have been a gap between her exit and Hemmings deciding to lay the fire. Mrs Hemmings would have been upstairs. A small window of opportunity, but the murderer had grasped it, and his hat, and disappeared without a trace.

Phyllida drew in a breath; the warmth of Lucifer's hand clasped around hers anchored her, steadied her. She looked down at Horatio's lined face and made a vow – a binding, resolute vow – that she would find whoever had hidden between the bookcases and watched her discover Horatio's body.

This was one murderer who would not escape.

Even as she made her silent declaration, she was aware another, very similar one was being made not a foot away. Lucifer's words to her father had rung with determination; she needed no convincing that he would regard his vow as seriously as she regarded hers.

They could work together – together they might succeed. Alone, even with her father's support, bringing a murderer to justice might well be more than she could accomplish. Despite his dubious talents, she was certain the reprobate beside her could achieve anything he set his mind to. So . . .

She slanted a glance at him. She needed to tell him all that had happened, even to admitting that it was she who had hit him over the head. Confessing to that wouldn't be comfortable, but he needed to know.

He especially needed to know about the hat.

Which meant she had to speak with Mary Anne straightaway.

She took in Lucifer's bleak expression, the planes of his face harsh without any lurking laughter to soften them. His large eyes were hooded. He'd been much closer to Horatio than she had.

Sliding her fingers from his, she retreated and left him with his grief.

Lucifer heard her go. Part of his mind tracked her movements; part of him relaxed when she turned deeper into the house. He remembered she'd mentioned speaking with the housekeeper. Reassured, he returned his attention to Horatio.

Their last farewell – there wouldn't be another. He let the memories spill through his mind, like water running through his fingers. Their shared interests, their successes, their mutual appreciation, the long afternoons spent on the terrace overlooking Lake Windemere. All good times – there'd been none bad.

At the last, he drew in a deep breath, then laid a hand atop Horatio's, clasped on his chest. 'Go twit Martha on her pansies. As for revenge, leave that to me.'

Vengeance might be the Lord's, but sometimes He needed help.

As he turned away, his gaze fell on the bookshelves lining the walls. Idly, he strolled along them, tracing the spines of volumes here and there, remembered friends. Toward the end of the room, he noticed three volumes jutting out from their shelf. He slid them back in, aligning them. He looked back along the tome-lined wall. How appropriate for Horatio to spend his final hours here, surrounded by his dearest possessions.

He was standing before the long windows, looking out on the garden that so puzzled him, when a discreet cough sounded in the doorway. He turned; a thin, spare man, hunched into his coat, was staring at the coffin. Lucifer left the window. 'Covey. Pray accept my condolences. I know how attached you were to Horatio – and he to you.'

Covey blinked watery blue eyes. 'Thank you, sir. Miss Tallent told me you were here. I regret that it's such a dreadful occasion that sees you with us . . . again.'

'A dreadful business, indeed. Do you have any idea . . . ?'

'None at all. I had no inkling, no reason to suppose . . .' He gestured helplessly at the coffin.

'Don't blame yourself, Covey – you couldn't have known.'

'If I had, it wouldn't have happened.'

'Of course not.' Lucifer interposed himself between Covey and the coffin. 'Horatio wrote to me about some item he'd discovered that he wanted my opinion on. Do you know what it was?'

Covey shook his head. 'I knew he'd found something special. You know how he'd get – his eyes all lighting up like a child's? That's how he was for the past week. I hadn't seen him so excited for years.'

71

'He didn't mention anything at all about it?'

'No, but he never did, not with his special finds. Not until he was ready to tell all; then he'd lay all the proofs out on his desk and explain it all to me.' A wistful smile touched Covey's lips. 'He'd take great delight in that, even though he knew I understood not one word in three.'

Lucifer gripped Covey's shoulder. 'You were a good friend to him, Covey.' He hesitated, then added, 'I'm sure Horatio will have made provision for you in his will, but whatever happens, we'll sort something out. Horatio would have wished it.'

Covey inclined his head. 'Thank you, sir. I appreciate the reassurance.'

'One thing. Have any of the other dealers stopped by recently? Jamieson? Dallwell?'

'No, sir. Mr Jamieson stopped by some months ago, but we've seen no one recently. The master hasn't – hadn't – been so active in dealing since we'd moved south.'

Lucifer hesitated. 'I imagine I'll be staying at the Grange for the next few days.'

'Indeed, sir.' Covey bowed. 'If you'll excuse me, I'll return to my tidying.'

Lucifer nodded in dismissal, wondering who Horatio's heirs would be. He made a mental note to have a word with them regarding Covey's long service and devotion. Returning to the window, he considered Covey's description of Horatio's recent excitement.

If he could understand why Horatio had been killed, he would know who had killed him. The 'why' was the key. It seemed possible, even likely, that the 'why' was the mysterious item Horatio had discovered; his violent death had followed so soon after the discovery. If the mysterious item was the key, then the murderer might have come from beyond the local area, as Lady Huddlesford insisted was the case. Luckily, they were deep in the country – 'outsiders' were noticed. He was sure he'd been noticed, perhaps not in Colyton, but certainly along the way.

Turning, he scanned the room. Horatio might have concealed his latest find in plain sight, amid the treasure trove of his collection.

When Phyllida returned to the drawing room, she found her nemesis examining the halberd responsible for the dent in his skull. He looked at her. 'Was it always kept here – behind the door?'

'I understand so.'

He studied her, then looked at the axe-head. Raising the halberd, he let it fall to his other hand, watching how the weighted head swung. 'I would have thought, if it had fallen or been wielded with intent . . .'

Then the axe should have cleaved his skull in two. Phyllida didn't want to think about it. 'This part here' – she pointed to the rounded side – 'was apparently what connected with your head.'

'Indeed?' He hefted the weapon fully upright, then looked at her. 'How did it fall?'

She met his eyes directly – and said nothing.

He held her gaze, and let the tension stretch.

And stretch . . .

She lifted her chin. 'I have to go to the church to sort out the flowers for the funeral, and then I must speak with the curate. You can stay here, if you like.'

Lucifer replaced the halberd. 'I'll come with you.'

He'd said his last good-bye to Horatio.

Contained and uncommunicative, she led the way through the garden. As they rounded the fountain, he paused. 'The flowers for the church – use some of these peonies. They were Martha's favorites.'

She stopped and glanced back at him, then at the flowers. Then she nodded and continued on.

They crossed the lane and started up the common. The expanse of green was kept clipped by the sheep allowed to graze over it; it rose in a gradual slope from the lane to the crest on which the church stood.

Lucifer matched his long strides to Phyllida's and breathed deeply. The air was fresh, sun-warmed; the scents and sounds of a June afternoon ebbed and flowed around them. The ache in his head was subsiding, and the best distraction Colyton had to offer was walking beside him.

He was intrigued, and couldn't entirely understand why. Indeed, he wasn't sure he approved. His preference, until now, had been for ladies of more bountiful charms, yet Phyllida Tallent's

74

slender grace acted powerfully on his ever-ready male senses. Being so easily aroused by a gently reared, intelligent, and stubborn virgin, one who was making no effort to attract him at all, had to be fate's idea of a joke. Perhaps being hit on the head had affected him more than he'd realized.

Whatever the cause, walking beside and a little behind her left him all too aware whenever the frolicking breeze plastered her gown to her legs and bottom, or when it flicked at the hem of her skirt, exposing slim ankles. Her svelte figure contained a suppressed energy one part of him – the wild, untamed pirate part of him – instantly recognized; he longed to wind it tight, then release it before plunging into its core.

Climbing the hill was easing his head at the expense of intensifying the ache in his loins. An ache destined to remain unrelieved. Drawing a bracing breath, he looked ahead, and deliberately shifted his thoughts.

She preceded him into the church and went straight to the altar. Picking up a vase, she headed through an open door into a small side chamber.

He lounged against a pew. The small church was well endowed with carvings and stained glass. The oriel window above the entrance was particularly pleasing. It was fitting that Horatio's funeral would be held here; Horatio would have appreciated the church's beauties.

A beauty of a different sort swept back in and effortlessly recaptured his attention.

Phyllida jumped when large hands covered hers as she wrestled with the urn on the font.

'Let me.'

She did. The reverberations of his voice played up and down her spine and left her nerves jangling. Wordlessly, she led the way through the vestry and out through the open back door. She indicated the pile of dead flowers. 'Just toss them there.'

He did. She retrieved the urn from his hands; without being asked, he wielded the pump handle so she could rinse it. With a nod of thanks, she swept back into the vestry; swiping up a cloth, she vigorously buffed the urn.

He halted in the doorway, almost blocking out the light; propping one shoulder against the frame, he watched her.

The vestry suddenly seemed very small. Awareness prickled over her skin.

'The funeral will be tomorrow, late morning. I'll send flowers over first thing – in this weather, they wilt so quickly.' She was babbling. She'd never babbled in her life. 'Especially if they're not picked before the sun strikes them.'

'Does that mean you'll be flitting among the flowers at dawn?'

She wanted to look at him but didn't. 'Of course not. Our gardener knows just how I like them picked.'

'Ah. No need, then, to get up too early.'

It was his tone, the deep resonance in his voice, that gave his words their full meaning. For an instant, she froze, her hands on the urn, then she sucked in a breath, grasped the urn, set it on the shelf, and swung to face him. Her expression, she was sure, remained calmly superior, unruffled, and serene. No one in the village ever saw beyond that, which made protecting herself and managing them very easy.

His gaze, however, settled on her eyes. He saw further, deeper – she wasn't at all comfortable with what he might see. 'I need to speak with Mr Filing, the curate. Given your injury, you should rest for a few minutes. I suggest you sit in a pew in the cool of the church. I'll collect you when I've finished with Mr Filing.'

He continued to study her face, her eyes. After an unnerving moment, he glanced back outside, over his left shoulder. 'Is that the curate's house?'

'Yes. That's the Rectory.'

He straightened away from the doorframe; the movement did nothing to reduce the sense of entrapment she felt. 'I'll come with you.'

Phyllida drew in a breath, and held it. With anyone else she would have argued, but there was an undercurrent in his voice that warned her she had no chance of swaying him. Not without a fight – and fighting with him was too dangerous. 'As you wish.'

He moved back and she stepped past him, into the sunshine. She led the way down the winding path to the Rectory, snug in a hollow just below the crest. Shutting the vestry door, he followed on her heels.

His intention was impossible to mistake. He knew she was hiding something; he was going to cling to her side – unnerve her as much as he could – until she told him what it was. Or until he uncovered her secrets for himself.

The latter, Phyllida decided, was not a fate to tempt. How soon could she see Mary Anne?

Lucifer followed her to the Rectory, too conscious of the lithe grace of her stride, the unfettered freedom with which she moved. To senses steeped in consideration of the feminine, she registered as something beyond the norm. Infinitely more desirable, and infinitely more elusive.

Why, he wondered, did she not wish him to be a party to her meeting with the curate?

That gentleman had seen them coming; he stood waiting for them at his front door. Fair, pale, and slightly built, his clothes fastidiously neat, Filing had the appearance of a gentleman aesthete. He greeted Phyllida with a smile, one that held the warmth of long-standing friendship.

'Good morning, Mr Filing. Allow me to present Mr Cynster, an old friend of Horatio's.'

'Indeed?' Filing offered his hand; Lucifer shook it. 'Such a sad occurrence. It must have been a shock to discover Horatio slain.'

Lucifer inclined his head.

'As you'll have heard, the funeral's tomorrow morning. Perhaps, as an old friend, you'd like to give the eulogy?'

Lucifer considered, then shook his head. 'With

this knock on the head, I'm not sure I'll be up to it, and frankly, I think Horatio would consider his connection with the people here of more importance to him over these last years than his professional associations.'

And he suspected he'd be of more use to Horatio by studying those attending the funeral.

'I see, I see.' Filing nodded. 'Well, then, if there's no objection, I'll give the eulogy myself. Horatio and I often shared a glass of port of an evening. He had a wonderful collection of ecclesiastical texts and kindly gave me free rein to browse through them. He was truly a gentleman and a scholar – that will be the theme of my eulogy.'

'Very apt.' Lucifer turned his gaze on Phyllida, and waited; Filing did the same.

Her expression calm, her eyes watchful, she glanced at him. 'There are a number of organizational matters I must discuss with Mr Filing.'

Lucifer nodded, as if giving her permission to speak. Shifting back, he let his gaze roam the common, down to the cottages lining the lane.

'Our discussion will take a few minutes. Perhaps you should rest on that bench over there.'

The bench was halfway down the slope overlooking the duck pond, well out of hearing range. He frowned and glanced at her. 'It might be wiser if we descend together. Just in case I'm overcome with giddiness.'

Her annoyance reached him in a wash of heat; anger glowed momentarily in her eyes. But she inclined her head, her expression cool, unconcerned – a perfect social mask. Filing glanced back and forth; he sensed something, but couldn't define it. Couldn't see past her facade.

Lucifer wondered why *he* could – and why he wanted to see so much further, to know so much more.

She turned to Filing. 'About the flowers for tomorrow . . .'

Fixing his gaze down the common, Lucifer let their discussion flow past him. There seemed a great deal to be said about the flowers. Then, with not the slightest shift in her tone to mark the shift in her subject, she continued. 'Which brings us to our other business.'

Lucifer suppressed a cynical smile. She was good. Unfortunately for her, he was better.

'You have the collection complete, I believe?'

From the corner of his eye Lucifer saw Filing nod – and shoot a glance at him.

'I assume you foresee no difficulties in the distribution to those deserving?'

'No,' Filing murmured. 'All seems . . . straightforward.'

'Good. Our next outing will be as scheduled. I've had a letter confirming there's been no change to the plans. If you could pass the word on to those interested?'

'Of course.'

'And do remind them that we'll need the group assembled in good time – we can't wait for

80

stragglers. If they're not there from the very first, then we really cannot include them in the group, so they'll miss out on the benefits of the excursion.'

Filing nodded. 'If any want to argue that point, I'll suggest they speak with Thompson.'

Phyllida shot him a glance. 'Do.' She straightened. 'Until tomorrow, then.'

Lucifer returned his attention to her, then nodded a farewell to Filing.

Phyllida gestured down the common. 'We should get back – you really should rest your head.'

He fell into step beside her; they descended the slope at an easy pace.

What in all Hades was the woman up to?

He assumed he was supposed to imagine that they'd been discussing some excursion for Filing's parishioners. He might have believed it but for her dogged attempts to keep the knowledge from him. While the correct interpretation presently eluded him, he couldn't believe it was anything heinous or illegal. She was the magistrate's daughter, devoted to good works, and Filing was patently honest and upright. So why didn't she want *him* to know what she was about?

If she'd been younger, he would have suspected some lark. Not only was she too old for that, but her behavior tended to the mature, the managing; she was no irresponsible hoyden.

The mystery about her had just deepened; the urge to take her somewhere private, back her against a wall, and keep her there until she told him all he wished to know, grew with every step.

He glanced at her and was rewarded with a full view of her face as she lifted it to the breeze, shaking back her tangling bonnet ribbons. He drank in her features, the resolution in her face, the challenge implicit in the defiant tilt of her chin. Facing forward again, he reminded himself that she was a gently reared virgin – no fit prey for him. She was not a woman with whom he could dally.

He would learn her secrets, then he'd have to let her go.

They stepped into the lane. A carriage was drawn up just ahead, the occupants – a large gentleman and an older lady – patently waiting to speak with them.

'Sir Cedric Fortemain and his mother, Lady Fortemain,' Phyllida supplied sotto voce.

'And they are?'

'Cedric owns Ballyclose Manor – it lies over the hill past the forge.'

They neared the carriage. Sir Cedric, in his late thirties and already tending portly with a florid face and thinning hair, rose and bowed to Phyllida, then leaned over the side to shake her hand.

Phyllida performed the introductions. Lucifer bowed to her ladyship and shook hands with Cedric.

'I hear you were the first to discover the body, Mr Cynster,' Lady Fortemain said.

'Shocking business!' Cedric declared.

They chatted inconsequentially about London and the weather; Lucifer noted Cedric's gaze rarely left Phyllida. His comments were a touch too patronizing, a touch too particular. When, contained and unresponsive, she stepped back, preparing to leave, Cedric caught her eye.

'I'm pleased to see, m'dear, that you're not rambling about the village on your own. There's no telling but that Welham's murderer is still about.'

'Indeed!' Lady Fortemain smiled at Lucifer. 'So comforting to see you're keeping an eye on dear Phyllida. We'd be devastated were anything to happen to our village treasure.'

That was accompanied by a beam of sincere approbation, which brought a frown to the village treasure's eyes. 'We must be getting on.'

Lucifer bowed to Lady Fortemain, exchanged nods with Cedric, then strolled beside Phyllida as she crossed the lane to walk along the cottages' front fences. 'Why,' he murmured, 'does Lady Fortemain think you a treasure?'

'Because she wants me to marry Cedric. And because I helped her to find a ring she misplaced at the Hunt Ball one year. And once I guessed where Pommeroy was hiding one of the times he ran away, but that was years ago.'

'Who's Pommeroy?'

'Cedric's younger brother.' After a moment, she added, 'He's much worse than Cedric.'

The rattle of carriage wheels came from behind them; they both slowed, stepping further to the side of the lane. The carriage swept past; a hatchet-faced, stony-eyed lady gazed haughtily down on them.

Lucifer raised his brows as the carriage rattled on. 'Who was that harbinger of sunshine and delight?'

He looked across in time to see Phyllida's lips twitch. 'Jocasta Smollet.'

'Who is?'

'Sir Basil Smollet's sister.'

'And Sir Basil is?'

'The gentleman approaching us. He owns Highgate, up the lane past the Rectory.'

Lucifer studied the gentleman in question; he was neatly, even severely dressed, and of an age similar to Cedric. But where Cedric's expression had been choleric yet open, Basil's was guarded, as if he had a lot on his mind, but was above explaining himself to anyone.

He tipped his hat in greeting. Introduced, he shook hands with Lucifer.

'Dreadful business, this. Sets the whole village on its ears. No rest for any of us until the villain's caught. Pray accept my condolences on the death of your friend.'

Lucifer thanked him. With polite nods to them both, Basil continued on his way.

'Punctilious,' Lucifer murmured.

'Indeed.' Phyllida stepped out again, looked ahead, and slowed. 'Oh. Dear.'

The words were uttered through her teeth; she might as well have cursed. Lucifer considered the cause of her consternation. Red-haired, in his late twenties, the gentleman strode toward them with a purposeful air. Only just taller than Phyllida, he was plainly dressed in corduroy breeches and riding boots, topped by a loose, flapping coat.

Phyllida's chin rose; she moved forward decisively. 'Good day, Mr Grisby.' She inclined her head, her intention plainly to continue on her way.

Grisby planted himself directly in front of her. Phyllida halted and smoothly turned to Lucifer. 'Mr Cynster, allow me to present Mr Grisby.'

Lucifer nodded coolly. Grisby hesitated, then curtly responded. He returned his gaze to Phyllida. 'Miss Tallent, please allow me to escort you home.' The glance he shot Lucifer brimmed with poorly concealed dislike. 'I'm surprised Sir Jasper hasn't forbidden you to roam, what with this knife-wielding murderer on the loose.'

'My father—'

'One never knows,' Grisby sententiously continued, 'from what direction danger may come.' Pugnaciously, he reached for her arm.

Phyllida reached for Lucifer's.

Bending his arm, covering her hand with his, Lucifer drew her closer. He caught Grisby's gaze, all humor flown. 'I assure you, Grisby, that Miss Tallent is in no danger from knife-wielding felons, or any others, while in my care.' He'd only been waiting for some sign from Phyllida before stepping in; if he hadn't been feeling his way, Grisby would already be flailing in the duck pond. 'We're on our way back to the Grange. You may rest assured I will see Miss Tallent safe into Sir Jasper's keeping.'

Grisby flushed.

Lucifer inclined his head. 'If you'll excuse us?'

He gave Grisby no choice, solicitously steering Phyllida, censoriously haughty, down the lane. He kept her close, her skirts brushing his boots. Under his hand, her fingers fluttered. They strolled on; eventually her fingers relaxed under his.

'Thank you.'

'It was entirely my pleasure. Aside from being an insensitive clod, who, exactly, is Grisby?'

'He owns Dottswood Farm. It's up past the Rectory, beyond Highgate.'

'So he's a prosperous gentleman farmer?'

'Among other things.'

Her disgusted tone gave him his clue. 'Am I to understand Mr Grisby is another aspirant to your fair hand?'

'They all are – Cedric, Basil, and Grisby.'

Her tone wasn't improving; Lucifer raised his brows. 'You have cut a swath through the local ranks.'

She cast him a repressive glance, one his aunt, the Dowager Duchess of St Ives, could not have bettered, then, head high, looked forward.

The common ended just ahead where the lane leading to the graveyard and the forge joined the village lane. Along the lesser lane lay a row of small houses, bigger than the cottages but not as large as the Manor or the Grange. Each house had its own garden with a fence and a gate.

A gentleman stepped through the nearest gate; in breeches, stockings, and high-heeled shoes, he minced down the lane toward them. In a bottle-green coat with a bright yellow-and-black kerchief tied in a floppy bow and sporting a periwig, the gentleman was unquestionably the most colorful figure Lucifer had seen for many a long year.

He glanced at Phyllida; she was deep in thought, her gaze fixed ahead; she'd yet to see the gentleman.

'I hesitate to ask, but is the gentleman to our right another of your suitors?'

She looked. 'No, thank God. Unfortunately, that's the best I can say for him. His name is Silas Coombe.'

'Does he always dress like that?'

'I've heard that in earlier years, he dressed as a macaroni. These days, he contents himself with adopting all the extremes of fashion and wearing them all at once.'

'A gentleman of independent means?'

'He lives off inherited investments. His main interest in life is posturing. That, and reading. Until Horatio arrived, Silas had the most extensive library in the area.'

'So he and Horatio were friends?'

'No. Quite the opposite.' She paused as the

gentleman neared; he crossed the corner of the common, sparing them not one glance. They continued to stroll; as they left the village behind, Phyllida mused, 'In fact, Silas is possibly the only one in the locality who sincerely hated Horatio.'

'*Hated* Horatio?' Lucifer shot her a glance. 'Horatio wasn't an easy person to hate.'

'Nevertheless. You see, for years, Silas had touted himself as a renowned antiquarian bibliophile. I think it was his ambition, and here in the country there was no one to challenge his claim. Not that it meant anything to anyone else, but it meant a lot to Silas. Then Horatio arrived and exploded his myth. Horatio's library eclipsed Silas's completely and Silas did not know books as Horatio did. Even to us, untutored though we are, the difference was obvious. Horatio was genuine; Silas, a poor imitation.'

The Grange drive appeared before them; as they turned through the gateposts, Phyllida drew her hand from his sleeve and turned to face him. 'You don't think . . . ?'

He met her gaze. 'I don't know what to think. At the moment, I'm merely gathering information.'

'Silas is effeminate. I wouldn't think him very strong.'

'Weaklings can kill quite effectively – rage can lend strength to the most ineffectual.'

'I suppose . . .' She frowned. 'But I still can't see Silas stabbing anyone.'

He was silent for a moment, then asked, 'So who do you think killed Horatio?'

The question hung between them; she lifted her head and looked him in the eye. 'I don't know who killed Horatio.'

She enunciated each word clearly. Their gazes held; it was she who turned away. Head high, she continued down the drive. After a moment, he fell in beside her, his stride longer and slower than hers. 'Tell me, how many more are there in the locality – people like the Fortemains who would have known Horatio socially?'

'Not that many. You've met about half.' They continued strolling down the winding drive, hemmed in by trees on all sides. Phyllida drew in a breath. 'Do you seriously think someone from the village killed Horatio?'

She glanced up; Lucifer caught her eye. 'Horatio was killed by someone he knew well – someone he let get close to him, well within arm's reach.' When she frowned, he added, 'There was no sign of any struggle.'

Her frown cleared as she remembered; refocusing, she saw the intensity in his gaze and looked away. 'Perhaps it was someone he knew from outside – another collector.'

'If so, we'll find out. I'll be making inquiries in all the surrounding towns.'

They walked on in silence. She felt his gaze on her face. They'd gone another fifty yards before he asked, 'Indelicate question though it is, why, with so many suitors, aren't you married?'

She glanced up but could see nothing in his eyes

beyond simple interest. The question was indeed impertinent, yet she felt no compunction in answering; she knew the answer so well. 'Because every man who has ever asked for my hand has wanted to marry me to suit his own ends – because having me as his wife would improve his lot. For Cedric and Basil, marrying me would be sensible – I'm suitable, I know the locals, and I could manage their households with my eyes shut. For Grisby, I can add that marrying me would be a step upward socially – he's ambitious in that sphere.'

She looked up and discovered Lucifer studying her. After a moment, he asked, 'Don't you have any wishes, any requirements of marriage – anything they might provide you?'

She shook her head. 'All they can offer is a household and a position – I already have both. Why marry and take a husband when I'd gain nothing I desire in the process?'

His lips twitched, then curved into a smile. 'How very clearheaded of you.'

The dangerous purr had returned to his voice; there was a look in his eyes she didn't understand. Facing forward, she kept strolling.

The house lay just ahead, screened by the last bend, when he stopped her with a hand on her arm. She faced him, her question in her eyes. He looked down at her, his gaze disturbingly direct. 'What actually happened?'

Phyllida held his gaze and thought about telling him. But it was a case of all or nothing – she'd seen enough of him to know she would have to tell him all once she admitted that she was there. He wouldn't let her keep anything back. And for once in her life, she doubted her ability to stand against a man.

This man was something else – some different species she hadn't before encountered. She was old enough, wise enough, to recognize the difference and acknowledge in her mind that she'd be unwise to challenge him.

Of course, not telling him was a blatant challenge, but that simply had to be. She would not break her word. She might prevaricate for a good cause, but her oath was absolute, and a vow given to a friend was sacred.

'I can't tell you. Not yet.' She turned away. He stopped her, long fingers closing around her elbow. Her temper flared; she looked up at him. 'I've kept my part of the bargain.'

He blinked. 'What bargain?'

'You didn't tell Papa you believed that I was there, in Horatio's drawing room, and so I took you around the village, introduced you to Horatio's acquaintances, and answered your questions about them.'

He frowned, the gesture more evident in his eyes than on his face. His hold on her arm anchored her before him; she didn't bother trying to wriggle free. He studied her eyes and she let him; emotionally, she had nothing to hide.

'Is that why you thought I invited myself along?'

'That, and so you could try to trip me up. Why else?'

He released her, but his gaze held hers. 'Couldn't I have wanted to spend time in your company?'

She stared at him. The suggestion was so unexpected, she couldn't at first imagine it. Then she did, and the truth washed over her – she would have liked it if he had. If he'd simply wanted to spend a summer afternoon strolling with her around the village, idly commenting, relaxed in her company. Her chest tightened; haughtily, she turned away. 'You didn't. That wasn't why you came walking with me today.'

Lucifer heard the calm statement but left it unchallenged. He watched her walk away, and let the impulse to correct her fade. She was such a contrary female – handling her was difficult, not to say dangerous; she was so different from the women he knew. God knew, he'd never before been so attracted to a virgin.

A stubborn, willful, innocent, headstrong, intelligent, far-too-untouched-for-her-own-good virgin.

It made everything so much more complicated.

CHAPTER 4

He caught Phyllida up as she negotiated the last bend in the drive. The side lawn of the Grange opened before them; a knot of people were gathered around tables and chairs, enjoying the late afternoon. They both halted, but they'd been seen; Lady Huddlesford beckoned imperiously.

'Who are they?'

'Some of the half you've yet to meet.' Phyllida searched the group; then she saw Mary Anne and felt giddy with relief. 'Come. I'll introduce you.'

They crossed the lawn. Lady Huddlesford, presiding over the gathering from a chair at a wrought-iron table, beamed delightedly. 'Mr Cynster! Excellent! I was just telling Mrs Farthingale . . .'

Phyllida left Lucifer to fend for himself, something he was patently well able to do; he smiled, effortlessly charming, and the ladies all preened. Directing a general smile on those present, she strolled to Mary Anne's side.

Mary Anne stared at Lucifer. 'He's . . .' She gestured.

'From London.' Phyllida slipped her arm through Mary Anne's. 'We need to talk.'

Mary Anne turned huge blue eyes her way. 'Did you find them?' she whispered as they turned from the group.

Mary Anne's fingers clamped like talons around her wrist; something close to panic filled her eyes. Phyllida inwardly frowned and drew her on. 'The rose garden's more private. Pretend we're simply strolling.'

Luckily, the entire gathering – Mary Anne's mother, Mrs Farthingale, Lady Fortemain, Mrs Weatherspoon, and a gaggle of other ladies, with Percy and Frederick for leavening – was hanging on Lucifer's every word. Phyllida glanced back as she and Mary Anne entered the yew walk that led to the rose garden. Lucifer's attention appeared fully engaged.

Surrounded by thick stone walls, the rose garden was a secluded paradise of lush growth, vibrant splashes of color, and rich, exotic scents. The instant they entered its privacy, Mary Anne's public demeanor crumbled. She swung to face Phyllida, gripping her hands tightly. 'Say you found them! *Please* say you did!'

'I looked, but . . .' Phyllida frowned. 'Come – let's sit down. We need to discuss this.'

'There's nothing to *discuss*!' Mary Anne wailed. 'If I don't get those letters back, my life will be *ruined*!'

Phyllida towed her to a seat set against the wall.

'I didn't say we won't get them back – I promised we would. But there's been a complication.'

'Complication?'

'A large one.' Over six feet tall and difficult to manage. Phyllida sat on the seat and pulled Mary Anne down beside her. 'Now, first, are you absolutely sure Horatio was the one your father sold the writing desk to?'

'Yes. I saw Horatio take it away last Monday.'

'And you definitely, positively, hid your letters in the secret drawer in the desk? You haven't by accident left them somewhere else?'

'They were too *dangerous* to leave anywhere else!'

'And it is your grandmother's traveling writing desk that we're talking about, with the rose leather on the top?'

Mary Anne nodded. 'You know it.'

'Just checking.' Phyllida considered Mary Anne, considered how much to tell her. 'I went to Horatio's on Sunday morning to search for the desk.'

'And?' Mary Anne waited; then understanding dawned. Horror replaced her panic. Her mouth opened, then closed, then she squeaked, 'You witnessed the murder?'

'No, not exactly.'

'Not exactly? What does that mean? You saw something?'

Phyllida grimaced. 'Let me tell it from the beginning.' She related how she'd invented a sick headache, then dressed in boots and breeches – Jonas's castoffs that she often wore when engaged in nonpublic activities that might necessitate running. 'Sunday morning was the perfect time because there shouldn't have been anyone at home.'

'But Horatio was sick.'

'Yes, but I didn't know that. I slipped through the wood and searched that outbuilding he used as his warehouse, then I went in through the kitchen and searched the storerooms. They were filled with furniture as well. I didn't see your grandmother's desk anywhere, so I assumed it was somewhere in the main rooms. I went back through the kitchen, into the hall—'

'And you saw the murderer.'

'No. I found Horatio just after he'd been killed.'

'After the murderer had hit Mr Cynster and left him for dead.'

Phyllida gritted her teeth. 'No. I got there before Mr Cynster.'

'You saw the murderer hit Mr Cynster?'

'No!' She glared at Mary Anne. 'Just listen.'

In the baldest terms, she recounted what had happened. By the time she finished, Mary Anne had traveled from horror-struck to aghast. '*You* hit Mr Cynster?'

'I didn't mean to! The halberd tipped and fell – I stopped it from killing him.'

Mary Anne's face cleared. 'Well, he's obviously recovered. He must have a thick skull.'

'Perhaps. But that's not the complication.' Phyllida caught Mary Anne's eye. 'He knows I was there.'

'I thought he was knocked unconscious.'

'Not entirely – not at first.'

'He saw you?'

Phyllida described what had happened.

Mary Anne bent a look of utter disbelief upon her. 'He couldn't possibly tell from a touch. He's bamming you.'

'That's what I thought at first. But he *knows*, Mary Anne – he knows and he wants to know what happened.'

'Well, why not just tell him that yes, you were there, and tell him what happened and that you had to leave?'

Phyllida fixed her with a direct look. 'I haven't admitted that I was there, because as soon as I do he's going to want to know *why*.'

Mary Anne blanched. 'You can't tell him that!'

'He's determined to find out what happened – he's investigating Horatio's murder. From his point of view, he needs to know everything that happened that morning.'

'But he doesn't – he doesn't need to know about my letters.' Mary Anne's lower lip protruded. 'And he can't make you tell him.'

'He can.'

'Nonsense.' Mary Ann tossed her head. 'You're always the one in charge – you're Sir Jasper's daughter. You can just look at him haughtily and refuse to say anything. How can he force you to tell?'

'I can't explain it, but he will.' She couldn't

describe the sensation of being mentally stalked, trapped, and held, the pressure of knowing he was waiting, watching . . . patient now, but how long would that last? On top of that, she felt she *should* tell him, that he deserved to know. 'He hasn't yet threatened to tell Papa that he knows I was there, but he could – he knows he could. It's like Damocles' sword hanging over my head.'

'That's just melodramatic. He's pressuring you. He doesn't have any evidence you were there – why would Sir Jasper believe him?'

'How often do I succumb to sick headaches?'

Mary Anne pouted; her expression turned obstinate. 'You can't tell him about my letters – you *swore* you'd tell no one.'

'But this is *murder*. Horatio was killed. Mr Cynster needs to know what happened and what I saw.' She hadn't mentioned the brown hat; that would only distract Mary Anne, who was distracted enough as it was. 'He needs to know about your letters so he can be sure they aren't anything to do with why Horatio was killed.'

Mary Anne stared at her. *'No!* If you tell him about the letters, he'll think Robert killed Horatio.'

'Don't be silly. Robert wasn't anywhere near . . .' Phyllida stared at Mary Anne. 'Don't tell me Robert was here on Sunday morning.'

'I walked home after church – it was a lovely sunny day.' Mary Anne slid her eyes from Phyllida's. 'We met in the Ballyclose wood.'

'It's impossible that Robert killed Horatio and

then made it there to meet you, so he can't be the murderer.'

'But we can't tell anyone we met in the wood!' Phyllida swallowed a groan. She wasn't getting anywhere; she tried another tack. 'What is *in* these letters?' She hadn't asked before – before, it had only mattered that Mary Anne was hysterical and getting the letters back – an easy enough task, it had seemed – would calm her down. She'd given her oath not to reveal the existence of the letters to anyone without a second thought. But now Horatio's murder had turned her simple plan to retrieve Mary Anne's letters into a nightmare – and she was still bound by that oath.

Mary Anne picked at her skirt. 'I told you – they're letters I sent Robert that he gave back, and some he sent to me.'

Robert Collins was Mary Anne's intended, not her betrothed. Her parents had stood firm against the match since Mary Anne and Robert first met at the Exeter Assembly when Mary Anne was seventeen. Robert was an articled clerk in a solicitor's office in Exeter. His fortune was nonexistent, but once he took his final exams next year, he would be able to practice and thus support a wife. Through the years, Mary Anne's devotion to Robert and his to her had never wavered. Her parents had hoped the attachment would wane. However, they'd known better than to feed their daughter's stubbornness; assuming that with Robert in Exeter, physical meetings would be rare, they'd allowed the usual exchange of correspond-ence.

The existence of the letters would therefore surprise no one; it was the content that consti-tuted the threat. Phyllida wasn't, however, convinced that the threat was all that serious – not compared with murder. 'I can't see why telling Mr Cynster that your letters were the reason I was in Horatio's house, searching for them because they'd been accidentally put in the writing desk and then forgotten, is going to cause a scandal.'

'Because if you tell him that, he'll want to know why you – or, more to the point, I – didn't simply call and ask Horatio for them.'

Phyllida grimaced. She'd asked precisely that question when Mary Anne, distraught and barely coherent, had come to her for help. The answer had been that Horatio might look at the letters before he handed them over – and then he might hand them to Mary Anne's parents instead.

'And,' Mary Anne continued, her tone increas-ingly obstinate, 'if Mr Cynster is half as clever as you think him, he'll guess why I want them back so desperately. He's investigating – if he finds them, he'll read them.'

'Even if he does, he wouldn't hand them to your parents.' Phyllida glimpsed a way out. 'Wait – what if I make him *promise* that if I tell him all and he finds the letters, he'll hand them to me without reading them?'

Mary Anne frowned. 'Do you trust him?'

Phyllida returned her gaze steadily. She trusted Lucifer to find Horatio's killer if that were humanly possible. She would trust him with any number of things. But could she trust him with Mary Anne's secret? She still didn't know what was in those damned letters. 'These letters – in them you described what happened at your meetings? How you felt – that sort of thing?'

Tight-lipped, Mary Anne nodded; she was clearly not going to say more.

A few kisses, a cuddle or two – how scandalous could that be? 'I'm certain that even if Mr Cynster read the letters, they wouldn't shock him. And he's a stranger. He'll leave after Horatio's murderer's found and we'll never see him again. There's no reason he'll feel any great need to hand even the most scandalous letters to your parents.'

Mary Anne pondered. 'If you tell him about the letters, you wouldn't tell him they were scandalous?'

'Of course not! I'll tell him they're private letters you don't want anyone else reading.' Phyllida waited, then said, 'So – can I tell him?'

Mary Anne shifted. 'I . . . I want to talk to Robert.' She lifted eyes clouded with worry to Phyllida's face. 'I haven't told him the letters are missing. I want to know what he thinks.'

Oh, how she wished she could infuse a little of her own steel into Mary Anne's backbone. But Mary Anne was, beneath her social veneer, nearly frantic with worry. Phyllida sighed. 'All right. Talk to Robert. But *please* talk to him soon.' She swallowed the words *I don't know how long I can hold Mr Cynster at bay*.

She looked up – and discovered the wolf a lot closer than she'd thought; her heart leaped to her throat, then somersaulted back into place.

He stood fifteen feet away, framed by the arch leading into the garden. White roses nodded above his dark head, the delicate blooms emphasizing his strength and the latent power in his stance. Hands in his trouser pockets, his gaze was fixed on them. Phyllida was relieved to see the tails of his coat settle – he'd only just arrived.

Summoning a serene smile, she rose and strolled toward him. 'We've been catching up. Have they let you escape?'

His dark blue eyes watched her approach. He waited until she halted before him to say, 'I escaped a while ago to check on my horses.'

His gaze went beyond her; Phyllida turned as Mary Anne nervously joined them. 'Allow me to present my close friend, Miss Farthingale.'

He bowed gracefully.

Mary Anne bobbed a curtsy. 'I should return to my mother – she'll be wanting to leave.'

He stepped aside and Mary Anne slipped past him. She glanced at Phyllida. 'I'll let you know as soon as I can.'

With that, she hurried away. Phyllida suppressed a grimace. From under her lashes she glanced at her nemesis. Drawing his gaze from Mary Anne, he fixed it on her. He studied her face; she kept her expression calm and collected. Lifting her lids, she gave him back stare for stare.

After an instant of hesitation; he raised one dark brow. 'My horses? No one here seems to know where they are.'

'They're in the Manor's stables. There wasn't enough space here, while the stables there were empty. I asked John Ostler from the Red Bells to look after them. He's very good with horses.'

He considered her, then nodded. 'Thank you for arranging it. Now' – he looked toward the lawn – 'I'd better head back to the Manor.'

There was a slight frown in his eyes; Phyllida didn't think it was due to worry about his horses. He took a step – she put a hand on his arm. He glanced at her, brows rising. She searched his eyes. 'Are you in pain?'

After a moment, he inclined his head. 'A little.'

'I don't suppose you'd consider waiting until tomorrow to see your horses?'

'No.' His lips curved just a little at the ends. 'You know how gentlemen are about their horses.'

She pressed her lips tight and considered. 'There's a shortcut through the wood. It's much faster than going via the village.'

His interest was immediate; his speculation that that was the route she'd used to go from the Grange to the Manor on Sunday morning gleamed in his eyes. 'Where does this shortcut start?'

Phyllida hesitated, but only for a moment. If his head was aching, she couldn't let him walk through the wood alone. She turned away from the lawn. 'I'll show you.'

He followed her through the wood, claiming her hand often, helping her over roots and up and down rocky dips. The path was clear, but not designed for strolling; long before the Manor's roof came into sight, Phyllida was wishing she was in her boots and breeches. Then she wouldn't have needed to let him take her hand – wouldn't have been so conscious of his strength prowling at her heels, all but surrounding her every time he steadied her.

She wouldn't have been so conscious that he could physically manage her without any difficulty at all.

Despite the fact she was neither tall nor large, she'd never felt at a physical disadvantage with any other man.

As they reached the trees bordering the back of the Manor and stepped into the mild sunshine, she reminded herself that this man was different – he was like no other she had met before, altogether a very different proposition.

She'd do well to remember that.

'Your horses will be in there.' She indicated the stone stables that stood to one side. 'I'll let the Hemmingses and Bristleford know you're here.' Evening was approaching. 'John will probably look in shortly.'

She headed on through the kitchen garden, aware that Lucifer's dark gaze lingered on her before he turned to the stables.

The Hemmingses were in the kitchen, Mrs Hemmings cooking, Hemmings by the fire. Hemmings immediately went out to the stables. Phyllida discussed the preparations for Horatio's wake, then excused herself and went into the house, ostensibly to take a last look at Horatio.

She did. Then she looked around the drawing room and Horatio's library across the hall. Mary Anne's grandmother's traveling writing desk had to be somewhere. It was small enough and ornate enough to be placed on a side table as an ornament, especially in a house full of antiques. Phyllida searched, but didn't find it. Going back down the hall, she checked in the dining room, then in the back parlor and its adjoining garden room. In vain.

Returning to the hall, she halted at the foot of the stairs and looked up. The thud of a drawer being shut reached her ears. Covey, most likely, tidying his late master's effects. Phyllida grimaced. The desk had to be upstairs. There were bedrooms on the first level with attics above. Covey and the Hemmingses had rooms in the attics, but that would account for only part of the space. She would have to find time, and some excuse, to search upstairs.

Retreating through the kitchen, she bade Mrs Hemmings an absentminded farewell and strolled out into the kitchen garden, pondering the how and when. No answers leaped to mind.

Standing before the stables, Lucifer watched her amble along the path. He'd glimpsed her in one of the back rooms. What had she been doing there? Yet another question to which she'd be giving him an answer. Soon.

His blacks were eating their heads off; John Ostler had just left. Hemmings nodded and headed back to the house. Phyllida looked up as Hemmings passed her, smiled a vague greeting, then saw Lucifer waiting. She moved forward more purposefully and joined him. 'Ready?'

He fell into step beside her. 'You were right – John Ostler knows his horses.'

She smiled; her gaze lingered on his eyes, then slid over his face. 'How's your head?'

'Better.'

She looked ahead. 'The fresh air should help.'

They walked into the wood and cool silence enveloped them. The westering sun threw slanting beams through the trees, golden shafts to light their way. The bustle of day faded as evening approached; birds settled on boughs, into nests; soft cooing filled the air.

Nearing the Grange, they reached a spot where the path dipped sharply. Phyllida halted, assessing it. Lucifer stepped past and over the gap; turning, he held out a hand. She took it and leaped – her narrow skirt restricted her stride; her sole slipped in the leaf mold lining the dip's edge.

He caught her around the waist and swung her clear. She landed against his chest.

The unexpected contact shocked them both. He heard her indrawn breath, felt the tensing of her spine. Felt his own inevitable reaction. She looked up, lustrous brown eyes wide . . . the procession of emotions through their depths held him spellbound.

Wonder – fleeting, innocent thoughts of what it might be like . . .

Her fingers, spread across his upper chest, fluttered, then stilled.

Her gaze dropped to his lips; his dropped to hers.

Her lips parted, just a little.

He bent his head and covered them.

They were petal-soft, and sweet – a delicate, fresh sweetness that hinted, not of innocence, but of innocent pleasures.

He hadn't intended this. He knew he should stop, draw back, let her escape even if she didn't know enough to run. He didn't. Couldn't. Couldn't bear to release her without tasting her, without giving his clamoring senses at least that much reward.

No easy task, to take that much in a first kiss without frightening her. The implicit challenge tantalized.

He kept the caress gentle, undemanding, waiting with the patience of one who knew for her curiosity to overcome her scruples. It didn't take long – she was inherently confident, with little reason to doubt her ability to cope, even if, in this arena, she was out of her league. Just how out of her league was not a point she appreciated. Not yet.

When her lips firmed, tentatively molding, gently

returning his kiss, the pirate within him gloated. He swooped, but was careful to disguise his attack. Skillfully fanning her interest, teasing, tantalizing, he set himself to captivate with simple kisses laced with potent temptation.

The promise of something new, illicit, sensual – a taste she'd not tried before.

She sank into his arms. He closed them around her, aware to his bones of her warmth, of the enticement of her soft flesh. He breathed deep and her scent wreathed through him – his arms locked. He shackled the sudden urge to seize. Instead, he traced her lower lip with his tongue, and waited.

She hesitated for a heartbeat, then parted her lips. He traced their contours, encouraging her further, until, almost giddy with need, with triumph, he could enter and taste her as he wished.

One taste was what he'd promised himself; he savored the moment, then, reining in his rakish impulses, drew back.

Their lips parted, by half an inch. Their breaths mingled; she didn't draw back. Her hands were fisted on his lapels. Her lids were heavy, veiling her eyes. As he watched, they lifted and she met his gaze.

Her eyes were darkened, sultry, yet filled with innocent surprise, and with a womanly wondering . . .

He kissed her again, not, this time, for his pleasure but for hers. To show her just a little more of what could be, a little more of the wonder.

Phyllida tightened her hold on his lapels and

gave herself up to the kiss, to the slow surge of his tongue, the intimate caressing and exploring. Warmth seeped through her; a sharp lick of sensation whipped to her toes and slowly curled them.

His head angled over hers and she clung; he deepened the kiss and she willingly followed. For years, she'd dreamed of being kissed like this, kissed as a woman, a woman desired. It was frightening and enticing. She couldn't breathe, she couldn't think. She certainly wasn't in control. Instead of scaring her, that thrilled her. Foolish, certainly, yet she felt no fear. Only a wanton eagerness.

Lips and mouths melded; tongues tangled, sliding, caressing . . . for one magical instant, the world fell away.

He tasted of heat and wildness, of something primeval, something barely tamed. Male – hard where she was soft, beast to her beauty. She sensed the leashed power simmering beneath his lips, held back behind his experienced facade.

Then he started to draw back, to retreat and end the kiss.

It was a surprise to realize she'd stretched up on her toes, that she'd pressed herself against him. Her knees had weakened, her skin felt too hot, her wits were whirling. His chest was a solid wall supporting her; she spread her fingers and pressed, enthralled by the resilient hardness beneath the crisp layers. His arms had locked, iron bands caging her; she didn't care.

She wanted to hold him, to prolong the precious moment – she knew she couldn't. She didn't know how.

On the instant their lips would have parted, he paused. Then he returned, surging deep, a swift, hard invasion that mentally rocked her – the hidden power she'd sensed was no lie.

Then he lifted his head and straightened, and she was standing on her feet, his hands rising to close about hers, clenched again on his lapels. She blinked and released her grip, then drew her hands from under his.

Dazed, she met his eyes, and wasn't at all certain what she saw. Something dark and dangerous prowled behind the blue. 'Why did you kiss me?'

That was suddenly very important to know.

He didn't smile, didn't try to turn the awkward question aside with some glib and charming quip. His eyes held hers; they'd widened slightly at her question – she could almost believe he was as dazed as she.

'Because I wanted to.' His voice was gravelly; he blinked, drew breath, and added, 'And to thank you for your help – yesterday and today.' He met her gaze. 'Regardless of all else, I sincerely appreciate all that you've done.'

Lucifer tried to find a charming smile and couldn't, so he clung to impassivity and gestured, urging her ahead of him along the path.

With one last, wondering glance, she acquiesced. He followed, breathing deeply, thanking his stars that she'd accepted his answer. Walking before him, she couldn't see the effort it took for him to reshackle his demons. He hoped she never guessed how close she'd come to meeting them.

At least he'd answered her truthfully. About that first kiss. There was no need for her to know his reasons behind the second, and even less his reasons for the third. He couldn't remember the last time he'd warned a woman away, but for her own safety, she should keep her distance.

Frowning, he strolled at her heels, through the gathering gloom. He'd taken what he'd wanted, that one simple taste, but what had it cost him?

He wasn't sure he wanted to know.

They'd reached the Grange lawns when he closed his fingers around her elbow and drew her to a halt. She faced him, brows rising, her expression all but blank. The shadows were too dense for him to read her eyes. 'I kissed you because I didn't want you seeing me as some ogre, bent on browbeating the truth out of you.' Releasing her, he held her gaze. 'I'm not the enemy.'

She studied his face, then her lips lifted as she turned away. She stepped out, heading for the house. Her cool words drifted back to him. 'I didn't think you were.'

CHAPTER 5

Phyllida knew why he'd kissed her. He wasn't an ogre, he wasn't her enemy, but he was a masterful seducer. She was a novice in that sphere, yet she realized he'd kissed her to rattle her, to weaken her resolve so she'd tell him all she knew. She'd asked him why, but she'd known the answer the instant she'd voiced the question.

Seated in the second pew, she glanced across the aisle of the church to where Lucifer sat. His expression was impassive as he listened to Cedric read the lesson. Covey hunched beside him; farther along, Mrs Hemmings wept into her handkerchief. Hemmings patted her arm awkwardly. White-faced, Bristleford stared straight ahead. While the rest of those present might have lost a friend and a neighbor, Covey, the Hemmingses, and Bristleford had lost a beloved master and their livelihoods had been rendered uncertain.

Phyllida returned her gaze to Lucifer's face – it wasn't expressive, yet she encountered no difficulty in following his thoughts. They were presently centered on the coffin resting before the altar, jeweled by shafts of light playing through the stained-glass windows. His thoughts, however, were not on Horatio but on who had put him in the box.

She faced forward once more. Cedric continued to drone. She let her mind slide back to its most urgent consideration – how to deal with Lucifer.

That name was the one that sprang to mind; it suited him so well. She'd known what type of man he was the instant she'd set eyes on him, although she hadn't fully appreciated the whole until she'd encountered him fully dressed and fully conscious. Then, what he was had been obvious.

The reason matrons preened and women lost their wits when he smiled was blatantly apparent – he didn't hide his light under any bushel. Even more to the point, his powerful aura of masculine energy, raw edges smoothed by graceful elegance, hadn't come about by accident – it was even more than cultivated – it was part of a practiced art.

An art he intended practicing on her.

Luckily, she knew it. She was confident and in control of her world, bar him. And his kisses hadn't rattled her in the least. She hadn't expected them, but, on consideration, she hadn't been surprised. He'd thought about kissing her when he'd held her trapped on his bed the night before. The woods had simply been a more amenable venue.

Would he kiss her again? The question hovered in her brain. She'd enjoyed the experience; she hadn't felt the least bit threatened, or coerced, or

113

even in danger. But wishing for more might be tempting fate.

Besides . . . She glanced sideways to where a small man in severe black sat, pinched features blank. Mr Crabbs was Horatio's solicitor, come from Exeter to read the will. And in Mr Crabbs's train had come his clerk, Robert Collins.

With luck, this evening, after speaking with Robert, Mary Anne would release her from her oath. Then she could explain to Lucifer what had happened in Horatio's drawing room and they could join forces to track down Horatio's murderer.

That was her aim and she wasn't about to be deterred, even if succeeding meant dealing with the devil. He was definitely the most fascinating devil she'd ever met, and deep down, she was convinced he'd never hurt her.

Impatient, she waited for Cedric to have done.

When the service was over, Lucifer stepped forward with Cedric, Sir Jasper, Thompson, Basil Smollet, and Mr Farthingale; they hefted the coffin and slowly carried it out to the graveyard. During the short burial ceremony, Lucifer noted the faces of the men he'd not yet met as they stood about the graveside. Was the murderer present? The ladies did not join them, but gathered in a dark group just beyond the side porch of the church.

When earth rained down on the coffin, Lucifer joined Sir Jasper and Mr Farthingale. As they walked back to the church, he learned enough to place Mr Farthingale as a minor Sir Jasper – backbone of the county, absorbed with his land and family, unlikely to have any connection with Horatio's murder.

Together with the rest of the men, they joined the waiting ladies; family groups formed and started down the common. Sir Jasper led the way, Jonas beside him. Phyllida followed; Lucifer fell in beside her. She slanted him a glance; her eyes held no hint of censure or trepidation. If anything, they held a question: What next?

'If you'd be so kind as to introduce me to those I don't know . . . ?'

She inclined her head regally. 'Of course.'

She acted as if he'd never kissed her. Lucifer hid a frown.

Followed by, as far as he could tell, the entire congregation, they went through the Manor gate, crossed Horatio's garden, and filed into the house.

The wake was the perfect opportunity, not just to meet the locals, but to have them explain their relationship to Horatio. Most discussed their last meetings with him without prompting, and aired their views on his murder.

Phyllida hovered near, graciously steering people his way, in each case providing him with the right information to place the person in the context of village life and establish his or her connection with Horatio. If he'd thought she'd played any role in Horatio's murder, he'd have been suspicious.

Instead, he stood by the side of the room and appreciated her social skills.

'Mr Cynster, allow me to present Miss Hellebore. She lives in the cottage immediately next door.'

Lucifer bowed over Miss Hellebore's hand. Old with a sweet, lined face, she stood no higher than his shoulder.

She clutched his hand. 'I was in church when it happened – *so* unfortunate. I might have heard something otherwise. They'd just dropped me off before they found you – what a to-do *that* was! But I'm so glad, dear, that you were not the one.' She smiled vaguely, her eyes dimming. 'Horatio was a dear soul. Such a worry, this happening.'

Her voice faded; Phyllida took her other hand and patted it reassuringly. 'You needn't worry, Harriet. Mr Cynster and Papa will find out who did it, and then all will be peaceful here again.'

'I do hope so, dear.'

'There's some asparagus on the table – would you like some?'

'Oh, yes. Which table?'

With a glance that said she'd be back, Phyllida steered the old lady away.

Lucifer watched them go. Despite the fact that Phyllida was unmarried and neither the oldest nor the most established lady in the room, it was to her the locals unhesitatingly turned – for reassurance, for order. Her character, her personality, cast her in the role – that calm, collected air of being perennially in control.

The desire to see her in an uncontrolled frenzy surfaced – again. He swiftly doused it and looked away.

'Mr Cynster.' Jocasta Smollet, as haughty as when she'd passed them in the lane the previous evening, approached on the arm of Sir Basil. She extended her hand.

Basil performed the introductions.

'I do hope,' Jocasta said, 'that you'll be remaining in Colyton for a few days yet. We'd be pleased to entertain you at Highgate – I'm sure there's little else hereabouts to interest a gentleman such as yourself.'

If Jocasta's nose rose any higher, she'd tip backward.

'I'm unsure how long I'll be staying.' Lucifer watched Phyllida returning through the crowd. She didn't see Jocasta until she was almost upon them. Her smile faded; she changed tack so she could slide past them.

Calmly, he reached out, caught her hand, and drew her to his side. Setting her hand on his sleeve, he looked at Jocasta. 'Despite the unfortunate circumstances, I've enjoyed meeting those round about. People have been very welcoming.' He glanced at Phyllida. 'Miss Tallent has been particularly helpful.'

'Indeed?' There was a wealth of meaning in the word. Jocasta drew herself up and stiffly inclined her head. 'Dear Phyllida is so good to everyone. If you'll excuse us, I really must speak with Mrs Farthingale.'

She glided away. Basil, embarrassed, didn't follow. He chatted inconsequentially; Lucifer determined that he'd been in church when Horatio had been murdered.

When Basil moved on, Lucifer looked down at Phyllida. 'Why does Miss Smollet so dislike you?'

She shook her head. 'I really don't know.'

Lucifer glanced across the room. 'There are three gentlemen I've yet to meet.'

The first proved to be Lucius Appleby. Phyllida introduced them, then left to chat with Lady Fortemain. Lucifer made no effort to disguise his purpose. Appleby answered directly, but was hardly forthcoming.

Collecting Phyllida, Lucifer guided her down the room. 'Is Appleby always so reserved? So self-effacing?'

'Yes, but he's Cedric's secretary, after all.'

His eye on their next target, Lucifer murmured, 'What was Appleby before he became Cedric's secretary? Has he ever mentioned?'

'No. I assumed he always was a clerk or something similar. Why?'

'I'm sure he's been in the army. He's the right age – I just wondered. Now, who's this?'

A moment later, Phyllida said, 'Allow me to present Pommeroy Fortemain, Sir Cedric's brother.'

Lucifer held out his hand.

Pommeroy's eyes bulged; he edged back. 'Ah . . .' Wide-eyed, he looked at Phyllida. 'I mean . . . well . . .'

Phyllida sighed exasperatedly. 'Mr Cynster did not murder Horatio, Pommeroy.'

'He didn't?' Pommeroy glanced from one to the other.

'No! This is Horatio's wake, for heaven's sake! We wouldn't knowingly have invited the murderer.'

'B-but . . . he had the knife.'

'Pommeroy' – Phyllida spoke very distinctly – 'no one knows who the murderer is, but the one thing we *do* know is that it could *not* be Mr Cynster.'

'Oh.'

After that, Pommeroy behaved reasonably, answering Lucifer's questions with, if anything, an overeagerness to please. He'd accompanied his mother to church on Sunday and, he assured them, knew nothing about anything.

'That last is unfortunately true.' Obedient to the touch on her arm, Phyllida moved to the side of the room.

'So I'd gathered.' Lucifer was looking ahead. 'Our last potential suspect is scanning the book-shelves.'

She'd guessed who it was before they stepped around the Farthingales and came face-to-face with Silas Coombe, fingering a gold-plated spine. He snatched his hand back as if the book had bitten him and stared at them, blank-faced.

'Good day. Mr Coombe, is it not?' Lucifer smiled. 'Miss Tallent mentioned you know something of books. Horatio's amassed quite a collection, don't you think?'

His glance along the shelves clearly invited Silas's opinion. It was a masterly stroke. Phyllida practiced self-effacement while Silas waxed lyrical, putty in the hands of a gentleman he didn't even realize was his interrogator.

'Well, I don't normally confess this, but you're a gentleman who knows a bit about life.' Silas lowered his voice. 'Not much of a churchgoer, you understand. Got out of the habit in my youth – can't see the point in rubbing shoulders with all the starched-up matrons, not at my age. I've better things to do with my time.'

Silas's gaze ranged the nearby shelves. 'I don't suppose you have any idea who will inherit these, do you?'

Lucifer shook his head. 'No doubt we'll learn soon enough.'

'Ah, yes – the solicitor fellow's here, isn't he?' Silas scanned the room, then frowned. 'He's staring at you.'

Lucifer looked; Phyllida did, too. It was instantly apparent that Mr Crabbs was hovering, hoping for a word.

'If you'll excuse us,' Lucifer murmured, 'I'll see what he wants.'

The instant they stepped away, Crabbs headed toward them. Lucifer stopped by the bookshelves and waited. Crabbs smiled perfunctorily as he joined them.

'Mr Cynster, I just wanted to be sure that it would be convenient to read the will immediately the guests leave.'

'Convenient?' Lucifer frowned. 'For whom?'

'Why, for *you*.' Mr Crabbs searched Lucifer's face. 'Well, dear me – I assumed you knew.'

'Knew what?'

'That, barring some minor bequests, you are the sole principal beneficiary of Mr Welham's will.'

Crabbs's statement had been uttered within the hearing of Lady Huddlesford, Percy Tallent, and Sir Cedric and Lady Fortemain. Within seconds, all of Colyton had heard the news. The wake terminated as if a gong had sounded. People quickly took their leave, their alacrity plainly due to a wish to have the unexpected details of the will disclosed as soon as possible.

Despite the fact that the reading had been attended by very few, for the last hour the attention of Colyton had been focused on Horatio's library.

Pushing back from the desk, Lucifer laid the will down. He'd just finished going through it a second time with Crabbs, making sure he understood the details. For someone familiar with the complex assignment of a ducal purse, Horatio's stipulations were straightforward. Leaning back in the leather chair, Lucifer scanned the room.

At one corner of the desk, Crabbs sat checking documents. At the sideboard, his assistant, Robert Collins, was carefully packing a satchel.

The Hemmingses, Covey, and Bristleford had slipped out after the reading, all intensely relieved, all clearly pleased with the outcome.

For himself, Lucifer was . . . faintly stunned.

'Ah-hem.'

He looked at Crabbs, then raised a brow.

'I was wondering if you planned to sell the Manor. I could get matters started if you wish.'

Lucifer stared at Crabbs without seeing him. Then he shook his head. 'I don't intend to sell.'

The statement surprised him more than Crabbs, but when impulse struck this strongly, it rarely served to fight it. 'Tell me.' He refocused on Crabbs. 'Were there any others who might have expected to inherit?'

Crabbs shook his head. 'There was no family – not even any legal connections. The estate was Mr Welham's outright, his to leave as he pleased.'

'Do you know who Horatio's heir was, who was in line for the estate, before this present will was drawn up?'

'As far as I'm aware, there was no previous will. I drew this one up three years ago, when Mr Welham came into these parts and engaged me to act for him. He gave me to understand he had not made a will before.'

Later, with the shadows lengthening, Lucifer strode back to the Grange through the wood. Hands in his pockets, gaze fixed on the ground, he stepped over roots and ditches blindly, his mind engrossed with other things.

Crabbs had taken his leave, retreating to the Red Bells. Given he was not presently residing under the Manor's roof, Lucifer had not invited him to stay there. He hadn't wanted to impose the duty of entertaining the solicitor on Bristleford, the Hemmingses and Covey, not tonight.

He'd instructed Crabbs to contact Heathcote Montague, man of business to the Cynsters. With Montague involved, the formal transfer of the estate would be accomplished quickly and efficiently. Lucifer made a mental note to write to Montague.

And Gabriel. And Devil. And his parents.

Lucifer sighed. The first tugs of the reins of responsibility. He'd avoided them most of his life. He couldn't avoid them now. Horatio had bequeathed them to him – the responsibility for his collection, the responsibility for the Manor, for Covey, Bristleford, and the Hemmingses. Together with the responsibility for his garden.

That last worried him more than the others combined.

Horatio had trained him in how to oversee a collection; his family had prepared him to manage an estate and servants. No one had ever taught him about a garden, much less the sort of garden Horatio had created.

He had a very odd feeling about the garden.

The path joined the Grange shrubbery, leading

into a maze of interconnecting walks. Lucifer checked he was taking the right one, then paced on, deep in thought.

Until a fury in patterned cambric came storming through a gap in the hedge and walked into him.

Phyllida lost all her breath in the collision. Even before she'd glanced up, her senses had recognized whose arms had locked around her. If she'd been the type of female who gave way to every impulse, she'd have shrieked and leaped away. Instead, she fixed him with a glittering glance and stepped back.

His arms fell from her. The reprobate had the gall to raise one arrogant black brow.

'My apologies.' Calmly correct, she whirled around and headed for the house.

He fell in beside her as she walked, with lady-like gentility, along the path. His gaze lingered on her face; she refused to look at him – refused to see if his lips were straight and what type of amusement lurked in his blue eyes. The fiend had just made her life immeasurably more difficult.

His, too, did he but know it.

'You do that very well.'

The murmured words were deliberately provocative.

'What?'

'Hide your temper. What was it that set you off?'

'An acquaintance who's being particularly trying. Actually, it's three acquaintances.' Him, Mary Anne, and Robert. He'd inherited the Manor,

Mary Anne had been thrown into a tizzy on the grounds that he might decide to stay, and Robert had unhelpfully confirmed that as fact.

She'd hoped the funeral would convince Mary Anne that her letters were a minor matter compared to murder. Instead, thanks to Mary Anne's sensitivities, she was now further away from being able to tell Lucifer why she'd been in Horatio's drawing room than she had been that morning. Fuming, she'd left Mary Anne and Robert by the fountain and stalked off. Only to run into Lucifer.

A sudden flush ran down her body at the memory of the impact. Under his elegant clothes he was all hard muscle; despite the fact she'd been going at full tilt, he hadn't even staggered. She glanced at him. 'I take it you have, indeed, inherited the Manor?'

'Yes. There are apparently no relatives, so . . .'

They stepped onto the lawn. Phyllida fixed her gaze on the house. 'If I might make so bold, what are your plans? Will you sell, or live here?'

She felt his gaze on her face but didn't turn to meet it.

'You may be as bold as you like, but . . .'

His tone had her glancing quickly his way.

He smiled. 'I was on my way to discuss matters with your father. Perhaps you could take me to him?'

Sir Jasper was in his library. Lucifer was unsurprised when, after showing him in and then disappearing, Phyllida returned with a tray bearing glasses and a decanter.

'Well, so you're now a landowner in Devon, heh?'

'Shortly to be so, it seems.' Lucifer accepted the glass of brandy Phyllida brought him. She handed a similar glass to her father, then retired to the sofa facing the chairs he and Sir Jasper occupied.

'Any thoughts on what you'll do with the property?' Sir Jasper regarded him from under shaggy brows. 'You mentioned your family's estate is in Somerset . . .'

'I have an older brother – the family estate will go to him. In recent years, I've lived primarily in London, sharing my brother's house.'

'So you have no other establishment demanding your attention?'

'No.' That was something Horatio had known. His gaze on the brandy swirling in his glass, Lucifer added, 'There's nothing to stop me from settling in Colyton.'

'And will you?'

He looked up, into Phyllida's eyes. It was she who had, with her habitual directness, asked the simple question.

'Yes.' Raising his glass, he sipped, his gaze never leaving her. 'I've decided Colyton suits me.'

'Excellent!' Sir Jasper beamed. 'Could do with a little new blood around here.' He went on at some length, extolling the benefits of the area; Lucifer let him ramble while he tried to understand the irritation in Phyllida's brown eyes. Her expression calm,

126

she sat watching her father, but her eyes . . . and a downward quirk at one corner of her lovely lips . . .

Sir Jasper wound to a halt; Lucifer stirred and faced him. 'One point I wanted to mention. I consider Horatio's bequest a gift, one I couldn't comfortably accept if I hadn't done everything I could to bring his murderer to justice.'

Sir Jasper nodded. 'Your feelings do you credit.'

'Perhaps, but I'd never feel at ease in Horatio's house, owning his collection, unless I'd turned every stone.'

Sir Jasper eyed him shrewdly. 'Do I take it that's a warning you intend turning every stone?'

Lucifer held his gaze. 'Every rock. Every last pebble.'

Sir Jasper considered, then nodded. 'I'll do whatever I can, but as you doubtless appreciate, it won't be easy to lay this murderer by the heels. The bare fact of the matter is no one saw him.'

'There may be other proofs.' Lucifer drained his glass.

Sir Jasper did the same. 'We can hope so.' As Phyllida collected the empty glasses, he added, 'You may investigate as you wish, of course. If you need any formal support, I'll do all I can.' He stood. 'Horatio was one of us. I suspect you'll find you'll have any number of people willing to help you find his murderer.'

'Indeed.' Lucifer rose, his gaze resting on Phyllida. 'I'm hoping that will be the case.'

★   ★   ★

He wanted her help in catching Horatio's murderer. He'd all but asked for it.

She wanted to help him. Even if he hadn't asked, he would have received her assistance.

Unfortunately, the promise of the morning, when she'd hoped to be able to tell him all soon, had given way to the frustration of the afternoon, which was now to be crowned by the disaster of the evening. For some ungodly reason, and she used the term advisedly, her aunt had decided to host an informal dinner for a select few who had attended the funeral. A funeral dinner. Phyllida wasn't impressed.

She'd had a good mind to wear black, but compromised with her lavender silk. It was one of her most flattering gowns and she felt in need of the support.

She was the last to enter the drawing room. Lucifer was there, startlingly handsome in a midnight-blue coat the exact same shade as his eyes. His hair appeared black in the candlelight; his ivory cravat was an exercise in elegance. He stood with her father and Mr Farthingale before the hearth; from the instant she'd stepped over the threshold, his gaze had remained fixed on her.

Regally inclining her head, she went to join the Misses Longdon, two spinsters of indeterminate age who shared a house along the lane to the forge.

They were sixteen at table. After checking with Gladys, Phyllida took her seat. Lucifer was at the table's other end, at her aunt's right and flanked by Regina Longdon. Regina Longdon was all but deaf, which left Lady Huddlesford with little competition. Mary Anne and Robert were both too far away to engage in conversation. Or persuasion. With nothing else to do, Phyllida applied herself to overseeing the meal.

Her father never dallied long over the port; he led the gentlemen back into the drawing room a bare fifteen minutes after the ladies had settled themselves. Those fifteen minutes had been spent listening to Mary Anne play the pianoforte. As soon as the gentlemen appeared. Mary Anne closed the instrument and came forward to join the conversing groups. Phyllida closed in on her.

Mary Anne saw her coming; agitation instantly filled her blue eyes. *'No!'* she hissed, before Phyllida could say a word. 'You must see it's impossible. You have to find the letters – you *promised*!'

'I would have thought that by now you'd see—'

'It's *you* who don't see! Once you find the letters and give them back to me, *then* you can tell him, if you're so sure you must.' Mary Anne literally wrung her hands, then her gaze flicked past Phyllida. 'Oh, heavens! There's Robert – I must rescue him before Papa corners him.'

With that, she all but fled across the room.

Phyllida watched her go, not entirely able to hide her frown. She'd never seen Mary Anne so overset. 'What on earth is in those letters?'

Swinging to face the room, she scanned the guests to see if any needed her hostessly attention, only to discover Lucifer crossing the room toward her, the look in his eye signaling that he required precisely that. She waited; he halted beside her, and joined her in considering the room.

'Your bosom-bow, Miss Farthingale – what's the situation between her and Collins?'

'Situation?'

He glanced at her. 'Farthingale looked ready to have an apoplectic fit when Collins arrived with Crabbs. Mrs Farthingale looked thoroughly taken aback, and then grimly, tight-lippedly, resigned. I've been following your father's lead in stepping in with distractions all evening – it would be helpful to know what game we're all playing.'

Phyllida met his eyes. 'Star-crossed lovers, but we're hoping this version will end without tragedy.' She looked across the room to where Robert Collins was speaking with Henrietta Longdon, who happened to be sitting beside Mary Anne on the *chaise*. 'Mary Anne and Robert have been sweethearts since they first met. That was six years ago. They'd be perfect for each other but for one thing.'

'Collins has no fortune.'

'Precisely. Mr Farthingale forbade the connection, but despite Robert living in Exeter, meetings always seem to occur, and Mary Anne has remained absolutely adamant.'

'For six years? Most parents would have yielded by now.'

'Mr Farthingale is *very* stubborn. So is Mary Anne.'

'So who'll win?'

'Mary Anne. Luckily, quite soon. Robert will shortly complete the requirements for registration. Crabbs has already offered him a place. Once Robert is practicing, he'll be able to support a wife, and then Mr Farthingale will capitulate because he won't have any choice.'

'So Farthingale's apoplexy is all for show?'

'In a way. It's expected, but it's not as if Robert isn't presentable.' He might be too meek, too conservative, too nonassertive, but his birth was acceptable. 'That said, the Farthingales wouldn't have expected Robert to be here this evening. Everyone hereabouts knows the situation; we all avoid doing anything to exacerbate it.'

'What happened tonight?'

Phyllida looked at Lady Huddlesford, holding court by the hearth. 'I'm not sure. It's possible my aunt, who spends two or three months here every year, forgot and innocently invited Robert along with Crabbs.'

'But . . . ?'

Phyllida's lips twitched. 'Under that careworn exterior, she's rather a romantic. I suspect she imagines she's easing the star-crossed lovers' path.'

'Ah.'

The syllable was heavy with worldly cynicism.

131

Phyllida glanced up – and saw Percy bearing down on them.

He nodded to Lucifer, his gaze fixed on her. 'I wonder, cuz, whether I could have a private word with you?'

About what? Phyllida swallowed the ungracious reply. 'Of course.'

Percy smiled at Lucifer. 'Family business, don't y'know.'

Lucifer bowed.

Inclining her head in reply, Phyllida put her hand on Percy's sleeve and let him escort her through the open French doors and onto the terrace. Withdrawing her hand from his arm, she walked to the balustrade.

'Not there.' Percy gestured along the terrace. 'They can see.'

Phyllida heaved a mental sigh and obliged, hoping Percy would cut line, tell her what he wanted, and let her return to the drawing room. If she got Robert alone, she might be able to salvage something from today. Robert might be meek, but he was also stultifyingly conservative, and as an almost solicitor, he should be law-abiding. Perhaps she could convince him—

'The thing is . . .' Percy halted outside the darkened library windows. Tugging down his waistcoat, he faced her. 'I've been watching you and thinking. You're what? Twenty-four?'

Leaning back against the balustrade, she stared at him. 'Yes,' she admitted. 'Twenty-four. What of it?'

'What of it? Why, you should be married, of course! Ask m'mother – she'll tell you. You're all but on the shelf at twenty-four.'

'Indeed?' Phyllida considered explaining that she was quite happy on her shelf. 'Why should that concern you?'

'Of course it concerns me! I'm the head of the family – well, once your father shuffles off, I will be.'

'I have a brother, remember?'

'Jonas.' With a wave, Percy dismissed Jonas. 'Thing is, you're here, unmarried, and there's no sense to it, not when there's an alternative.'

Phyllida debated. Humoring Percy was probably the fastest way to bring this scene to an end. Folding her arms, she settled against the balustrade. 'What alternative?'

Percy drew himself up and puffed out his chest. 'You can marry me.'

Shock held her speechless.

'I know it's a surprise – hadn't thought of it myself until I came down here and saw how it was. But now I can see it's the perfect solution.' Percy started to pace. 'Family duty and all that – offering for you is what I should do.'

Phyllida straightened. 'Percy, I'm perfectly comfortable here—'

'Precisely. That's the beauty of it. We can be married and you can stay down here in the country – daresay your father would prefer it. He wouldn't want to have to run the Grange without you.

On the other hand, *I* don't need a hostess. I've never had one.' He nodded. 'I'll be perfectly happy rattling 'round London on my own.'

'I can quite see that. Let's see if I fully understand your proposal.' Her terse accents had Percy tensing. 'Are you, by any chance, currently at *point-non-plus*?'

Stony-faced, Percy glared at her.

Phyllida waited.

'I might, at present, have outrun the constable a trifle, but it's merely a temporary setback. Nothing serious.'

'Nevertheless. Now, let's see . . . you came into your inheritance from your father some years ago and you have no further expectation from our side of the family.'

'Not with Grandmother making you her beneficiary and Aunt Esmeralda leaving her blunt to you and Jonas.'

'Quite. And, of course, when Huddlesford dies, his estate will pass to Frederick.' Phyllida fixed her gaze on Percy's now petulant face. 'Which means that beyond any inheritance from your mother, who everyone knows enjoys the best of health, there's no pot of gold waiting just over your horizon.' She paused. 'Am I right?'

'You know you're right, damn you.'

'And am I also right in thinking that the centpercents will no longer advance you funds – not unless you can show them some evidence of further expectations – like a wife with various inheritances attached?'

Percy glowered. 'That's all very well, but you're straying from the point.'

'Oh, no! The point is you've run aground, and you're looking to me to tug you out of the mire.'

'And so you *should!*' Face mottled, fists clenched, Percy stepped close. 'If I'm prepared to marry you out of family duty, you should be pleased to marry me and resurrect my fortunes.'

Phyllida shut her lips on an unladylike utterance. She gave Percy back stare for glare. 'I will *not* marry you – there's absolutely no reason that I should.'

'Reason?' Percy's features contorted. '*Reason?* I'll give you reason.'

He grabbed her, clearly intending to kiss her. Phyllida jerked back and wrestled half out of his hold. She'd never been afraid of Percy; he was three years older, but she'd run rings around him from her earliest years – she'd grown accustomed to treating him with contempt.

To her shock, he was much stronger than she'd realized. She struggled, but couldn't break his hold. With a growl, he hauled her back into his arms, cruelly pressing her back into the balustrade, trying to force her face to his—

Suddenly he was gone, literally plucked off her.

Phyllida collapsed against the balustrade, dragging in air, one hand at her heaving breast. She stared at Percy, dangling, choking, at the end of one long, blue-suited arm.

'Is there a pond or lake closer than the duck pond? I believe your cousin needs to cool off.'

Tracking along his arm, Phyllida located Lucifer's face in the dimness. Then she looked back at Percy, feet still swinging helplessly four inches clear of the flagstones. His face was turning purple. 'Umm – no.'

Lucifer's lip curled. He shook Percy, then flung him away – he landed with an 'Ooof!' and a clatter of limbs. He lay wheezing on the flags, shaking his head weakly, not daring to look up.

Reluctantly accepting that that was the worst he could do, Lucifer slammed a door on the chaos of emotions whirling inside him and looked at Phyllida. She was still breathing rapidly, but her color, as far as he could judge in the poor light, was acceptable. Her gown and hair were still neat – he'd been in time to spare her that much of the ordeal. He resettled his coat and cuffs, then offered her his arm. 'I suggest we return before anyone else misses you.'

Looking up at him, she swallowed, then nodded. 'Thank you.' Placing her hand on his arm, she straightened, stiffening her spine and lifting her head. Her mask of calm composure slid into place, hiding her shock – the sudden comprehension of her physical vulnerability – that had, until that moment, sat naked on her face.

It was not a look he had ever liked seeing on any woman's face. He would have given a great deal to have saved her from the realization entirely.

She shouldn't need to know that men could physically harm her. Her physical safety, here in her home, in and around the village, was something she'd taken for granted all her life. Percy had violated the 'comfort' she had alluded to – the sense of security she enjoyed in this place.

As for Percy's so elegant proposal, just the thought of it made Lucifer see red. Grimly clinging to his own mask of calm indifference, he steered Phyllida along the terrace. They reached the French doors and she stepped into the light. He let his gaze slide over her, from her pale, hauntingly lovely face, over the slender frame and feminine curves concealed beneath lavender silk, down to the tips of her satin slippers. Other than her breathing, still too shallow, there was no overt evidence of any distress.

Chest tightening, he looked into her eyes. They were shuttered, all emotions locked away.

As he handed her over the threshold, then followed, Lucifer wondered if it was too late to slip out again and thrash Percy to within an inch of his life.

CHAPTER 6

The emotions stirred by the incident on the terrace did not rapidly subside. Later that night, with the moon riding the sky, Lucifer paced before his bedchamber window.

Tomorrow, he'd remove to the Manor. Tomorrow, he'd start investigating Horatio's murder with a great deal more intensity than he'd yet employed. Horatio had been killed on Sunday morning. Tomorrow would be Wednesday. The first rush of shock and speculation would have died; people would have had time to think and, he hoped, remember.

Pausing before the window, he glanced out. The moon broke free of the wispy clouds and shone down; the night was a cauldron of shifting shadows stirred by the pale light.

A figure left the house, striding purposefully across the back lawn. Lucifer stared. A low cap hid the man's head – or was it a youth? The stride was swinging, graceful, and easy, long legs encased in breeches and boots. A hacking jacket hung to hip length. Jonas?

The figure neared the entrance to the shrub-bery; the graceful stride faltered, slowed.

That instant of hesitation ripped the veils from Lucifer's eyes. 'What the *devil* . . . ?'

He didn't wait for an answer. His quarry was into the wood before he had drawn close enough to be sure of not losing her. He trailed her; he wanted to see where she was going.

And then he would want to know why.

He would have wagered a great deal that her goal would be the Manor – she knew he would be taking up residence there tomorrow. Instead, she turned left off the main path onto a narrower one heading into the village.

He followed, closing the gap so he could keep her in sight; the path twisted through the trees – it would be easy to lose her. Head down, she tramped along, apparently absorbed in her thoughts.

The path became an alley running between two cottages to join the lane. Without pause, Phyllida crossed the lane and continued up the common. Lucifer hung back in the alley, letting the distance between them increase. The common was open ground, and there was little doubt now of her destination. She was making for the church.

Her peculiar conversation with the curate replayed in his mind. What in all Hades was going on?

On reaching the graveyard, he saw faint light spilling from the church's side door. Using gravestones for cover, he crept closer, exercising greater caution than before.

Phyllida was no longer alone.

A tall gravestone stood by the path leading from the side door; concealed in its shadow, Lucifer watched Phyllida standing beside Filing in the narrow porch before the open door. Both had ledgers in their hands; heads down, they were making notes, occasionally comparing entries.

Lucifer looked down the path to the lane bordering the graveyard. The lych-gate was shrouded in gloom; eyes straining, he could make out shapes and movement in the lane beyond. Then figures separated from the shadows and came up the path – men toting small barrels, boxes, packages. They passed his hiding place. Swiveling, Lucifer watched as Phyllida checked each box and barrel, speaking in low tones to the men and to Filing.

Then the men carried their loads into the church.

Lucifer slumped back, his shoulders against the gravestone. *Smuggling?*

The daughter of the local magistrate running a smuggling gang, aided and abetted by the local curate?

It was too hard to swallow, especially given what he knew of the daughter of the local magistrate.

Phyllida checked each item brought to the church door against the bill of lading. Beside her, Mr Filing created a separate list, noting which men were assisting tonight and who brought what up to the crypt.

One of the men, Hugey, held a package up for her perusal. 'This be almost it.'

Phyllida nodded. 'Good. That can go down now.'

Hugey bobbed his head and trudged past them. She heard his boots clatter on the stairs down to the crypt.

'This be the last for tonight.' Oscar, another heavy, hulking man, sat a barrel on the step.

Oscar was the leader of the band and a solid supporter of their enterprise. Smiling, Phyllida bent to check the barrel's markings. 'A quiet and uneventful night?'

'Aye – just how I likes it.' Oscar grinned back. At Phyllida's nod, he hefted the barrel to his shoulder. 'I'll stow this, then we'll be away.'

Phyllida closed her ledger and turned to Mr Filing.

He smiled. 'It's all running so smoothly.'

'Thank heaven.' Phyllida headed for the crypt stairs. 'I want to get these figures into the accounts.' She and Filing stood back as Oscar and Hugey came back up the stone steps. With nods and good-byes, the men trudged down the path to join the others. They would quietly disperse, returning the ponies to their respective stables, then go home to their cottages and their beds.

It would be an hour or so before she could do the same. Phyllida led the way down into the crypt. 'I expect to be busy over the next few days, so I'll bring all the accounts up-to-date and work out the payments in advance. That way, once you've collected the money, you can disburse the men's share without having to find me first.'

'A very good notion.' Filing looked around as they reached the crypt floor. 'I'll just make sure everything's where it ought to be.'

Phyllida crossed to the sarcophagus she used as a desk. It was built flush to the wall, with various niches carved above it, presumably for offerings. The niches presently contained a set of ledgers, assorted writing implements, and the other paraphernalia she required to keep the accounts. There was a wooden stool beside the sarcophagus; she drew it out and sat, winding her boots around the stool's legs. Moving the lamp that had been left on the sarcophagus to a higher perch on a stack of boxes nearby, she checked that the light thrown on her ledger was even, then settled to her task.

Behind her, Filing moved between the rows of goods which largely filled the crypt. Phyllida transcribed numbers, then worked through the calculations. The sound of something sliding on stone reached her. She glanced back at the stairs. No one came down. Then Filing stepped out from one row, concentrating as he counted boxes. He rounded the next row; Phyllida turned back to her columns.

Fifteen minutes later, the intensity of light increased. Phyllida looked up. Filing stood beside her.

'Everything's as it should be. Thompson and

I should encounter no problem sorting the next delivery.'

'Good.' Phyllida looked at the ledger before her. 'I'll be a little while yet, so I'll wish you a good night.'

She glanced up. Filing frowned.

'I don't like to leave you here at this hour, alone . . .'

'Nonsense!' Phyllida made the disclaimer with a confident smile, although, for the first time in her life, she wasn't sure she wanted to be alone, away from her home at this hour. She wasn't, however, about to display her fear – doubtless an irrational one – to Mr Filing.

'I'll be perfectly all right and, truth to tell, I work faster in complete silence. If you shut the church door, no one's likely to come in. I'll be quite safe.' She returned her attention to the ledger. 'I'll probably only be another fifteen minutes.'

Mr Filing hesitated, but she'd spoken realistically. Why would anyone climb to the church so late at night?

'Very well – if you're sure . . . ?'

'I'm sure.'

'Then . . . good night.'

'Good night.' Phyllida nodded without looking up; as she corrected a figure, the light from Mr Filing's lamp receded. A moment later, she heard him on the stairs, then heard the scrape of the church door closing.

She was alone.

In silence, her concentration absolute, she finished adding the figures in five minutes, then calculated and recorded the payments due to the men in another five. Pleased, she sat back, surveying her handiwork.

A shadow loomed on the page.

With a gasp, she swung around—

Lucifer stood beside the lamp, arms crossed, dark blue eyes narrowed. Her heart thudding in her throat, she stared at him.

'Would you care to tell me what this is all about?'

She drew breath into her lungs – and narrowed her eyes back. 'No. And might I suggest that, given you intend to reside in this village, you'd do well not to prowl around at night scaring the occupants out of their wits!' She'd started her tirade evenly; the last word was shrill. Swinging back to stare at her ledger, she concentrated on breathing. Grabbing a piece of blotting paper, she blotted her figures.

After a moment, he replied, 'You might have momentarily been frightened, but you haven't lost your wits. And you may as well tell me what's going on, because you know I won't leave you be until I know.' She did know that; he wasn't easily deflected. And there really was no reason he couldn't know the truth, especially as he was remaining in Colyton. Shutting the ledger, she returned it to its niche. 'I'm running an import business.'

He hesitated, then asked, 'Is that the new name for smuggling?'

'It's all perfectly legal.' Rummaging in a niche, she drew out a sheet of printed paper and handed it to him.

He took it and read, 'The Colyton Import Company.' He looked up. 'A legal importing company that operates in the dead of night?'

His incredulity was transparent; nose in the air, she slid from the stool. 'There's no law against it.'

She reached past him for the lamp – he anticipated her and lifted it. Laying the paper on the sarcophagus, he waved her to the stairs. Head high, she led the way; as she climbed she became increasingly conscious of the side-to-side sway of her hips. She scampered up the last stairs, but with one step he was beside her, looking beyond her to the church door. Phyllida shut the small door to the crypt; he extinguished the lamp, set it aside, and pulled open the church door. Together, they went out into the night.

He tugged the door shut. She felt his gaze on her face.

'Explain.'

Phyllida headed for the common. He fell in beside her, his dark presence more comforting than unnerving. He had the sense not to repeat his command; if he had, she might not have obliged. 'This is a smuggling coast. There's always been smugglers here, running goods either heavily taxed or, in more recent times, prohibited because of the war with France. The end of the war led to trade resuming, so the goods previously prohibited could once again be openly imported.'

Leaving the graveyard, she continued down the common. 'Virtually overnight, smuggling was no longer, or only marginally, profitable. Selling smuggled goods became difficult because merchants could buy the same goods legally at a reasonable price – there was no longer any incentive to take risks. Most of the smugglers are farm laborers – they turn to the night trade to supplement their incomes and support their families. Suddenly, that extra income was no longer there, and the whole' – she gestured – '*balance* of things hereabouts was in jeopardy.'

They crossed the lane and headed down the alley; she waited until they were in the wood before continuing. 'The only way I could see to help was to set up the Colyton Import Company. Papa knows all about it – it's entirely legitimate. We pay our excise duties to the Revenue Office in Exeter. Mr Filing is an accredited collector.'

He was following close at her shoulder, head bent as he listened. She glanced his way and saw him shake his head.

'Legitimized smuggling.' Through the gloom, he caught her eye. 'You arranged it all?'

She shrugged. 'Who else?'

A fair answer, Lucifer supposed, but it led to the next question. 'What do you get out of it?' An impertinent question, but he wanted to know.

'Get out of it?' The concept puzzled her; she halted and looked at him, then moved on again. 'I suppose peace of mind.'

Not what he'd expected. Excitement, the thrill of being in charge, something along those lines, but . . . 'Peace of mind?'

'Just consider the alternative to smuggling in these parts.' Her voice hardened. 'We're two miles from a coast riddled and raked with reefs and sandbars.'

'Wrecking?' His blood ran cold.

'That's what happened before. I wasn't having it happening again – not with Colyton men.' Even through the dark, she exuded determination. Now he understood. Peace of mind.

'So instead, you organized this entirely legitimate enterprise.' Not a question but a statement, one tinged with surprise and more definitely with approval.

She inclined her head.

They walked on in silence as he digested it all. 'But why work at night?'

The sound she made, half snort, half sigh, was distinctly patronizing. 'So it *looks* like the men are still smuggling, of course.'

'Why is that important?'

'It isn't, not to anyone but them.' Resigned frustration colored her tone. 'Other than myself, only Papa, Mr Filing, Thompson, and the men involved – and now you – know that the business is legal. In the company's name, I organize the rendezvous with the ships – most French captains are happy to unload without having to lay into an English port. The gang keeps the rendezvous and brings the goods up to the church –'

'And you store them in the crypt.'

She nodded.

'What happens then?'

'Mr Filing takes the signed bills of lading to the Revenue Office and pays the duties owed, then brings back the stamped clearances. Thompson isn't involved with the incoming goods, but his brother, Oscar, is the gang's leader. Once Mr Filing has the clearances, the gang comes back one night and loads the goods onto Thompson's dray. The next day, Thompson drives the goods into Chard, where the Company has an arrangement with one of the major merchants. He sells the goods on commission and the funds come back to Mr Filing, who pays the men their share.' She gestured. 'That's it.'

'But why do the men pretend they're still smuggling?'

'They pretend they're still members of the brotherhood essentially to save face. They've got used to a regular income and a comfortable existence free of any threat from the Revenue, but the mystique of smuggling runs deep in these parts – they don't want it known they're no longer involved, no longer taking risks. There are other smuggling gangs still operating in the district. The gang that operates to the west of Beer is all but legendary.'

Eyes on the ground, she strode on. 'When I suggested the Company, the men were adamant that they'd only be part of it if the legality of the operation was kept secret. I had to agree to them continuing to operate like smugglers.'

She shot him a glance; he sensed her contemptuous air. 'Male egos are nonsensical things.'

Lucifer grinned. The woman came out night after night to spare those selfsame male egos. He looked ahead. The Grange shrubbery was just discernible through the gloom.

Crack!

He reacted instantly, grabbing Phyllida, hurling them both forward.

A long groan and the sounds of roots and earth tearing followed them down; the next instant, with a massive *crash!* a dead tree thumped down across the path where a few seconds before they had stood. One skeletal branch trapped Lucifer's boots. Turning, glancing back at the tree, he kicked and the brittle twigs snapped.

He'd flung them against the rising bank that bordered the path at that point, Phyllida first, his body protectively over hers. They'd landed roughly horizontal, stretched full length on a narrow shelf in the bank. Lucifer slowly turned over, assessing their state. He slipped and slid down, ending on the path, flat on his back.

Phyllida, who'd been trying to push herself away from the bank, lost his support behind and beneath her. With a muffled shriek, she followed him down. She landed on top of him, her shoulder digging into his chest.

He winced. Gasping, she wriggled around; they ended literally nose to nose, lips and eyes mere inches apart.

They both froze, stilled . . . waiting . . . thinking . . .

He started to raise his arms to close them about her, then stopped. Percy had grabbed her only hours before and tried to force his attentions on her. He wanted to seize, to hold, to capture, but the last thing he wanted was to remind her of Percy.

His night vision was good. Her face was a pale oval, her expression not her usual serene mask but carefully blank. Eyes wide, she was staring at his face. Considering . . . wondering . . .

He knew what he'd like her to consider – what he wanted her to wonder. 'I believe' – his voice had deepened – 'that I deserve a reward for that.'

Phyllida stared at him and tried to marshal her wayward wits. His hands were at her waist, but not gripping. She lay fully upon him; he lay passive beneath her. She knew that he was infinitely more dangerous than Percy. Why, then, did she feel so much safer, all but in his arms, lying atop him, entirely alone in the dark wood late at night?

It was a conundrum, one she felt she should solve. But she couldn't, not now, not with his dark gaze on her eyes, with the hard warmth of him beneath her, threatening, in the most tempting way, to surround her.

He did deserve a reward. If she'd been alone, she would have stopped and looked around, and probably have ended being hurt. Even killed. He deserved a reward, and she didn't even have to think to know what it was he would like.

His wish was the glint in his eyes, the tension in the hard body beneath her – an almost discernible hum of desire. Of its own volition, her tongue came out; she licked her lips, leaving them slightly parted.

His gaze lowered; her lips throbbed. She waited . . .

His gaze rose to her eyes. He held her gaze, then slowly raised one brow.

You may be as bold as you like . . .

His earlier words returned to her; their true meaning – the meaning his deep, purring, seductive voice had invested them with – rang crystal-clear. She hesitated no longer. Framing his face with her hands, she set her lips to his.

They felt as they had before, alive, firm, tempting; they made her lips tingle. She kissed him and he kissed her back, pressure for pressure but no more. She kissed him again and the same thing happened – she was in control. Some part of her mind tried frantically to remind her just how dangerous he was; the rest gloried in the unexpected possibilities. There were so many things she'd always wanted to know, sensations she'd wanted to experience.

She traced his lower lip with her tongue and he

obediently parted his lips. She ventured in and was immediately lost in a carnival of delicious delights, slipping from one to the next and back again. Whatever she asked, he gave; wherever she ventured, he followed. The texture of his tongue against hers, the heated wetness of the kiss, were all still new to her. She reveled in each novel delight, then, confident and secure, explored further.

Lucifer lay there and let her have her way with him. He had to concentrate to maintain his passive state, given she was a mature twenty-four and every development in their kiss apparently necessitated a wriggle or a squirm. Luckily, she provided a distraction, too – her naivete coupled with her blatant curiosity left him wondering what the local gentlemen had been doing for the past six years. Asking for her help, apparently – certainly not kissing her. Especially not kissing her as she deserved to be kissed.

She was twenty-four – the warm swells that tantalizingly brushed his upper chest, the warm weight of her hips pressed to his waist, the long sweeps of her thighs riding down, over his hips – He abruptly cut off that train of thought and focused again on her hungry lips, on satisfying her and satisfying himself.

He felt they'd succeeded very nicely when she finally raised her head.

Phyllida looked down at him, and felt her heart thud. Her skin, all her nerves, had come alive; she was intensely aware of his body, and hers, of the masculine power he exuded yet controlled so effortlessly. It surrounded her, yet she didn't feel trapped, didn't feel like pulling away. She felt like plunging deeper in.

Temptation might well be his middle name.

She frowned, then struggled, just a little. 'Let me up.'

His lips curved. 'I'm not holding you.'

She stared at him; heat rose in her cheeks. His hands on either side of her waist might be burning her – they weren't gripping her. She tried to push away, to roll off him. His fingers gripped lightly and he lifted her from him.

Scrambling upright, she brushed herself down, tugged her cap firmly on her head, then, with barely a glance to confirm he was on his feet, she strode on toward the house.

Lucifer followed, careful, even in the darkness, not to grin too triumphantly. Close behind her as they navigated the shrubbery, he felt more than victorious. He felt honored, curiously so, as if she'd bestowed something on him that was worth more than words could define. In one way, she had – she'd gifted him with a degree of trust she'd never given to any other man.

He'd invited it, true, but it wasn't something he could have forced from her. Inordinately pleased with himself, and her, he stepped onto the back lawn.

She'd trusted him in one way – that augered well for his plan, a plan that was simplicity incarnate.

She knew something about Horatio's murder and she was a sensible, intelligent female; the only reason she hadn't told him all was because she didn't yet trust him that far. Once she'd learned more of him and convinced herself that he was an honorable man, then she would tell him her secret. Simple.

Grinning, he walked on by her side.

His next thought came out of nowhere, unheralded – unwanted. It destroyed his triumph, leaving a bitter taste on his tongue. Was he any better than the others who courted her, not out of real desire, but out of a desire for something she could give them?

The question clanged in his brain. The sensual memory of her body lying flush atop his washed over him.

Jaw setting, he willed both memory and question away.

The house rose before them, silent and still. Without words, they made their way inside, and parted for what was left of the night.

CHAPTER 7

Late the next morning, Lucifer walked into the front corner bedchamber at the Manor and looked around. His brushes were on the dresser. If he opened the wardrobe, he would, he was sure, find his coats neatly hanging. Covey had been busy.

He'd breakfasted at the Grange with Sir Jasper and Jonas; Phyllida, he assumed, had still been abed. Or perhaps, after last night, she'd decided to avoid meeting him quite so soon. If so, he was grateful. Taking leave of his host, he'd walked through the woods to the Manor to take up the reins Horatio had willed him.

After speaking with Covey, Bristleford, and the Hemmingses, assuring them that he would, indeed, be residing permanently at the Manor and that he was happy to have them continue in their present positions, he'd allowed himself to be shown around the house and had chosen this room as his.

Leaving Mrs Hemmings and Covey to organize and fuss – which had reassured them as no words could – he'd settled in the library to write letters.

One to his parents, one to Devil, one to Montague, and a summons to Dodswell to join him here. He didn't know where Gabriel and Alathea were, so he couldn't write to them. Had it really been only four *days* since their wedding? It felt like weeks.

Leaving the letters for Covey to take to the Red Bells for collection, he'd wandered up here.

He'd chosen this room because of the windows, the light. The room Horatio had occupied, similarly large but at the back, was shady and quiet.

Here, the front windows looked over the flower garden, the drive, and the gates to the lane, while the side windows gave views of the shrubbery, the lawns, and the lake. Between the side windows sat a large four-poster bed invitingly arrayed with plump pillows and a rich red-and-gold tapestry bedspread. Curtains of the same fabric were gathered at the four corners and tied back with tasseled gold cords.

All the furniture gleamed; the faint scent of lemon polish hung in the air.

Walking to the window facing the common, Lucifer gazed out, mentally assembling a plan, one that didn't involve pressuring Phyllida Tallent into telling him all she knew. She could come to trust him of her own accord; he refused to seduce her into it.

Shaking aside all memories of last night, including the hours during which he'd been unable to sleep, he focused on the lane. He recalled driving into the village, halting, and looking around . . . he'd seen no horse or carriage, no one on foot. . . . How had the murderer left the scene?

'If by horse . . .' Crossing to the side window, he studied the shrubbery.

Two minutes later, he was striding across the side lawn. The shrubbery entrance was wide but shaggy; inside, the hedges were overgrown. Making a mental note to speak to Hemmings about hiring more help for the grounds, Lucifer pressed on along a path leading, he hoped, to the lane.

He discovered an archway in the hedge running parallel to the lane. Pushing through, he found himself on a narrow path winding between the shrubbery hedge and the hedge bordering the lane. Topping him by more than a foot, both hedges were so poorly tended that arching new growth met and tangled overhead. Even though the path was wide enough to walk freely, when he'd stopped in his curricle only yards farther along the lane, he hadn't had any inkling this path was here – it had appeared that the shrubbery hedge and the lane hedge were one and the same.

Presumably the path started by the Manor's drive. Turning, Lucifer paced in the other direction.

He found what he'd suspected he might just beyond the shrubbery. The side and back shrubbery hedges met in a corner; a grassy area wide enough to accommodate a horse lay between the back of the shrubbery and a briar-filled ditch marking the edge of a paddock. Hard by the lane, the ditch closed over and the path led on, hugging the lane hedge to swing out of sight around a bend.

Turning his attention to the grassy area, he looked, then squatted and parted the grass to study the impressions in the earth beneath.

A horse had stood there, not long ago. He didn't think it had rained since Sunday. As the grass sprang back, he saw that some tufts had been chomped. So – a horse had stood there recently, for at least a little while. Why?

There seemed only one likely answer.

Lucifer rose and continued along the path. He was out of sight of the shrubbery when he came upon a place where the lane hedge had partly died. There was a gap, wide enough for a horse to push through.

Twigs were snapped on both sides of the gap. He twisted one free and studied it. It had broken, not this morning, not even yesterday, but not long ago.

From the other side of the hedge came a rustle of skirts, a quick, light step. Lucifer looked up. His senses prickled.

The steps halted. A small hand appeared, fingers extended to touch a broken twig.

The owner of the hand stepped into the gap.

She gasped and nearly stepped back when she saw him.

Lucifer stared at her.

Phyllida stared back.

For one wild moment, her consciousness of their kiss in the night flared in her eyes; he felt the same awareness tug, hot and strong, in his gut. Then she blinked and looked down – at the twig he still held in his fingers. Her gaze swung up to his face. 'What have you found?'

Sharing would make her trust him sooner. He glanced back down the path. 'I think a horse was ridden through here and left waiting at the back of the shrubbery.'

She pressed into the gap, craning to see; the curve of the lane prevented that. 'The back of the shrubbery?'

'There's a clearing there.'

'Show me.' She began to push through the hedge. Branches grabbed at soft curves protected only by her delicate blue gown.

'No!' He waved her back. 'Use your parasol as a shield.'

She looked at him inquiringly. He showed her how; holding the open parasol before her, she maneuvered through the hedge without sustaining any serious damage. Shaking out her skirts, she raised the parasol again. 'Thank you.'

He said nothing but waved her down the path; it wasn't his pleasure – he wasn't at all sure he wanted her this close, alone and private again. He had to keep reminding his rakish senses that she was more innocent than her behavior painted her. Not an easy task when he could all too clearly remember the sensations of her lips on his, her tongue . . . He shook his head. 'The clearing's beyond those briars.'

She stopped at the spot. He hunkered down and showed her what he'd found, the clear impressions made by front hooves neatly shod.

'Can you tell anything from the hoofprints?'

He shook his head and stood. 'The back hooves were on harder soil, and the horse was here long enough to shift about a good deal. There's no imprint with any distinctive mark.' He frowned, still looking down. 'But the shoes are good quality – clean, good lines.'

'So it's unlikely to be a workhorse, a plow horse . . .'

'No, but any decent mount would fit the bill.' He moved back, onto the path. Phyllida joined him. Without further words, they strolled toward the Manor.

Temptation whispered; Lucifer ignored it. He glanced at her; there was no evidence of aware-ness in her face – but then, there rarely was. Her face was a mask; only her eyes would tell him what she was feeling, and she was being careful not to meet his gaze. Being very careful not to touch him as they strolled.

He looked forward and drew in a breath. 'Let's hypothesize that on Sunday morning, the murderer rode here, pushed through the hedge, and left his horse waiting at the back of the shrubbery while he went on to the Manor. Where could he have ridden from?'

'You mean from which towns?'

He nodded.

'Lyme Regis is close, about six miles, but the route is by the coast, so if they'd come from there, they would have ridden through the village.' She glanced at him. 'Old Mrs Ottery lives in the cottage by the Bells. She's chair-bound and spends her Sunday mornings looking out over the common. She swears no one rode through the village.'

Lucifer eyed her calm profile. 'If not Lyme Regis, where else?'

'Axminster is the closest town, but it's not very large.'

'I passed through it on my way here. Chard is further, but might be worth considering. I saw a few stables there.'

'Chard is the most likely place where someone from outside would hire a horse to ride here. The mail coaches to Exeter stop there.'

'Very well. Let's consider nearer at hand. Who rides in from this end of the village?'

She glanced at him; a frown filled her eyes. 'The households of Dottswood and Highgate – their lane joins the main lane back by the first cottages.'

Lucifer remembered the lane beside the ridge. 'Who else commonly rides into the village?'

She hesitated. They'd passed the archway into the shrubbery; the end of the path lay just ahead. 'Most of the men living outside the immediate village ride in. Papa and Jonas rarely ride in the village. Silas Coombe and Mr Filing I've never known to ride at all. All the rest, even Cedric, would normally ride in.'

Stepping through the ragged entrance to the path, she halted on the lawn. He followed, glancing around. They were some yards from the main gates, the hedge bordering the lane still to their immediate right. The gravel path leading to the front door started twenty paces away.

He returned his gaze to Phyllida. 'Could a man from any of the other estates – not Dottswood or Highgate – easily circle the village and reach the lane at that spot?'

'Yes. Bridle paths link all the lanes, although you'd have to be a local to know them.'

No one wanted to think the murderer was a local, yet . . . 'Ignoring that gap in the hedge, could the horse have been ridden to that clearing from the other direction?'

'By coming up the field?' When he nodded, she shook her head. 'That field – in fact, all your fields – runs down to the river. The Axe. It's not far and it's too deep to ride across without getting thoroughly wet. To come along this side of the river, they'd have to cross the Grange fields first – a lot of fields, most bordered with briar ditches.'

Lucifer looked across the drive to the colorful blooms nodding in Horatio's garden. 'So we're looking for some outsider who hired a horse, most likely in Chard, and rode in, then out, or it could have been any of the local gentlemen.'

'Bar Papa, Jonas, Mr Filing, and Silas Coombe.

And the other gentlemen who were at church, of course.'

He'd forgotten. 'Basil and Pommeroy. I haven't checked the others, but that should narrow the list.'

Phyllida threw him a glance. 'Don't count on it.'

Lucifer grinned. He was about to twit her on the comment when the rumbling of a carriage reached them.

They glanced toward the lane, then looked at each other. Their gazes met, held . . .

Without a word, they stepped into the drive – into the open. Where anyone could see them and no one could suggest they'd been 'private'.

They were standing in the middle of the drive, facing the gate, when the carriage slowed and halted.

Lady Fortemain leaned over the side and beamed. 'Mr Cynster. *Just* who I was looking for!'

Lucifer quashed an urge to flee. With an easy smile, collecting Phyllida with a glance, he strolled to the barouche.

'I've just heard the *wonderful* news!' Lady Fortemain's eyes gleamed. 'Now you've decided to remain among us and fill the void left by dear Horatio's passing, you must – positively you *must* – allow me to host an impromptu dinner to introduce you to your neighbors.'

He'd been born in the country and lived among the ton; there was no need to ask how Lady Fortemain had heard.

She leaned forward, including Phyllida in her bright gaze. 'Our summer ball is just over a week away – I'll send you a card, of course. But I thought, seeing as we're so very quiet hereabouts, that there would be no harm in holding a small dinner tonight.'

'Tonight?'

'At seven – Ballyclose Manor. You can't miss it – just take the lane past the forge.'

Lucifer hesitated for only an instant; such a gathering would provide excellent opportunities to further investigate his neighbors' activities last Sunday morning. He bowed to Lady Fortemain. 'I'd be honored.'

Delighted, her ladyship turned to Phyllida. 'I'm just going to Dottswood and Highgate, dear, and then I'll be calling at the Grange. I'm expecting everyone to attend – your papa and brother, as well as dear Lady Huddlesford and her sons. And, of course, you, my dear Phyllida.'

Phyllida smiled. To Lucifer, the gesture was superficial – mild, distant, it said nothing of her thoughts.

Her ladyship saw it otherwise; she beamed warmly at Phyllida. 'Perhaps you'd like to accompany me to Dottswood and Highgate, and thence to the Grange?'

Phyllida's smile didn't waver as she shook her head. 'Thank you, but I must call on Mrs Cobb.'

Lady Fortemain sighed fondly. 'Always so busy, dear. Well, I must leave you and spread the word.'

She tapped her coachman; she waved as the carriage jerked forward. 'Until seven, Mr Cynster!'

Lucifer raised his hand in salute; smiling, he watched the carriage rumble away. Then he turned to Phyllida, unsurprised to find that her smile had faded, leaving a frown investing her dark eyes.

'So why aren't you delighted?' He gestured to the flower garden; brows rising haughtily, she strolled beside him onto a secondary path that wound its way through burgeoning beds to the central fountain.

He waited – he had no intention of withdrawing the question. He wanted to know the answer.

After a moment, she pulled a face. He inwardly blinked – she rarely displayed her feelings so blatantly.

'Would *you* be delighted to know you were destined to spend the entire evening listening to a pompous windbag?'

'Which windbag is that?'

'Cedric, of course.' They strolled on, she admiring the blooms, he, more covertly, admiring her. Her consciousness of their interlude the previous night was still there, but had faded, receded, as they'd talked. Stopping to examine a rose, she went on. 'I told you Cedric wants to marry me – Lady Fortemain is determined that I should marry him. That alone would render this impromptu dinner less than appealing, but, of course, Pommeroy will be there, too, doing his best to be off-putting.'

'Why off-putting?'

165

'Because he *doesn't* want Cedric to marry me.'

'Pommeroy wants to marry you, too?'

She smiled. 'No – it's simpler. Pommeroy doesn't want Cedric to marry at all. There's fifteen years between them – Pommeroy therefore has expectations that Cedric's long bachelorhood have fueled.'

'Ah.'

They wandered on through the garden; Lucifer said nothing more. Her tone whenever they touched on the subject of marriage grated, although why he, of all men, should feel compelled to defend the institution was difficult to comprehend. Or, more to the point, he didn't want to comprehend the reasons behind the impulse, to study his motives too closely. Yet the fact remained.

Courtesy of her self-centered suitors, she'd developed a cynical, not to say negative, view of marriage that seemed considerably more cynical and deeply entrenched than his own. He, at least, knew all marriages were not like those offered her. Did she? 'When did your mother die?'

Halting by the fountain, she blinked at him. 'When I was twelve. Why?'

He shrugged. 'I just wondered.'

She bent to sniff a burst of lavender spikes. Leaning one shoulder against the fountain's rim, he watched her.

After a moment, he said, 'This garden . . .'

She glanced up at him, her face shaded by her parasol, her expression serene yet interested, eyes dark, unknown and unknowing . . .

166

That dark gaze caught him. She was aware of him, yet so . . . innocent of all else. All that she had a right to know, to experience – all she deserved to enjoy.

'I haven't any idea how to . . . manage it.' He heard his words as if from a distance.

She smiled and straightened. He pushed away from the fountain.

Turning toward the gate, she gestured to the glorious displays on all sides. 'It isn't that hard.' Pausing beneath a delicate arch covered with rioting white roses, she looked back at him. Her smile curved her lips, still warmed her eyes. 'Horatio learned how – I'm sure you could, too. If you truly wished to.'

Lucifer halted beside her; for a long moment, he looked into her eyes. Her dark gaze was direct, open, honest – assured and confident and also so aware. A bare inch of air was all that separated his body from hers, nevertheless, she stood, a serene goddess as yet untouched, certain, not of his control, but hers. 'If I were to ask, would you help me?'

His voice had deepened, his tone almost rough. Tilting her head, she studied his eyes. Her answer, when it came, was considered. 'Yes. Of course.' Smoothly, she turned away. 'You have only to ask.'

Lucifer stood beneath the arch watching her hips sway as she headed for the gate. Then he stirred and followed.

★ ★ ★

167

Lady Fortemain's dinner proved more interesting than Phyllida had expected, even if, for the most part, she was relegated to the status of mere observer. From the side of the Ballyclose drawing room to which she'd retreated to escape Cedric's patronizing possessiveness, she watched Lucifer move gracefully through the gathering.

At dinner, she'd been seated at Cedric's right at one end of the long table; Lucifer had been guest of honor at the other end, beside their hostess. He'd returned to the drawing room with the rest of the gentlemen a good half hour ago. Since then, he'd been on the prowl, indefatigably hunting, yet no one seemed defensive in the least.

He would pause beside a group of gentlemen and, with some question or comment, neatly cut his quarry from the pack. A few questions, a smile, perhaps a joke and a laugh; having got what he wanted, he'd let them return to the group and he'd move on, an easy smile, his elegantly charming air, masking his intent. Why they couldn't sense it, she did not know; even from across the room, his concentration reached her.

Then again, she knew what it felt like to be stalked by him, to be the focus of that intensely blue gaze. She hadn't expected to meet him that morning; throughout the interlude, she'd waited for him to pounce, to once again ask what she knew of the murder. She'd hoped he wouldn't, that he wouldn't mar the moment – the odd sense of ease, of shared purpose, that seemed to be growing between them.

To her considerable surprise, he'd walked her to the garden gate, held it open, and let her escape with nothing more than a simple good-bye.

Perhaps he, too, hadn't wanted to disturb the closeness that had enveloped them in Horatio's garden. His garden now.

She watched him weave through the other guests. That sense of closeness puzzled and intrigued her. Lifting her head, she considered the other gentlemen – all her prospective suitors and the others from the village – all men she'd known most of her life; the exercise only emphasized the oddity. She'd known Lucifer for a handful of days, yet she felt more comfortable with him, less inhibited, infinitely freer to be herself. With him she could be open, could speak her mind without any mask, any concession to society. That he saw through her mask had certainly contributed to that, but it wasn't the whole explanation.

Jonas was the only other person she felt that comfortable with, yet not by the wildest stretch of her imagination could she equate the way she reacted to Lucifer with her all but nonreaction to her twin. Jonas was simply there, like some male version of herself. She never wasted a moment wondering what Jonas was thinking – she simply knew.

She also never worried about Jonas – he could take care of himself. Lucifer was similarly capable. The same could not be said of anyone else in the room. Perhaps it was that – that she considered Lucifer an equal – that made her feel so at ease with him?

Inwardly shaking her head, she watched him prowl the room. Sometimes she could tell what he was thinking; at other times – like in the garden this morning – the workings of his mind became a mystery, one she itched to solve. Regardless of the danger she knew that might entail.

Putting out a hand, Mrs Farthingale stopped him. He paused, smiling easily, exchanged some glib quip that had her laughing, then smoothly moved on. As far as Phyllida could tell, his sights were set on Pommeroy.

She left him to it, turning to greet Basil as he strolled to her side.

'Well.' Taking a position beside her, Basil scanned the room. 'There are some who are now wishing they'd been more regular in their devotions.'

'Oh?'

'I overheard Cedric speaking with Mr Cynster – they were discussing estate management and Cedric mentioned he'd started using Sunday mornings to tackle his accounts.'

'Cedric wasn't at church last Sunday?'

Basil shook his head. His gaze shifted to Lucifer. 'I have to say, I'm quite impressed with Cynster. I suspect he's gathering information as to who might have killed Horatio. Thankless task, of course, but his devotion does him credit. Most would accept the inheritance and let be. Nothing to do with him, after all.'

Phyllida viewed Lucifer with increasing appreciation. It had never occurred to her that he wouldn't pursue the murderer, yet Basil was right. Most men would have shrugged and let be. Indeed, she suspected Basil would have shrugged and let be, and Basil was the most morally upright of her suitors.

At no time had she doubted Lucifer's resolve. He'd called Horatio friend and she'd known without question that he valued friendship highly. He was that sort of man – an honorable man.

Inwardly, she grimaced. She wasn't, to her mind, acting honorably at present – she was caught on the prongs of an honor-induced dilemma, damned if she did and damned if she didn't.

'Is Lady Huddlesford planning a long stay?'

Phyllida replied; conversing with Basil was always stultifying, given there was no chance of any challenging surprise. Mundane topics were Basil's specialty, but at least he was innocuous.

That changed when Cedric came charging up, much in the manner of a lowering bull. His short neck contributed to the unflattering image.

'I say, come and talk to Mama.' Cedric grasped her elbow. 'She's on the *chaise*.'

Phyllida stood her ground despite his tug. 'Did Lady Fortemain ask to speak with me?'

Cedric's face darkened. 'No, but she's always pleased to speak with you.'

'I daresay.' Basil's expression turned as haughty as his sister's. 'Miss Tallent, however, might prefer to converse with someone who actually wishes to converse with her.'

Miss Tallent would prefer an empty room. Phyllida

171

swallowed the words. 'Cedric, what were you doing last Sunday morning?'

Cedric blinked at her. 'Sunday? While Horatio was being murdered?'

'Yes.' Phyllida waited. Cedric responded well to directness. Subtlety was entirely beyond him.

He glanced at Basil, then back at her. 'I was doing the accounts.' He paused, then added, 'In the library.'

'So you were in the library at Ballyclose all morning?'

He nodded, his gaze straying to Basil. 'From before Mama left until after she got home.'

Phyllida artfully sighed. 'So you couldn't have seen anything.'

'Seen what?'

'Why, whatever there was to be seen. The murderer must have slipped away somehow.' She glanced at Basil. 'You were in church.' She looked from one to the other. 'Of course, you do both hire laborers who might have been out and about – or their children. Papa would be very grateful for any information.'

'I hadn't considered that.' Basil drew himself up. 'I'll ask around tomorrow.'

'So will I,' Cedric growled.

'If you'll excuse me, I must have a word with Mary Anne.' Phyllida left Basil and Cedric scowling at each other. If any of their farm workers had seen anything useful, she could be assured they would learn of it and come to lay the information at her feet.

She'd glimpsed Mary Anne and definitely wanted to speak to her, but Mary Anne didn't want to be spoken to. Short of chasing her around the room, there was nothing Phyllida could do. Robert had returned to Exeter. Halting, she considered the crowd, wondering who else she might conscript. Would anything be gained by enlisting the ladies of the village?

'Miss Tallent. I've been waiting for an opportunity to speak with you.'

Whirling, Phyllida came face-to-face with Henry Grisby. 'Good evening, Mr Grisby.' She inwardly sighed; she'd managed to avoid him thus far.

Henry bowed. 'My mother sends her greetings. She heard about the recipe for gooseberry tart that you gave the Misses Longdon. Mama wondered if you'd be so kind as to share the recipe with her.'

'Of course.' Phyllida added it to her mental list. Recipe for cough syrup for Mrs Farthingale; speak to Betsy Miller, one of Cedric's tenants who Lady Fortemain believed was having difficulties; recipe for Mrs Grisby; letters for Mary Anne; one murderer for Lucifer.

Henry tried to catch her eye. 'My mother would be deeply honored if you would call at Dottswood.'

Phyllida looked at him. Henry's eyes met hers, then slid away. 'I don't think that would be appropriate, Henry.' *He* would be deeply honored; Mrs Grisby would not.

He regarded her challengingly. 'You call at Ballyclose and Highgate.'

'To visit with Lady Fortemain and old Mrs Smollet, both of whom have known me from the cradle.'

'My mother's lived here all your life, too.'

'Yes, but . . .' Phyllida searched for a polite way to point out that Mrs Grisby, at present, was not pleased with her. Mrs Grisby, who rarely ventured beyond Dottswood Farm and therefore relied on Henry for her view of village life, was intractably opposed to Phyllida marrying Henry. Being Henry's mother, it had not occurred to her that Phyllida was of a similar mind. In the end, Phyllida simply looked Henry in the eye and said, 'You know perfectly well your mother would not be pleased if I called.'

'She would be pleased if you accepted my proposal.'

Another lie. 'Henry—'

'No – listen. You're twenty-four. It's a good age for a woman to marry—'

'My cousin informed me just yesterday that at twenty-four, I was firmly on the shelf.' Percy might as well be useful for something.

Henry scowled. 'He's got rocks in his head.'

'The pertinent point you fail to grasp, Henry – you and Cedric and Basil, too – is that I intend to cling to my shelf for all I am worth. I like it there. I am not going to marry you or Cedric or Basil. If you could all regard me as an old maid, it would simplify matters considerably.'

'That's nonsense.'

Phyllida sighed. 'Never mind. I'm prepared to wait you out.'

'Ah, Mr Grisby.'

Phyllida turned to find Lucifer almost upon them. His dark blue eyes met hers; a rush of prickling warmth washed over her skin. Halting beside her, he looked at Grisby and smiled – like a leopard eyeing his next meal. 'I understand,' he purred, 'that you've been agisting on some of the Manor's fields.'

It was clear Henry would have preferred to scowl; instead, he nodded stiffly. 'I keep part of my herd on some of the higher fields.'

'The fields overlooking the river meadows? I see. Tell me, how often do you shift the herd?'

Despite Henry's resistance, Lucifer extracted the information that Henry's herds had been rotated last on Saturday; on Sunday, both Henry and his herdsman had worked in his barns. The questions were sufficiently oblique that Henry didn't recognize their intent.

He still glowered; he had not expressed any great joy at the news that Lucifer was to join their small community.

Henry's visual daggers bounced harmlessly off Lucifer's charm. He glanced at her. 'I wonder, Miss Tallent, if I might avail myself of your understanding of the village. A small matter of traditions.' He looked at Henry. 'I'm sure Mr Grisby will excuse us.'

Left with no choice, Henry gave an exceedingly stiff bow and pressed her fingers too fervently.

Phyllida tugged her hand free and placed it on Lucifer's sleeve. He led her away, strolling easily. She glanced up at him. 'On what subject did you wish to ask my advice?'

He smiled down at her. 'That was a ruse to whisk you away from Grisby.'

Phyllida wondered if she should frown. 'Why?'

He stopped before the French doors that opened to the terrace. 'I thought you might be in need of some fresh air.'

He was right; the night air outside was wonderfully balmy, warm against her skin. The terraces at Ballyclose were handsome and wide; they ran around three sides of the house. Lucifer and Phyllida strolled through the twilight.

'Are there many who were not at church last Sunday?' she asked.

'More than I'd expected. Coombe, Cedric, Appleby, Farthingale, and Grisby, and they're just the ones here tonight. If I included those not of the gentry, the list would be longer, but I'm concentrating on Horatio's peers.'

'Because whoever it was struck from so close to him?'

'Precisely. More likely someone he regarded at least as an acquaintance.'

'Why were you after Pommeroy? I thought he accompanied Lady Fortemain to church.'

'He did. I wanted to ask if he'd spoken to Cedric or Appleby when he returned. It seems they were both out.'

'Out?' Phyllida slowed. She looked at Lucifer.

He raised a brow. 'What?'

Phyllida halted. 'I suggested Cedric and Basil ask their farm workers if they'd seen anyone – meaning the murderer – about on Sunday morning.'

'An excellent notion.'

'Yes, but while discussing last Sunday, Cedric stated quite definitely that he'd been in the library all morning and was there when his mother returned.'

Lucifer looked into her eyes, then shrugged. 'Both Cedric and Pommeroy could be telling the truth. Cedric could have left after he heard his mother return, but before Pommeroy went looking for him.'

Relieved, Phyllida nodded. 'Yes, of course.'

They started strolling again, then Lucifer asked, 'What's the name of the head groom here?'

A knot of suspicion pulled tight in Phyllida's chest. But he was right – they had to be sure it wasn't Cedric. 'Todd. He'd know if Cedric had taken a horse out.'

'I'll speak to him – perhaps tomorrow.'

Phyllida said nothing. The seriousness of the murder seemed to be growing. How terrible for the village if the murderer was one of them.

How horrible if that suspicion firmed, but they never learned who.

'You're very determined to find Horatio's murderer.'

'Yes.'

One word, no embellishments. It didn't need any. 'Why?' She didn't look at him, but continued to stroll.

'You heard me explain it to your father.'

'I know what you told Papa.' She walked a few more paces before she said, 'I don't think that's all your reason.'

His gaze slid over her face, sharp, not amused. 'You're an exceedingly persistent female.'

'If your middle name is Temptation, then mine is Persistence.'

He laughed; the sound tugged at something inside her.

'All right.' He halted and looked down at her. She raised a brow at him, then turned to pace back toward the drawing room. He fell in beside her. 'I'm not sure I can explain it simply. Not in a way that'll sound rational to you. But it's as if Horatio was mine – part of me – certainly under my protection, even if that wasn't actually so. His murder is as if someone has taken something from me by force.' He paused, then went on. 'My ancestors conquered this country – perhaps it's some primitive streak that hasn't fully died. But if anyone dared take one of theirs, vengeance, justice, would have been guaranteed.'

After a moment, he glanced at her. 'Does that make any sense?'

Phyllida arched a brow. 'It makes perfect sense.' His ancestors might have conquered the land, but hers had civilized it. Horatio's murder violated her code in precisely the same way it offended his. She understood his feelings perfectly – indeed, she shared them.

She halted. For a moment, she stared straight ahead, then she drew in a deep breath. 'There's something I must tell you.' She turned to him—

'*There* you are, Mr Cynster!'

Jocasta Smollet swept up to them, flashing stiff silks and feathers. 'We were all wondering where you'd disappeared to. So naughty of Phyllida to monopolize your time.'

That last was said with open spite. Phyllida silently sighed. 'We were about to return inside—'

'No, no! So much more pleasant out here, don't you agree, Miss Longdon?' Jocasta turned to the French doors as the Longdon sisters stepped through, followed by Mrs Farthingale and Pommeroy. Others joined them, milling about, exclaiming at the pleasantness of the evening.

Phyllida shot a glance at Lucifer; he caught it. *Later?* was what his look said.

Almost imperceptibly, she nodded; it didn't really matter if she told him tonight or tomorrow.

She was threading through the guests, wondering where her father was, when someone grabbed her sleeve and unceremoniously tugged.

'Please, Phyllida, *please*! Say you've found them.'

Phyllida turned, and watched Mary Anne's face crumble.

'You haven't, have you?'

Taking Mary Anne's arm, Phyllida drew her into the shadows by the house. 'Why *are* you in such a panic? They're just *letters*. I know you've worked yourself into a pelter over them, but truly, nothing terrible will come of it even if someone else discovers them before I do.'

Mary Anne swallowed. 'You only say that because you don't know what's in them.'

Phyllida opened her eyes wide and waited. She couldn't be sure, but she thought Mary Anne blushed.

'I . . . I can't tell you. I really truly can't. But' – she was suddenly talking so fast she tripped over her words – 'I've had the most *horrendous* thought.' She grabbed Phyllida's hands. 'If Mr Cynster finds them, he'll give them to Mr Crabbs!'

'Why would he do that?'

'Mr Crabbs is his solicitor – he knows him!'

'Yes, but—'

'And even if he only gives them to Papa, now Papa will show them to Mr Crabbs – they met at the Grange last evening. You *know* Papa would do *anything* to stop Robert from marrying me!'

Phyllida couldn't argue with that, but . . . 'I still don't see why—'

'If Mr Crabbs reads the letters, he'll expel Robert from the firm! If Robert doesn't complete his registration, we'll *never* be able to get married!'

Phyllida started to get an inkling of what might be in the letters. She wished she could reassure Mary Anne that it really wasn't that serious – not compared to murder. Unfortunately, she wasn't sure herself just how damning the revelations might be – not to Mr Crabbs.

Mary Anne tried to shake her. 'You have to get the letters back!'

Phyllida focused on her face, on the huge eyes overflowing with so much panic it was evident even in the gloom. 'All right. I will. But I haven't even seen the desk yet. It's not downstairs anywhere, so I'll have to wait for a time when the upper floors are clear.'

Mary Anne drew back, making a heroic effort to reassemble her previous, subdued expression. 'You won't tell anyone, will you? I don't think I could *bear* it if I couldn't marry Robert.'

Phyllida hesitated; Mary Anne's eyes widened. Phyllida sighed. 'I won't tell.'

Mary Anne's lips lifted in a pathetically weak smile. 'Thank you.' She hugged Phyllida. 'You're such a good friend.'

CHAPTER 8

'What was it you wanted to tell me?' Lucifer glanced at Phyllida, perched beside him on his curricle's box seat. 'When we were talking on the terrace last night.'

They were on the road to Chard, his blacks pacing eagerly, a picnic hamper in the boot. He'd called at the Grange midmorning and without much difficulty prevailed upon Phyllida to join him on his investigative excursion.

He'd given her a few miles to broach the subject, but she hadn't.

The breeze flicked her bonnet ribbons as she glanced his way, giving him the barest glimpse of her face. 'The terrace?'

Her tone suggested she couldn't recall the moment. 'You *said* there was something I should know.'

His tone stated he wouldn't forget.

After a moment of tense silence, she lifted her chin. 'I have it now. I wanted to tell you that I feel just as strongly over unmasking Horatio's murderer as you do, and that you may count on me for whatever aid I can give.'

He narrowed his gaze on the sliver of pale cheek that was all he could see beneath her bonnet rim. Eventually she glanced up, avoiding his gaze. There was nothing to be read in her calm expression. Bowling along with the blacks in an exuberant mood and his hands consequently full, his chances of forcing her to meet his eyes were slight.

He eyed her bonnet with increasing distaste. 'I already knew you want to catch Horatio's murderer, and I fully intend to call on you for assistance. I'm doing precisely that at this moment.'

He got another fleeting glance. 'By taking me along so I can help question the stable masters?'

'And anyone else you can think of.'

'Hmm.' She sounded mollified, although he couldn't think why.

Who had invented poke bonnets? Any reasonably tall gentleman had the devil of a time seeing a lady's face when she was sitting or standing next to him wearing one.

He glanced at her again. She was surveying the fields and hedgerows, transparently enjoying the outing. He doubted Cedric or Basil, much less Grisby, had thought to squire her about, to woo her. More fool they.

His thoughts returned to the previous evening. Damn Jocasta Smollet. She'd interrupted at precisely the wrong moment. Jocasta clearly harbored some deep antipathy toward Phyllida, although no one, not even Basil, seemed to know why. But Jocasta had achieved what she'd wanted. She'd clung to his side for the rest of the evening; he'd lost sight of Phyllida when the crowd had invaded the terrace.

He'd seen her briefly in the hall as they'd all prepared to depart; she'd given no indication of having any burning information to convey to him.

He hadn't imagined that moment on the terrace. She'd been about to entrust him with the truth. Something had happened to change her mind, yet she hadn't retreated from trusting him. He tried to imagine what could hold enough power to prevent a woman like her from doing something he was increasingly sure she felt she should. She wanted to tell him, but . . . What was it that had stopped her?

The question went round and round in his mind but found no ready answer.

Chard appeared before them. They'd driven straight through Axminster and made for the larger town.

Phyllida straightened as they passed the first houses. 'There's three stables here. Perhaps we should start at the one furthest north?'

They did. No gentleman had hired a horse on the Saturday or Sunday in question. No unknown gentleman had stayed at the inn. They drove back into the town. The other two stables were off the main street. After receiving negative answers at the Blue Dragon, they left the curricle there, the blacks resting, and strolled to the Black Swan.

'Nah!' The innkeeper shook his head. 'We got two nags, but there's rarely much call for 'em. Later in summer, p'r'aps, but right now we haven't hired a horse to any gen'leman for months.'

In answer to their second question, he opened his eyes wide. 'Ain't *seen* any gen'leman – nought but the locals – not for weeks.'

As they stepped outside, Phyllida murmured, 'We don't get many visitors down here.'

'Which means any visitor would have been noted.' Taking her arm, Lucifer turned her toward the Dragon. 'I think we can conclude no visitor used Chard as a base.'

They strolled along; Phyllida halted when they reached the Dragon. 'This hasn't taken us long. If we drive back and check at Axminster, and then drive down to Axmouth and check there, then if no one's seen any unknown gentleman about . . . well, it really leaves few options.'

'Honiton, perhaps.'

'Perhaps. But why would anyone come from that direction?'

'I understand the tendency to imagine any nefarious wrongdoers essay forth from London. That isn't, however, necessarily true.'

'Is it likely the person who killed Horatio came from Honiton or Exeter – from somewhere to the west?'

Lucifer fell silent. Phyllida watched him. 'Well?'

He refocused. 'I was trying to recall if any

collectors, or anyone connected with collecting, lived out that way.'

'And?'

'I'd have to agree that if the murderer rode in from beyond the village last Sunday, then they probably came from the east. Nevertheless, we'll need to check Honiton, but we can do that some other day.' Looking up, he saw a dapper little man hurrying across the street, flourishing a piece of paper to attract their attention. 'Who's this?'

Phyllida turned. 'Mr Curtiss – he's the merchant the Colyton Import Company deals with.'

Mr Curtiss reached them; he nodded politely to Lucifer, then beamed at Phyllida. 'Miss Tallent – well met! I wanted to send this' – he held out a letter – 'to Mr Filing. My customers have been very pleased with the quality of goods Mr Filing's company provides. So rare to find quality one can rely on. I've decided to increase our order. With word getting around, I'm sure I can sell more. If I could presume – I know you assist Mr Filing – could you see this missive reaches him?'

Smiling serenely, Phyllida took the letter. 'Of course, Mr Filing will be thrilled.' She tucked the letter into her reticule.

Mr Curtiss bowed. 'A pleasure, my dear. Do convey my best wishes to Sir Jasper.'

'I will, indeed.'

With a nod to Lucifer, Mr Curtiss, still beaming, withdrew.

'Mr Filing's company?' Lucifer asked as they

186

entered the Dragon's courtyard and headed for the curricle.

Phyllida unfurled her parasol. 'Of course. No mere female could operate an import company.'

Lucifer smiled. 'Naturally not.'

He handed her into the curricle. Minutes later, they were bowling back toward Axminster. 'Tell me – just so I don't inadvertently cause a problem. Am I right in assuming no one other than those involved knows of your involvement in the Company?'

'Of course not. There's no reason for others to know. In fact, not all of the men know – most think Filing runs it and I'm just his amanuensis. I'm not *sure* how much Papa understands . . .'

He could imagine. She was the linchpin, the person around whom all else revolved, yet she preferred anonymity. Her tone, subtly amused, said as much.

Her role, however, extended much further than the company. He'd been in Colyton only a few days, yet he'd lost count of the times he'd seen someone – man, woman, even child – approach Phyllida with some request.

He'd never seen her turn anyone down.

The impulse to watch over people, to be actively involved, doing, helping, was one he understood. In his case, it derived from *noblesse oblige* – part learned, part inherited, part instinctive. Phyllida's impulse was, he suspected, wholly instinctive. Wholly giving. He was, however, getting the distinct impression that the village took her – and her help – for granted. 'How long have you been ruling the roost at the Grange?'

The glance she slanted him was sharp. 'Since my mother died.'

Twelve years? No wonder her influence was so pervasive. She waited, but he said nothing more, content to drive through the sunshine with her beside him. And to consider . . .

Her impulse to help him would lead her to tell him whatever she knew soon enough. She was too intelligent to hold back information that would allow a killer to run loose; he accepted that she did not know the murderer's identity. She had a clue, nothing more; the best way forward was to continue his inquiries and keep her closely involved. Ironically, the less he learned, the more she'd feel compelled to resolve whatever matter was preventing her from being open with him, and to tell him all she knew.

'That was how to proceed on that front. For the rest, now that he'd committed to residing in Colyton . . .

He had a house – one too large for just him. It was a family house – a family was what it needed. That was what Horatio would have envisioned. *He* certainly hadn't envisioned a family, not before he'd come to Colyton. But now he was here, and Horatio was gone, but the Manor still stood along with its garden.

The outlying houses of Axminster appeared – a welcome distraction. They were thorough in their inquiries, but, as they'd assumed, no gentleman visitor had ridden through or driven through Axminster on Sunday morning.

''Cept for you.' The grizzled veteran slouching outside the small inn eyed him suspiciously.

Lucifer grinned. 'Quite. I drove through that morning. But you're sure no one else was before me?'

A quick shake of the head. 'Don't get that many carriages or horsemen going south of a Sunday. I'da noticed. And I was here from first light.'

Lucifer nodded and tossed him a coin. The man caught it deftly and bowed to them both.

Phyllida led the way back to the curricle. 'Where now?' he asked as he lifted her up.

'South. To the coast.'

She directed him down a road; a mile or so south, a river came into view, winding along to their right.

'Is that the Axe?' When she nodded, he asked, 'Are those my fields on the other side?'

'Not yet, but a little further and they will be.'

They rattled through the early afternoon, the lush green of the river valley about them. The sun was screened by light clouds; it was warm but not hot. The first intimation that the coast was near was a cool breeze. They rounded a curve – at a crossroads before them stood an old inn. Phyllida pointed to the left. 'That's the road to Lyme Regis.

189

If anyone came past from Lyme on Sunday morning, the children would have noticed.'

'Children?'

A tribe ranging in age from about twelve to two, mostly girls. He left the questioning to Phyllida, content to lean against a stone wall and watch.

The innkeeper's wife had looked out at the sound of their wheels on the cobbles. She recognized Phyllida and came forward, beaming, wiping her hands on her apron. Without waiting for assistance, Phyllida jumped down. In seconds, she and the woman were discussing what sounded like the recipe for some poultice.

The innkeeper stuck his head out; Lucifer waved him away, tied the blacks to the rail, then settled to observe.

Laughing, Phyllida gestured to an opening in the worn stone wall. The woman nodded and smiled; together, she and Phyllida strolled through. Lucifer trailed after them. Stopping in the gap, he leaned against the wall.

Beyond lay the remnants of a garden, stunted by the sea breeze whipping across the open fields. A vociferous crowd gathered around Phyllida, greeting her shrilly; she laughed, patted heads, tweaked braids. Then she sat on a stone bench in the sun and the children pressed around her.

He couldn't hear what she asked, how they answered. He didn't bother trying to hear. Instead, he drank in the sight of Phyllida with the children

190

like fairies surrounding their queen, all eager for her blessing.

She gave it unstintingly with smiles, laughter, and an effortless understanding. With sincere interest and a deep caring. It glowed – in her eyes, like an aura all about her. The children, the woman, basked and drew it in; Phyllida simply gave.

He was sure she didn't realize – she certainly didn't realize how much he could see.

Finally, after much teasing, she stood and the children, made to mind by their mother, let her go. She strolled toward him, still smiling softly, her gaze on the path. As she neared, she looked up. He kept his expression impassive. 'Did they see anyone?'

She shook her head. Looking back, she waved, then, side by side, they headed for the curricle.

'They were out on Sunday morning. It was glorious weather, if you recall. They play out there most of the time. The chances of anyone slipping by and being missed by all those sharp eyes . . .'

He handed her up to the seat. 'So we've accomplished what we set out to do – we've confirmed no visitor, no one from outside, rode into Colyton on Sunday, at least not from the east.'

Phyllida was silent as he set the blacks in motion and turned them out onto the road. 'Now where? I'm ravenous. We need a place to do justice to Mrs Hemmings's picnic.'

She pointed south. 'Down to the coast. It's wonderful on the cliffs.'

The road took them down through the village of Axmouth, then wound up onto the cliffs. She directed him along a rutted track that led to a stand of scrubby trees. 'We can leave the horses here. It's not much further.'

Carrying the basket, he followed her onto the windswept cliff. The view was magnificent. He stopped to drink in the majestic sweep of the cliffs westward. The Axe spilled into the sea virtually at their feet, distance miniaturizing the houses of Axmouth. The estuary itself was peaceful, but beyond the breakers the Channel swell ruled, surging powerfully.

The gray-green sea stretched to the horizon; the cliffs dominated on either side. Phyllida stood watching a little way ahead; when his gaze reached her, she smiled and beckoned with her head. She led the way around a hillock; a patch of grass lay protected by the hillock, large boulders, and trees. It was a pretty spot, partly sheltered yet still open, still blessed with panoramic views.

'Jonas and I found this place when we were children.' Phyllida drew the rug from the basket, then spread it on the grass. As she straightened, Lucifer's hand appeared before her. She hesitated, then put her fingers in his and let him hand her down to the rug. He placed the basket beside her. She busied herself unpacking and arranging their feast.

He lounged on the other side of the basket and reached for the bottle wrapped in a white napkin.

Sliding it free, he rummaged for the glasses. When she finished laying out their repast, he had a glass ready to hand to her.

'To summer.'

She smiled and clinked glasses, then sipped. The wine slid down her throat, cold and refreshing; a tingle slithered down her spine. A whisper of anticipation echoed in her mind while a pleasurable warmth spread through her.

They ate. He seemed to know her needs before she did, offering her rolls, the chicken, pastries. At first, she felt unnerved; then she hid a self-deprecatory smile. He wasn't deliberately trying to rattle her – he wasn't even aware he was. Such attentions were simply second nature to him.

Not so to her. No other man treated her like that – ready with a steadying hand, a protective shoulder, not out of any intent to impress her but simply because she was she.

It was unnerving, and rather nice.

'Does the Colyton Import Company bring its goods ashore near here?'

She waved to the west. 'There's a path to the beach a little way along. It's easy to find; there's a knoll beside it. If we need to light a beacon, we put it up there.'

How dangerous is it along this stretch?'

'Not too bad if you know it. But there are reefs close.'

'So the Colyton men go out and bring the goods in?'

193

'They've been sailing these waters since they could stand. There's very little risk for them.'

She repacked the basket. The wind was freshening, tugging at napkins, but it was still pleasant beneath the screened sun. She'd left her parasol in the curricle and was glad she had. She couldn't have used it in this wind.

With everything returned to the basket, she stood. The wind frolicked about her face, flirting with her hair, teasing the ribbons of her bonnet. Lifting her face, she drew in a deep breath, then wrapped her arms about her. She'd worn a lilac cambric carriage dress, normally perfectly adequate in this weather, but here the wind rushed at her, sliding chill fingers through the fabric and along her body.

Beside her, Lucifer uncoiled his long length and stood.

She shivered.

An instant later, warmth fell around her; his coat settled over her shoulders. 'Oh—' She half turned. He'd side – stepped the basket and now stood just behind her. She met his gaze briefly and prayed her reaction didn't show. She managed a small smile. 'Thank you.'

His body heat was trapped in the fabric; it slid like a warm hand down her spine. She turned further toward him. 'I'm really not that cold. You'll freeze without your coat.'

Before she could slide out of it, he caught the lapels and drew the coat more firmly around her. 'I'm not cold.'

Taking a firm hold of her wits, she looked up, into his eyes. 'Are you sure?'

Even as the words left her lips, she sensed the answer. She couldn't have missed it – his hard body was near enough to feel his heat, the all-too-tempting warmth. The wind pushed her, urging her into it. Into his arms.

His eyes, intensely blue, searched hers; his lips kicked up at the ends. 'Why,' he murmured, his hands sliding from between them, his head bending nearer, 'do you think they call me Lucifer?'

If she'd been wise, she'd have stepped smartly back and told him she had no idea. Instead, she stood still, face tilted up, and let his lips settle on hers.

The kiss was pure heat – a source of wonderful warmth. It spread through her; she could almost believe she was thawing – nerves stretching, unfurling, luxuriating. The kiss teased, tantalized. She moved closer, drawn to him, needing to feel his chest solid against her breasts. They tingled, then ached, yet it wasn't with pain. His shirt was under her hands; she spread her fingers, feeling the fine fabric shift like a veil over hard muscle, over the roughness of hair; the flat disk of his nipple burned under her palm.

She felt that tempting power surge through him. She parted her lips and opened her mouth to him, and shuddered when he entered. So hot. She drank it in; she wanted more. She pressed her palms to his chest, pushed them up to his shoulders. Everywhere she touched was like a furnace, the steady pulsing heat of hot coals.

Her breasts were pressed to that heat; his hands had slipped beneath his coat and fastened about her waist. He held her tight against him, his thighs like granite columns on either side of hers. He was hard, ridged, rampant against her belly.

A wanton urge to shift her hips and caress that rampant hardness gripped her; in something near panic, she tamped it down, like putting out a fire. The flaring urge died; she sighed into his mouth and sank a little more against him.

He shifted, one hand rising to her throat. She felt a tug – he was pulling at her bonnet ribbons. She drew back from the kiss – the bow under her chin unraveled—

'Oh!' She grabbed at her hat as the wind whipped it from her head. She whirled and caught it.

Her feet twisted in the rug; she tipped backward, stumbled, and crashed into Lucifer. He caught her, tried to steady her, took a step back—

They tumbled over the picnic basket, large and solid in the middle of the rug. Lucifer ended sitting behind it with her in his lap. Shaking with laughter. Swinging his legs free of the basket, he lifted her – and turned her and sat her back in his lap.

He grinned at her. 'We seem to be making a habit of landing on the ground with you on top of me.'

She blushed. She should definitely have made every effort to struggle free, to escape from his arms and stand up. Safe. Instead, she sat there, warm to the core, her gaze fastened on his lips, a mere inch in front of her nose.

'Here – let me have that.' He tugged her bonnet from her nerveless fingers; bemused, she watched as, reaching around her, he tied the ribbons around the basket's handle. 'Now you won't worry about losing it.'

He was a man who definitely understood women.

He straightened, his gaze fastening on her lips. He bent his head, fingertips sliding across the sensitive skin beneath her chin. She swallowed. 'I'm not sure this is a good idea.'

'Why not?' His lips brushed hers lightly – too lightly to satisfy the hunger welling inside her.

'I don't know.' She couldn't drag her gaze from his lips.

They murmured, 'Do you trust me?'

Her heart was pounding in her ears. Her lungs were so tight she couldn't breathe. She couldn't think, but she knew the answer. 'Yes.'

His lips lifted. 'Then relax.' They closed the distance and brushed hers; his voice was a whisper in her mind. 'And let me show you what you want to know.'

It was easy, so easy to do just that, to give him her mouth, to let herself flow, boneless in his arms. They held her, but not tightly. She felt cradled, protected, cared for.

Worshipped.

The thought floated through her mind as his fingers gently trailed her cheek. The touch was as wondering as hers had ever been; she suddenly understood how he had known it had been she who had touched him in Horatio's drawing room. She'd never forget his touch, either – it was such a revealing, oddly innocent, gesture.

His fingers drifted lower and he framed her jaw, his tongue surging boldly. Not innocent at all. She met him, knowing now what he wanted, what he liked. A dangerous knowing – so tempting to use it, to learn a little more. Her hands lay passive against his chest – she pushed them up, over his shoulders, fingers spreading over the powerful muscles, then sliding further to tangle in his hair.

It was soft, silky, black as a night sky. She sank her fingers into the thick locks, holding tight as he slowly, unhurriedly, plundered her mouth, taking, certainly, but giving more.

Addictive. Another word that drifted through her mind. It had to be that – the sweetest craving – that held her to the kiss even when he released her jaw.

Forbidden – he was surely that. She shouldn't be kissing him at all, yet the idea of stopping seemed totally foolish, something she never was. His fingers trailed, just the tips tracing tantalizingly down her throat, tightening nerves she hadn't known she possessed. His fingers trailed on, lower; flames followed, heat spread.

Her breast was swollen long before he touched it; once he had, she didn't want him to stop. His touch was light, excruciatingly insubstantial – she wanted more, much more.

Experienced – thank heavens he was that. His hand settled, hard palm cupping the weight of her breast. Delight was all she felt as his fingers firmed, then eased. His hand shifted, caressed. She sighed into their kiss and sensed his satisfaction, felt the hand at her back firm.

The kiss grew more demanding, a fire that needed tending. She gave it her full attention, only dimly aware when the warmth of his hand about her breast slid away.

Need was growing within her, but for what she didn't know. The compulsion was not one she recognized. Then she felt the top button of her bodice give, and knew. A thrill of pure excitement raced through her. That was what she needed – a scandalous need, assuredly, yet . . . her breasts were swollen, aching with the heat of their kiss. Her wits were awash on the swelling tide that lapped about them. A languorous thing, it whispered promises of things she'd never known, of pleasure beyond imagining.

The touch of cool air on her breasts, the light tracing of his fingers as he brushed her bodice wide, drew her from the mesmerizing warmth of their kiss. She should stop him, she knew it, yet . . . she couldn't recall why. There was no threat, no danger – he'd told her to trust him and she did.

If she wanted this to end, wanted to bring the simple pleasure to a halt, she only had to say.

She didn't say – she had no reason to. She wanted to know, to feel, to be touched and savored. Just once to be a woman desired.

He gave her what she wanted, that and much more.

She hadn't known that his lips would feel like that, there. That the hot wetness of his mouth could scald her so and rip her wits away. Hadn't known that her body could grow so hot and heavy, so wanton with desire.

It was desire that thrummed through her, that pounded in her blood, that rose to every touch, every tantalizing caress. His lightest touch was sharp delight; more explicit caresses left her senses reeling. Heated pleasure was what he conjured; purposely, he wrapped her in it, pressed it upon her, and let it sink into her.

Until she was filled with it, until her mind rode on the warm waves and her body was melting.

His lips returned to hers, and she welcomed him back. His hand closed possessively about her naked breast and her body sang.

He drew back from the kiss, just enough to look down at her. He studied his hand, firm and still about her breast; her flesh filled and heated even more. His gaze lifted to rove her face, her eyes. He glanced past her.

His gaze steadied, fixed beyond her. Then he blinked; she saw his eyes widen and alter focus, saw his features harden. She felt the changing tension in his body.

Lucifer looked back at her – and tried to think. Tried to breathe past the tightness in his chest. She lay relaxed in his arms, her nipple furled between his fingers, her skin hot silk against his palm. He felt dazed. Rational thought had left him long ago; desire rode him – potent temptation flicked a whip.

He knew what he wanted, the need sharp as spurs, as clamorous as any demon.

A tempest was bearing down on them, racing over the sea, piling thunderheads before it, yet looking into her eyes, drowning dark beneath heavy lids, with her body supple and heated in his arms, he wasn't sure in which direction danger lay.

It had been a long, long time since he'd surrendered so completely that he'd lost all sense of self-protection.

Stifling a curse, he bent his head and kissed her, passion-deep, fire-hot. He closed his hand over her breast, fingers kneading, tightening . . . then easing. He drew back – from the kiss, from the caress, his fingers reluctantly leaving her. He brushed a last kiss to her lips as he drew her bodice closed.

Her eyes blinked wide, revealing surprise . . . disappointment.

Features setting grimly, he nodded out to sea. 'There's a storm blowing in – we have to go back.'

CHAPTER 9

Late the next morning, Lucifer tramped through the wood behind the Manor and tried not to think about the previous day. He'd told Phyllida the truth; they'd had to go back, to retreat. He'd gone charging into unchartered terrain, far too fast for her, and much too fast for him.

Thank God for storms.

He'd started today with breakfast at a table too empty for his liking. He'd never lived alone; the solitary life did not suit him. He'd repaired to the library and started sorting through Horatio's desk. He'd spent two hours reading accumulated correspondence.

After that, he'd had to get out. Walking through the wood to explore the lay of his land all the way down to the Axe seemed a sensible, and sufficiently physical, exercise.

He felt like the energy of last night's storm was bottled up inside him.

The storm had brought rain; they'd gained Colyton in the teeth of a downpour. Although the sun was now out, the wood remained damp;

the tang of rain-washed greenery rode the light breeze. He'd headed east from the rear of the stable block, leaving the lake on his left. The trees ahead thinned; he'd trudged for less than half a mile. Fifty paces more and he stood on the edge of a wide field, gently sloping down; beyond lay a lush meadow. Beyond that lay the Axe, a gray – blue ribbon glimmering in the sunshine.

He ambled down the sloping field. A flash of movement to his left caught his eye. He looked, then halted.

Phyllida was marching – no, *storming* – through his field. Her skirts frothed about her, whipped by the violence of her stride. Her gaze was fixed in front of her. Her dark hair gleamed. She held her poke bonnet in both hands.

She was mangling the bonnet, twisting it, hands clenched on the brim.

He stepped out to intercept her.

She didn't see him until he was almost upon her. She recoiled, eyes flaring, one hand rising to her breast. A squeak escaped her; it would have been a scream if she hadn't recognized him and smothered it. Gulping in a breath, she stared up at him through huge dark eyes.

'What's wrong?' He smothered an urge of his own – to haul her into his arms. 'What happened?'

She dragged in another breath and looked at her bonnet. She was shaking. 'Look!' She thrust her finger through a hole in the crown. 'The ball just missed my *head*!'

Her tone made it clear she wasn't shaking with fear. She was shaking with fury. She whirled and looked back the way she'd come. 'How *dare* they!' If both hands hadn't been clenched on the bonnet, she would probably have shaken her fist. 'Stupid hunters!'

The words trembled; she bit them off and hiccuped.

Lucifer reached out and wrapped his hand around one of hers, tugging until she released the bonnet. He enveloped her small hand in his and drew her to face him.

Her expression was blank, not calm and serene but blank, as if she couldn't maintain her usual mask but was fighting not to let her feelings show. Her eyes, wide and dark, were turbulent, awash with emotions. Fear was there, very real; she was using her fury to counter it.

He drew her nearer still, until she stood close enough to feel his heat and the shield of his physical presence. She was wound tight, her control so brittlely fragile he didn't want to risk even putting an arm around her; she wouldn't thank him if she broke. 'Where did it happen?'

She dropped her gaze to his chest, drew a tight breath, then gestured with her bonnet. 'Back there. Two fields back.' After a moment, she added, 'I was returning from visiting old Mrs Dewbridge – I go there every Friday.'

A chill touched his spine. '*Every* Friday morning?'

She nodded.

His grip on her hand tightened; he forced himself to relax it. He looped her arm through his. 'I want you to show me where.'

He turned her back along the track, an old right-of-way. She resisted. 'It's no use – they won't still be there.'

'I know.' He kept his tone calm, even; that wasn't how he felt, but it was what she needed. 'I just want you to show me where you were. We won't go any further.'

She hesitated, then nodded. 'All right.'

He guided her along and helped her over the stile. A sliver of blue fabric was caught in the crossbar where she'd ripped her gown in her haste.

Despite her fury, she'd been very frightened.

She still was.

They reached the boundary of the next field and she stopped. 'I was there.' She waved with her ruined bonnet. 'Right in the middle of the field.'

Lucifer held her hand and looked, gauging distances. 'Can I have your bonnet?'

She handed it to him; he took it and raised it – there were *two* holes punched through the crown. Without a word, he handed it back. His face felt like stone. She'd glanced down at the critical moment; the ball had entered through the back of the bonnet just below the crown seam, then exited through the bonnet's top, on the other side of the seam. 'Let me check your head.'

'I didn't get hit,' she grumbled, but she let him look.

Her hair lay like mahogany silk, sleek and undisturbed – no wound. He imagined the way her bonnet would sit, then touched his fingers to her hair. Grit, very fine, came away on the pads of his fingers. He sniffed them. Powder – the bullet had come that close.

He looked back at the field. The path didn't run directly across but angled away toward the river. 'Did you hear anything? Glimpse anyone?'

'No, but . . .' She lifted her head. 'I ran. Silly, I know, but I just did.'

Running might have saved her life. He said nothing, just drew a breath and held it until his violent reaction faded. She'd been walking this way; the only possible place of concealment was a copse on the far side of the field.

'I'll walk with you to the Grange.'

The glance she shot him said she felt she should protest. Instead, after a moment's hesitation, she inclined her head and acquiesced.

Sir Jasper was out when they reached the Grange. Lucifer delivered Phyllida into Gladys's hands, making sure, despite Phyllida's dismissive remarks, that Gladys understood that her mistress had had a severe shock.

He left with Phyllida glaring at him; he didn't care. She was safe.

He strode back to the Manor via the wood, and was pleased to find Dodswell had arrived with the rest of his horses. Dodswell had paced the string well; they had enough in reserve to go for a quick gallop.

Taking Dodswell with him, he rode back to the copse. Dismounting at the edge of the field, they tethered their mounts while he told Doswell what they were looking for.

They found it close by one side of the copse, the side screened from the walking track.

'Just the one horse.' Dodswell examined the hoofprints in the rain-softened earth. 'Nice, clean front shoes.'

Lucifer stared at the ground farther back. 'I can't find any impressions of the back hooves.'

'Nah. That turf there's too thick, more's the pity.'

Grimly, Lucifer nodded at the hoofprints they had found. 'What do you make of them?'

'Decently looked-after horse, fresh shoes, no nicks or cracks, well-filed hooves.'

'A gentleman's horse.'

'A horse from a gentleman's stable, anyway.' Dodswell studied Lucifer's face. 'Why are we interested?'

Briefly, Lucifer told him of the horse that had stood at the back of the Manor's shrubbery. Told him who had a hole in her bonnet. He didn't tell him why.

'Wasn't no hunter. What would they be shooting at? No quail or skeet yet, and they'd be too far from the wood for pigeons. Rabbits won't be out at present.' Grim-faced, Dodswell scanned the area. 'Nothing here to shoot at.'

Only one female given to solitary walks and addicted to doing good deeds by a regular schedule. Lucifer looked at the hoofprints and tried to ease the tension in his shoulders. 'Let's get back. We've learned all we can here.'

Bristleford was waiting when he walked into the front hall.

'Mr Coombe has called, sir. I put him in the library.'

'Thank you, Bristleford.' Lucifer walked straight to the library door and opened it. Silas Coombe jumped back from one of the bookshelves, his hand raised. Lucifer would have wagered Horatio's entire collection that Coombe had been fingering the gold-encrusted spines. Face impassive, he nodded, shut the door, and stalked to the desk. 'Gold leaf doesn't wear all that well – but then, you'd know that, wouldn't you.'

He arched a brow at Coombe, who drew himself up and tugged at his waistcoat; its black-and-white horizontal stripes made him appear more rotund than he was.

'Oh, quite. Quite! I was just admiring the tooling.' He approached the desk.

Waving him to a chair, Lucifer sank into the one behind the desk. 'Now – to what do I owe this pleasure?'

Coombe sat, making a great show of settling his coattails. Then he looked at Lucifer. 'Naturally, I feel Horatio's loss keenly. I daresay I'm one of the few hereabouts who truly appreciated his greatness.'

A wave indicated the room about them; Lucifer was left in no doubt that in Coombe's eyes, Horatio's greatness had resided in his possessions. Coombe's gaze drifted along the shelves. 'It must be quite puzzling to you that someone would spend his life gathering all these musty tomes. Such a fantastic number of them.'

Lucifer kept his expression impassive. He'd told only Sir Jasper and Phyllida of his interest in collecting; clearly, neither had talked.

'Now, it may seem odd to you, but I've an interest in books myself, as you might have heard around the village. I'm viewed as quite the eccentric because of it, y'know.'

'Indeed?'

'Yes, oh, yes. Now, to come to my point, I realize you'll want to be rid of these – doubtless you'll start clearing them soon. They take up such a great space. All through the ground floor and even, I daresay, abovestairs?'

Lucifer pretended not to hear the question.

'Yes, well.' Coombe shifted, tugging at his coat. 'That's where I believe I could help you.'

He sat back and said nothing more. Lucifer was forced to ask, 'How?'

Coombe leaned forward like a well-rehearsed puppet. 'Oh, I couldn't take them all, of course! Dear me, no! But I would like to add just a few of Horatio's books to my collection.' He brightened. 'In memorium, you might say. I'm sure Horatio would have wanted it that way.'

Smiling, Coombe sat back again. 'I'll just come and take a look at the books as you're packing them – I wouldn't want to inconvenience you.'

'You won't.' Lucifer tried to imagine Coombe with a knife in his hand. The picture wasn't convincing. If there was any man in the village liable to swoon at the sight of blood, he would have bet it was Coombe. Still, he hadn't been in church last Sunday. 'I haven't thought about selling the books, but if I do, I'll probably call in an agent from London.'

A frown creased Coombe's brow. 'I hope that you'll agree, when the time comes, to grant me first refusal?'

Lucifer shrugged. 'I'll have to see how things fall out. Some agents may not take the commission if they believe the juiciest plums have already been picked.'

'Well, my word!' Coombe puffed like an agitated hen. 'I must say, I think Horatio would have wanted me to have some of his gems.'

'Is that so?' His dry tone had Coombe deflating. He held the man's gaze. 'Unfortunately for you, Horatio is no longer here. I am.' He rose and tugged the bellpull, then looked at Coombe. 'If there's nothing else, I've a considerable amount of business awaiting my attention.'

The door opened; Lucifer glanced up. 'Ah, Bristleford – Mr Coombe is leaving.'

Coombe got to his feet, face mottling. But he drew himself up and bowed from the waist. 'Good day, sir.'

Lucifer inclined his head.

As Coombe neared the door, Lucifer signaled to Bristleford; Bristleford almost imperceptibly nodded, then ushered Coombe out and shut the door.

Lucifer was sorting correspondence when Bristleford returned.

'You wanted something, sir?'

'Send Covey to me.'

'At once, sir.'

Covey slipped into the room some minutes later. Lucifer sat back. 'I've a job for you, Covey.'

'Yes, sir?' Covey stopped before the desk, hands clasped before him.

Lucifer glanced at the bookshelves. 'I want you to take a complete inventory of all Horatio's books.'

'All of them?' Covey looked at the long, high bookshelves.

'Start in the drawing room, then in here, then in the other rooms. For every book I want the title, publisher, and date of publication, and I want you to check for inscriptions or page notes. If you find any notations, set those books aside and show them to me at the end of each day.'

Covey squared his shoulders. 'Indeed, sir.' He was transparently pleased to be following orders again. 'Shall I use a ledger for the list?'

Lucifer nodded. Collecting a fresh ledger and a pencil from a chest, Covey headed for the drawing room. Lucifer watched the door close; he sat back – leather squeaked.

The books he'd found misaligned in the drawing room – now he thought of it, they'd been tight in the shelf. They couldn't have accidentally slid forward.

Now Silas Coombe was requesting first dibs on Horatio's books. Could Coombe be the murderer?

Lucifer looked down at the pile of correspondence he'd stacked on the blotter. He had other questions, too, at present equally unanswerable.

What was it Horatio had wanted him to appraise? And where on earth was it?

Late that evening, he stood looking out from his bedchamber window, watching the moonlight play over the common. He'd spent half the afternoon searching the house in the hope that something, some piece, would strike him as unfamiliar and unique enough to have been Horatio's mystery item. He'd learned the extent of his inheritance, but was no nearer to solving the mystery.

The house was a treasure trove, understated in its magnificence. Every piece had a history, had a value greater than its functional worth. Yet, as was common with many great collectors, Horatio's best items were used as they'd been designed to be used, not hidden away. So where was his mystery item? In full view? Or hidden away in some other item designed to provide a hiding place?

That was a possibility. Lucifer made a mental note to check.

Identifying the mystery item – possibly the reason

Horatio had been killed – was only one of his problems. The most pressing, the most critical, was learning why some man, riding a horse that might well have been the same horse that had waited in the shrubbery while Horatio was killed, had attempted to kill Phyllida.

Lucifer rotated his shoulders, trying to ease the knots that had been there since late afternoon, when he'd gone back to the Grange to speak with Sir Jasper.

And Phyllida, of course, but she hadn't been there.

Not in the library, not in the drawing room, not lying on her bed prostrate with shock. The damned woman had ordered out the carriage and gone to visit some other deserving soul. At least she hadn't walked.

Of course, she'd been the first to Sir Jasper with the story – her version had stressed that it had been some misguided hunter; she had clearly downplayed her fright.

He'd tried to correct those impressions, but had been severely handicapped by two things. First, as Sir Jasper did not know of Phyllida's presence in Horatio's drawing room, he therefore had no reason to suppose Horatio's killer would have any interest in her. Without telling Sir Jasper all, without exposing Phyllida, there was no point making the connection between the horses, and without that, his ability to invest the situation with suitable gravity was severely compromised.

The second obstacle was the fact that Sir Jasper

had been well trained to accept everything his daughter told him, at least about herself. With all that against him, shaking Sir Jasper out of his complacency and into a sufficiently protective frame of mind had been beyond him. All he'd managed was to convey his own deep unease over the shooting, and over Phyllida's safety in general.

Sir Jasper had smiled too knowingly and assured him that Phyllida could take care of herself.

Not against a murderer. He'd held the words back, but only just.

He'd stridden back through the wood in something perilously close to a temper; the emotion had converted to a nagging disquiet by the time he'd reached the Manor.

Gazing out at the moonlit common, he felt decidedly grim. Tomorrow, he'd find her—

A figure crossed the lane and started up the common.

Lucifer stared. He knew what he was seeing, but his brain refused to take it in. '*Damnation!* What in *Hades* does she think she's *doing*?'

Swinging on his heel, he went to get an answer.

She was standing on the side porch, ledger in hand, when he reached the church.

Phyllida saw him emerge from the shadows, large, dark, and menacing, like a god not at all pleased with a disciple. She lifted her chin and fixed him with a warning glance; Mr Filing stood beside her.

'Mr Cynster!' Filing shut his ledger.

'It's all right,' she reassured him. 'Mr Cynster knows all about the Company and how we operate.'

'Oh, well, then.' Reopening his ledger, Filing smiled at Lucifer. 'It's quite a little enterprise.'

'So I understand.' Lucifer didn't return the curate's smile. He stalked past Filing, circled her, and halted on her other side, hands on his hips, doing an excellent imitation of a disapproving deity. 'What are you doing?'

He'd bent his head so his words fell by her ear in an angry rumble. She didn't look up. 'I'm checking the goods against the bill of lading – see?' She demonstrated as Hugey lumbered up with a box. 'Put that to the left of the Mellows' sarcophagus.'

Hugey nodded circumspectly to the looming menace beside her and headed into the church.

Oscar took his place, eyeing Lucifer more directly. She felt forced to introduce them. Oscar bobbed his head, his arms locked around a small tun.

Lucifer nodded. 'You're Thompson's brother, I hear.'

'Aye, that be right.' Oscar grinned, pleased to have been known. 'Hear tell you've decided to make Colyton your home.'

'Yes. I don't plan to leave.'

Bent over her ledger, Phyllida pretended not to hear. Oscar shuffled on to be replaced by Marsh. He coughed and she had to introduce him, too. Before the night's cargo was stored, all the men had been introduced to Lucifer; he'd been accepted by them all far too easily for her liking.

She glanced at him as she headed for the crypt – and had to grudgingly admit that he was a commanding figure, especially in the shadowy night. Like his namesake, dark and forbidding, he followed her down the stone stairs.

Nose elevated to a telling angle, she pointedly settled to her accounts. He hovered for a moment, then made his way to where Mr Filing was shifting boxes. She heard him offer to help, heard Filing's ready acceptance. Boxes scraped on stone; she concentrated on her figures.

Finally shutting the ledger, she stretched her back; only then did she realize Lucifer and Filing had finished moving boxes long before. Turning, she saw them leaning against a monument, talking earnestly. Filing was facing away from her; Lucifer's voice was too low for her to hear.

Quickly clearing her 'desk', she went to join them.

Lucifer watched her approach. 'So, other than Sir Jasper and Jonas, Basil Smollet and Pommeroy Fortemain. the bulk of the males were not at church.'

Filing nodded. 'Sir Cedric is an irregular attendee, as is Henry Grisby. The ladies I can count on' – he smiled at Phyllida – 'but I'm afraid the males of the parish are rather more recalcitrant.'

'Inconvenient, in this case.'

Phyllida looked at Filing. 'Indeed. I've entered everything. All is in order, so I'll bid you a good night.'

'And a good night to you, my dear.'

Filing bowed. Phyllida smiled and turned away.

Lucifer straightened. 'I'll walk you to the Grange.'

She wasn't the least bit surprised to hear that. She inclined her head and started up the stairs. 'If you wish.'

She led the way out of the church and onto the common. He lengthened his stride until he was pacing beside her, almost shoulder to shoulder. Her skin prickled; awareness rushed over her and left all her nerves standing on end.

Their mad dash from the cliffs to Colyton – a careening drive – had left no time, let alone breath, for embarrassment or consciousness, but once she'd regained her bedchamber, consciousness had swamped her. She'd been sure she could not possibly meet his eyes again – look at his lips again – not without blushing so fierily everyone would guess why. She'd almost made up her mind to avoid him – certainly to avoid his arms.

Then someone had shot at her and he'd arrived – and she'd wanted nothing more than to fling herself into his arms and feel safe. The urge had been so strong she'd quivered with it; only by a supreme effort had she quelled it.

It was utter nonsense to feel so – to feel that the only place she would truly feel safe was in his arms. Dangerous, too, when she knew his interest in her was transient. Once she told him what she knew, he would have no reason to seduce her.

She'd spent the afternoon lecturing herself, pointing out that she'd survived perfectly well until now, that she would still be safe in the village. All she needed to do was exercise a little extra caution and all would be well. She'd find Mary Anne's letters, tell Lucifer everything, then they'd unmask the murderer and life could go on as it had before.

Except that Lucifer would be living in the village. He wasn't going to leave. She wouldn't be able to avoid him.

There was only one solution – to behave with her usual confidence and pretend nothing out of the ordinary had happened on the cliff. Pretend he didn't affect her at all.

Not too easy when he was glowering at her.

'You can't possibly be so witless as to believe that it was some benighted huntsman who shot at you.'

'You can't argue that it's not a possibility.'

'It became much less of a possibility when we found hoofprints, just like those behind the Manor's shrubbery, beside the copse in that field.'

Her stride faltered; she slowed. 'Someone rode there . . . it could still have been a huntsman.'

'There was nothing to hunt in the field.'

Except her. A cold hand gripped her nape; icy fingers trailed her spine. Phyllida suppressed a shiver. She continued walking. Her mind darted, sifting, rearranging the known facts in light of that new one.

She'd almost convinced herself it *had* been a careless hunter – despite her instinctive fear, there'd been no logical reason to think otherwise. Now . . . could the murderer be trying to kill her?

Why? She'd seen the hat, true, but it was just a brown hat – she'd know it again if she saw it, but

218

she couldn't recall seeing it before. She'd kept her eyes peeled, but she hadn't sighted it again. In fact, until they'd confirmed otherwise, she'd assumed some outsider must have ridden in and stabbed Horatio. That no longer seemed likely. If Lucifer was correct and the same horse that had been tethered by the shrubbery on Sunday had been by the copse this morning, then she could only agree with him.

The murderer was a local and had tried to kill her.

He must think she could identify him, but surely not because of the hat? He'd have burned it by now, and as she hadn't said anything, it must be obvious she hadn't recognized it. Was there something else she'd seen?

Frowning, she walked on.

A disgusted sound came from beside her. She felt Lucifer's gaze on her face and swiftly banished her frown.

'I should tell your father of your connection with the murder.'

She rounded on him. 'You haven't?'

He scowled at her. 'No – but I should. I *will*, if that's the only way to ensure you remain safe.'

She breathed easily again. 'I'll take care.'

'Take *care*? Just look at you! Traipsing about in the dead of night – alone!'

'But no one knows I'm out here.'

'Except all those involved.'

She snorted softly. 'None of them is the murderer and you know it.'

A charged silence ensued.

'Are you going to tell me that no one ever notices the light shining from the church every few nights?'

'Of course they notice – they think it's smugglers.'

'So everyone knows you're there.'

'No! No one even *imagines* I'm there – I'm a *woman*, remember?'

That shut him up. Only for a moment. 'Believe me, that's one thing I'm highly unlikely to forget.'

She tripped. He caught her arm, hauling her up, swinging her to him. She steadied, facing diagonally down the common. 'Good Lord!' She stared. 'A light just winked in your drawing room.'

They both froze, staring down at the Manor. All was dark, then a pinprick of light flashed again. Before they could blink, a faint glow suffused the windows of the drawing room. A lamp had been lit and turned low.

Phyllida sucked in a breath. 'It must be the murderer!'

'Stay here!'

Releasing her, Lucifer plunged down the slope.

'Hah!' Phyllida headed after him, in his wake, trusting that if there was a place to stumble, he'd find it first.

They skirted the duck pond, then picked their way across the lane, careful to avoid loose stones. Gaining the cottages' front fences, they hugged the shadows, ducking low as they rushed along the Manor's garden wall. Lucifer reached the gate before her; he stood and swung it open—

It creaked.

The sound seemed loud enough to wake the dead.

Lucifer flung himself up the path, gravel crunching under his feet. Phyllida followed at his heels.

The light in the drawing room abruptly died.

They skidded up against the front door, Lucifer juggling a set of unfamiliar keys. From within came the sound of footsteps fleeing across the tiles. Lucifer stopped, lifted his head, listened . . .

He swore and shoved the keys back in his pocket. He focused on her. 'Dammit! Stay here!' He turned and charged along the front of the house.

Phyllida followed.

Lucifer rounded the corner and stopped; Phyllida cannoned into him. Steadying herself against his back, hands clutching his coat, she peered around his shoulder—

And caught a glimpse of a fleeing figure at the edge of her vision. 'There!' She pointed.

The moon sailed free as the man fled across a stretch of open lawn. He was heading for the shrubbery. shrubbery.

'*Stay here!*' Lucifer took off after him.

Phyllida hesitated. There were only two other exits from the shrubbery – one to the lake, one . . . She looked at the entrance to the narrow path beside the lane. Dragging in a quick breath, she raced for it.

It was the fact that she wasn't following him that made Lucifer glance back. At first, he couldn't see her – then he did; she was a shadow streaking across the stretch of lawn by the main gates. His heart stopped.

'No!' he roared. 'Come back!'

She dove into the dark entrance of the path.

Swearing violently, he swerved and headed after her.

He plunged along the path. It twisted and turned, a tunnel whose walls were impenetrable black, whose ceiling was the night sky obscured by dark branches. He could barely see the ground beneath his pounding feet. Branches grabbed at his coat; he pressed on at full tilt.

Phyllida was fast – faster than he'd expected – unencumbered as she was by skirts. She was still ahead of him, but he thought he could hear her footfalls over his own and the pounding in his ears.

The pertinent question was not how fast she was, but how fast the murderer was. And whether he was armed or not.

Would they reach the end of the shrubbery in time?

Would he catch Phyllida before she ran headlong into the murderer's arms?

Then he rounded a bend and saw her; exerting every last ounce of strength, he forged ahead. He caught up with her where the shrubbery hedges ended; shoulder to shoulder, they burst into the clearing beyond.

The mocking thud of retreating hooves greeted them.

They halted, sagged. Chest heaving, hands on his hips, Lucifer looked at Phyllida. Half bent over, hands on her knees, she puffed and puffed.

He waited, then asked, 'Did you recognize him?'

She shook her head, then straightened. 'I barely glimpsed him at all.'

They'd been too late to even catch a glimpse of the horse. Beneath his breath, Lucifer swore. He scowled at Phyllida, then brusquely gestured back up the path. He'd give her his opinion of her behavior later – after he'd caught his breath.

They retraced their steps. At the end of the path, they emerged onto the lawn. Phyllida looked ahead, sucked in a breath, and stepped back.

Lucifer halted. Dodswell and Hemmings were prowling the lawn. Inwardly sighing, he murmured, 'Stay here.' He began to walk forward, then paused and added, 'You don't want to know what I'll do if you are not in that precise spot when I get back.'

He thought he heard a haughty sniff, but he didn't look back. Pushing into a lope, he crossed the lawn, waving when Dodswell saw him.

'An intruder – I gave chase but lost him.' He waited until Hemmings came up, then said, 'I'm going to prowl around a bit more. You can check through the house, see how he got in and out, then lock up. I've got my keys – we can compare notes in the morning.'

Both Hemmings and Dodswell were in their nightshirts; they nodded and started toward the house.

Lucifer waited until they'd gone indoors, then turned and headed back to the path.

CHAPTER 10

Phyllida was waiting where he'd left her, just inside the entrance to the path. Arms folded, she might have been scowling at him; he couldn't be sure in the dark.

He halted beside her, looming over her, deliberately intimidating. She gave not an inch.

'Do you always have such difficulty following orders?'

'There are very few people who give orders to me.'

They stood, gazes locked, then he stepped back and gestured to the lawn. 'I'll walk you through the wood.'

She glanced at the house. 'It might be better to go through the shrubbery and out by the lake path.'

He waved her on, and followed.

Phyllida retraced their steps, then turned into the shrubbery, all too conscious of the poorly suppressed male energy prowling at her back. She tried to tell herself he was doing it only to intimidate, to pressure her into revealing all and following his orders hence forth, but she knew it wasn't that. If he'd wanted to intimidate her, he would have been more forthright.

Not that the sense of something dangerous, something violent and not fully under control, stalking on her heels, wasn't intimidating enough.

They skirted the lake and traversed the wood in silence. She paused when they reached the Grange's shrubbery, but he frowned and waved her on.

The back lawn lay just ahead when he caught her arm and drew her to the side, onto one of the connecting paths. He released her; she faced him, her back against the hedge, luckily one of a small-leaved conifer. Neatly trimmed, it formed a cushion at her back. He leaned one shoulder into the hedge, just beside hers, and looked down at her. 'When are you going to tell me what it is you know?'

She wished she could read his eyes, but they were lost in shadow. He stood there, so close, yet there was no sense now of intimidation. Invitation was what reached her. No pretense, no guile, simple dealing, him and her. To her, that was so much more appealing. She blew out a soft breath. 'Soon.'

'How soon?'

'I can't say, but not long. A few days, perhaps.'

'Is there anything I can do to shorten the time?'

'If I could tell you . . .' She paused. 'But I can't. I gave my word.'

'Is this knowledge of yours the reason the murderer now has you in his sights?'

'I don't think so. I can't see how it could be any threat to him.'

He considered, then nodded. 'I'll make a bargain

with you.' He straightened, and suddenly the sense of physical menace was back; a leashed predator stood before her.

'I'm not aware of any need to make any bargains.'

'Believe me, there's a need.'

The growl in his voice warned her against challenging the statement. 'What, then?'

'I want a promise from you that until we've laid this murderer by the heels, you will not roam about alone, either by day or by night.'

She lifted her chin. 'And in return?'

'In return, I won't tell your father that you were there, and know something to the point.'

She relaxed. 'You won't tell Papa anyway.'

He frowned; his eyes narrowed. 'Are you so sure you're prepared to risk it?'

She was, but this didn't seem a wise time to admit it. 'I'll be careful.' She would have moved on again, but he was in the way.

'"Careful."' His features hardened. 'Someone tries to kill you and you talk of being *careful*? I should tell your father and have him lock you in your room.'

'Nonsense! We can't be absolutely certain it was the murderer who shot at me.'

'Who else? And don't say it was a hunter.'

'There's no *reason* for the murderer to kill me!'

'He must think there is.' He searched her face. 'This thing you know must identify him.'

'Well, it doesn't.' She didn't try to hide her chagrin.

'I thought at first it might, but I can't see how it can, not now.'

'It doesn't matter whether it identifies him or not, only that he believes it might. That's enough to put you in danger.' As he said the words, Lucifer felt their weight – for the first time fully realized their truth. She was in danger. Real, acute danger. She could be killed by the same killer who'd taken Horatio from him.

He drew a tight breath. 'You have a choice. Either you can promise me you won't set foot outside the Grange except on urgent matters, and then only with a male escort, or we can go inside right now and speak with your father and lay all the pertinent details before him.'

For once, she allowed her irritation to show. 'This is ridiculous. *You* are not my keeper.'

He stared down at her, and let that point lie.

'I'm going inside.'

He didn't move.

She glared, then darted out—

He wrapped an arm around her waist, swung her back to the hedge, then trapped her against it. He looked into her smoldering eyes. 'You are not safe.' He'd meant from the murderer, but it suddenly occurred to him that he was speaking literally. He lowered his head. 'You're a woman – the murderer's a man.' He breathed the words along her cheek, his lips tracing down to her jaw. Her scent rose, wreathed his senses – and ensnared him.

Muscles bunched, locked. The temptation to

taste her rose within him, more compelling than ever before. On the hedge beside her shoulder, his fist clenched as he fought the urge – and won.

He was a man, too. In the heat of the moment, he'd overlooked that fact. Steeling himself, tightening his reins, he tensed to draw back.

'Kiss me.'

The words were a whisper in the dark, a soft plea so unexpected he felt stunned. Raising his head, he looked at her face, unsure he'd heard aright.

His jacket had been open; her hands had come to rest on his shirt-clad chest. Now they slid to his sides, gripping, urging him nearer.

'Kiss me again.' He saw her lips move as she stretched up; they touched his jaw. 'Kiss me like before . . . just once more . . .'

She didn't have to ask a fourth time, but it wouldn't be just one kiss. Bending his head, capturing her lips, he assumed she knew that, that her last words were simply part of her entreaty. He wanted to kiss her a million times, over and over again. He'd never get tired of her taste, of the sweet, innocent, trusting way she yielded her lips, her mouth.

She did it again and captured his senses. He fell into the kiss, into her.

He was ravenous.

The springy hedge was soft enough to press her into. He did; the feel of her supple body taut against his inflamed his need. Her hands slid further, searching, then spreading over his back.

She clung and he kissed her more deeply. His hunger exploded. She arched against him, instinctively offering, and then she kissed him back.

She was still new to the game, enough so to distract him. He took the time to coax, to tease, to tutor, until, lips melded, tongues tangling, they were satisfied with the depth of the shared intimacy.

It wasn't enough – not for him.

It wasn't enough for Phyllida, either. When he ventured nothing more but simply remained, a hot, vibrant, intensely exciting male all but wrapped around her in the dark, she presumed it was her turn to take the lead. Sliding her hands around from his back, savoring the hard muscles, the tension she felt invest them as she stroked, she searched and found the buttons of his shirt. Quickly, she worked her way up, sliding the small buttons from their moorings, all the while kissing him, taking him in, then returning his hot caresses with heated caresses of her own.

The give-and-take – the reciprocity of it all – was something she hadn't foreseen. It intrigued her and spurred her on. He'd seen her breasts, stroked them, played with her nipples; it had all been gloriously pleasurable. Now was her chance to return the gift.

The last button gave; she slipped her hands inside the soft fabric. Splaying her fingers, she pressed her palms to the broad muscle that was the equivalent of her breasts.

He reacted as she had; a sharp tensing all but

instantly converting to heat, to a curious thrumming resonance of the flesh. Pleased, she caressed, shifting her hands, fingers flexing, digging in, releasing; she wondered if that thrumming resonance was desire – his desire.

Hair rasped against her palms. She found the flat disks of his nipples, so unlike hers yet they still budded as hers did. She played, intrigued by the discovery, by the welling reaction she sensed in him. Their lips remained fused, her mouth trapped beneath his. She sensed his control, his holding back. Boldly, she caressed him with hands and tongue and tempted him more.

The dam broke; heat washed through her in a burning tide.

She'd been right – it was desire; she knew it in her bones. It filled her, warmed her. She basked in its heat and bravely drank it in, as much as he would give her.

She wanted this – desperately wanted to know about all the things she'd feared she never would. She wanted to feel, wanted to know what mutual desire was like, how it felt to burn with that flame.

Tonight might be her last chance to find out – once she told him her secret, he would no longer be interested in her, not like this. He would have no cause to compel her, no reason to seduce her. Once she found the letters, she would have to tell him all; the instant she did, this brief moment – her opportunity to be the object of a man's desire – would be over.

She didn't want it to pass. The realization shook her; she pushed it aside, too confusing to deal with now. Now when she had so many new sensations, not just physical but ethereal, to deal with. To experience, to understand – it was like plunging into a new world with new wonders, new customs. There was so much she had to learn.

He pressed her back into the hedge; his hands tugged at her shirt. It didn't button down the front. She sank back, easing her hold on him. He yanked the shirt from her breeches and then his hands were underneath it.

They encountered the bands wound tight over her breasts; his hands froze. She thought she heard him groan. Then his hands slid around, locking over her back, and he hauled her against him. That she understood. She pulled her hands free, wound them around his neck, and pressed herself to him, giving him back kiss for wild kiss, caress for heated caress.

She wasn't sure her feet were touching the ground. She didn't care. All she wanted was to get closer, to combine her heat with his.

His hands slid lower, over her hips, until they cupped her bottom. He lifted her against him, into him. His desire was very evident. She let her body press like a hand to him, as if with her soft stomach she could caress him there.

Something changed. Not in a flash, but in a steady rush of power. Something new rose between them, something so vital, so intense, she ached to hold it, to know it. She tightened her arms about his neck and kissed him more deeply, sharing the driving need. He kissed her back. The power swelled and spread through them until she was glowing with it, aching with it, and he was the same.

Their lips parted. They both needed to breathe. A curious hiatus held them; she glanced at his face. His eyes were shut; his breathing was as ragged as hers. What next? She had no idea. She was quite sure he did.

She brushed her lips against his. 'Teach me.'

His harsh laugh was mostly groan. 'Dammit – I'm trying to *spare* you!'

'Don't.' She would have frowned, but his eyes were closed. Was he being chivalrous? Or pigheadedly protective? Was there any difference? And did she care? 'Stop making my decisions for me.'

'You don't even know—'

'Stop arguing and *show* me.' She kissed him – hard, forcefully. He reacted instantly and kissed her back fiercely. Her head spun. She didn't draw back, she refused to retreat – she kept kissing him, sinking against him, using her body against him. She sensed the moment when she won, when desire triumphed over whatever misguided male notions he'd held.

A shudder went through him, then heat and glory welled between them again, even more powerful than before.

The tenor of their kiss changed – the giving and

taking shifted to some deeper level of intimacy. She gave readily, took gladly, and refused to back away.

A deep sigh coursed through him and his hands firmed about her bottom. His fingers flexed, then kneaded; heat spread in a prickly wave over her skin.

He backed her further into the hedge. One hand cradling her bottom, he held her there, pinned by his weight, while, with fingers quick and sure, he undid the buttons closing her breeches.

She should have been shocked, but she wasn't – she wanted to know. Now. Tonight. Here. With him.

Long fingers splayed over her stomach; they gently pressed and she lost her breath. His lips firmed and she took her breath from him, and rode the spiraling sensation of his touch, of his exploration.

He didn't hurry. He took the time to savor, to learn. Nerves tightening to excruciating sensitivity, she followed his every move.

Followed his fingers through the springy thicket of her tangling curls, felt the long slide of his fingers between her thighs. Sensed the heat, the curious dampness he encountered, thrilled to the flash of pure sensation that speared her when he caressed, then fondled.

His knowing fingers touched her, parted her, explored her – waves of pleasure rose and swamped her. They pushed her on. On toward something; the urge to reach it grew, swelled, until a near-mindless want consumed her.

She didn't know what she wanted; she was sure he did. Holding tight to him, to their anchoring kiss, she tilted her hips, opening herself to his hand, begging . . . she knew not for what.

He cupped her, fingers sliding slick in a soothing caress; then, very slowly, he entered her.

So slowly she felt the intrusion keenly – no force, no pressure, just the yielding of her body to his penetration. He reached deep, then stroked.

The heat within her tightened, coalesced, then contracted even more. He stroked again, finger within her, thumb upon her – she would have gasped, cried out, but he drank the sound. And stroked again.

Her heat fractured, imploded, then erupted. Hot glory and pleasure spilled down every vein. Fierce delight, tangible in its sharpness, ran across her skin, through her body, scattered her wits and left her senses sighing.

Clinging tightly, she gave herself up – to him, to the splendor of desire.

Lucifer watched her face as the pleasure rolled through her, his awareness centered within her, savoring the rippling caresses as she eased. Every demon he possessed was slavering, expecting its customary reward; he didn't know how he was going to hold them back, only that he would.

Somewhere, a line had been crossed, some Rubicon beyond which there was no turning back. He didn't know where or when, but there was no longer any point pretending he hadn't, at least partly deliberately, taken the fatal step. Whether it had been fifteen minutes ago, when the realization that he'd already nearly lost her had hit, whether Horatio's garden was to blame, or the inheritance as a whole – or if he'd decided in that instant when first he'd laid eyes on her face – didn't matter. She was his. So the only matter he had to concentrate on right now was not giving in to his demons.

Not easing her breeches farther down, lifting her, and taking her here, now, against the hedge.

Studying her face, eyes closed, her expression beatifically serene, helped – so did easing his fingers from her, gently drawing them from between her thighs.

Her musky scent rose, teasing, taunting his demons. He slammed a mental door on them, shut his ears to the howls.

He'd have her – he'd decided that days ago, even if he hadn't let himself think of it – but not here, not tonight. For all that she'd insisted, she deserved better than a shrubbery hedge. And he seriously doubted, when the time came, that once would be enough – not now. He'd known from the first that abstinence was not a good idea.

A whole night. If he exercised appropriate caution and skill . . .

Leaning into the hedge beside her shoulder, he was still watching her, her breeches done up, his hand resting on her hip on top of her loose shirt, when she drew in a deeper breath and opened her eyes.

She blinked. Her gaze flew to his face.

Even in the dimness, he saw awareness bloom; through his hand on her hip he felt tension reinvest her spine. She stared into his eyes, then swiftly scanned his face before once more meeting his gaze.

His lips curved, not so much a smile as a gesture of intent. He leaned into her. 'That was just the appetizer.'

He brushed a kiss across her swollen lips, then captured her wide-eyed gaze. 'Next time, I'll have you naked, on a bed, and I won't let you go until I've had you. Multiple times.'

At eleven the next morning, Phyllida closed the side door of the church and started down the path. The vases were done for the services tomorrow – one item she could cross off her list.

Jem, the Grange's youngest groom, was lounging in the lych-gate; he straightened as she neared. She'd requested his presence on her errand to protect her from the murderer or to protect her from Lucifer – she wasn't sure which. If the latter, then she'd failed. A pair of blacks pranced before the lych-gate; she had not the slightest doubt who would be holding their reins.

Jem opened the gate and she stepped into the lane. Lucifer was listening to Thompson, standing beside the curricle, but his blue gaze was all for her.

Thompson saw her and broke off to nod.

Lucifer seized the opportunity. 'Good morning,

Miss Tallent. Would you prefer to drive back to the Grange?'

No one would believe her if she said she wouldn't; in truth, she was perfectly amenable to meeting him again. In public. 'Thank you.' She sent Jem home, then strolled to the curricle's side. Although still engaged with Thompson, Lucifer held out a hand as she neared. She considered it, then calmly put her hand in it and allowed him to help her up. In public, she'd be safe.

Settling beside him, she shamelessly eavesdropped.

'So you want new locks on all the doors and windows, the kind that can't easily be slipped.'

Lucifer nodded. 'I haven't any idea how many will be needed, but I want every window secured.'

'Aye, well – no point otherwise.' Thompson straightened. 'I'll be along this afternoon to count up. I knows just the sort you want, but it'll take a week or more to get 'em in. Come from Bristol, they do.'

Lucifer nodded. 'Get the job done as fast as you can.'

'I'll do that.' With respectful nods to them both, Thompson stepped back.

Lucifer clicked the reins and the blacks stepped out. He glanced at her, but had to look back to his horses. They passed Jem, swinging down the lane. 'You have no idea,' Lucifer said, 'how pleasantly surprised I am to see you with Jem in your train.'

'Why? I didn't say I wouldn't.'

'You didn't say you would, either, and you are the most contrary female I've ever met.'

She couldn't decide whether to be pleased or insulted. 'Why are you ordering locks? Because of last night?'

His gaze touched her face. 'Because of the intruder.'

A frisson of awareness raced through her; she carefully kept it from her face. She wasn't going to let what had happened last night inhibit her from continuing with their joint investigations. She had a shrewd notion he'd be quite happy to see her retreat from the field, a victim of consciousness. But last night had come about by her insistence; just because he'd given her precisely what she'd wanted – even though, as he'd observed, she hadn't known for what she was asking – she wasn't about to convert into some mindless ninny.

She wasn't about to let his warning about the next time worry her, either. It would be up to her if ever there was a next time, and she hadn't yet made up her mind.

Shocking, of course, but there it was. She should be swooning, not sitting beside him, calmly if warily. She might not have appreciated last night's possibilities, not until she'd been in the middle of them, but she was twenty-four. She knew what he'd meant by his final words.

They'd been uttered like an oath. One that had carried a great deal of conviction. After a tense moment, face hard, all angular planes, he'd stepped back and let her slip past him, out onto the lawn. She'd looked back just once and seen him standing, a dark, forbidding shadow at the entrance to the shrubbery. Lucifer, indeed. All hot desire.

Temptation *was* his middle name.

And she'd felt safe, utterly and completely safe – safe not just physically, but at some much deeper level – while in his arms.

Why that should be so was a mystery, but it was pointless to cavil. Just how far that sense of safety might tempt her she didn't know, but in all her twenty-four years, he was the first to make her feel that being a woman desiring and desired was an experience available to her.

Deep in her mind lay a very strong feeling that just as he was the first, he might also be the last.

'The intruder' – she grabbed the curricle's rail as he took the corner into the main lane – 'how did he get in?'

'There was a window with a loose latch – the one in the dining room facing the side lawn.'

'So that's how he got out so fast.' After a moment, she asked, 'Do you think he'll return?'

'Not immediately, but sometime. Whatever he was after, he hasn't found it. If it was enough to commit murder for, then he'll be back.'

'Are you sure the intruder is the murderer?'

He grimaced. 'No. But unless there were *four* people visiting Horatio on Sunday morning – the murderer, you, me, *and* the intruder – and we've found absolutely no trace of the murderer, then the intruder is the murderer.'

The gates of the Manor appeared around the bend; he didn't slow. 'Bear with me.' He flicked her a glance. 'Bar your father and brother, you're the only sane and definitely innocent person I can talk to about this, and for obvious reasons, I can't yet talk to your father or brother.'

She regarded him calmly.

He had to look to his horses. 'I believe Horatio was killed because of some book. Everyone knew that on Sunday morning, the Manor should have been deserted. The downstairs doors were never locked. The murderer – a local who was not at church – left his horse behind the shrubbery and went to the drawing room. He started examining books, pulling them from the shelves – then Horatio disturbed him. On Monday afternoon, I noticed three books not properly pushed in.'

'Where?'

'Bottom of the last bookshelf against the inner wall.'

Near the gap where she'd surmised the murderer must have hidden. 'So – the murderer is after a book.'

'Or something in a book.'

'Could the book be the item Horatio wanted you to appraise?'

'No. Horatio wouldn't have asked me to appraise a book. *He* was the foremost authority in the field. If he'd found something spectacular, and all the signs suggest he had, he wouldn't have needed my opinion to be sure.'

They'd reached the road to Axmouth; he slowed and turned the curricle. When they were rolling back to Colyton, Phyllida asked, 'Why did you say something *in* a book?'

'Many books are valuable, not because of the book itself, but because of what's subsequently been written in them. Sometimes it's the notational information that adds the value, but most often it's the identity of the writer.'

'You mean inscriptions – that sort of thing?'

'Inscriptions, instructions, messages – even wills. You'd be amazed at what you come across.'

'So at present it appears that the motive for the murder is some information noted in a book?'

'That's my best guess.' The Grange gates loomed; deftly, he turned through them.

'What about the item Horatio wanted you to look at?'

'That remains a mystery. The fact that Horatio was killed just after he'd discovered it is looking more and more like coincidence. No one beyond myself and Covey knew he'd found anything. Covey knows no more than I.'

'We'll have to search all the books.'

'I have Covey doing that. He's used to handling old and valuable tomes – he'll be careful yet thorough.'

He drew up before the Grange steps; the blacks pranced. Phyllida climbed down without assistance.

On the steps, she turned and met his blue gaze. 'Thank you.' She didn't add anything more.

One black brow arched; he searched her face, consideration in his eyes.

She smiled, inclined her head, and turned toward the door. 'Until next time.'

She didn't look back to see how he reacted, but his wheels didn't start turning until she'd stepped over the threshold and Mortimer was closing the door behind her. Still smiling, she headed for her room. Why she was teasing him, she didn't know. She knew it wasn't safe.

She didn't know if she was teasing, either.

By the time she reached her room, her smile had converted to a frown. Lucifer was focusing on Horatio's books, which meant he'd be unlikely to go inspecting a writing desk. But he'd ordered new locks and he'd order them used, at least until the murderer was caught.

So she had a week's grace – the time it would take for the locks to arrive. She would have to search the Manor's upstairs rooms one night soon. Mrs Hemmings had told her Lucifer had taken the room at the front right corner, leaving Horatio's room as it was.

Phyllida grimaced. 'All I can do is pray that damned writing desk is not in the front corner bedroom.'

CHAPTER 11

Not to be outdone by the Fortemains, the Smollets had arranged to host a dance that evening. It was a large affair with guests driving in from miles around. Many Lucifer hadn't met; he spent half the evening being introduced and exclaimed over – he was the main attraction, after all.

While doing the pretty, he kept an eye on Phyllida. She'd arrived in good time with her father, brother, and Miss Sweet. Lady Huddlesford had swept in later, Frederick at her heels. Percy Tallent had not appeared.

In her gown of bronze silk, a simple gold chain around her throat and gold drops in her ears, Phyllida was the least fussily dressed woman in the room, and easily the most stunning. She drew many men's eyes, yet few, Lucifer realized, properly appreciated the sight. Cedric, Basil, and Grisby – those he paid most attention to – clearly viewed Phyllida as a desirable chattel, one that, if possessed, would add to their consequence. None of them seemed to see *her* at all. Fools, the lot of them.

Her expression serene, she did her best to ignore

them, chatting instead with the many others present – doubtless dispensing aid and succor in various forms. Yet she could not entirely avoid her would be suitors.

She danced the first dance with Basil, their host. By dint of superior strategy, Lucifer avoided the reciprocal fate; Jocasta Smollet danced the measure with Sir Jasper. Phyllida then danced a cottilion with Cedric; later, he saw her going down a country dance with Henry Grisby.

Her attitude at the conclusion of the dance – that of relief that her duty had now been done – failed to puncture Grisby's self-absorption. Less than impressed, Phyllida retreated to speak with the Misses Longdon.

From the side of the room, Lucifer watched her, and considered his best avenue of approach.

'There you are!'

He turned as Sir Jasper joined him.

'Wanted to ask – have you uncovered anything about this blackguard who stabbed Horatio?'

'Nothing positive. There's no evidence anyone rode in from beyond the village, at least not from the east. I've yet to check in Honiton, but at present, all signs point to the killer residing locally.'

'Hmm. This intruder you surprised last night . . . ?'

'May well be the murderer.'

Sir Jasper let out a long sigh. He looked away, over the room. 'I'd hoped, y'know, that it wouldn't be someone from round about. But if they're still searching . . .'

'Precisely. It can't be anyone from far afield. They'd be noticed.'

'By the same token, given the way we all go about down here, riding day in, day out, it'll be hard to pin anyone down.'

Lucifer inclined his head in agreement.

Sir Jasper remained beside him, a frown gathering on his face. Eventually, he drew breath and faced Lucifer. 'This business of that hunter shooting at Phyllida . . .'

'Exactly what I want to know, too.'

Sir Jasper and Lucifer glanced around as Jonas ambled up. Hands in his pockets, he met Lucifer's gaze. As usual, he appeared relaxed, ready for any lark. It occurred to Lucifer that, as Phyllida's calm serenity was often a mask, so, too, Jonas's insouciant good humor concealed something more. There was certainly nothing insouciant in his hazel eyes.

'I know Phyl *said* it was a hunter, but I can't see it myself. Ridiculous time and place to go shooting. And whyever did she burn that bonnet?'

'She burned her bonnet?' Sir Jasper gazed across the room at his daughter.

'So Sweetie said.' Jonas studied Phyllida, too.

'Why on earth would she do that?'

Because she'd been frightened and destroying the bonnet had been her way of putting the incident from her. Lucifer could understand that. For all her intransigence, Phyllida was too intelligent not to be afraid.

'What I want to know is: Is she in any danger?'

It was Jonas who voiced the question. To Lucifer's relief, it wasn't directed specifically at him; he couldn't answer truthfully. He shifted; it went against his grain to keep Sir Jasper and Jonas in the dark. To his mind, they had a right to know – had a right to protect daughter, sister.

Lips shut tight against any unwary word, he canvassed his options, but there wasn't any way to warn them that it looked like the murderer was indeed after Phyllida – they'd immediately ask why. 'I saw her out walking, coming back from the church. I noticed she had a groom with her.'

'Did she? Now that's a first.' Jonas glanced at him. 'I wonder why.'

'Perhaps the shock of being shot at.' Lucifer kept his tone light. 'Who knows what goes on in the minds of women?'

Sir Jasper snorted. Jonas grinned.

After a moment, Sir Jasper said, 'I don't like this business of a murderer running loose among us. No telling where it might end. I might just have a word with the male staff – no need to let Phyllida know.'

'A general increase in watchfulness wouldn't hurt.'

'She'll hear of it,' Jonas said. 'You know she will. Then she'll just reorganize things her way.'

'Humph!' Sir Jasper's frowning gaze remained on his daughter. 'I'll do it anyway. With luck, by the time she learns of it, we'll have this miscreant by the heels.'

Lucifer hoped so. Leaving Sir Jasper and Jonas, he strolled down the room to negotiate with the musicians laboring in a corner. After that, he headed toward the *chaise* Phyllida was sharing with the Misses Longdon.

He bowed to all three ladies. They had barely exchanged five words before the opening bars of a waltz filled the room. The Misses Longdon tittered; neither danced, but they eagerly scanned the room to see who of their neighbors would partner whom.

Lucifer caught Phyllida's eye and bowed again. 'If you would do me the honor, Miss Tallent?'

She inclined her head and gave him her hand. He raised her and drew her into the dance, into his arms. The Misses Longdon twittered furiously.

Phyllida danced well and was thankful for it – at least she didn't need to mind her steps. One less problem on her plate. The most pressing, literally, had her trapped in his arms and was whirling her effortlessly around the floor. For some silly reason, her wits and her senses seemed intent on following her feet into some realm of giddy delight, and that was far too dangerous.

There was an aggravated frown in Lucifer's eyes, a tightness about his lips, a tension in his body as it tantalizingly brushed hers – unquestionably all danger signs. She kept her expression mild, her gaze on his face.

'I've just had a most *uncomfortable* conversation with your father and brother.'

She felt her eyes go round, her jaw drop. 'How on earth did Papa, let alone Jonas, learn of last night?'

Lucifer stared at her, then his lips thinned. 'We weren't discussing our interlude in the shrubbery. They don't know about that.'

Phyllida sagged with relief. 'Thank heavens!'

Lucifer all but shook her as they went around the turn. 'We were discussing whether you are in danger. Which you are.'

'You didn't tell them?' She searched his eyes.

They glittered back at her. 'No, I didn't. But I should.'

'There's no reason for them to be worried—'

'They have a right to know.'

She narrowed her eyes at him. 'I don't want them to know. It's pointless. As you saw, I'm perfectly capable of taking appropriate steps, and with luck I'll be able to tell you all soon, and then, one way or another, we'll catch the murderer and all will be well.'

He studied her face, her eyes. 'It would be better if you told me what it was you saw in Horatio's drawing room.'

She considered it.

I saw a brown hat.

A brown hat?

Just a brown hat. I didn't recognize it and no one's worn it since.

Then it can't be that that the murderer's worried about. What else happened? What were you doing? Why were you there?

'I can't tell you. Not yet.'

His gaze remained steady, vibrant dark blue, focused on her eyes. 'I think you can.'

His voice was soft, low; it sent shivers down her spine. Her impulse was to lift her chin and step back from his arms; before she could, he drew her nearer.

Near enough so the silk over her breasts brushed his coat with every breath; close enough so that his hard thighs brushed hers at every turn.

She was suddenly very conscious of just how physically powerful he was – although he never hid it, he hadn't before projected it, not like this. Some part of her mind was pointing frantically, urging her to understand how threatening he could be, and give in. Instead, she simply frowned at him. 'Not yet. I'll tell you as soon as I can.'

Her tone was calm and even. An expression of surprise – as if he couldn't quite believe his ears – passed swiftly through his eyes. Then the blue hardened. Slowly, arrogantly, he lifted one black brow.

She knew that look – could interpret it with ease. 'Nothing you can do will change my mind.'

The music stopped; they swirled to a halt by the side of the floor, but he didn't let her go. His hand at her waist burned through the silk, threatening to bring her hard against him. He lowered their linked hands, lacing his fingers through hers, and looked into her eyes. 'Nothing?'

Just that one, soft word.

Phyllida suddenly felt faint. Her knees felt weak. If she didn't say something soon, he was going to kiss her – right here in the Smollets' ballroom in front of half the county. He would do it, and delight in the doing. Her heart was thudding; her eyes were trapped in midnight blue. She couldn't think – not well enough to concoct any evasive plan. And she couldn't break away.

His gaze grew more intent; his lips lifted a little at the corners. The hand at her back tensed—

'Ah, Phyllida, my dear.'

It was Basil. He walked toward them, not looking at them but surveying his guests. Lucifer was forced to release her. Phyllida edged back.

Reaching them, Basil glanced at them and smiled perfunctorily. 'I wonder, my dear, if I could prevail on you to give your opinion of the punch. I'm just not sure . . .'

'Of course!' Seizing Basil's arm, Phyllida turned him. 'Where's the punch bowl?'

She steered Basil down the room, away from Lucifer, and didn't once look back.

Despite that, she knew he watched her – kept watching her, waiting for another chance at her. No matter where in the room she went, she felt his gaze on her. Consequently, she was forced to conscript some gentleman – one of her village suitors or one of the others from farther afield who would gladly pay court to her if she gave the slightest sign – as bodyguard. They, unfortunately, didn't know they were guarding her.

One, a Mr Firman from Musbury, insisted on fetching her a glass of punch; he left her by a window. Phyllida scanned the crowd; she couldn't see Lucifer. But the sense of being in danger grew . . . retreating to the withdrawing room seemed a good idea. She turned toward the door—

And walked into a familiar chest.

She all but leaped back. She glared at him. 'Stop it!'

He raised his brows, all innocence. 'Stop what?'

'This! You know you can't' – she gestured with both hands – '*seduce* me in a ballroom.'

'Who wrote that rule?' He studied her eyes, then added, 'I'll admit it's a greater challenge, but . . .'

His voice had deepened to a suggestive purr. Phyllida flashed him a repressive look and turned to scan those nearby, hoping to see Mr Firman or some other useful soul. . . . Robert Collins was standing quietly by the wall.

Lucifer had followed her gaze. 'I thought the hostesses hereabouts didn't encourage Mr Collins.'

'They don't and Jocasta's no different, she's just more cruel. She knows inviting Robert will irritate Mr Farthingale, reinforcing his opposition, which quite ruins Mary Anne's delight in having Robert here. Robert, of course, is helpless to decline the invitation – he gets so few opportunities to see Mary Anne in such surrounds.'

Phyllida was conscious that, just for a moment, Lucifer's attention drifted from her. She glanced at him; he was studying the guests.

'Miss Smollet,' he murmured, 'seems to have a rather peculiar notion of what constitutes entertainment.'

Phyllida quietly humphed. She was saved from having to find some other distraction by Mr Firman's return. He handed her her glass; to gain a moment, she introduced him to Lucifer, only to discover that Mr Firman had been waiting to talk to Mr Cynster all evening.

Mr Firman, it transpired, was the owner of a cattle stud. Phyllida learned that that was a subject on which Lucifer wished to extend his knowledge. Not only did Mr Firman talk, but Lucifer listened and asked questions.

The opportunity was too good to pass up. Phyllida edged away; Lucifer shot her a glance but was trapped in the ongoing discussion. Mr Firman was not someone he wanted to offend.

Phyllida gave her glass to a footman, then joined Robert Collins by the wall.

He glanced at her – there was a painful intensity in his eyes that Phyllida didn't like to see. He pressed her hand. 'Mary Anne told me about the letters.' He looked across the room to where Mary Anne stood chatting with two young ladies. 'How I *wish* I'd never urged her to write to me.'

The bitterness in his words had Phyllida frowning. 'It's the letters I wanted to speak to you about.'

Robert's head whipped around, hope naked in his face. 'You've found them?'

'No. I'm sorry . . .'

Robert sighed. 'No – *I'm* sorry. I know you will and I'm grateful for your help. I've no right to press you.' After a moment, he asked, 'What did you want to know?'

Phyllida took a deep breath. 'I have to ask you this because it's important, and whenever I try to talk to Mary Anne on the subject, she becomes quite hysterical. But I need to know this, Robert – and if I don't get a sensible answer, I don't know that I can keep searching for those letters in secret. So tell me – what is it about them that makes them so dangerous to you and Mary Anne?'

Robert stared at her, the image of a rabbit cornered. Then he swallowed and looked away. 'I can't tell you – not in so many words.'

'Generalizations will do – I'll extrapolate.'

He fell silent; eventually he said, 'Mary Anne and I have been meeting secretly for nearly a year. You know how long we've waited and . . .' He dragged in a breath. 'Anyway, Mary Anne used to fill in the time between my visits by writing to me about our last meeting – about what we'd done and what we might do the next time – well, she wrote in a very *detailed* way.' He cast Phyllida an anguished glance.

She met it, blank-faced. After a moment, she said, her tone flat, 'I think I understand, Robert.'

Thanks to Lucifer, she now had some inkling of what could transpire between a lady and a gentleman where desire was involved. And she had no doubt Mary Anne desired Robert – she always had. Phyllida cleared her throat.

'I used to bring the letters with me to our next meeting and we'd try to . . . well . . .' Robert hauled in another breath and rushed on. 'So you see, if Mr Farthingale got hold of the letters, it would be very . . . bad. But if he showed them to Mr Crabbs – if *anyone* showed them to Mr Crabbs . . .'

'Hmm.' A vision of the starchily conservative, stern-faced solicitor flashed into Phyllida's mind.

'I wouldn't get my registration, and then we'd never be able to marry.' Robert looked at her, his plea in his eyes.

She forced a reassuring smile. 'We'll find them.'

Robert squeezed her hand. 'I can't thank you enough – you're such a good friend.'

Phyllida took back her hand, and wished she could be a bad friend. But she couldn't. On top of that, she'd given her word. She turned from Robert – and found Lucifer almost upon her.

She met his eyes. 'No!'

A violin sang – they both glanced toward the musicians. Then Phyllida looked back. She considered Lucifer, then stepped closer and flicked a hand against his chest. 'Waltz with me.'

He looked at her, arrested. 'Why?'

'Because you might as well be useful and I don't want to waltz with anyone else.'

His arm closed around her and he steered her into the whirl. His eyes searched hers. 'You're trying to distract me.'

254

'Perhaps.' She was also trying to distract herself, and he was simply perfect for the task.

How *could* Mary Anne have been so idiotic as to write such things down? Love-induced stupidity – that was the only reason Phyllida could imagine.

The sun shone brightly, the air was fresh and clean as she strolled briskly down the common. Behind her, the Sunday-morning congregation was streaming home. Ten paces to her rear, Jem strode, her concession to male notions of feminine vulnerability. Her aunt and the rest of the females of the Grange were rolling home in the carriage, but she had elected to stroll back via the wood.

And the Manor.

All the Manor's household bar Lucifer had been in church, even the newcomer, his groom. Bristleford had informed her that Mr Cynster had elected to watch over the house in light of the recent intrusion.

Phyllida wondered if that was the real reason or whether, given his name, he would prove any less irregular than the other gentlemen of the parish when it came to Sunday services.

Her parasol protecting her from the sun, she crossed the lane and turned toward the Manor. Nearing the front gate, she slowed, considering what excuse to give for calling.

From the shadows beyond the open front door, Lucifer watched her hesitating by the gate. He'd been deep in Horatio's ledgers when some force had metaphorically jogged his elbow, breaking his concentration. He'd glanced up, then stood and strolled to the library window. His gaze had been drawn to the figure heading purposefully down the common, neatly encased in Sunday ivory, her parasol shading her face, Phyllida's destination wasn't hard to guess.

He'd waited in the hall – he didn't want to seem too eager to see her. That wouldn't help his cause. His gaze lingered on her figure, on the sweet curves of breast and shoulder, on the dark hair that framed her face. With the glory of Horatio's garden between them, he studied her, then stepped forward.

She saw him and straightened; her grip on her parasol tightened. Not fear but alertness – a keen anticipation he could feel. He crossed the garden but stopped short of the gate, halting beneath the rosecovered archway. There was a convenient spot where his shoulder could prop; availing himself of it, he crossed his arms and looked at her.

She studied him, trying to gauge his mood. He gave her no assistance.

She tilted her head, her eyes on his. 'Good morning. Bristleford said you'd stayed to watch the house. I take it the intruder didn't reappear?'

'No. All was quiet.'

She waited, then said, 'I was wondering if Covey had discovered anything – any wildly precious volume or one containing a reason for murder.'

How much to tell her? 'Have you ever heard any rumors concerning Lady Fortemain?'

Her eyes widened to dark saucers. 'Lady Fortemain? Good heavens, no!'

'In that case, possibly.'

Phyllida waited. When he continued to simply stand there, his gaze steady, his face uninformative, she prompted, 'Well? What was it?'

A moment passed before he answered, 'An inscription in a book.'

So she had imagined. 'What did it say?'

'What did you see in Horatio's drawing room last Sunday?'

Phyllida stiffened. The undercurrents in the present scene were suddenly clear. 'You know I can't tell you – not yet.'

His eyes were very dark; they remained fixed on her face. 'Because it concerns someone else?'

She pressed her lips together, then nodded. 'Yes.'

They stared at each other across the gate to Horatio's garden. He stood relaxed but still, dark, dangerous, and devilishly handsome, framed by white roses. The sun beat down on them; the breeze wrapped them in its warmth.

Then he stirred, straightened. His eyes hadn't left hers. 'Someday I hope you'll trust me.'

He hesitated, then inclined his head, turned, and walked back toward the front door.

Three paces and he stopped. He spoke without turning. 'Walk back through the village. Until the murderer's caught, the woods and the shrubberies are no place for you.'

He waited for a heartbeat, then continued on.

Phyllida watched until he'd disappeared into the house. Then she turned. Her mask firmly in place, she beckoned to Jem, who had hung back on the common, and set off – through the village.

Of course she trusted him – he *knew* she did! Phyllida slapped the brass vase she'd just emptied down on the vestry table, then swept back into the nave. She headed for the font.

The flowers she'd arranged on Saturday had only just lasted through Sunday. Wrapping both arms around the heavy urn, she hefted it. Balancing the weight carefully, she slowly edged toward the vestry and the open door beyond; the last thing she needed was dirty water streaks down the front of her muslin gown.

That would be the last straw.

How could he not know that she trusted him? He did know – he *must,* after their little interlude in the shrubbery. He knew, but he was using the question of trust – her trust in him – as a lever to pressure her.

He wasn't really talking about trust at all – he was talking about dominance. About the fact that she hadn't weakened and told him what he wanted to know. If he wanted to discuss trust, what about him trusting *her*? She'd told him she couldn't tell him, but that she would as soon as she could, and that what she knew was of no consequence anyway!

And just what had he meant by his parting comment about shrubberies not being safe for her?

'I'll go into the shrubbery any time I like.'

The words, uttered through clenched teeth, echoed in the empty vestry. Feeling ahead with one foot, she located the threshold, then stepped out into the grassy area at the back of the church.

The sky was overcast, at one with her mood. Peering around the urn, she turned toward the pile of discarded flowers—

Black cloth fell over her head.

The weight of a rope fell against her collarbone.

The next instant, it jerked tight.

And tightened.

She flung the heavy urn aside – it clanged against a headstone. Lashing back with her elbows, she connected, and heard a satisfying 'Ouff!'

It was a man, and he was bigger, heavier, and stronger than she was. She didn't stop to think; years of wrestling with Jonas flared in her mind. She scrabbled at the rope with both hands, bending forward from the waist, hauling on the rope, forcing the man to reach over her, forcing him off-balance. Before he could pull back on the rope, she straightened. The back of her head hit his jaw. More important, the rope eased enough for her to hook her hands inside it.

He brutally yanked it back again, but she pulled with all her strength, dragged in a breath, and screamed.

The scream bounced off the church walls; it echoed from the stones all around them.

A door crashed; footsteps pounded, heading their way.

A rough curse fell on her ears. Her attacker flung her aside.

Phyllida fell over a grave. Rough stone grazed her calf, then she toppled, catching her upper arm on another sharp stone edge before tumbling blindly back. She landed across a marble slab, still shrouded in the heavy black cloth, the rope still hanging around her shoulders.

'Here! You! *Stop*!'

Jem's yells broke through Phyllida's stunned daze. She heard him run past and on down the path. Struggling to rise, she batted at the black fabric hanging heavily all about her. Panic clawed at her throat. She couldn't break free.

Then she heard another curse, more forceful, more virulent. Heavy footsteps strode quickly toward her.

Before she could gather her wits, she was swept up like a child in a pair of strong arms, then he sat, and she was deposited in his lap.

'Stop struggling – you're only tangling it. Hold still.'

Her panic left her in a rush. She started to shiver. The rope was unwound from her shoulders. The next instant, the black shroud was lifted away.

She stared into Lucifer's face, blue eyes dark with concern.

'Are you all right?'

She drank in the sight of his face for one more moment, then slid her arms around him, ducked

260

her head to his chest, and clung. His arms closed comfortingly about her. He rested his cheek on her hair and rocked her.

'It's all right. He's gone.' He held her tight, safe. A minute passed, then he asked, 'Now tell me, are you hurt?'

Without lifting her head, she shook it. She gulped in air and struggled to find her voice. 'Just my throat.' Her voice was hoarse from the scream and from the rope. She put a hand to her neck and felt roughened skin and the puffiness of swelling.

'Nothing else?'

'Just a graze on my leg and a bruise on my arm.' She didn't think she'd hit her head on the slab, but her leg was stinging. Lifting her face, fists clenched in his coat, she peeked at her legs – her skirts were rucked up to her knees.

She blushed and tried frantically to flick them down.

Lucifer caught her hand, returned it to his chest, then reached out and straightened the flowing muslin for her. He noticed the graze and paused. 'It's just a scratch – no blood.' He arranged her skirts so they covered her calves.

Then he looked up, his gaze fixing on the path leading down to the lych-gate. 'Here they come.'

He looked down at her, then his arms tightened and he rose to his feet. Settling her in his arms, he set out, negotiating the narrow path between the graves to the grassy area by the vestry door. He stopped and waited. Mr Filing and Jem joined them.

Thompson was with them, a heavy hammer in one hand. 'What's to do?'

'Someone attacked Miss Tallent.' Lucifer glanced back at the slab where he'd left the black cloth and rope. 'Filing – if you would?'

Frowning, clearly upset, Mr Filing was already on his way. He returned a moment later, distress very evident on his face. 'This is my robe.' He held up the black shroud, shaking it so it fell into a more recognizable shape. 'And this' – he held up the rope; it was gold, about half an inch thick – 'is the cord from one of the censers!'

Outrage rang in his tone.

'Where were they kept?' Lucifer asked.

'In the vestry.' Filing looked at the open back door. 'Good God – did the blackguard attack you in the church?'

Phyllida shook her head. Trying to hold it steady and not rest it on Lucifer's chest was an effort. 'I was clearing the vases. I walked out . . .' She gestured to the area beyond the open door. She swallowed, and it hurt.

Lucifer was frowning at her. 'Filing, I think we should take Miss Tallent back to the Rectory so she can rest. We can discuss the matter more fully there.' He glanced at Jem and Thompson. 'I take it he got away?'

Jem nodded. 'I barely got a glimpse of him. He was already through the lych-gate when I got here.'

'Where were you?'

Phyllida waved. 'I told Jem he could sit out at the front of the church and watch the ducks. I never imagined . . .'

'Indeed.' Lucifer tightened his hold on her, tipping her slightly so it seemed natural to lean into his chest.

'I heard the scream and grabbed my hammer and came running,' Thompson said, 'but by the time I got to the lane, he was in the wood.'

'I followed into the wood a ways,' Jem said, 'but then I couldn't tell which way he'd gone.'

Lucifer nodded. 'You did well. If he's following his usual pattern, he would have had a horse waiting. No sense running on.'

Jem ducked his head, clearly relieved.

Filing had taken the robe and cord back into the vestry; now he fetched the urn, emptied it, and returned that, too, to the church. Phyllida watched as he shut the vestry door; the curate's face was pale and set.

Lucifer turned and headed toward the Rectory. Filing caught him up and fell in just behind; Jem and Thompson brought up the rear.

As they started down the sloping path, Phyllida leaned closer and whispered, 'I'm sure I can walk. You don't need to carry me.'

Lucifer's eyes met hers; the look in them suggested she'd missed the point entirely. 'I do need to carry you.' His jaw tightened; he looked ahead. 'Believe me, I do.'

They trooped into the Rectory; Lucifer made for the *chaise* in the parlor. He lowered Phyllida, laying her along it so she could lie back. The loss of his heat, his muscled strength protectively around her, made her tense. She fought the urge to cling. She'd never clung to any man in her life.

But sudden panic rose as he drew his arms from her and straightened. Fright flowed like a chill through her and she shook. She knew he was frowning down at her, but she didn't meet his eyes.

Mr Filing appeared with a glass of water. Gratefully, she took it and sipped.

Lucifer stepped back, then prowled around the *chaise*. Without looking, she knew he came to stand just behind her, a protective presence hovering over her.

Mr Filing paced back and forth before the hearth. 'This is shocking – most shocking. That anyone would *dare* – !' Words failed him; pressing his hands together in silent prayer, he stood for a moment, then turned to Phyllida. 'Perhaps, my dear, you could tell us what happened.'

Phyllida took another sip of water. 'I was emptying the vases—'

'Do you always do that on Monday mornings?'

She glanced up and back at Lucifer. 'In this weather, yes. Mrs Hemmings brings flowers up on Tuesday, and then I change the vases again on Saturday. That's what we usually do – last week was different because of Horatio's funeral.'

Lucifer looked down into her wide eyes, still dark,

still huge, still frightened. 'So it was common knowledge that you'd be at the church, most likely alone, with the vestry door open this morning?'

Phyllida hesitated, then nodded. She looked at Filing.

'If we could start at the beginning,' Filing suggested. 'You reached the church . . . ?'

Phyllida sipped, then lifted her head. 'I reached the church and as usual entered through the main door from the common. I left Jem outside, sitting on the steps.'

'There was no one inside?' Filing asked.

Phyllida shook her head. 'I picked up the vase from the altar and carried it through to the vestry. I opened the vestry door, propped it open, and took the vase out to empty it. Then I took it back inside.'

'You didn't see or hear anyone about?' Lucifer asked.

'No. But . . .' Phyllida glanced up at him. 'I was . . . absorbed. Someone might have been near, but I wasn't paying attention.'

The fleeting awareness in her eyes told him what she'd been absorbed with – she'd been annoyed at him, which was exactly what he'd intended. He'd wanted to irk her, to prod the temper he'd sensed and occasionally glimpsed behind her calm facade; wanted to bring it to life and use it to get her to tell him the truth. Instead, he'd distracted her and made her an even easier target for the murderer.

No more games. Jaw setting, he looked at Filing as Phyllida did the same.

'And then . . . ?' the curate prompted.

Phyllida drew in a deeper breath. 'I fetched the urn. It's heavy and cumbersome – I have to wrap both arms about it. I reached the door and stepped out . . .' She paused, then went on. 'That's when the cloth fell over my head. Then the rope—' She broke off and took another sip of water.

'Quite, quite,' Mr Filing soothed.

After a moment, she added, 'He was behind me. I struggled, then I screamed – I heard a door crash.'

'That was here.' Filing glanced at Lucifer. 'Mr Cynster and I were considering the list of men who did not come to church last Sunday when we heard your scream.'

'What happened next?' Lucifer asked.

'He flung me aside and ran off.' Phyllida glanced back at Lucifer. 'I never saw him.'

He looked down at her. 'Think back. He was standing behind you – how tall was he?'

She considered. 'He was taller than me, but not as tall as you.' She glanced across the room. 'About Thompson's height.'

'Did you get any sense of build?'

'Not as heavy as Thompson' – her gaze swung to Filing – 'but not as slim as Mr Filing.'

Lucifer turned to Jem, standing by the door. 'Does that sound right for the glimpse you caught, Jem? A man about Thompson's height but of average weight?'

Jem nodded. 'Aye. And he had brown hair – leastways, not dark like yours.'

'Good. What about clothes? Any idea?'

Jem scrunched up his face. 'Neat. Couldn't rightly say gentl'man or not, but neat. Not a smock or anything shabby.'

Lucifer glanced down at Phyllida. She'd gone quiet, withdrawn. She was not moving, barely breathing. 'Phyllida?'

She raised her face; her eyes were drowning dark pools filled with revisited fear. 'A coat,' she said, then shivered and looked away. 'When I was struggling . . . I think he was wearing a proper coat.'

Lucifer left Phyllida with Filing and strode back to the Manor to fetch his curricle. Returning to the Rectory, he carried Phyllida out to the carriage, ignoring her hissed protests, and set her gently on the seat.

When he flung a rug over her knees, she stared at him. 'It's summer,' she said as they rattled down the Rectory drive.

'You're in shock,' he replied, and said nothing more.

Silence was definitely wise; God alone knew what might tumble out if he let the chaos of emotions inside him free.

He concentrated on driving as quickly as he dared; he wanted her safe indoors again as soon as possible. They reached the Grange gates in a few minutes; a minute later, he pulled up before the steps.

Phyllida flicked back the rug and clambered out

before he could tie off the reins. Jem, who had hustled back earlier, came running; Lucifer threw him the reins and followed Phyllida. He caught up with her on the porch.

She stopped him with a look. 'I am not going to faint.'

This was her home; she should be safe here. 'All right.' His tone was grudging, precisely how he felt. He looked up as Mortimer opened the door. 'Miss Tallent has been attacked – she'll need Gladys and Miss Sweet. If Sir Jasper's at home, I'd like to speak with him immediately.'

An hour later, Lucifer stood before the window in Sir Jasper's study and stared out over the Grange lawns. Behind him, seated in the big chair behind his desk, Sir Jasper raised a glass and sipped, then sighed heavily.

Summoned by a horrified Mortimer, Miss Sweet and Gladys had descended on Phyllida and borne her off upstairs. Lady Huddlesford had swept majestically after them, declaring her intent to see that her niece did not play fast and loose with her nerves. Whose nerves, Lucifer wasn't quite sure.

Miss Sweet had popped her head into the study half an hour ago. She'd informed them that Phyllida was resting quietly on her bed and had agreed to the wisdom of remaining there for the rest of the afternoon.

That much he'd accomplished. She was fussed over and safe, at least for the time being.

Lucifer turned. Sir Jasper had aged years in the past hour. The lines in his face had deepened; fretful worry had taken up residence in his eyes.

'What's this place coming to, that's what I'd like to know.' Sir Jasper set his glass down with a snap. 'Dreadful business when a lady can't go to fix the church flowers without being attacked, what?'

Lucifer opened his mouth, then shut it. Again he felt compelled to bite his tongue. Telling Sir Jasper that the attack was not general but quite specific might dampen his concerns as local magistrate, but would only escalate his fatherly fears.

Sir Jasper fixed him with a frowning glance. 'From what you said, it seems unlikely this was some itinerant laborer passing through. Not a gypsy or a tinker.'

'No. Phyllida's impression that the culprit wore a coat tallies with Jem's description of him being neatly dressed. In Jem's words, "not a smock or anything shabby."'

'Hmm.' After a long moment of staring into space, Sir Jasper looked at him. 'Any chance this attack is connected to Horatio's murder?'

Lucifer looked down into eyes that were very like Phyllida's but had seen a great deal more. 'I can't say.'

That was the literal truth.

He turned back to the window. He felt even grimmer than his grim expression showed. 'With your permission, I'd like to talk to Phyllida tomorrow morning.' He glanced at Sir Jasper, meeting his gaze. 'There are a number of matters I'd like to discuss with her, and if I could speak with her privately, I think there are various points we might clarify.'

Sir Jasper held his gaze, then turned back to his desk. 'Privately, heh? Well, you might be right – not easy to get her to open her budget.' He paused, then asked, 'Should I mention you'll be dropping by to speak with her?'

Lucifer looked out of the window. 'It might be better if my visit came as a surprise.'

CHAPTER 12

Midnight. Phyllida lay in her bed and listened to the clocks throughout the Grange chime. The last echoes died and left her in silvered darkness.

She'd slept through half the afternoon, then, after dinner, she'd been harried and hounded until, simply to gain some peace, she'd retired early to her room and her bed. She'd slept. Now she was wide awake.

Nothing hurt. The scrape on her calf and the bruise on her arm were distant irritations.

Her thoughts were more tortured.

Being shot at across a field was something she'd been able to push aside – despite the evidence of the horse Lucifer had uncovered, it *could* still have been a hunter. Being shot at was distant; she hadn't seen her attacker.

At the church, she hadn't seen him, but she'd felt him.

Felt his strength, and known the threat was real.

Fear. She could still taste it at the back of her tongue. She'd never known real fear before – not here in her peaceful, maybe not quite happy but content, existence.

That existence was under threat; she felt it like cold iron at her back. Her life was not something she'd thought of before – she'd taken it for granted. Just like all those around her. How ironic.

She didn't want to die. Especially for no reason. Especially at the hands of some cowardly murderer. Lucifer had been right. The murderer obviously thought she knew more than she did. He was after her in earnest.

Dragging in a breath, she held it, forced the chill from her skin, waited until the shivery tremors had died. She couldn't go on like this – she hated the sense of not being in control, of not being safe. She hated the taste of fear.

So – what to do?

It should have been an easy question; thanks to her promise about Mary Anne's letters, it was anything but. Phyllida lay on her back and stared up at the shadows dancing on her ceiling.

She would bet her best bonnet Lucifer would be back tomorrow morning; this time, he wouldn't let be. He'd insist she tell him all, and if she refused, he would speak to her father. She felt confident in predicting how he would react, certainly in those circumstances where honor and duty ruled. He might be many things, a reprobate, a rake, an elegant charmer of questionable constancy, but at his core he was a gentleman, one of the highest caliber.

It would not be in his lexicon to allow her to endanger herself – that was how he would see it. That, for him, would be the crux of the matter, regardless of how she felt.

After nearly being strangled, she could hardly argue. She would have to tell him all tomorrow. She would tell him about the hat – and then she would have to tell him about the rest, too.

But what of her promise to Mary Anne, her sworn oath that she'd say nothing to anyone about the letters?

What price an oath to a friend?

She'd never imagined facing such a decision. Finding the letters should have been so easy. Even now, if only she could search upstairs at the Manor. She'd been thinking of going one night, when the servants were abed. She knew which room to avoid, but the other rooms . . . Mary Anne's grandmother's traveling writing desk had to be in one of them. She doubted it had been put in the attic. No – it would be sitting on some chest somewhere, looking dainty and delicate, just waiting for her to retrieve the letters . . .

Lifting her head, she looked across her room. The moonlight was bright; she could see her dresser clearly, even make out the scrollwork around her mirror's rim.

She pushed up onto her elbows.

Before tomorrow morning dawned and brought Lucifer with it, she had at least four hours of deep night. Time enough to search the first floor rooms at the Manor, find the letters, and return home. And the window in the Manor's dining room still had a loose latch.

She flung aside the covers. If she didn't find the desk tonight, then tomorrow she'd tell Lucifer all and ask for his aid in finding the letters. Despite Mary Anne's and Robert's paranoia, she felt confident that if he bothered to read them at all, the contents of the letters would gain no more than a raised eyebrow from Lucifer; she couldn't imagine him giving the letters to Mr Crabbs.

But for Mary Anne, and to honor her promise, she'd make one last attempt to find the letters.

Struggling into her clothes, she glanced out at the shifting shadows of the wood. She'd be safe. No one, not even the murderer, would imagine she'd be out tonight.

She was still repeating that thought when she reached the edge of the wood and looked across at the Manor. She'd worked her way farther around the house; across the lawns stood the dining room. To reach the corner window, she'd have to pick her way across the gravel drive.

Steeling herself, she started across, carefully placing each foot before transferring her weight to it. Luckily, her enforced sleep and the brisk walk through the wood had left her physically alert. She reached the beds before the dining room with barely a crunch.

The latch was certainly loose; just a jiggle and

the window swung wide. She hauled herself up onto the wide sill, then sat and swung her legs in.

Easing down to the floor, she closed the window, then listened. The house was asleep – she could feel the silence like a heavy cloak hanging undisturbed all around her. Shadows draped the furniture, rendered deeper by the moonlight slanting through the uncurtained windows. Like all the ground-floor rooms, this room was lined with bookcases. Once her eyes had adjusted enough to pick out the books, she moved silently around the large table.

The door to the front hall stood wide; beyond was a sea of shadows. She paused before the doorway, gathering her courage.

Movement. Just by the foot of the stairs. She froze.

A foot above the floor, a disembodied plume came swaying through the shadows, then the cat lifted its head; its eyes gleamed.

She sagged with relief. The cat considered her, then, unperturbed, paced down the hall, tail raised, still swaying.

Phyllida dragged in a calming breath. It had to be a good sign – a cat would sense any evil intruder. Presumably she was the only intruder tonight. She hadn't expected the murderer to be here, yet . . .

Putting the nagging worry aside, she crossed the hall, treading lightly, then started up the stairs. She trod close to the banister to minimize the chance of any telltale creak. Reaching the landing, she paused and looked up.

The gallery above was dense with shadow. She took a moment to reorient herself. The last time she'd been upstairs at the Manor was before Horatio had bought it. She knew he'd remodeled and refurbished extensively, but the basic layout of the rooms remained unchanged.

On the way through the wood, she'd distracted herself by planning her search. Horatio had been ill for a week before his death. He'd written to Lucifer in that time, and he'd always had a deal of correspondence. He might have been using the desk himself.

The idea had given her heart. There was no point looking anywhere else before she searched Horatio's room, so she would search it first, even though it was separated from the room Lucifer occupied only by a narrow dressing room.

Reaching the head of the stairs, she stepped into the corridor. Hugging the wall, she slid along, tensing with each footstep, praying for no creaks. The door to the front corner room loomed out of the darkness; it was shut.

She halted, sparing a moment to take it in and breathe a little easier. The image of her nemesis sprawled on his stomach in the big bed at the Grange flashed into her mind. She'd survived the sight once. Even more to the point, tonight she wasn't going to open his door.

She swiveled her gaze to the opposite door, the

one to Horatio's room. It stood open – another piece of luck. Mrs Hemmings had told her that, other than tidying, they'd left the room as it was. Confidence welling, Phyllida resisted the urge to hurry; keeping to her careful glide, she covered the last yards to the door and moved inside.

Halting, she listened, senses straining for any sound, any hint she'd alerted anyone to her presence. Around her, the huge house remained silent, inanimate yet with a presence of its own. Nowhere in that presence could she sense any threat.

Drawing in a steadying breath, she looked around. The room was large, the curtains drawn. She could see enough to avoid the furniture, but not enough to be certain what it was. Grasping the doorknob, lifting to minimize any scrape, she eased the door into its frame. She didn't push it fully closed, didn't want to risk the sound of the bolt falling home. But it was shut enough for her purpose, wedged tight enough that it couldn't swing open.

She still needed to move quietly, but she no longer needed to skulk. Surveying the room, she blew out a breath. Searching thoroughly was going to take more than a few minutes.

The huge bed stood foursquare between twin windows overlooking the lake. A large blanket chest stood at its foot; another heavy chest stood back against one wall. There were two large tallboys, both with deep lower drawers, and three huge armoires. The traveling writing desk could be in any one of them.

An escritoire filled one corner; a comfortable armchair sat before the hearth. The long bay window overlooking the kitchen garden was fitted with a window seat.

Moving past the bed, Phyllida parted the curtains at one side window. The moon was high; silver light streamed in. She looked up – the curtains hung from large wooden rings; both rings and rod were polished from frequent use.

Holding her breath, she drew the curtains evenly back. The rings didn't rattle. Exhaling, she circled the bed and did the same with the other side window, then, for good measure, with the bay window as well.

The result was good – not daylight, but sufficient to search without worrying that she would knock something she hadn't seen to the floor. Fate was on her side tonight. Confidence brimming, she knuckled down to her task.

The desk was nowhere in open sight, but both Mrs Hemmings and Covey had tidied – they might have tidied it away. Phyllida started with an armoire. The deep shelf at the top looked promising; she fetched the chair from the escritoire and checked, but the shelf held only boxes. The chest by the wall held only clothes. She spent minutes wrestling out the bottom drawers of the tallboys, all without making a sound; they were filled with books. The other two armoires were similarly disappointing. By the time she reached the blanket chest, her spirits were sinking. The chest was filled with blankets and linen.

Closing the chest, she sank down on it. The confidence that had fired her thus far – the conviction that tonight she had to find the letters and would – had faded. Yet as she glanced around the room, she couldn't quite believe that the desk wasn't here. She'd felt so sure it would be.

Her scan of the room had her swiveling around; she ended staring at the bed. She rose and looked under it.

Nothing. Heaving a dejected sigh, she clambered to her feet. One boot toe scraped on the polished boards; the sound wasn't loud, but she warned herself to be careful. She still had to search the rest of the rooms on this floor.

She headed for the door, then halted. What about the curtains – would anyone notice if she didn't close them? She frowned at the wide bay window and decided those curtains, at least, she would have to close.

Only fear of detection kept her from trudging dejectedly across the floor. Rounding the window seat, she reached up to the curtains bunched at that end. Her gaze fell on the window seat. Her hand froze on the curtain.

The window seat was a chest in disguise. The padded, chintz-covered top was hinged. Hope flared anew. Phyllida left the curtains wide and moved to the center of the window seat. Sliding her fingers under its edge, she gripped, then lifted. The long seat lifted up.

It was a weight, but she eased it over – at the

very last, her fingers slipped and she lost her grip. The padded edge hit the windowsill with a muted thud. Muted enough to ignore. Phyllida looked down at the length of dark chest and prayed: *Please, let it be here.*

The interior of the chest was deeply shadowed. The lid shaded it and the side windows were too far away to throw much light inside. She would have to search by feel.

She started at one end. The chest was divided into three compartments. Finishing one, she stood and massaged her back, taking a few steps before bending to the compartment at the other end. That, too, proved disappointing.

Standing before the middle section – the last place in this room left to search – she stared into the shadowed chest. Then she sighed, bent, and reached into it.

Her fingers touched polished wood. Her heart leaped. Instantly, she quelled it, reminding herself of the need for care. If she shifted wooden objects around, there'd be bumps and knocks – just the sort of sounds to wake people she didn't want to wake. Like one blind, she felt with her hands, fingers outlining the shapes for her mind.

Walking sticks. A shooting stick. Wooden boxes – could this be it? No – too small. She reached further, easing her fingers between the boxes, trying to ascertain if there was a bigger boxlike object underneath.

Her fingers touched the planks at the bottom of the chest.

At the same instant, a light breeze wafted past her cheek, stirring her hair. Phyllida froze.

No window was open. The only door was the one to the corridor – the one she'd wedged shut.

That door, behind her, was now open.

Slowly, she straightened. Her wildly flickering senses screamed the information that there was someone in the doorway, blocking it. The murderer?

She felt him step forward and whirled—

'Well, well. Why am I not surprised?'

Her breath came out in a rush. Her mind all but wilted with relief. *Thank God, thank God* – the refrain filled her head, then abruptly died.

Her eyes flared wide, then wider; her wits tripped over themselves, then seized. Her lungs already had; they squeezed tight. She stood and simply stared.

Lucifer was standing just inside the room. His broad shoulders did indeed block the doorway. The moonlight washed over him, lovingly illuminating every muscle, every angle, every plane.

He was naked.

One part of her mind wanted to ask where his nightshirt was; the rest considered the point irrelevant. Wherever it was, it wasn't on him, and that was all that mattered.

Her gaze slid helplessly over him, from his face, limned in silver, over his shoulders, his chest. The muscles of chest and forearms were shaded by dark hair, while those of shoulders and upper arms formed smooth, sculpted curves. She could imagine their heat beneath her palms. The band of hair across his chest coalesced to a dark line that trailed down, over his ridged abdomen. His waist was narrow, as were his hips. She couldn't stop herself; she didn't even try. Her gaze lowered. Her mouth dried.

She felt her lips part, her jaw drop; she couldn't summon a single coherent thought. By the time her gaze reached his bare feet, her face was aflame.

In his right hand he was carrying a naked sword, its edge winking silver in the moonlight. He held it in a relaxed grip, as if he were used to wielding it. It was presently pointing at the floor.

Not so that other part of him, equally naked, equally unsheathed. That was pointing—

She wrenched her gaze upward and fixed it on his face. Even then, she couldn't breathe. She could feel his gaze like a living thing, a warm weight on her skin. He was watching her, considering her, his eyes heavy-lidded.

Then he smiled, a flash of white in his dark face. It wasn't a comforting smile. With the sword in his hand, he looked like a pirate. A naked pirate. Fully aroused. With wicked thoughts filling his mind.

He stepped forward; she stepped back – the backs of her booted calves struck the chest.

Without taking his eyes from her, he reached behind him and closed the door. The click of the latch sounded loud in the suddenly warm dark.

'I suppose,' he murmured, his voice deep, his

tone languidly conversational, 'that you're going to be stubborn and refuse to tell me what you came here looking for.'

What she came here looking for. The letters? An alternative truth rose in her mind; she quickly buried it.

He stalked slowly toward her; she struggled to keep her gaze on the naked blade – the one the moonlight was glinting on. She'd seen Jonas in various stages of undress, but nothing had prepared her for this.

The letters. She'd intended telling him about them in the morning. Why not now? She looked into his face. He was close enough now that she could see his eyes glinting, could appreciate the subtle changes – changes she'd seen before.

Desire – he desired her with an almost brutal intensity. A thrill slithered down her spine. What was he planning – what would he do to her if she refused to tell?

'I . . .' Her voice wavered; abruptly, she lifted her chin and looked him in the eye. 'I don't want to tell you yet.'

He halted in front of her, a yard away. He held her gaze, then his lips curved. His expression held no disappointment, only a keen anticipation.

'I'll just have to torture it out of you, then.'

The intent was there, ringing in his voice, yet the promise was not one of pain but of pleasure – pleasure too tempting to resist, too powerful to withstand. The threat filled her mind with images of warm flesh, hard muscle, silk sheets, and burning touches.

She licked her lips. 'Torture?'

His eyes had never left hers. They searched briefly, then he nodded. 'Hands up.'

The sword flashed upward between them. Phyllida jumped.

'Up.' He gestured with the sword.

Frowning inwardly, she raised her hands, palms facing him, up to shoulder level.

'Higher.'

The sword flashed again; she frowned openly, but raised her hands to head height.

The sword tip hovered level with her nose, then slowly lowered . . . she followed it with her eyes. It stopped, resting on the top button of her shirt, just above her breasts.

She looked up – the sword flashed. Openmouthed, she watched as the button rolled over the floor and under the bed. '*What* . . . ?' The word came out as a strangled squeak.

She looked back at his face.

He grinned. 'I've always wanted to do this.'

The sword flashed again – once, twice – *pong, ping*. Her shirt gaped fully open. Instinctively, she reached to pull it closed.

'Oh, no.' The sword flickered warningly before her, quicksilver in the moonlight. 'Keep your hands up.' He paused, studying her face. 'You're not ready to confess yet, are you?'

She looked into his eyes, glinting beneath heavy

lids, pure temptation in the night. If she told him all, he'd stop. If she told him, he wouldn't have any reason for continuing . . . and then she'd never know. 'No.'

His head tilted, just a little; his gaze grew more intent. He hesitated, then asked, 'Are you sure?'

The words were quiet, direct; she understood what he was asking. The night shimmered around them, filled with desire so potent she could taste it. It didn't all come from him. They stood three feet apart, bathed in moonlight, he completely naked, she in breeches with her shirt gaping. And both of them were thinking of taking that next step – of closing the distance between them, of feeling skin against naked skin.

Her fingers itched, her palms burned, her skin heated.

'I'm sure.' She heard the words, felt them fall from her lips, sensed them deep inside her. She was sure – she wanted to know and with him she could learn and still feel safe. If the murderer had been a better shot, or if she hadn't fought so hard this morning, she might have died not knowing; that seemed a fate too sad, too pathetic, to contemplate. Lifting her chin, she fixed him with a direct and, she hoped, challenging look. In for a penny, in for a pound. 'What next?'

Humor lit his face, then was gone. 'If you're not going to confess, then you'll have to do exactly what I say.' The 'exactly' was invested with particular emphasis. 'To begin with, you have to stand . . . absolutely . . . still.'

His gaze dropped as he said it. The sword flashed again – a quick zigzag. The two buttons closing her breeches flew off into the night.

The breeches gaped. Phyllida sucked in a breath and fought the urge to lower her hands.

'Keep them up,' he murmured as if reading her thoughts. 'Now . . . what have we here?'

His deep purr made her toes curl. His gaze remained fixed below her waist.

The sword rose, its tip lifting one side of her jacket. His gaze rose with it to lock with hers. 'Slip it off. One arm at a time. Keep the other hand up.'

She kept her expression bland; her nerves were skittering. Her stomach was one tight knot. His face right now branded him all pirate – all male predator – but it was desire that burned in his eyes. She did as he said, sliding the jacket off – it hit the window seat behind her. The instant it did, he was busy with the sword again, tangling it in one side of her loose shirt. He lifted, and drew the shirt – slowly – from her breeches, then slid the fabric over her shoulder, tugging it sideways until the seam lay over her upper arm, trapping her arm by her side. He repeated the exercise, trapping her other arm in the same way.

That accomplished, his gaze did not return to her face but fastened on her breasts, firmly bound in linen bands.

Phyllida swallowed.

'You were brave coming here tonight.' Eyes narrowing, he brought the sword tip in to rest at the top of the band between her breasts. 'Brave – and reckless.'

He lifted his gaze to hers fleetingly, then drew the sword down and away. She glanced down. He'd sliced cleanly through just one layer.

'Take a deep breath – now!'

His voice rang with such command that she'd obeyed before she'd thought. The bands slipped, slid, then unraveled in a rush. They clung for an instant, then gave up their hold, collapsing around her waist.

Leaving her breasts naked, exposed to his gaze. She quaked; she couldn't bring herself to look into his face.

But she knew he was looking – she could feel the warmth of his gaze. A slow flush suffused her. Her nipples crinkled, then puckered tight.

He moved then, transferring the sword to his left hand. He stepped closer – his lower body came into view and she quickly raised her gaze. To his chest, to the fascinating pattern of silver-etched muscle and shadow. He bent his head; his lips traced lightly along her temple. He shifted closer, so that all along one side she could feel his heat.

She was breathing quickly, as if she'd run a race.

His right hand rose; he trailed the backs of his fingers along her collarbone, then reversed his hand. It lowered; she watched him cup her breast, then slowly close his fingers about it. His voice was a dark whisper, his lips close to her ear. 'Now let's see how much of my torture you can take, before you beg for mercy.'

His fingers tightened; she looked up on a gasp. His lips closed over hers.

Lucifer took her lips, took her mouth. He deliberately let passion flare, let the smoldering embers catch fire, then drew back.

He was operating on instinct, primal instinct – a primitive blend of wants, needs, and desires. He wanted her – wanted to possess her, to brand her unequivocally his. After the shock of the morning, and the consequent realization that he'd come within minutes of losing her – of never having her at all – he needed to make her his.

But he also needed her with him, needed her to share the moment fully, needed her to want him as much as he wanted her. To desire him as deeply as he desired her. He desired her as he had no other – wanted her and needed her in myriad ways, some entirely new to him. That emotion he'd hoped never to feel had sunk its claws deep, so deep he didn't even want to shake free.

He was a willing captive – he wanted her to be one, too.

So he drew back from the kiss until their lips parted, not even by an inch but enough to breathe. Enough for her to be fully aware, to feel, to know. To watch from beneath heavy lids.

His hand at the back of her waist still held the sword; the hilt was pressed to her back. Releasing her breast, he slipped his fingers into the folds of her bands; slowly, he drew the linen strip free, then let it fall to the floor. He splayed his hand across her naked midriff, then, lightly caressing her breast on the way, trailed his fingers to her shoulder. He traced the bare roundness; her skin shimmered pale in the moonlight. Instinct prodded; he bent his head. With his lips, he followed the line his fingers had laid over her shoulder, then continued lower, fingers artfully stroking, lips following, until he cupped her breast and lifted the tight peak to his mouth.

Her gasp shivered through the room. Her knees weakened; he tightened his arm about her, bringing her hip against his thigh. He'd warned her he would torture her and he did – rasping her sensitive flesh with his tongue, then suckling hard enough to make her cry out.

The evocative sound ripped through him and set his instincts racing. He shifted across her, trapping her thighs between his, and turned his attention to her other breast, repeating the torment until her hands, trapped low by her shirt, reached for him. Her fingers gripped, then sank into his flanks.

He raised his head and kissed her, took all she offered, all she gave; the flames of desire licked hotly, hungrily. Lifting the sword, he stood it in the open chest behind her. Then he spread his hand across the back of her hips and drew her fully against him.

She murmured, not in protest but in discovery. He held her close, letting her feel the flagrant promise of his body, the heady certainty of pleasure to come.

Her clothes chafed. He lifted his head, then lifted both hands to her shoulders, caressing briefly before sliding his hands down her arms, taking the shirt to her wrists. Her eyes were open but screened beneath lids sensuously heavy; her breathing was rapid, shallow. He paused, hands light on hers. She drew in a deeper breath, held it, and drew her hands from his, tugging them from the sleeves.

He held the shirt until she was free, then dropped it in the chest behind her. Closing his arms around her, he slid his palms along her back, urging her to him, glorying in the exquisite sensation of her silken skin, already heated, brushing, then settling, then sinking against his chest.

She looked up at him briefly; her gaze came to rest on his lips. Her hands rested lightly on his arms; she pushed up, fingers tracing, flexing, over the muscles, then up and over his shoulders. Stretching on her toes, she lifted her lips and touched them to his.

He waited; their breaths mingled. Then she angled her head and kissed him. He opened his mouth and welcomed her in, teasing and tempting her. He held tight to their reins and let her play, let her explore, let her learn.

When she was totally enthralled, he closed both

hands about her waist, then slid them lower, easing her breeches down. They didn't fall from her – she was too curvaceous for that – but they now gaped front and back. Their kiss had become a heated melding; he caressed her boldly, then slid both hands deep beneath her breeches and closed them about the firm hemispheres of her bottom. Her skin was flushed; he kneaded, deliberately possessive. Her hands clenched on his nape, then speared into his hair and fisted.

She moved against him, her body lifting, caressing – a siren's song as old as time. He understood; gliding one hand from her bottom, over the curve of her hip, he splayed his fingers over her stomach, pressing until she moaned and repeated her instinctive demand. Then he gave her what she wanted.

He'd caressed the soft flesh between her thighs before; Phyllida wanted to feel the magic again. He traced and played, then entered her, one finger sliding deep and stroking, but it wasn't enough – not nearly enough.

She wanted more, much more – she knew exactly what she wanted.

Drawing back from the kiss, she lifted her weighted lids and looked down. Then she reached down, and closed her fingers gently about him. He tensed; the fingers caressing her slowed. Fascination washed over her.

So hard, so male, yet so delicate. Her fingers brushed, reached, traced, lingered on the softest skin she'd ever touched, then she closed her hand again.

A groan reached her. She glanced at his face just as he raised his head. The moonlight highlighted features set, hard-edged, etched with desire. She tightened her grip and watched his face grow taut, felt his body react.

It was too tempting not to experiment. To see just how much tenser she could make him, how much pleasure she could lavish on him with just that simple touch. Rigid became more rigid; his whole body hardened against her.

He drew in a huge breath, looked down at her, then his head swooped and he took her lips, her mouth, in a kiss that poured fire down her veins. His hand left her; his fingers locked around her wrist and he drew her hand from him. He bent, wrapped both arms around her hips, and lifted her against him.

She didn't want to end that kiss; she framed his face with her hands and, now above him, kissed him hungrily as he walked to the bed. He stopped by its side; he juggled her – she felt him blindly groping, then he flung the covers back. His arms locked her to him. Holding her tight, he kissed her back – a heated duel ensued – it quickly spun out of control. Desire raged through them in a hot tide.

He pulled back with a gasp. He stared up at her face, his breathing ragged, his eyes black pools. They searched her face, her eyes. She looked steadily back at him, her pulse racing, her breathing fragmented.

He reached up again as if to kiss her, but held off with less than an inch between their lips.

'Tell me you want this as much as I do.'

A command and a plea – she heard both, felt both.

She slid her hands into his hair. 'I want it more.' She kissed him ravenously, letting all she felt flow freely, letting the wild desire, the wanton rush of feeling, the excitement, the sensual joy, the anticipation, pour from her to him.

He drank it in, then broke from the kiss and tossed her across the bed. His brief laugh was harsh. 'That's impossible.'

She didn't argue, but he was wrong. He'd done this before; he knew what was to come, but she'd never experienced it. And she wanted to – with him, tonight.

It felt right, so very right.

He reached for her boots; she let him slide them off. He reached for her breeches and she lifted her hips. He pulled the breeches from her, then let them fall, his gaze locked on her.

She lay naked – as naked as he – and let him look.

He couldn't seem to look away. He knelt on the bed, first one knee, then the other. A ripple of excitement shivered down her spine as he crawled on all fours to come over her. Then, slowly, he lowered himself to her.

It was a shock – a sensual shock – feeling his hard weight settle upon her, sensing his strength, the reined power in his body, feeling the rasp of crisp hair against her sensitive skin. He caught her hands and moved them to his shoulders. He looked into her eyes, then dipped his head.

'We're going to take this slowly. Very, very slowly.'

Was he murmuring to her, or repeating an injunction to himself? His lips brushed hers, then slid along her jaw until he nuzzled her throat. His hands pressed down into the mattress, easing beneath her. They traced down her back, caressing as they went. They stopped at her hips, closing possessively.

'This is going to hurt. You know that, don't you?'

She lay beneath him, feeling his heat surround her, feeling her own heat rise in response. His hips lay across her thighs, his erection hot and heavy between them. She closed her eyes and whispered, 'Yes.'

He said nothing more, asked nothing more. His hands slid lower, tracing the backs of her thighs, then gripping and parting them. He settled between, reached between.

He caressed her, over and over until she thought she'd scream. Her body arched beneath his and still he stroked, probed. She was slick and wet, all but melting when he withdrew his hand; gripping her hips, he eased into her.

It did hurt, but from the first touch of that incredibly soft skin at the entrance to her body, where she so longed to feel him, she knew she couldn't live without having him inside her. The conviction was so strong that despite the discomfort, she tilted her hips to urge him in.

He stilled, fingers clamping hard about her hips, anchoring her. 'No – just lie still.' The words were strained, uttered against her throat. He waited until she eased back before pressing inward once more.

Slowly, steadily, he filled her. She felt her body stretching and marveled. Then he stopped. He lifted his head, found her lips, and kissed her deeply. She responded eagerly, breathless and yearning – quite for what, she wasn't sure.

She had only an instant's warning – the sudden coiling tension that gripped him. He drew back and thrust into her.

Her scream spilled into their mouths; she arched beneath him, but almost immediately the sharp pain receded. She eased back, into the bed, tensed muscles gradually releasing. He lay still, upon her, within her, and kissed her. She kissed him back, letting him catch her up in the caress, willingly following his lead.

His experienced lead; she realized that when he finally lifted his head. Her body felt invaded, he lay heavy within her, but the pain was gone. He looked down at her, dark eyes glinting. His expression was one she'd never seen before, set and locked, passion driven. He searched her face – she had no idea what he saw, but it seemed to reassure him. Bending his head, he set his lips to hers. Her hands resting lightly on his shoulders, she gave herself up to the kiss, up to him. Then he moved.

Until he did, the sensation of being so stretched, so filled, hadn't fully registered. As he withdrew, then returned, riding her slowly, the sensual realization impinged again and again.

Her body stirred beneath him. She found his rhythm and matched him, rising to meet him. The effortless joining, the repetitive glide of his body into hers, became her reality. His body shifted against hers, crisp hair rasping her sensitized skin. She slowly heated as if he were fanning a furnace deep within her. Her senses swirled, whirled; the surge of his tongue into her mouth mirrored his possession of her body.

She was his – her fingers tightened, sinking into the muscles of his upper arms. She held tight as the world fell away and only they remained, skin to heated skin. Desire lapped, a warm sea washing over them, through them.

He said it would be slow – she'd felt no sense of urgency, not at first. But something – some compulsion, some blinding physical need – was steadily swelling inside her. Something hot, tight, coiling inside her – with every thrust he touched it, stoked it, fanned the flames higher.

She drew back from the kiss with a gasp; pressing her head back, into the bed, she arched and struggled to breathe, struggled to urge him nearer. Deeper. She needed him there, deep and hard – suddenly, she was sure of it.

He raised up, arms bracing, lifting his chest from hers; his next thrust rocked her.

She gasped again; her fingers trailed, nails sharp, down his chest. The crisp hair that brushed her palms focused her mind on the feel of crisp hair rasping between her widespread thighs. Spreading her hands, she ran them over his ribs, then around – the heat inside her coiled tighter, almost painfully tight . . . she rose, hands sliding to his back, then clinging tight as she lifted her lips to his.

He took them in a kiss that was almost savage – his weight shifted. He leaned on one arm, his other hand curving over her bottom, tucking her hard against him, holding her there as he thrust deeply – again, again.

The heat inside her exploded; her lower body clenched. A silvery sensation, brittlely intense, speared through her, then the spasm dissolved in a burst of glory. A river of feeling welled and washed through her, soothing away her compulsive heat, leaving a different warmth in its place.

She clung to him and rode the warm tide.

He laid her down, then followed, but he rolled onto his side, then onto his back, taking her with him. She ended sprawled atop him with him still hard within her. She'd melted – she couldn't move. Resting her head on his chest, she lay and luxuriated in heavenly delight.

How much time passed before her wits re-engaged and she realized she still lay naked atop him, with his hand lazily, yet somehow intently, stroking her naked bottom, she didn't know. The realization was suddenly there, along with another – he was still hard within her, filling her. His body was still strung tight with that tension she now recognized. He hadn't . . .

She lifted her head and looked into his face. He studied her eyes, then raised a brow. She blushed, grateful he couldn't see it in the moonlight. 'What now?' Presumably there was a next step.

His lips curved, his eyes glinted. 'I did say we'd take it slowly.'

Her skin was still heated, dewed where he caressed; in contrast, the air felt cool. She had felt relaxed to her toes, but tension was returning along with her wits. She licked her lips. 'What does that mean?'

His wicked smile flashed. 'It's easier to demonstrate.'

He reached down and curled his hands around her thighs. He tugged, and she let him bend her knees up, shift her and mold her – she ended sitting astride him, knees bent, calves tucked to his flanks, hands on his chest, looking down at him. His face held more pain than smile as he lifted her hips slightly, then let her sink down again.

'Oo-oooh.' Exhaling slowly, she closed her eyes and let her head fall back.

'Does that hurt?'

'Hurt?' Opening her eyes, she looked down at him. She couldn't find words to describe how it felt. 'It doesn't hurt.'

'Good.' He lay back, sinking deeper into the bed beneath her. 'So do it again.'

She did, lifting up without his help, although his hands still rode her hips, guiding her. He would let her rise only so far before he stopped her. She sank down and watched his lids fall, watched desire deepen the lines in his face. A new eagerness gripped her – she rode him slowly, concentrating on the feel of him pressing into her softness, concentrated on caressing him like that.

The tension investing his body increased; she felt it through her hands, through her thighs – saw it in his face. She was heating, too. His hands left her hips to close over her breasts; his fingers played – her urgency grew.

Then he rose beneath her and brought his mouth to her breasts. Sharp sensation speared her; she nearly died. Nearly saw rapture again. She clung desperately to her wits as he laved, sucked, teased. The wet spots felt cool against her burning skin.

One hand returned to her hip – he gripped and slowed her. Slowed her until she was nearly frantic, mindless with the need to take him deeper, harder, faster. She spread her thighs and pressed down on him. She rose again – he halted her and pressed her down. And took one turgid nipple into the hot wetness of his mouth and suckled.

She cried out and plunged down, pressing him high inside her. Her world came apart, fragmenting into glimmering shards of rapturous wonder. They penetrated her skin, spread, and melted, until she was a mass of glowing heat with him hard and vibrant at her core.

With a sob, she put her arms around his shoulders, held his head to her breast, curled herself around him, and clung tight.

Gradually, he moved back, drawing her down with him. His breathing was harsh in her ear. Every muscle in his body was locked tight.

'Why?' She whispered the word against his skin.

Lucifer lay beneath her and couldn't think enough to form a coherent thought. 'I wanted you more than once, but . . .' He lost the thread. She was hot and so tight around him. He brushed a kiss to her temple. 'In a moment.' His voice was a gravelly rumble, almost hoarse with need.

He'd wanted her more than once, but she'd been untried, untutored. If he'd had his wicked way with her, he'd have had her three times, and she'd have cursed him in the morning. Instead, once inside her, he'd stayed deep, moderating the length and thus the force of his thrusts to minimize the abrasion and pressure to her delicate flesh. So he'd been able to enjoy having her come apart in his arms with him sunk inside her twice . . . thus far.

Lifting her, he withdrew from her, sliding from beneath her. She murmured, tried to clutch and hold him. He soothed her with a kiss along her back. 'You have to do all I say, remember?'

She slumped onto her stomach. 'So what should I do?'

He reached for a pillow. 'Absolutely nothing. It's my turn now.'

She lay boneless and let him lift her hips and stuff the pillow beneath them. He knelt between her legs and bent one slender limb, nudging it to the side, knee almost level with her waist. Then he touched her, leaned over her, and slid home.

Her breath fell from her in a gasping moan.

'Did that hurt?'

She shook her dark head and pressed back against him. He took what she offered, sinking deeper into her body. Arms braced, he lowered his head and dropped a kiss on her shoulder.

'Just lie still and let me love you.'

She did – he would have thanked her if he'd been able to form the words. Instead, he thanked her with his body. She lay hot, naked, and completely open before him; he filled her, his hips pressed to her firm derriere, the smooth hemispheres glowing palely in the moonlight. The curves caressed him, her body welcomed him, enclosing him in slick, sweet heat. The musky scent of her rose and wreathed through him; he drew it deep, and felt the beast within him slip its leash.

Beneath him, he felt her stir. She didn't move, but her body tightened about him. He reacted instinctively, pressing his hips to her bottom, thrusting deep, rotating just enough to lift her hips in a roll.

She caught her breath and pushed back, then eased down again. He gritted his teeth, withdrew further, held back, then filled her slowly. He sank home, rolled, withdrew – she moaned.

Filled with feminine entreaty more primitive than words, the sound shredded his much-tried control. He rode her hard, plunging even deeper; she met him, urging him on. He'd meant to be gentle, but she was wild and wanton – he responded in the same way.

She shattered beneath him in a climax so intense he felt it in his bones. She spasmed so hot and tight about him, he thought he'd lose his mind. And then he did. Lost all touch with reality as he lost himself in her. Lost his soul to her heat, lost his heart to her.

CHAPTER 13

Phyllida woke. She lifted her lids; through the nearby window she could see the sky. A gray light washed over the darkness, presaging dawn, but dawn was not yet here.

Her lids fell; she snuggled deeper into the warm cocoon of the covers. Every muscle in her body felt stretched, released. The heavy arm across her waist was comforting.

She half sat up with a jerk – or would have, but that hairy arm tensed and held her down.

Lying on her side, she sent her senses searching. Lucifer lay sprawled on his stomach alongside her, one arm flung over her. And he was awake. And naked. And so was she. Escaping this while maintaining her composure was not going to be a simple matter.

Unfortunately, rack her brains though she did, she could recall no teachings on the etiquette of leaving a gentleman's bed. If he'd been asleep, she'd have slipped away – and worried about meeting him face-to-face later. Fully clothed, she'd have managed with tolerable calm.

But naked? With him naked beside her?

If she lay there thinking about it anymore, she'd end in a witless panic. She turned; his arm slid over her waist. On her back, she glanced sideways at his face, half buried in the pillow. 'I have to go.'

Only one of his eyes was visible; it opened and regarded her – far too intently for her liking.

'You haven't yet told me what you were looking for, which is presumably why the murderer is after you.'

'It's not, but it's nearly dawn. I have to get through the wood and into the Grange. If you call later this morning, I promise I'll tell you everything.'

He didn't lift his head – he just shook it. He looked stunningly handsome with his black hair rumpled; had she done that? Her fingers itched.

'I was going to come and interrogate you this morning, but the present situation has a great deal to recommend it in terms of extracting information.'

She frowned. 'What do you mean?'

'I mean that you won't be leaving this bed until you've told me all.'

'Don't be silly – I have to leave before your household gets up. You won't want your servants to know I'm here.'

Lucifer shrugged. 'If you don't mind, why should I?' He was going to marry her; in the circumstances, everyone would turn a blind eye.

She stared at him, blank-faced, then her eyes flashed. 'Well, I *do* mind!'

She tried to push his arm from her. He sighed and turned – and drew her into his arms. She quieted. He rolled her until she lay on her side, all but nose to nose with him, his arms locked around her, her legs tangled with his, his erection pressed to her soft belly. He looked into her eyes. 'In that case, you'd better start talking.'

Her expression was impossible to read; only her dark eyes, still wide, still lustrous with lingering satiation, showed her awareness of his state. Of his unstated threat. Her lips firmed, obstinate to the end.

He held her gaze and waited, while the sun rose.

Phyllida capitulated. 'I've been searching for a packet of letters. Not mine – someone else's.'

'Mary Anne's.'

The leap of logic was hardly great. 'Yes. She hid the letters in her grandmother's writing desk, and then her father sold the desk to Horatio and it was delivered here before Mary Anne realized.'

'What's so threatening about these letters?'

'I don't know. All I know is that Mary Anne and Robert are desperate to get them back without anyone knowing anything about them, much less reading them.'

He searched her eyes. 'You promised not to tell anyone?'

'I swore I wouldn't reveal the existence of the letters to anyone at all.'

After a moment, he nodded. 'All right. So you were looking for the letters . . .' His gaze sharpened. 'That's why you were in Horatio's drawing room on Sunday last.'

Phyllida sighed. 'Yes.' It felt good to be able to tell him. And he'd understood about her promise; she'd thought he would. 'I was searching for the writing desk and walked into the drawing room – and saw Horatio lying there, dead.'

'Where was I?'

'You hadn't arrived yet. I'd just turned Horatio over and realized he really was dead when I heard you striding up the path.'

'And?'

'I thought you might be the murderer coming back for the body. I hid.'

A frown formed in his eyes. 'Where?'

She kept her eyes glued to his. 'Behind the door.'

His eyes hardened; so did the planes of his face. The arms about her tightened. She'd imagined telling him that she'd been the one who had hit him with the halberd a hundred times, but she'd never imagined doing it while naked in his arms.

'*You* hit me?'

'I didn't mean to! I realized you weren't the murderer and stepped forward to speak to you, and the halberd overbalanced.'

He stared into her eyes for a long, long minute; then the muscles in his arms relaxed. 'You tried to stop it. That's why it didn't kill me.'

She let out the breath she'd been holding. 'I tried, but I *couldn't*. I only managed to turn it a bit.' The remembered panic washed through her; it must have shown in her eyes.

He bent his head and touched his lips to hers.

'It's all right.' His hands smoothed over her back. 'A bit was enough.'

The comfort in his tone, in his touch, wiped away all resistance. She relaxed in his arms. Her gaze dropped to his lips. 'Well, now you know.'

His lips quirked. 'I now know a great deal that I didn't go to bed knowing, but . . .'

She blushed and looked back at his eyes – away from those devilish lips.

'I don't know why the murderer is after you.'

'I think it's because of the hat.' She told him, describing it briefly. 'But I don't know whose it was, and I haven't seen it since.'

A board creaked directly above them. They both looked up. Phyllida paled. 'Oh, Lord!'

Lucifer pulled her to him and kissed her soundly, long and deep, his hands playing over her back, her bottom. Then he released her. 'Go.'

Dazed and blinking though she was, she didn't wait to be told twice. She scrambled from the bed. Her breeches were at her feet; she swiped them up and sat to struggle into them. Crossing his arms behind his head, he lay back and watched her.

She stuffed her feet into her boots, then raced across the room and grabbed her shirt. Neither shirt nor breeches had buttons anymore. Horrified, she turned to him, arms wide, demonstrating. He raised a brow.

She glared, picked up her jacket, and shrugged into it. She stooped to pick up her bands, stuffed them in a pocket, then made for the door, one hand clutching the jacket closed, the other beneath it, holding up her breeches.

'I'll call on you later in the morning. Don't go *anywhere* before then.'

His tone gave her pause; from the door, she looked back, then nodded, hauled it open, and fled.

Lucifer listened, but she was quiet as a mouse. None of his household were yet up – he always heard them going down the stairs. She'd be safe getting out of the Manor and safe enough through the wood; no one could know she'd spent the night in his bed. Both attacks on her had been planned; their murderer was not the sort to hang around on the off chance where someone might see him and grow suspicious. She'd be safe getting home; he trusted her to reach her room undetected, not that it was of any truly great moment, but she would worry if she were seen.

The thought gave him pause. He lifted the sheet and looked down. Blood spotted both sheets.

He lowered them, then looked across the room to his exceedingly sharp cavalry saber, standing propped in the chest. Obviously, he'd been unable to sleep, thought he'd heard a noise, and gone to investigate, carrying the saber. He'd nicked his leg, but hadn't noticed in the dark. Then he'd decided to try out Horatio's bed, to see if sleep came easier there. It had. Simple enough.

Leaning back, he closed his eyes and let his mind revisit the night. His lips curved in a wicked smile.

★ ★ ★

'I want to ask for your daughter's hand in marriage.'

The words were amazingly easy to say. Lucifer turned from the window overlooking the Grange lawns and faced Sir Jasper.

Seated behind his desk, Sir Jasper beamed. 'Excellent!' Then his smile faded. He cleared his throat. 'Of course, Phyllida herself will have the final say. Headstrong female. Runs her own life, y'know.'

'Indeed.' Lucifer claimed a chair facing his father-in-law to-be. 'Apropos of that, it appears her suitors to date have left her with a distinctly jaundiced view of marriage.'

'Indeed, indeed – she's been adamant she'll have none of it.' Sir Jasper eyed Lucifer consideringly. 'Not sure if it's some odd kick in her gallop or not having a mother for so long, or what, but there it is – she declares she has no interest in marrying.'

'With due respect, she's been given little incentive to be interested. Everyone expects her to marry, assumes she will, and her suitors have sought to turn that to their own advantage.' Lucifer paused, then added, 'Few women appreciate being taken for granted.'

Especially not intelligent ladies of managing disposition. 'Because of that,' he continued, 'while I wished to make my intentions known to you, I have not yet spoken to Phyllida. We first met only nine days ago, and although I'm sure of my own mind on the matter, I'm equally sure that the way to gain Phyllida's agreement to the match lies in giving her time to convince herself of its rightness.'

'So you propose waiting before putting the question to her, heh?'

'I propose wooing her before, metaphorically, going down on bended knee. A few weeks – I'm in no urgent hurry.' An all-too-physical memory of Phyllida beneath him seared across his brain; he blocked it off, ignored his reaction, and continued. 'I believe the most inimical step I could take at present would be to press my suit.'

If he did, she'd immediately want to know why – why he wanted to marry her. He'd be forced to trot out all the conventional reasons, which would paint him in precisely the same unappealing colors as all her other suitors. The reasons were sound, but he knew they were not what she would want to hear. She would not be swayed by them.

He did have one obvious reason no other had ever had – he'd bedded her and therefore should, by all honorable tenets, make all right by marrying her. Although in some respects – the ones pertaining to honor – that struck a chord with him, it wasn't, to his mind, a wise or valid reason to advance in support of his cause.

No woman wanted to hear that she was being married because of honor's dictates. To let Phyllida believe that – to even suggest it – would be both cruel and cowardly. It was nowhere near the truth. He'd bedded her *because* he intended to marry her, not the other way around.

'I believe,' he said, 'that a course of gentle persuasion is in order.'

Sir Jasper nodded. 'You may be right. Can't hurt to try that tack.' He looked at Lucifer; his expression hardened. 'I won't hide it from you – right now I'd appreciate all the help I can get with Phyllida. This business of her being attacked – very possibly twice – has me more than worried. Can't see rhyme or reason to it myself.'

'I think we must assume that the attacker is Horatio's murderer. There's no reason to believe Colyton is harboring two men with malicious intent. But the reason he attacked Phyllida is certainly a mystery.'

'She says she has no idea why he wants to kill her.'

'Hmm. I will, of course, be continuing my investigations into Horatio's murder. With your permission, I'll extend that to include the attacks on Phyllida. It must be the same man.'

'Hard to get one's mind around any of it, but yes, I agree. It's most worrying.'

Lucifer rose. 'Again with your permission, I'll keep an eye on Phyllida. I'll be better placed than others to do so.'

Sir Jasper rose, too, shrewd consideration in his eyes. He regarded Lucifer, then nodded and held out his hand. 'Whatever permission you need, consider it given. No one I'd rather welcome as a son.'

Lucifer grasped Sir Jasper's hand.

'Well, then,' Sir Jasper said. 'Now you can get to it with a clear conscience, what?'

311

Suppressing a smile, Lucifer inclined his head. 'Indeed.'

He left Sir Jasper's study, fully intending to get to the matter forthwith. His conscience, however, wasn't entirely clear. He was concealing his real reason for marrying Phyllida; he intended to do so indefinitely. He knew what it was, yet he could barely let the concept take shape in his brain – stating it out aloud, to her or even to himself, would remain, he was convinced, forever beyond him.

It was simply too much to ask. Not now. Not ever.

He found the object of his thoughts – the object of his lust, his desire, and a great deal more – in the rose garden. She was lopping blooms and laying them in a basket. He stood under the arched entrance and watched her. Watched the sunlight play on her dark hair, striking red lights in the silky strands. Watched the pale gold gown she wore swing and sway around the slender body that had writhed beneath him last night.

Pushing away from the archway, he stepped down to the flagged path.

Phyllida rounded a bush and saw him. She waited, watching him approach with the graceful strength of some large hunting cat. As always, he was the picture of male elegance, this time in a dark coat over pale breeches that molded to his thighs before reaching into polished Hessians. Her heart thudded as he neared; she seized the moment to calm it and strengthen her hold on her emotions. She knew exactly where she stood, where he stood; she would not allow herself to imagine anything more. She inclined her head. 'Good morning.'

He halted a foot away and studied her eyes. 'Good morning.'

There was a light in his eyes, a sliding purr in his voice that warmed her more than the sun. She looked at the bush and concentrated on snipping a nicely opened rose. 'Have you found the letters by any chance?'

'I looked, but I couldn't find any writing desk, not on the first floor and not in the attics, either. Are you sure it's not downstairs?'

She frowned. 'I don't think I missed it.'

'Perhaps you should visit the Manor this afternoon and check the downstairs rooms.'

She glanced up, then nodded. 'It would be a relief to solve at least one mystery.'

'As for the question of who murdered Horatio – tell me what happened from the time you walked into the front hall to the time you left the Manor.'

'I already told you.'

'Humor me. There could be something, some little thing, that you'll remember this time.'

Laying the clippers in the basket, she turned. She recounted her movements as they strolled to the arbor at the end of the garden.

'So reaching for the hat was the very last thing you did?' He handed her to the stone seat in the arbor.

'Yes. I thought it was yours.'

'Mine?' He sat beside her. 'My coats are either black or dark blue. What would I be doing with a brown hat?'

'I didn't know your sartorial preferences at the time.' She paused, holding tight to her calm, looking at the roses nodding in the heat rather than at him. 'Anyway, I went back in the afternoon to arrange about your horses. I thought I would fetch the hat for you. I asked Bristleford. He was certain there'd been no hat in the drawing room when they found Horatio's body.'

'And mine.'

She inclined her head. 'And yours.'

She waited for him to say something about how he'd come to be a 'body.' Instead, he sat silently for some minutes, then said, 'It has to be the hat. The murderer must be convinced you'll recognize it.'

'But I haven't. That ought to be obvious by now.'

'True, so he must think you *will* recognize it – that you'll suddenly remember. Which means—' He stopped.

She looked at him. 'Means what?'

He met her gaze. 'That it's someone you've seen often, in that hat.'

'So' – she drew a tight breath – 'definitely no stranger.'

'It's someone you know.'

The words hung in the air between them, chill despite the heat. Phyllida held herself rigidly upright and fought the sudden urge to take refuge in his arms. The seat was short; he'd stretched one

314

arm along its back, behind her shoulders. His chest was temptingly near. The impulse to lean into him, to press her shoulder to his chest, to feel his arms close about her, waxed strong.

She knew what it felt like to be held in his arms. It felt safe. But . . . she wasn't the clingy sort.

She was about to look away, to switch her gaze to the safe subject of the garden, when he shifted. His arm left the seat back and curled about her shoulders; his other hand tipped up her face. His lips were on hers before she knew it, and then she was kissing him back.

When he raised his head, she frowned at him. 'What was that for?' She wriggled upright.

Lucifer released her. He searched for a light answer; only the truth filled his mind. 'Reassurance. You looked frightened.'

She gazed into his eyes, then lightly shivered and looked away. 'I am frightened – a little.'

'A little frightened is wise, but the murderer is not going to have you, too.'

She slanted him a glance. 'You sound very sure.'

'I am.'

'Why?'

'Because I won't allow it.'

Before she could utter the 'Why?' he could see in her dark eyes, he drew her to him and kissed her again. After an instant's hesitation, she relaxed and let herself flow into the kiss. The rose garden was private; too tempting. Her bodice was open, his fingers fondling one breast when she pulled back on a gasp and looked down.

'What are you doing?'

He circled her nipple with one fingertip. 'I'm sure you can guess.'

The gaze she lifted to his face was shocked. 'But . . . I've told you all I know.'

She drew back; he let his hand fall. Puzzled, he tried to see her eyes as she fussed, rebuttoning her gown. Her expression was still calm, if just a little determined. Determined about what, he couldn't guess. 'What—?'

'There's nothing I've left out.' Gown neat again, she picked up the basket and stood. 'You know it all.'

Rising, too, Lucifer was certain that last wasn't true. An unwelcome suspicion formed in his brain.

Lifting her head, she stepped out. 'I assure you there's nothing more to be gained from continuing to seduce me.'

She'd taken only two paces when his fingers locked around her elbow and he swung her back.

'What did you say?' Eyes narrowed, he looked down at her.

She returned his gaze; irritation swam in her eyes. 'You heard perfectly well.' She twisted her arm; he let her go.

'Why do you think I seduced you?'

She drew herself up – suddenly, he could no longer read her eyes. 'You seduced me in order to learn what you wanted to know. Now I've told

316

you all, there's no need . . .' She gestured and swung away.

'That isn't why I seduced you.'

His tone stopped her. She took a deep breath, then turned to face him.

'Why, then?'

Her challenge rang clearly. Yet she'd asked the very question he didn't want to face, the one he couldn't bring himself to answer truthfully. He looked into her dark eyes, and he didn't want to lie.

A gong bonged, the sound carried on the breeze from the house. They both looked, then Phyllida turned. 'That's the gong for lunch.' After an instant's hesitation, she walked on.

A moment later, he caught up and fell in beside her.

She didn't speak again until they were climbing the steps from the sunken garden. 'If you meant what you said about allowing me to search the Manor, I'll come by this afternoon.'

'I meant what I said, but we can walk back together.' Lucifer halted on the top step. 'Your aunt invited me to lunch.'

Phyllida turned toward the house. 'How convenient.'

His hand on her arm halted her. She glanced back.

He held out a small pouch. 'Before we go in, you'd better take these.'

Puzzled, she took the pouch. And felt the buttons inside. Heat rose to her cheeks. 'Thank you.'

Without meeting his eyes, she tucked the pouch under the roses in her basket, then continued along the walk.

Three hours later, Phyllida sat in a chair before the desk in the Manor's library, carefully scanning entries in the ledger open on her lap. Seated in the chair behind the desk, Lucifer watched her from beneath his lashes.

They'd left the Grange after lunch and walked to the Manor through the wood. All the way, Phyllida had maintained her usual calm composure, answering when spoken to but otherwise treating him – reacting to him – as if he were any other reasonably intelligent gentleman. She hadn't, admittedly, attempted to treat him with the dismissive air she employed with her other suitors, but by the same token, she definitely wasn't treating him like the man she'd shared a bed with last night.

He'd spent enough nights with more than enough women to know how they should greet him the next day.

Not Phyllida.

Irritation simmered, fed by frustration. He'd turned away from seducing her into telling him all, yet because of her rash actions, and his reactions, he now appeared to have done just that. If truth were told, *she* had seduced *him* into seducing her. It hadn't been his doing that she'd turned up at the Manor in breeches after midnight, searching

Horatio's room. Once he'd found her – well, what was he supposed to have done? Bowed and shown her the door?

Suppressing a snort, he tried to focus on the ledger before him. The undeniable fact that he'd used his wish to learn her secret as camouflage, a superficial, flippant covering for the deeper, darker truth, continued to niggle and irk. The situation and Phyllida had conspired to trip him up; the reality of his need, the driving urge to make her his, had completed his downfall.

Why had he seduced her? Because he'd wanted to – *needed* to. If he told her that, she'd sniff and look away, and continue believing the worst.

His gaze flicked to her; he was careful not to stare too intently.

At least she was here, safe and, for the moment, occupied. She'd gone around the downstairs rooms, but the writing desk had not materialized; she'd returned dejected, making sounds about going back to the Grange. He'd suggested she look through Horatio's ledgers to see if he'd sold the desk.

He was also going through the ledgers, searching for any entry that might qualify as Horatio's mystery item. He hadn't found anything yet.

His gaze fastened once more on Phyllida's calm face. He definitely did not like being classed with her other suitors, those who wanted her for material or social reasons, reasons that had little to do with her fair self. They were the ones who had made her lose faith in marriage. The fact that she believed he was like them irked – indeed, irked worse because, from her point of view, he'd been exploiting her, the woman – her emotions, her femaleness – all those qualities the others failed to even see.

Even if she hadn't accused him of that, he didn't like the idea that, in her mind, she might.

How to correct her misconception? There really was only one answer. Having successfully seduced her once, he was going to have to do it again. And the bar on the jump had just been raised. Indeed, now he thought of it, she'd just become an even greater challenge.

The thought made him feel immeasurably better. He thrived on challenges.

Focusing on the page before him, he realized it was the one he'd been on when Phyllida had walked into the room. Stifling a sigh, he fixed his gaze on it, and scanned.

Minutes later, the latch clicked; Bristleford walked in. 'Mr Coombe wishes to speak with you, sir. Shall I inform him you are engaged?'

'Coombe?' Lucifer glanced at Phyllida. 'Show him in, Bristleford.'

Bristleford withdrew, closing the door. In reponse to Phyllida's pointed look, Lucifer murmured, 'Coombe called a few days ago wanting first refusal on Horatio's books.'

'You're going to sell them?' She looked shocked.

Frowning fleetingly, Lucifer shook his head; his gaze swung to the door as it opened. Silas Coombe minced in; Bristleford shut the door.

'Coombe. You know Miss Tallent, of course.' Rising, Lucifer held out his hand.

Silas bowed extravagantly to Phyllida, who nodded. Then he grasped Lucifer's hand.

'What can I do for you?' Lucifer waved Silas to a chair.

'I won't keep you long.' Silas glanced at Phyllida as he sat, then faced Lucifer. 'As I mentioned, I'm interested in acquiring selected works from Horatio's collection. As you're a busy man and will doubtless have many other calls upon your time, I wondered if I might propose an accommodation that would suit us both.'

'What accommodation?'

'I would be prepared to act as your agent in selling the collection.' Silas rushed on. 'It will be a very large job, of course, quite a commitment in time, but in the circumstances, I feel the arrangement will serve us both.'

For a long moment, Lucifer said nothing; then he asked, 'Let me see if I understand your proposal correctly. You're suggesting I should consign Horatio's entire collection to you, and you would arrange the sales for a commission. Is that right?'

'Precisely.' Coombe beamed. 'It'll make life much easier for you, especially with settling in – new county, new house.' His gaze drifted to Phyllida, then he looked back at Lucifer. 'Why, I'll even arrange to have the books removed to my house in the interim.'

'Thank you, but no.' Lucifer stood. 'Contrary to

your expectations, I have no plans to dispose of any part of Horatio's collection. Indeed, if anything, I shall be adding to it. Now, if there's nothing else?'

Forced to rise, Coombe stared at him. 'You don't mean to sell?'

'No.' Lucifer rounded the desk. 'Now, if you'll excuse us, Miss Tallent and I have various accounts to check.' He steered Coombe to the door.

'Well! I mean – well, fancy that! It never occurred . . . I do hope I haven't given the wrong impression . . .'

Coombe's protestations died away. Lucifer handed him to Bristleford, waiting in the hall, then shut the library door. He strolled back to the desk. Phyllida was sunk in thought. 'What?' he asked.

She glanced up, then waved at the door. 'I was just thinking. I don't think Silas has ever worn brown.'

Lucifer resumed his seat behind the desk.

Phyllida continued to frown. 'What was he after the first time he called?'

'A book – at least one. Other than that, he was exceedingly careful to give no indication.'

'Hmm.'

Lucifer waited, but she said nothing more. After another minute of puzzled frowning, she returned to the ledger in her lap.

An hour later, Phyllida snapped the last of the recent ledgers closed. 'Horatio did not sell that writing desk.'

Lucifer looked up. 'In that case, it must still be here somewhere.'

'Humph!' Placing the ledger on the desk, she glanced at the window. 'I'll search upstairs tomorrow, but I should return home now.'

Lucifer rose as she did. 'I'll walk back with you.'

She looked at him. 'I'm perfectly capable of walking through the wood on my own.'

His jaw set. 'I daresay.' Rounding the desk, he waved her to the door. 'Nevertheless, I'll accompany you.'

She held her ground and held his gaze.

He stood there, rocklike, and looked calmly back.

When it became clear he was prepared to stand there all night, she lifted her chin, turned, and swept to the door.

She left the house with him prowling at her heels.

Lucifer didn't let her get out of arm's reach. If anything happened to her . . .

It was just as well she couldn't see his face. If he looked half as grim as he felt, she'd probably stop and demand to know his problem. Not something he could easily explain without telling her she was his. She hadn't realized it yet, but she would. By the time he finished seducing her again, she would be perfectly ready to marry him without any further explanations.

He certainly didn't need any further discussion, not with himself or with her. His role felt just right – it fitted him like a glove. Protecting women had always been his role. Even those he tempted to his bed – there was more than one form of protection. But this, following on a woman's heels ready to screen her from any danger – this was him. The essential him. A part of him that needed – demanded – almost constant exercise. He'd never gone for long without a woman to protect.

The twins, his fair and beauteous cousins, had most recently been his release, but they'd turned into harpies and insisted he leave them to their own devices. Under considerable duress and the none-too-subtle threat behind the smothering attention of society's mesdames, he'd retreated to Colyton – only to discover here the perfect answer to his need.

What, after all, was he supposed to do with his life if not to have a wife – and a family, too – to protect? What else was he, under the elegant glamour, if not a knight – protector? Until the twins had refused him and his cousins' marriages had left him too exposed to brave the ton, he hadn't fully appreciated his own nature.

To Have and to Hold, the Cynster family motto – he understood it now, appreciated all that it meant.

For him, it meant Phyllida.

He followed her through the shadows of the wood, and considered how best to break the news to her.

⋆　⋆　⋆

324

Phyllida plunged a gladiolus spike into the heart of the vase and stepped back. She eyed the arrangement through narrowed eyes, studiously avoiding the lounging presence darkening the vestry door. Collecting a handful of cornflowers, she started setting them in the vase.

She'd arrived at the Manor midmorning and searched the first-floor rooms, all except Horatio's and Lucifer's. Horatio's she'd already searched; Lucifer's . . . she didn't need to check there. While not large, the traveling writing desk wasn't so small it was difficult to see.

'How thorough was your search of the attics?'

He seemed to be following her train of thought.

'Very thorough. So now you've looked, and I've looked – the desk isn't there.'

She didn't look at him – she'd sworn she'd give him no encouragement. If he insisted on clinging to her skirts against her clearly expressed, not to say forcefully stated, wishes, she wasn't going to put herself out to entertain him.

Descending from the attics, disappointed yet again, she'd run into Mrs Hemmings in the front hall. The housekeeper had been flustered. She had a pot of jam at the crucial stage and didn't dare leave it, but she hadn't yet done the church flowers. Hemmings had picked the best blooms that morning; they were in a pail in the laundry.

She'd gladly agreed to do the vases. The notion that the murderer might be haunting the church she'd dismissed as irrational; a brisk walk up the common followed by the soothing ambience of the church had sounded just perfect. Unfortunately, the door to the library had been open. Lucifer had materialized in the doorway – he'd insisted on coming, too.

A short argument had ensued. Once again, she'd lost. It was becoming a habit – one she indulged in with no one else. Losing arguments was not her forte.

By not one word would she encourage him further.

Sticking a finger in the vase, she checked the water. 'Too low.' Grasping a jar, she walked to the door, looked out, then stepped into the sunshine. She crossed the few feet to the pump – and listened to hear if he followed. No sound – he must still be brooding darkly in the doorway.

Indeed, he seemed to find her as irritating – that was not the right word, but it was something very similar – as she found him. Irritating, puzzling, unaccountable. Utterly impossible to comprehend.

She filled the jar, then lowered the pump handle. As she turned away, her gaze swept the graveyard – a vase on a grave had blown over. She tsked and went over to the grave. Righting the vase, she filled it from her jar and resettled it against the grave-stone. Straightening, she approved of the alignment, then turned to retrace her steps.

In the lane beyond the lych-gate, Silas Coombe clicked sedately along in his high-heeled shoes.

Phyllida hesitated, then waved. He didn't see;

she put the jar down on a nearby slab and waved both arms.

Silas noticed – Phyllida beckoned.

She thought furiously while he made his way under the lych – gate and up the path. Halting before her, he bowed extravagantly, flourishing a silk handkerchief.

When he straightened, she was smiling. 'Mr Coombe.' She curtsied – Silas liked the formalities. 'I was wondering . . . I couldn't help but overhear your conversation with Mr Cynster last afternoon.' She summoned her most sympathetic expression. 'He seems quite set on not selling any of Horatio's treasures.'

'Indeed.' Silas frowned. 'A great pity.'

'I hadn't realized you were interested in Horatio's volumes.' Sinking onto the marble slab, she gestured, inviting Silas to join her. 'I had thought your own collection was quite extensive in its own right.'

'Oh, it is – indeed, it is!' Silas flicked his coattails and sat beside her. 'Just because I wish to purchase one or two of Horatio's more interesting tomes is not to say my own collection needs them for validity.'

'I had wondered . . .'

'No, no! I do assure you. My collection is quite worthy as it stands!'

'So what is it that attracts you to buying certain of Horatio's books?'

'Well—' Silas blinked. 'I . . .' He focused on her

face, then leaned closer, raising a finger to tap the side of his nose. 'There's more reason for buying a book than just to read it, m'dear.'

'Oh?'

'Can't say more.' Silas sat back, clearly pleased with Phyllida's intrigued expression. 'But I'm not one to be interested for no reason, m'dear.'

'A mystery,' Phyllida murmured. 'I do so love secrets. Surely you could tell me – I would tell no one else.'

Striving to appear foolishly fascinated, she leaned closer, then wished she hadn't. Silas blinked; the look in his eyes changed. His gaze lowered to her lips, then drifted lower still.

Phyllida fought a blush – fought the urge to jerk upright. Leaning forward as she was, the scooped neckline of her gown was revealing more to Silas than she'd intended. But . . . Silas knew something. 'Isn't there anything you'd like to tell me, Silas?'

She uttered the question gently, encouragingly. Silas wrenched his gaze up to her face. Then he grabbed her.

Phyllida gasped and tried to straighten, but Silas had his arms around her.

'My dear, if I'd known you preferred more elegant men – more sophisticated gentlemen – I'd have gone down on my knees years ago.'

'Mr Coombe!' Crushed against his chest, Phyllida dragged in a breath. His cologne nearly suffocated her.

'My dear, I've waited and watched – you'll need

to forgive the strength of my passions. I know you're unversed in the art of—'

'*Silas*! Let me go!'

'Coombe.'

The single word fell like the sound of doom. A vengeful, threatening doom.

Silas started. He uttered a sound like a shriek, released her, and leaped to his feet – almost landing against Lucifer. Silas whirled, clutching his chest, ruining his floppy bow. 'Oh, my! My word. You – you startled me.'

Lucifer said nothing at all.

Silas looked into his face and started to back down the path. 'Just having a friendly word with Miss Tallent. No harm in it – none at all . . . you'll have to excuse me.' With that, he whirled around and clattered down the path as fast as his high heels would allow.

Still seated on the slab, Phyllida watched him go. 'Good Lord.'

She knew when Lucifer's gaze left Silas's retreating figure and fixed on her. 'Are you all right?'

The words sounded like they'd been said through clenched teeth. She regarded him calmly and stood. 'Of course I'm all right.'

'I assume the impression Coombe was laboring under was mistaken?'

She shot him a frosty look, straightened her skirts, lifted her head, pointedly stepped past him, and headed up the path. 'Silas knows something – something about one of Horatio's books.'

He fell in beside her, a large, hard, darkly masculine presence pacing by her shoulder. 'Perhaps I should pay him a visit. I'm sure I could persuade him to reveal his precious secret.'

There was a wealth of menace in his tone; Phyllida was grateful Silas wasn't there to hear it – he'd have fainted on the spot. 'Whatever it is may have nothing to do with Horatio's murder. We know Silas is unlikely to be the murderer, and he certainly isn't the man who attacked me – he's too short.' She paused before the vestry door and glanced at Lucifer. 'You can't go around intimidating everyone into doing as you wish.'

His midnight-blue eyes met hers. The message in them was simple: *You think not?*

Raising her chin, she stepped into the vestry – and stopped dead. He walked into her – she would have fallen but for the arm that wrapped around her, effortlessly lifted her, then put her down two feet farther into the room.

She caught her breath and swung around. 'I left the water jar outside.'

He raised one hand – it held the water jar.

'Thank you.' She took it – her fingers brushed his. She blocked the sensation, wiped her reaction from her mind. Turning to the vase, she filled it.

The sense of menace behind her didn't abate.

'Don't do that again.'

'Don't do what?'

'Slip away where I can't see you.'

Amazed, she turned. '*Where you can't* . . . Who appointed you my keeper?'

His face hardened. 'Your father and I—'

'*You discussed this with Papa?*'

'Of course. He's worried. I'm worried. You can no longer' – he gestured sweepingly – 'waltz around the village as if you don't have someone trying to kill you.'

'You have absolutely no right to – to *dictate* to me!' She whirled, snatched up the vase, and headed into the nave. 'I'm my own person and have been for years. I'm *astonished* Papa—' She broke off; she couldn't think of words to express the jumble of her feelings. Not precisely betrayal, but certainly a sense of having been handed over . . .

She plonked the vase down on the shelf beside the pulpit, breathed in, then rearranged the disturbed blooms.

She didn't need to think to know where Lucifer was – she could feel him right behind her. After a moment, he stepped around to her side. She felt his gaze on her face, sensed him trying to glimpse her eyes. She refused to look at him.

Finishing the flowers, she brushed her hands, then tensed to step away—

Hard fingers slid beneath her chin; he turned her face to his.

He held her gaze, studied her eyes. 'Your father is seriously worried about you. So am I. He cares for you . . .' He paused, then his face hardened. 'And just so you can get your astonishment over

331

all at once, your father has agreed to let me watch over you. In his words: "Whatever permission you need, consider it given."'

She stared at him – into that harsh face, all hard angles and planes, into his eyes, filled with ruthless candor. A weight – some power – amorphous but unrelenting, invincible, inescapable, settled around her and held her. She didn't need to wonder if he was telling the truth – his eyes told her he was.

'And what of *my* permission?' Her voice was calm, steady – much more so than she felt. Her heart was thudding in her ears, in her throat.

His gaze held hers, then it lowered. To her lips.

'As far as I'm concerned, I have your permission already.'

The words were dark and low. The weight around her closed in.

Phyllida stiffened. Lifting her chin from his fingers, she looked him in the eye. 'In that, you're quite definitely mistaken.'

She stepped past him, out of the circle of that dark embrace, and walked – calmly – out of the church.

CHAPTER 14

After lunching alone, Lucifer strode into the wood and headed for the Grange. Phyllida had insisted on returning home immediately after leaving the church. He'd insisted on accompanying her. He'd seen her onto the Grange's front porch, then returned to the Manor via the wood. Now he was retracing his steps – because he couldn't bear the thought of her being simultaneously in danger and out of his sight.

Ten days since they'd first met, and look what he'd been reduced to.

He'd already visited Silas Coombe. Although almost incoherent, Silas had said enough to convince him he knew nothing about any specific volume in Horatio's collection; he'd simply hoped to lay his hands on some treasures at bargain prices. Silas was not the murderer.

Lucifer swung along the leaf-strewn path; he moved quietly, an innate hunter. There was a point where the path curved sharply, thick bushes limiting the view ahead. He rounded it – and stopped, just in time to avoid mowing Phyllida down.

She ran into him instead.

He caught her, steadied her – he had to fight not to close his arms around her. Her breasts pressed to his chest were a remembered delight; lust, desire, and that simple need she and only she evoked poured through him.

She must have felt his instant reaction. Her breath caught in her throat, then she stiffened, dragged in a breath, and stepped back.

'My apologies.' She sounded breathless; she didn't meet his eyes as she flicked her skirts straight. Lifting her head, she looked past him. 'I was on my way to your house.'

He felt her gaze touch his face; his own gaze was fixed on the empty path behind her. She hadn't brought any escort. His temper rose; hot words burned his tongue – an elemental need to lash her with them gripped him.

He swallowed the words, resisted the urge; the effort left him feeling like a beast caged. At least she'd been coming to see him. After this morning, he should probably be grateful.

Stepping aside, he gestured her on. He fell in behind her, on her heels, and waited to hear why she wanted to see him. To say she understood? To admit that she was wrong to wander about alone and that she appreciated his watchful care?

They reached the edge of the trees and she walked into the sunshine. 'I came to ask,' she said, 'if you would mind if I look through the outbuilding and storerooms.' She surveyed the former across the

334

kitchen garden. 'They're stuffed with furniture – it's possible I missed the writing desk when I searched that Sunday.'

Lucifer looked at her face, but she didn't – wouldn't – look at him. After a moment, he drew breath. 'If that's what you wish, then by all means . . .' With a bow that was cuttingly polite, he waved her on. 'You will, however, have to excuse me – there are other matters requiring my attention.'

She inclined her head haughtily and headed for the outbuilding. He watched until she entered it, then turned to the house. He marched through the kitchen, curtly dispatched Dodswell to keep watch on the outbuilding, then retired to the library, leaving strict instructions he was not to be disturbed.

Phyllida stepped into the outbuilding and finally managed to draw a full breath. Her nerves were still twitching; she stood in the silence and willed them to settle.

What was going on? In the space of a few days, her life had changed from humdrum to unpredictable, from mundane to exciting, from sleepy to intense. And it had very little to do with Horatio's murder. That might be part of the drama about her, but it was not the source of the whirlwind of change.

A hot wind named Lucifer.

Luckily, he'd left her alone. If he'd stayed, she –

335

or he – would not have been able to resist reopening their unfinished discussion. The result would not have been a happy one. She was still smarting from learning that he'd discussed her safety with her father rather than with her. No one – not Cedric, not even Basil – had simply and so arrogantly *assumed* control of her.

The thought made her so angry, she thrust it aside, bundled the whole question of Lucifer away. She looked around. The long building was filled with boxes and furniture stacked along the walls and also down the center, leaving a path circling the room.

She'd searched here first on that fateful Sunday. She'd thought she'd been efficient, yet, as she studied the jumble, hope flickered to life. The traveling writing desk wasn't big – about twelve inches wide, twelve deep, maybe nine inches tall at the back. The sloping lid had leather the color of rose lavender set into it. A handsome piece, she could recall seeing it on Mary Anne's grandmother's knees innumerable times.

She could have missed it. Determination renewed, she started checking each stacked piece, each box, moving counterclockwise around the room. Her eyes searched; her hands touched, reached, poked.

Her mind wandered.

She should never have allowed him to seduce her, of course, but even now she didn't – couldn't – regret that night. She had wanted the experience, had yearned for the knowledge. Thanks to him, she'd got her heart's desire. That, however, should have been the end of it – a bargain of sorts, an exchange completed. One night filled with passion for the answers he'd wanted. The exchange had been made, yet something lingered.

Something else. And she wasn't even sure it had been born of that night. His possessiveness was a tangible thing – she had to wonder, given his recent behavior, if it had been there before and their night of passion had been driven both by his wish for answers and by his wish to . . .

Lips thinning, she shook her head. If he'd thought that would help his cause, he would need to think again. She wasn't a possession – not his, not any man's, not even her father's. She was herself – her own woman – and she would remain so, come what may.

As long as she stayed out of his arms so she wasn't visited by that all-but-overwhelming compulsion to spread her hands over his chest, she'd be safe. Safe from him. As for the murderer, they'd have to work together to ensure he was caught. On that they did not differ. Regardless of what lay between them, finding the murderer remained a shared goal.

That thought was comforting – she didn't want to ponder why. Shifting her mind back to the task at hand, she continued steadily searching.

She was almost at the far end of the building when Lucifer paused in the doorway. He saw her and stopped, hesitated.

He wished he knew what he was doing – what he was going to do. He was operating totally on instinct, an instinct that told him she didn't understand. She thought he'd seduced her for information. Regardless of the truth of that, did she seriously imagine that after that night he'd simply shrug and walk away? That he'd stop wanting her?

While he did not wish to examine, much less explain, his deeper motives, he was more than willing to correct that particular misconception.

Stepping over the threshold, he closed the door. Light slanted through narrow windows set high in the walls; Phyllida did not notice the dimming of the light behind her. He strolled toward her, watching her shift a box and peer under a table. She bent over; lilac muslin pulled tight over her hips. He considered the sight as he neared.

She straightened; he heard her sigh. Then she replaced the box and stepped back. Into him.

She tripped backward over his boots. His arm about her, his hand splayed across her midriff, he steadied her against him. She caught her breath; dark hair sliding like silk over his shoulder, she looked up, into his face.

Their eyes met, held for an instant, then her gaze lowered to his lips. His gaze slid to hers, then to the expanse of ivory breasts revealed by her neckline. The sweet mounds rose and fell. He bent his head, turning her to him.

She stopped him, her fingers light on his cheek.

He held her in one arm, her breasts against his chest, her thighs between his. Her lips were parted, her eyes wide; her gaze was fixed, not on his eyes, but on his lips.

'Why?' The whispered question overflowed with genuine puzzlement. She lifted her eyes to his.

He looked into them and searched for a true answer. 'Desire.' He lowered his head. 'Hasn't anyone told you of that?'

He kissed her; she kissed him back, not hungrily so much as wonderingly. Her lips were soft and full, warm, tempting. They parted tentatively – a hesitant invitation; when he immediately accepted, she softened in his arms, surrendering her mouth, inviting further conquest.

Conquest of whom, by whom, was moot; he pushed the question aside and sank into her, into the delight of her, letting the feel of her awaken him fully, letting his desire for her unfurl. It was a deliciously wicked moment, and even more delicious in its promise. He closed his arms about her, bringing her fully against him. The kiss deepened; their senses swirled, whirled, waltzed.

When they came up for air, she didn't pull away. Her dark eyes searched his face, then settled once more on his lips. 'Is this desire?'

'Yes.' He brushed her lips with his. 'But there's more. You've heard the music, but that's just the introduction. There's more steps, many more movements to the dance.'

She hesitated; desire shimmered about them, a

silvery anticipation hovering, waiting . . . She drew a short breath. 'Show me.'

He drew her closer; she let him. Let him hold her hard against him so her breasts caressed his chest and her thighs met his. His hands firmed about her waist; hers slid up to his shoulders. Their gazes were locked on each other's face; slowly, he bent and covered her lips with his.

Phyllida gave her mouth, her body, readily, too intrigued, too enthralled to draw away. Walk away. Did he truly desire her? No one else ever had. Was it possible? Was it desire that lingered after their night of passion?

Those weren't questions she could leave unanswered, yet it wasn't them alone that drove her. Drove her to spread her hands and flex her fingers, sinking them into the broad muscles of his shoulders as she stretched upward against him. Their kiss deepened, heated, and she wanted to get closer, to feel his desire as more than heat – as flesh and blood, muscle and skin, hunger and yearning.

Desire flowered between them, not just his, but hers, too – a new, very delicate bud. He skillfully coaxed it and she knew he did, knew he was waiting for it to bloom. When it did, in a rush of warmth and longing that flowed over her skin, he drew back from the kiss, lips sliding to trace her jaw, then her throat, as if he could taste it.

Their breaths mingled, warm, rushed, eager yet controlled. His lips touched hers again. 'Open your bodice for me.'

A warm shiver skittered over her skin. She glanced down; three buttons fastened the front of her gown. His arms eased. Her pulse sounded heavy in her ears as she lowered her hands and set her fingers to the buttons.

She knew what she was doing; she knew why she was doing it. There was something here, between them, that explained all – excused all. Something that prompted her to feed his desire, and hers.

The third button slipped free and the gown gaped, revealing her chemise, fastened with a row of tiny buttons. She unfastened them, too. After an instant's hesitation, she drew the layers aside; she could feel his gaze on her breasts as she bared them. A heated touch, it swept them and they swelled.

She would have looked up, but he bent his head, his temple against hers as his hand rose to caress her. The arm about her tightened, holding her hips against him; his fingers touched, traced, then fondled.

He'd touched her breasts before, but only in the night when shadows had shrouded them, hiding so much from her view. His face, close by hers, showed his leashed desire in the hard angles and planes, in the dark glow of his eyes beneath their heavy lids, in the sensual line of his lips.

He touched her gently, the pads of his fingers warm and vital, circling her aureoles, teasing her nipples into bud with just a brush. He watched as her skin heated, then glowed, brought to life by his ministrations; she watched, too, watched the reverence with which he invested each caress, not seizing but worshipping – a different face of desire.

She lifted one hand to his cheek, then turned his face so she could see his eyes. They burned darkly, turbulent yet banked. Controlled. He turned his head and pressed a kiss to her palm. She stretched up and kissed him, soft, deep, as temptingly as she could, then she drew back, leaned back, pressing her breast into his hand.

She didn't need to spell out her invitation; his head bent and his lips fastened on her heated flesh, hot, wet, burning. He kissed, licked, and she shuddered, fingers tangling in his hair. She closed her eyes, waiting . . . she tensed, nerves jumping when he rasped one nipple with his tongue. Then he took her into his mouth and her body melted, then tightened as he suckled, only to ease again.

The level of heat between them rose steadily; desire thrummed. She felt it in her fingertips, felt it spread under her skin.

He raised his head and drew her close, his breathing as unsteady as hers. He breathed deeply, chest expanding, coat rasping against her naked breasts. Lips close by her ear, he murmured, 'Do you want more?'

'Yes.' The word left her lips as she lowered her hands. She plucked the sapphire pin from his cravat, anchored it in his lapel, then tugged at the folds around his throat. At the edge of her vision, she saw his lips curve. Cravat loose, she started on his shirt buttons and flicked him a glance. 'What?'

The curve deepened into a wicked smile. 'Not quite what I had in mind, but . . . do carry on.'

She did, tugging his shirt loose and baring his chest. She stared. Moonlight had not done him justice – not at all. There was a warm tone to his skin that made her palms ache; she set them to the heavy muscle band across his chest and pressed, stroked outward. He closed his eyes. She stroked down, fascinated by the contours, the ridges, by the contrast of smooth skin roughened by crisp hair. He was heavy yet lean, sleek but solid. So very real.

She skimmed her hands back up to the flat disks of his nipples; greatly daring, she pressed closer, nearer, bringing her breasts, bare and sensitive, against his lower chest. Her skin tingled; her breasts ached. Easing them against him, she circled his nipples with her thumbs.

His hands clenched at her waist; he bent his head. His lips traced a line from her temple to her ear. He gave a short laugh – a little harsh, a little shaky. 'My turn.'

He drew her closer, his hands sliding down her back. At the backs of her thighs, he stroked her skirts upward, not lifting them but frothing them until they spilled and fell over his hands – leaving his hands beneath her skirts, riding over bare skin.

She caught her breath – he stroked – heat washed over her in a prickling wave. Her senses focused on the areas he touched; she leaned her head against his chest, slid her arms around him, and let her senses follow his lead.

He cupped her bottom, fingers tracing, learning, then caressing until she shuddered and clung. Head bowed against his chest, she put out her tongue and licked – and felt him tense. She turned her head and found a nipple, and licked again. His hands clenched, then eased, then kneaded provocatively.

He bent his head and breathed against her cheek, 'More?'

She nodded, eyes shut as she savored the feel of him wrapped all around her – savored the building urge to have him closer still. 'I want you inside me.' The words left her lips before she'd thought; she might have blushed, but she was already so warm she couldn't tell. But she didn't take the words back; she couldn't lie. Not about this. 'Is all this desire?'

'Yes.' After a moment, he added, 'This, and what's to come.'

He looked up, then under her dress, his hands rose to fasten about her hips. He backed her, steering her a few steps past a rolltop desk to where a high sofa table stood by the aisle; the table touched the back of her waist.

'I take it that's not the desk in question.'

Fingers on the buttons closing his buckskin

breeches, she barely glanced at it. 'No.' She looked back at his waist. 'Wrong sort of desk.'

He looked down; his fingers tightened on her hips. 'No – not yet.'

'Yes. Now.'

He didn't argue – he moved his hands. One to her bottom, splaying, then pressing and lifting to tilt her hips. His other hand slid down her stomach until his fingers tangled in her curls, then he touched her.

Sensation speared her. She slumped, her head against his chest. 'No.' But her protest lacked strength. Another argument she'd lost. She licked her lips, her senses already following the drift of his wicked fingers. 'If you . . . I won't be able to think, later.'

'You will.' He pressed a kiss to her temple. 'I promise.' His fingers stroked. 'This time, you'll know it all.' Gently, he probed the soft flesh between her thighs, then bent his head and nudged hers; his lips found hers in a languid, open-mouthed kiss that was hot enough to scald. 'Open for me.'

The whispered words sighed through her. She moved her feet, then, as she felt him reach between her thighs, she curled one ankle around his booted calf; that gave her better balance.

'Yes.' The encouragement came with another kiss. She ran her hands, trapped between them, up over his chest, his shoulders, and clasped them at his nape. Her breasts tingled, abraded by his hair-roughened chest; exquisitely sensitive, they felt hot and tight. The kiss ended and he laid his cheek against hers; she glimpsed his face, eyes closed, expression blank.

She rested her head on his chest and gave herself up – to him, to the thrills of sensation his fingers pressed on her, to the desire that beat about them, strong and growing stronger.

He held it back – held her anchored, safe from being taken and consumed too soon. She wanted to know, to learn, to experience desire in its full glory, so he reined himself in, and reined her in, too, so she could feel and know all that was, and anticipate all that would be.

He'd touched her before as he was touching her now, yet only now did she fully realize, fully feel, the true intimacy. The slickness of her flesh, its swollen state, the growing sense of aching emptiness – these had happened before, yet only now did she appreciate them.

'Desire,' she breathed; it wasn't a question.

She lifted her head and looked into his face. She stretched up and kissed him. Brief, hungry. Their lips parted. She leaned her forehead against his jaw, and he slid one finger slowly into her.

She closed her eyes and felt her body tighten, clasping him within her. Her eyes opened and she relaxed, then he stroked. His lips brushed her temple. 'You do that when I enter you.'

He continued to stroke slowly, then withdrew and explored, only to return to slide within her again.

Whether he was learning her or teaching her, she wasn't sure, but she felt every touch, every circling glide.

Heat fell from them in waves; desire rode the tide. She could feel it all around them, a welling sea rising to swamp them. It beat in her blood and his, in an increasingly compulsive tattoo.

It was she who lifted her head and breathed, 'Now.'

From beneath heavy lids, he looked at her face, then met her eyes. His were so drowning a dark blue they seemed black. His fingers didn't cease their slow, repetitive motion. 'Can you think enough?'

For a moment, she was lost, then she remembered. She drew in a short, tight breath and nodded. Tracing one hand slowly down his chest, she felt at his waist, then slipped the buttons free.

Hot, iron-hard, he filled her hand. She closed her fingers slowly, then slid them down, then up, marveling anew at the contrast of velvety softness encasing rigid strength. She ran her finger around, then over, the broad head.

His breath shivered by her ear. Fingers closing, she looked up; eyes shut, his expression was tight, fraught.

'Does that hurt?'

'No.'

Smiling, she looked down and closed her hand again.

He bore with her torture for only a minute more.

'Enough.' His hands left her, then gripped her hips. He lifted her and balanced her on the edge of the sofa table.

She grabbed his shoulders; she wasn't far enough back to sit securely. Wild panic gripped her – exhilaration and anticipation raced through her. But she didn't want to lose her wits – not yet. There was more she'd yet to see, more she'd yet to appreciate. She wanted it all – every moment. She sucked in a breath. 'How?'

Her question snapped his attention back to her face; he met her gaze – in his eyes she saw the fight he waged to releash his need, to bring it back under control. He paused, then drew in a long breath and nodded. 'Wait.'

Fingers sinking into his shoulders, she did.

He lifted her skirts and chemise, pushing them back, catching them under her so they pulled tight across her hips and stomach. She looked down and blushed; the dark locks below her stomach curled wildly, a soft nest between her bare thighs. Her stockings were gartered just above her knees; hands closing on the bare skin above her garters, he eased her thighs wide and stepped between. He'd loosened his breeches, releasing himself fully.

She ran her hand down, fingers trailing the length of his chest, then down still farther, until she coiled her fingers around his length. He caught her wrist and moved her hand away. He grasped her hips, drew her right to the table's edge, then held her there.

He stepped closer and she caught her breath. 'Watch.'

She did.

Lucifer watched her, watched the total absorption in her face as he pressed against her soft flesh. He found her entrance, and let her feel the pressure build before, with a gentle nudge, he slipped inside. Only a fraction. Just enough for her to catch her breath, then shudder and tense. He waited, expecting her to relax again. Then he realized.

'It won't hurt – not this time. Not ever again.' He whispered the words against her hair and willed her to believe them. His control was exceptional, but so was she – exceptionally hot, exceptionally wet, exceptionally trying. 'When you relax, I'll slide into you – you already know I'll fit.'

She let out a shuddering breath. 'Yes.'

He felt her body ease, little by little, around him. At last she was open and accepting. Slowly, very slowly, he pressed into her.

Head bowed, she watched him enter her, ultimately sliding home. She shivered. He pressed deep, then settled her. Then he withdrew. Because she was watching, he withdrew all the way, then reentered her and slowly sank home. She watched him penetrate her twice more before, with a shuddering gasp, she broke.

He was waiting when she clutched his shoulders and lifted her head blindly. He caught her, caught her lips in a searing kiss, and let their reins loose. She came to him like a wanton, eager, abandoned.

She pressed herself to him, bare breasts hot against his chest, nipples tight, taunting as she shifted with each thrust.

'Put your legs about my hips.'

She did; wrapping her arms about his shoulders, she lifted herself against him. He spread his hands beneath her bottom and held her as he thrust deep, then withdrew, only to return harder, deeper. She clung to him; he filled her mouth, filled her body, bathed in her wet heat.

That heat was exquisite, burning bright, hot enough to cinder their senses. He shattered deep within her, drowning in her glory. An instant later, she followed, shuddering in his arms.

He held her close; she curled around him, resting her head on his shoulder. Their hearts thundered; his chest swelled as he dragged in a breath. He eased her down, resting the backs of his hands on the tabletop, then placed a soft kiss in her hair.

For long moments, they remained still in the silence, locked in the comfort of that intimate embrace.

Phyllida couldn't believe the depth of the pleasure that washed through her. She was floating on a sea of golden joy, anchored, held safe in his arms. Throughout the entire interlude, that was how it had been – desire, intimacy, pleasure, and joy, all safe in his arms.

They still surrounded her. Beneath her cheek, she could hear his heart beating strongly, gradually slowing as they returned to earth. Her only wish was that, rather than here, still clothed, they were naked in his bedroom. Then there would be no reason to pull away – to disturb the moment. She could lie in his arms forever, bask in his heat forever. Play desire with him forever.

Only it hadn't, really, been play. The desire that had held them, driven them, and, at the last, consumed them – that desire had been very real. Hers and his – theirs.

She lay in his arms, and wondered just what lesson he'd really meant her to learn.

'Where are you leading me?' The most pertinent question.

'You know where.'

In her heart, she did. She had known, but not believed. Now she had to. 'Where?'

Better he say it, so she couldn't pretend otherwise.

'I would never have made love to you if I didn't intend to marry you.'

He hadn't wanted to tell her – she could imagine why. 'I haven't agreed.'

He let the silence stretch, then he pressed a kiss to her hair. 'I know – but you will.'

CHAPTER 15

'You said Covey had uncovered something about Lady Fortemain. I forgot to ask – what was it?'

Seated at his desk, a stack of books before him, Lucifer glanced across the Manor library to where Phyllida sat on a straight-backed chair facing one of the bookcases. She was working along one shelf, checking each book for notations, then entering the book's details in a ledger. Covey was working likewise around the drawing room. Lucifer had started on the shelves behind the desk.

'It was an inscription in a book. "To my dear Letitia, with fond memories of our recent time together, etc. Humphrey." I understand Lady Fortemain's husband was Bentley. It appears Horatio bought some volumes from the Ballyclose library and that book was among them.'

Phyllida looked at him. 'Well, it's hardly a sensation to find such an inscription. I daresay it dates back to before Lady Fortemain married.'

'The book was published after Cedric was born.'

'Oh.'

'Indeed. However, we haven't stumbled on any

other such protestations of affection for her ladyship, so I'm not setting much stock in that at present.'

Phyllida swung back to the bookshelf. After a moment, she shrugged and continued her cataloguing. Lucifer returned to his.

His campaign to win her, to woo her into marrying him, was progressing in a slow if not steady manner. He hadn't intended to state his decision to marry her so soon, but their interlude in the outbuilding had made it imperative she know – so she couldn't imagine he'd had any other motive in seducing her. Again. He was well aware that repeating the exercise had been easy only because she desired him with an uncomplicated directness that, at least while in his arms, she made no effort to deny.

He'd worried that after they'd left the warm stillness of the outbuilding, she'd grow skittish and even more difficult. Instead, she'd unsettled him with her continuing calm, as if she were coolly considering him and the question he hadn't yet asked. He wouldn't ask – not until he was sure of her answer; that was the strategic course. As long as she hadn't refused him, he could continue to press his suit, albeit carefully.

He wasn't fool enough to take gaining her agreement for granted; she had an entrenched belief that marriage was not for her. Her cool appraisal suggested he'd made her revisit that belief, but she hadn't yet changed her mind.

He needed to tread warily. Seducing a lady into matrimony was not a game he'd played before; he wasn't sure of the rules. But he'd never yet failed in a seduction – he wasn't going to start with Phyllida Tallent. How to seduce a lady of managing disposition? Thanks to her previous suitors, she had no appreciation of her womanly charms, much less their effect on him; the notion that her sweet self held the power to sway him was bound to be attractive. He'd need to make an effort to be more manageable than he was, but if that was her price, he'd pay it. He'd unblinker her vision, show her what might be, then leave her to convince herself how desirable that was.

Desire, in all its forms, was on his side. He only had to touch her to feel it flare – sometimes he only had to meet her dark eyes to be conscious of their mutual need. He could afford to give her time to decide that, despite her qualms, marrying him was an excellent idea.

For the past two days – yesterday and today – he'd pursued the strategy of propinquity, the notion that being constantly with him would help quell whatever qualms she possessed. On both mornings, he'd called at the Grange after breakfast; yesterday, after finishing her search of the outbuilding and storerooms, she'd joined him here. They'd spent the hours since making inroads into Horatio's book collection. Unexpectedly, they'd stumbled on a shared interest, stopping every now and then to exclaim over some plate in an old tome, to share some discovery. Her excitement yesterday over the illuminations in a prayer book had had him smiling – he'd caught a glimpse of his own youthful enthusiasm in her face. Thus must Horatio have seen him. They'd parted that evening when he'd walked her home before dinner, closer, more relaxed, the understanding between them broadening, deepening.

Propinquity was definitely working. It hadn't escaped him that, just now, she'd felt sufficiently comfortable to not bother looking at him when asking her question. A sign of growing ease. Little by little, even if she didn't know it, she was leaning his way.

They broke for lunch, a cold collation Mrs Hemmings had laid out in the dining room. Afterward, returning to the library, they found Covey stacking books on the desk.

'I've finished one wall in the drawing room. These are the books with notes written in them – I forgot to give them to you the last couple of days.'

'That's all right, Covey. We'll go through them now – it'll give us a break from the shelves.' Lucifer lifted a brow at Phyllida.

She nodded and headed for the desk. They settled in, he behind the desk, she in a comfortable chair before it, and knuckled down to decipher the often illegible notations.

'Hmm.' Phyllida sat up and scanned the desk, picked up a scrap of paper, placed it as a bookmark in the book on her lap, then set the book on the floor by her chair.

She glanced up; Lucifer looked his question.

'A recipe for plum sauce – I must take a copy.'

Lucifer smiled. They returned to the books. Companionable silence wrapped around them. The clock on the mantelpiece ticked on.

Then Phyllida sat up. Lucifer glanced at her; she was frowning. 'What?'

'This has another inscription to Letitia from Humphrey. "my dearest heart, my love, my life." It's dated February 1781.'

After a moment, Lucifer asked, 'How old is Cedric?'

Phyllida looked at him. 'In his late thirties.'

Lucifer raised his brows and held out a hand for the book; when Phyllida gave it to him, he set it aside. 'One to think about later.'

Five minutes later, Phyllida humphed. 'This is another one "to my dearest Letty." The wording is quite . . . warm. It's signed "Pinky."'

'Date?'

'1783.'

Lucifer added that book to the 'later' pile.

Fifteen minutes later, the pile had grown by three more volumes. Handing over the last, a book of poetry sent to dearest Letty from a gentleman who'd signed himself 'Your fated lover,' also with a date of 1781, Phyllida viewed the pile with consternation. 'This is really rather worrying.'

Lucifer eyed the stack of books with notations they'd yet to check. 'From what we have already, it would appear Cedric, certainly, has cause to be concerned over what might be found in Horatio's collection.'

Phyllida stared at him. 'You mean that Cedric might not be Sir Bentley Fortemain's legitimate son?'

Lucifer nodded. 'If that could be proved, and if Sir Bentley's will is the usual simple affair, then Pommeroy could claim that Sir Bentley's estate should be his.'

'Pommeroy is not fond of Cedric.'

'So I gathered. That gives Cedric a definite motive to clandestinely remove books from Horatio's collection.'

Silence fell. Phyllida stared at Lucifer; he looked steadily at her. 'I can't believe Cedric's a murderer.'

'What does a murderer look like?'

'Even worse, Cedric wears brown. Most of the time. I know he wears brown hats.'

'Think back – have you ever seen him wearing the hat you saw in Horatio's drawing room?'

Phyllida considered, then shook her head. 'I can't recall seeing him in that particular hat.'

'Are you sure you'd remember it?'

'The hat? Yes, definitely. I looked directly at it. I nearly picked it up. If I saw it again, I'd know it.'

Lucifer sat back. 'If Cedric's our murderer, he won't still have the hat.'

'No. He'll have got rid of it. Cedric may bluster, but he's not stupid.' Phyllida frowned. 'Did you ask Todd who rode out from Ballyclose that Sunday morning?'

'Dodswell asked. Unfortunately, Todd not only went to church, but then visited his brother-in-law's farm. He has no idea who rode that morning.' Lucifer considered. 'Could Cedric have been the intruder we chased?'

Phyllida grimaced. 'Cedric used to be more athletic. If pushed, he could probably run as fast as the intruder.'

'So Cedric's a possibility.'

Phyllida fell silent; after a moment, Lucifer prompted, 'Penny for your thoughts.'

She glanced at him, then looked away. 'Cedric wants – wanted – to marry me. If he's the murderer, then . . .'

Lucifer glanced at the clock, then stood and rounded the desk. 'Come on.' He held out his hand.

Phyllida looked up, her fingers slipping into his even without the answer to the question in her eyes.

Lucifer looked down at her. 'You've forgotten the summer ball at Ballyclose Manor tonight.'

'Good heavens!' Phyllida glanced at the window. 'I *had* forgotten.' She looked at Lucifer. 'Perhaps . . . ?'

He met her gaze. 'We'll need to go carefully, but we can certainly test Cedric's interest in Horatio's books, and all they may contain.'

★   ★   ★

Five hours later, stylishly gowned in pale blue silk, Phyllida stood by the side of the Ballyclose ballroom and watched the only one of her suitors who had succeeded in getting her to consider marrying him. He was standing across the room, charming the Misses Longdon; clinging to the shadows thrown by a large palm, she considered his tall frame, considered the dark locks rakishly framing his brow, the elegant black coat and trousers set off by his ivory cravat and an ivory silk waistcoat. Along with most of the women in the room, she savored the aura of strength and masculine confidence he so effortlessly exuded.

She'd hoped distance would help her gain perspective. With an inward sniff at her own susceptibilities, she forced her gaze from him and scanned the room. She'd sent Basil to fetch her a glass of orgeat; she hoped he would find some distraction along the way.

She needed time to think. Spending day after day by Lucifer's side was undeniably pleasant, but it made thinking sensibly about him difficult. And she definitely needed to think – about him, about marrying him. About what she wanted, about if she would.

His statement that he would never have seduced her if he hadn't intended to marry her had opened her eyes, not to his motives but to hers. *She* would never have *allowed* him to seduce her if she hadn't already loved him, even if she didn't understand what love was.

She'd always found the subject of love – love between a man and a woman – confusing.

Her mother had not lived long enough for her to form any useful view of her parents' marriage. The only other married couple she knew well were the Farthingales, and their relationship was based on mutual acceptance, not on any stronger emotion. Lady Fortemain's apparent excursions outside matrimony only muddied the waters further – she had always viewed her ladyship as the epitome of a gentlewoman.

No one had explained love to her. As for her reaction to Lucifer, she'd been suffering from self-assured blindness, convinced such an emotional development – the sort that looked set to bind Mary Anne and Robert for the rest of their lives – could never happen to her.

Out of the blue, it had. Lucifer had arrived and affected her life like an earthquake – everything had changed and was still changing. The new landscape hadn't yet taken final shape. She hadn't yet allowed it to do so.

Desire might have temporarily fogged her brain – it still did with just a touch, just one look from those midnight-blue eyes – but she was still her own woman, still in charge of her life. Letting the matter slide as she had with her other suitors was not an option with Lucifer. She couldn't ignore him; he'd created and occupied a place in her world that none of the others had. He was her lover.

He was, however, a great deal more.

A ruthless pirate at heart, a protective tyrant – all that she could easily see. She'd also experienced his gentleness, his tenderness. In teaching her of his desire and hers, he had, time and again, put her needs ahead of his wants. She might have been innocent, naive, a virgin, but she'd overheard enough over the years to know not all men were so considerate. With him, it had gone far beyond consideration – he had cared.

The emotion, the impulse, was so much a part of her, she'd recognized it instantly with no possibility of error. He cared for her. That truly unnerved her – everyone else expected her to be the one who cared.

She had wondered whether he'd seduced her intending to use the fact to pressure her into marriage, yet he hadn't done so. She was under no illusion that he expected to win her, to ultimately gain her agreement to their wedding, but she'd read his character accurately – he'd play fair. He was so much stronger than she, yet in his arms she never felt threatened. In his arms she felt safe – safe from everything, even him. So it was still her life, her choice, although he would do all he could to influence it.

It was still possible to say no, to turn her back and retreat to safer ground, but she was no longer the woman she'd been when he'd arrived, and so much of what he was offering was tempting. But there was one major hurdle to accepting that new future: How would their marriage work? If like the Farthingales' or Lady Fortemain's, then her answer would be no. He'd asked her what she wanted of marriage. She'd always known what she didn't.

She couldn't make up her mind, not without the answer to that major question. Could it work? Could she retain her sense of self while being the object of his overpowering protectiveness and the associated, highly possessive ramifications? Could she accept being cared for, rather than being the active carer? Could she adjust? Could he? If both of them were willing . . . that raised the question of how willing he was.

When he'd asked what she wanted of marriage, she hadn't had a clue. Now she did. She wanted to share. She wanted to work together, live together, love together – to make a difference together – to share his life and have him share hers. That was a prize worth the risk of binding herself to a protective tyrant.

If she told him what she wanted, would he give it? Would he let her take the driving seat sometimes? Was he truly capable of sharing the reins?

Smiling, she turned to greet Basil, all her questions still weaving through her mind.

Basil had brought her orgeat; she rewarded him with the next dance. Lucifer had strolled up the instant she'd stepped into the ballroom; they'd agreed to let the ball get under way before sounding Cedric out. So they were both dancing, chatting, and waiting for the time to pounce.

Lucifer watched Phyllida curtsy and link hands with Basil, then was forced to pay attention to his own partner, a Miss Moffat. Lady Fortemain had been exceedingly busy on his behalf – she'd invited every unmarried young lady for miles around. He was sorely tempted to tell her she didn't need to bother. He knew who his wife would be.

The word used to make him shudder; it no longer did. He was beyond fighting this fate – it was too desirable to reject. But he knew his social role and he played it well, charming the ladies, conversing with the gentlemen, acting as the perfect guest. Around him, the large crowd swayed and dipped. Lady Fortemain had pulled out all the stops; the occasion exuded a festive air. Her neighbors had joined in enthusiastically; the faces about him glowed.

The Grange household was well represented. Sir Jasper stood chatting with Mr Farthingale and Mr Filing. Mrs Farthingale and Lady Huddlesford were similarly occupied. Jonas, Percy, and Frederick were engaged on the dance floor. Percy had condescended to attend. Frederick was making an effort to be pleasant. Jonas, on the other hand, had an easy smile on his face – only his eyes flicking every now and then to Phyllida gave him away.

Lucifer twirled Miss Moffat; he could dance a cotillion without thought. Like Jonas's, his thoughts were on Phyllida and the man who had her in his sights. He had spoken to Jonas. If, for some reason, he wasn't watching Phyllida, then Jonas would be. No matter her intentions, no matter her fear, she too often forgot the danger. The village was her home; she'd been safe here for all her twenty-four years. It was hard to change a lifetime's habit. So he or Jonas would keep watch over her until the danger was past.

This was the second cottilion, the fourth dance; as he changed sides in the set, Lucifer scanned the crowd.

Cedric was standing in a patriarchal pose, watching his guests with an approving eye. Lady Fortemain was the center of a knot of voluble ladies. Pommeroy was dancing despite the exigencies of his ridiculously high cravat. Lucius Appleby was lending his assistance entertaining the guests and doing a much better job than Pommeroy.

The local ladies considered Appleby an enigma; Lucifer read the signs with ease. Appleby ranked as handsome; despite his reserve and an attitude that suggested he had no interest in stepping over anyone's line, his success with the ladies was assured. A Miss Claypoole was dancing with him, eyes and lips smiling. Appleby deflected her interest with a confidence that had Lucifer wondering.

With a flourish, the cottilion ended; Lucifer bowed and excused himself from Miss Moffat's side.

He headed for Phyllida's. She welcomed him with a smile that warmed him and a look so eager he pressed her fingers warningly. He exchanged nods with Basil.

'How opportune, Mr Cynster. I was about to mention that I understand Phyllida's been forced to spend the past two days at the Manor for safety's sake. That must be both boring for Phyllida and a distraction for you, what with all you have to do to settle Horatio's estate.' With a patronizing air that stated louder than words that he believed every word he said, Basil smiled at Phyllida. 'I'll send the carriage around tomorrow morning, my dear. Mama would be delighted to have you spend the day.'

Lucifer glanced at Phyllida's face, calm as always, and resisted the urge to applaud. She returned Basil's smile. 'Thank you, Basil, that's a kind thought. But I have other plans for tomorrow.'

'Indeed?' Basil clearly considered asking what; instead, he said, 'Then perhaps—'

'The day after tomorrow is Sunday, so that's out of the question. After that . . . well, the endeavors with which I'm assisting Mr Cynster have yet to be completed, so I'll still be helping him at the Manor.'

Her tone as she uttered that last sentence was enough to give even Basil pause. After a moment, he bowed. 'My apologies, my dear, if I did not properly understand—'

There was no apology in his tone, only irritation and faint rebuke; Phyllida stopped him with a raised hand. 'There's a great deal you fail to properly understand, Basil, usually because you don't wish to understand it.'

A violin hummed, then screeched. Phyllida turned to Lucifer. 'I believe that's our waltz commencing.'

Lucifer bowed and took her hand. He nodded to Basil. 'You'll excuse us, Smollet.'

No question, of course; Basil bowed stiffly. With a bob, Phyllida turned on Lucifer's arm and let him lead her to the floor. She went into his arms, following his lead without thought; after a moment, she felt his hand stroke her back.

'Relax.'

She threw him a glance – one she knew he would interpret correctly. 'Where he ever got the idea that he *owned* me, that he could simply appropriate me and dictate my life, I have no notion.'

Lucifer said nothing. He drew her closer, just enough so their bodies brushed lightly as they whirled. She softened, relaxing into his embrace. 'Not all men are like that, surely?' She glanced around them. 'Well, of course they're not, but just look at Basil, and Cedric, and Henry Grisby. No woman of sense would marry such a man.' After a moment, she added, 'Perhaps it's something in the water hereabouts.'

Lucifer held her protectively tighter as they went through the turn, then he murmured, 'Appleby. How long's he been with Cedric?'

'Appleby?' Phyllida scanned the dancers. 'He's been here . . . well, it seems a long time, but he only joined the household last February. Why?'

'I wondered before if he'd been in the military –

I think he must have been. He seems popular with the ladies.'

'He is. They approve of his style and his person, and his behavior is such as must please.'

'You don't sound particularly taken.'

'I've never seen the attraction, I must confess.'

Lucifer was glad to hear it; her tone left no doubt she found the other ladies' interest puzzling. Her comments on Basil were less reassuring.

'I think,' she said, 'that it's time to speak to Cedric.'

Lucifer glanced at their host, now listening to Lady Huddlesford. 'At the end of this dance. Follow my lead.'

'What tack do you intend to take? You can hardly walk up and ask if he was aware he might be illegitimate.'

'I thought I'd ask if he was interested in acquiring any of Horatio's tomes.' Lucifer looked to where Silas Coombe, resplendent in a green silk coat and a canary-yellow waistcoat, stood conversing. 'How likely is Coombe to have mentioned to anyone that I don't intend to break up Horatio's collection?'

'Silas is an inveterate gabblemonger.'

'In that case, I'll have to watch my phrasing.'

The music ended. Lucifer released Phyllida, raised her from her curtsy, then tucked her hand in his arm and strolled toward Cedric. He was with Lady Huddlesford. Everyone exchanged bows; then her ladyship, overwhelming in bronze bombazine, regally glided away. Cedric smiled at

Phyllida, then looked at Lucifer. 'Well, sir, I hope our simple country gathering measures up in some small way against what you're accustomed to.'

'It's been a thoroughly felicitous evening,' Lucifer returned. 'Your mother is to be congratulated, as I've already told her.'

'Indeed, indeed. Mama delights in these sorts of affairs. She used to be a feature in the capital before the pater's health forced them to retire here. You may be sure she's pleased to have reason to entertain in such style again.'

'If that's so, then I'm pleased to have been of service.' Lucifer considered the bluff geniality that colored Cedric's expression. Was it a facade, or his true nature? 'I don't know if you've heard, but I've decided to keep Horatio's library essentially intact.'

'Ah, yes! I did hear Silas bemoaning that fact. He seemed to think some of Horatio's collection would be better housed with his own.'

'Unfortunately for Coombe, my mind is made up, in the general sense. However, in checking Horatio's records, I noticed he'd acquired some volumes from your library.'

Cedric was nodding. 'Before his death, the pater – greatly taken with Horatio, he was – went through the library and sold quite a few tomes to him.'

'Indeed. As your father is now dead, and as I'll be preserving the collection more as a memorial to Horatio than from any real interest of my own, I wondered if you wished to repurchase any of those books. At the same price Horatio paid your father, of course.'

Cedric pulled a face. 'Not much of a book man myself. I always thought it wise of the pater to get rid of a few of the books. There's a blessed lot left if you're interested.'

Lucifer smiled easily. 'It's not my field.'

'Ah, well, worth a try.' Cedric turned to Phyllida. 'Now, my dear, we've been neglecting you shamefully. I hear you've been spending your days at the Manor.'

Cedric glanced at Lucifer; Phyllida stiffened. If he intimated she just sat there, twiddling her thumbs . . .

Cedric looked back at her. 'Daresay there's all manner of things you've been helping Cynster with, heh?'

Her stiffness easing, Phyllida inclined her head. 'Indeed.' She glanced at Lucifer. 'All manner of things.'

Lucifer's dark eyes smiled at her, then his gaze went past her and he bowed. 'Miss Smollet.'

Phyllida turned as Jocasta joined them. Jocasta exchanged greetings with Cedric, then glanced at her. Phyllida inclined her head.

Jocasta mirrored the movement, then, smiling a touch brittlely, fixed her gaze on Lucifer. 'I understand, Mr Cynster, that you're considering life as a farmer. Basil tells me you're talking of setting up a stud.'

'It's one of the possibilities I'm investigating. The

fields and meadows of the Manor are currently underused.'

'True, very true.' Cedric frowned. 'Tend to forget how much land there is, back of those woods of yours.'

Lucifer regarded him. 'Have you been that way recently?'

Cedric shook his head. 'Can't recall being down that side of the valley for over a year. Not hunting country.'

'Cedric hunts with the local pack,' Jocasta said. 'Will you be joining them, Mr Cynster?'

Lucifer smiled. 'I only ride hounds to ride, rather than to hunt.'

Phyllida swallowed the observation that, for him, a fox was the wrong sort of prey. She stood and pretended to listen while inwardly she plotted. Eventually, Lucifer excused them; they left Jocasta with Cedric. Her hand on Lucifer's sleeve, she strolled with him through the milling crowd.

'Was it my imagination, or was Cedric less . . . fixated on you than when last we met?'

Phyllida blinked. 'Now you mention it, yes. In fact, he seemed rather relaxed. He didn't seem perturbed that I've been helping you at the Manor.'

'You know him better than I, but I would almost say he was *relieved* you were spending so much time at the Manor.'

Phyllida looked forward. Lucifer was right. And how did she feel about that? 'If he's relieved, then

I'm relieved.' She glanced at Lucifer. 'I've known Cedric all my life. I've always considered him a friend; I never wanted him as a suitor.'

Lucifer held her gaze, read her eyes. 'And you don't think he's a murderer, either.'

'No.' She sighed. 'It's so horrible, knowing how you feel about people but logically knowing it's possible.'

'I detected not the slightest degree of consciousness over the books, or about my fields beyond the wood.'

'No, that was simply Cedric. What you see is what there is.'

'Speaking of facades' – Lucifer steered her toward the side of the room – 'Jocasta Smollet was making an effort to be conciliating. I can't help suspecting she's the victim of some sad story.' She struck him as a woman who'd missed her chance at happiness, yet still searched for it every day. 'Perhaps that's the reason for her normally acid tongue.'

Gaining the side of the room, Phyllida faced him. 'Having usually been a target for her acid tongue, but then, almost everyone in the village is, you know, I hadn't really thought of it, but she does seem sad. I've never seen her smile or laugh, not happily, not for years.'

'You don't know her story?'

'No. And that's really rather odd, because if I don't know, then it must be a secret, and in a village this size . . . that's amazing.'

For a moment, they both pondered, then Phyllida shook aside her thoughts and looked into Lucifer's face. 'I think we should search Cedric's room for the hat.'

Lucifer's blue gaze fixed on her eyes. 'Why? I thought we'd agreed he'd passed our tests.'

Phyllida grimaced. 'I *like* Cedric. I don't want him to be the murderer. Or my attacker. But you know as well as I do that beneath Cedric's genial *bonhomie* is an intelligent man, and the threat implied by those inscriptions is a real motive for him. It would destroy his life.' She gestured about them. 'It would destroy all this. And this simple country life is important to Cedric.'

She studied Lucifer's face, then narrowed her eyes. 'And despite what you just said, you haven't crossed him off the top of our list of suspects.'

Lucifer's lips thinned. 'No, but—'

'We owe it to ourselves, the village, and Cedric to turn every possible stone to determine whether he's the murderer or not.'

'Searching his room for the hat.' Lucifer fixed her with a gaze too patronizing for her liking. 'As you yourself pointed out—'

'I know he *should* have got rid of it, but what if he hasn't? This isn't London – decent hats aren't easy to come by. He might have laid it aside, intending to get rid of it, but I've made no mention of the hat – even of being there that Sunday. He might reason nothing will ever come of it. Who knows – he might even have forgotten about the hat. It might be something quite different that he thought I saw.'

She turned toward the ballroom door. 'If you wish to remain here, *I* will go and search Cedric's room.'

She took one step. Long fingers curled about her elbow and stopped her in her tracks.

'Not. Alone.' The two words rumbled just above her ear; they carried a weighted warning she could not have described in words, but her senses translated effortlessly. She waited, her gaze fixed on the door.

A sigh brushed her ear. 'Where is Cedric's room? Do you know?'

'Upstairs to the right – the last door along the corridor.'

'Very well.' He drew her to face him. 'In a moment, we'll part. I'll head for the refreshment table. You stroll a little – not enough to get caught – then go out as if heading for the withdrawing room. I'll be watching. I'll give you enough time to reach Cedric's room, then I'll follow.'

Phyllida looked at him. 'You've done this before.'

He simply smiled, then he bowed and they parted.

Phyllida followed his instructions to the letter – not something that came naturally, but she could see no good reason to do otherwise. He'd agreed to search Cedric's room – that was what mattered. And not only in terms of their investigation. It meant he could be reasoned with, which, did he but know it, was a definite point in his favor.

Henry Grisby tried to solicit her for the next dance; she politely declined and headed for the withdrawing room. No one was about to see her glide up the stairs. Once in the gallery, she turned right. She reached Cedric's room; her hand was on the knob when she heard a distant footfall. Glancing back, she saw Lucifer step up from the stairs.

He saw her; she waved, then opened the door and walked in. Less than a minute later, he joined her, easing the door closed behind him. Phyllida watched him straighten, watched him prowl toward her, his gaze scanning the room; it came to rest on her.

Moonlight slanted through the uncurtained windows and lit his face. She suddenly recalled how he had looked three nights before, when he had crossed such a room toward her. The same heavy-lidded eyes, the same sensual lips. His gaze dropped to her lips; she could swear he was having the same sensual, wicked thoughts.

Her breath caught in her throat.

He stopped before her, less than a foot away. His heat reached her; his gaze rose to her eyes. He studied them. His hand rose; one thumb brushed her lips and she shivered.

His lips curved, just a little – not taunting, but self-deprecatory. 'Hats,' he murmured. 'Where would Cedric store his hats?'

Phyllida blinked. Weakly, she waved to a small door. 'In his dressing room. There's a hat shelf.'

Lucifer looked at the small door, half ajar, then back at her, one brow rising.

'This was Sir Bentley's room – he was ill for years. I often visited.'

Phyllida bustled to the door, ignoring the tempting warmth that had slid under her skin. She tried to ignore the presence following at her heels, but that was beyond her.

Lucifer stepped into the dressing room – long and narrow, it ran the length of the main bedroom. A hat shelf was fixed along the wall facing him at head height. It was packed with hats.

'This *isn't* London.' He glanced at Phyllida. 'Cedric owns more hats than any gentleman of fashion I know.'

'All the more reason to check – it looks like he's never thrown one away in his life.'

That was true. Phyllida couldn't reach the hats. He stood there, her assistant, and handed them to her, one by one. She took each specimen in both hands, studied it, held it at arm's length, then shook her head and handed it back. In the moonlight streaming through the high single window, all the hats appeared the same color – brown.

Slowly, they progressed the length of the shelf. With a sigh, she handed the last hat back and shook her head. He was reaching up to the shelf, setting it back, when a faint sound – not a click, not a tap – reached his ears. He froze.

Phyllida froze, too, head tilted. Then she

looked at him. He held a finger to his lips, then turned.

The bedroom had two doors – the one they'd entered by, near to the wall of the dressing room, and another, leading to the adjoining room, presumably a sitting room. They would have heard someone coming along the corridor. Had someone just entered from the sitting room?

Cedric? But would a host leave a country ball?

If he was a murderer, he might.

Lucifer drew in a breath and stepped into the bedroom.

A rush of air, a faint whistle, warned him – he ducked back – a heavy rod cracked across his left shoulder.

The impact drove him to his knees; he caught himself, bracing with his right arm on the door-frame, and saw a man's figure, shrouded in shadows, whip around the door into the corridor. The sound of fleeing footsteps thudding on the corridor runner reached them.

'Good Lord! He's getting away!' Trapped behind him, Phyllida lifted her skirts and leaped over him.

He caught her in mid-leap and hauled her back. '*No!*'

She fell on him. 'But—' She wriggled furiously, silk skirts a-froth in his lap. 'I might catch him!'

'Or he might catch *you!*' He tightened his arm around her and she quieted.

'Oh.'

'Oh, indeed.' Teeth gritted, he shifted her so her

hip wasn't grinding into him, then tried to ease his shoulder.

She turned to him. 'He was waiting.'

'With this.' Lucifer reached out and pulled a cane toward them, then lifted it so they both could see. The top of the cane was a lion's head, brass and very heavy.

'It usually sits in the corner by the door.' Phyllida looked at the corridor door, and tried not to think about what might have happened if Lucifer's reflexes hadn't been so honed. If he hadn't ducked and the cane had connected with his skull, he might have died, or at least lost consciousness. Leaving her facing the murderer.

She turned to Lucifer and saw the same realization in his gaze. 'We have to get back to the ballroom.'

CHAPTER 16

'Jonas, I wonder if we might have a word.' Phyllida by his side, Lucifer smiled at the two young ladies with whom Jonas had been conversing.

The young ladies giggled; they bobbed curtsies, then bustled away, casting coy glances over their shoulders.

Jonas met Lucifer's eyes. 'Any trouble?'

'As a matter of fact, yes.' Lucifer smiled as if they were bandying observations.

Jonas looked at Phyllida. 'I thought Phyl was with you.'

'I was,' Phyllida put in. 'But that's not the trouble.'

Jonas raised a brow. Phyllida looked away and decided to leave the explanations to Lucifer.

'Did you notice any of the gentlemen slipping away about fifteen minutes ago?'

Jonas raised both brows. 'Cedric left, then Basil left. Filing had left before that. And Grisby, too. There had to be others missing as well, because there was a dance and there weren't many couples on the floor and not many men standing out. Lady Fortemain was beating the bushes.'

'Has Cedric returned?'

'He came back a few minutes ago – Basil returned a bare minute before that. They both looked a trifle choleric. I haven't seen any others slipping back, but I wasn't watching.' Jonas looked at them. 'What happened?'

Briefly, Lucifer told him. Phyllida scanned the room, trying to determine which gentlemen were present. The crowd was still considerable. 'Do you think,' she said, when Lucifer fell silent, 'that we might engineer a trap?'

They both looked at her, identical expressions of male incomprehension on their faces, as if she'd spoken in an alien tongue.

'What sort of trap?' Lucifer eventually asked.

'I didn't get a glance at the murderer this time and you only got the barest glimpse. He must know that – there's no reason for him to flee. Assuming he's still present, perhaps we can encourage him to show himself again.'

Lucifer stared at her. 'With you as bait?'

'If you both keep watch, then there's no reason I should be in any danger.'

'If we're both watching – if either of us is anywhere near – he won't make a move. We've known from the first he's not stupid.'

'You don't need to hover so obviously. There's more dances to come. Everyone will expect us to separate.'

Lucifer quelled his rising panic and studied Phyllida's calm face. What she was suggesting was . . .

reasonable. He couldn't give way to his instinctive urge to plant his foot solidly and say no. He didn't dare. '*If* you promise to remain in the ballroom—'

'I fully intend to remain in sight.' She tilted her chin challengingly; her dark eyes flashed a warning. 'I'm perfectly capable of playing my part. All you need do is watch from a distance. Now, I'll take myself off.'

She drew her hand from his sleeve – he had to fight the urge to grab it back. With a gracious nod and a smile, she turned and strolled into the crowd.

Lucifer watched her go. Under his breath, he swore.

Jonas humphed. 'I wish you'd said no.'

He hadn't had a choice. Not if he wanted her to marry him.

'I'll go watch from the other side of the room.' Jonas ambled off.

Phyllida danced and chatted, and danced some more. She circulated through the room at her brightest, her most charming. She spoke again to Cedric, Basil, and Grisby. She pretended to a faulty memory and conversed with Silas as if their meeting in the graveyard had never been.

All for nought. No gentleman approached her with any, even slightly nefarious, proposition.

At one point, Lucifer stopped by her side. 'Enough. I don't like this. He'll be feeling under pressure. He might be at his most dangerous.'

'He's more likely to be off-balance and at his

most vulnerable.' She strolled on, not waiting to hear his opinion of her logic.

Fifteen minutes later, Lucifer joined the circle about Phyllida; with practiced ease, he excised her from it. Her hand on his sleeve, he ambled down the room. 'I think we should call it a night.' He had had enough. He could feel the tension locked between his shoulder blades; his left shoulder was aching as well. 'If he hasn't approached you by now, there's no reason to think he will.'

She stopped and swung to face him. Her expression was calm and serene; her eyes glinted dangerously. 'You know perfectly well that, other than finding that hat, we have no evidence to identify our man. There's not much we can do other than tempt him to try again. Here, where I'm surrounded by friends, is the safest place to do it. You're here; Jonas is here. This is too good an opportunity to pass up.'

She held his gaze steadily; Lucifer swallowed a low growl. He was feeling increasingly caged. 'This is *not* a good idea.'

Her chin rose; her eyes flashed. 'This is *my* idea and it's a perfectly sensible one.'

With that, she swanned off.

Lucifer gritted his teeth and let her. It was that or risk showing her how mildly possessive her other suitors truly were. Compared with a Cynster, they did not rate. Fate had to be laughing hysterically.

Jaw clenched, he strolled to a wall and propped

his uninjured shoulder against it. He watched her dance another country dance, then she chatted with a group of ladies. After that, she drifted. Then he saw her hesitate, looking down the room. He followed her gaze – he couldn't see whom she was staring at.

Then she stepped out; from her stride, she'd either seen something or had an idea. He wasn't enamored of her ideas. Chest tightening, he started after her.

He lost her in the crowd. Panic sank its claws deeper. He stopped and looked over the heads – he saw Jonas. Jonas shook his head. He'd lost her, too. Lucifer cursed, turned, and glimpsed her. At the other end of the ballroom, she stepped onto the terrace beside Lucius Appleby.

Appleby? Lucifer didn't stop to consider her reasoning. He doubted Appleby had invited Phyllida outside. If he had, she wouldn't have gone. No, she'd inveigled him out, God only knew why. But outside with only one gentleman was impossibly dangerous. Who knew who might be concealed by the night?

The distance to the nearest French door seemed a mile – a mile of obstacles, all smiling and nodding and wanting to chat. He reached it – it was locked. He had to plunge down the side of the room to the doors through which Phyllida and Appleby had disappeared, all without raising a dust.

He gained the terrace; Jonas, who'd been even

farther down the room, was following. He glanced around and caught the smallest, most fleeting glimpse of blue skirt disappearing around the far end of the terrace. He strode after her, making no attempt to mute his footsteps. Rounding the corner, he discovered Phyllida a few yards away, leaning back against the balustrade, talking with Appleby, who was standing before her.

Behind the balustrade was a thicket of bushes, just the right sort to conceal a man with a knife.

Lucifer reached out, locked a hand around Phyllida's wrist, and yanked her to him, away from the bushes. He ignored her shocked expression and turned to Appleby. 'Do excuse us, Appleby. Miss Tallent is just leaving.'

Appleby returned his look blank-faced, the epitome of a well-trained employee. With the barest nod, Lucifer turned, let Phyllida get a good glimpse of his face, then stalked back around the corner of the terrace, dragging her with him.

'What are you doing!' she hissed. She twisted her wrist; he tightened his grip and strode on.

'I'm saving you from yourself! What the devil did you think you were doing, going off outside like that?' He pulled her close, moderating his stride so his body shielded her as much as was possible. 'It's black night out there!' He waved at the lawns rolling away from the terrace. 'He could take a shot at you without risk of being seen.'

She glanced at the lawns. 'I hadn't thought of that.'

He ground his teeth. 'Well, *I did.* That's why I made you promise not to go out of the ballroom.'

'I didn't promise.' Her nose rose. 'I said I'd remain in sight. I thought you were watching.'

Her tone, hinting at sudden vulnerability, made him bite his tongue. 'I *was* watching. So was Jonas. But we both lost you for a moment, and then you were stepping outside. We nearly lost you altogether.'

The thought made his blood run cold. It made his voice deeper, darker, a great deal more menacing. 'I repeat, what the *devil* did you think you were doing?'

He stopped; she stopped, too, and faced him, head up, gaze direct. Her tapered chin was set. 'I admit I forgot about the dark, but my reasons were perfectly sensible. I couldn't think where else to take Appleby.'

'So this *was* your idea?'

'Of course! Appleby is the one person most likely to know which men had slipped out and returned. He's Cedric's right hand – he helps with all the arrangements and acts as Cedric's second. If Cedric left the room, then Appleby would have been alerted and watching the other guests in case someone needed anything.'

'So,' Lucifer grudgingly extrapolated, 'Appleby's unlikely to be the murderer. He would have been on duty, as it were—'

'Precisely! So I was in no danger from him. Appleby doesn't like me any more than I like him, so I wasn't risking receiving any unwelcome advances. And you did say he'd been in the military, so he was probably the safest person, aside from you, to be with on the terrace.'

Lucifer bit back the information that she wouldn't have been safe with him – still wasn't safe with him. He gestured brusquely toward the ballroom. 'Let's get inside.'

With a distinctly irate sniff, Phyllida turned. He wrapped the wrist he still held about one arm and stalked beside her. Jonas had stuck his head out, seen them, and gone in again. As they neared the open door, Lucifer asked, 'Well? Did Appleby know anything to the point?'

Phyllida stepped over the threshold, nose in the air. 'No.'

'I wondered if you'd care to accompany me on a drive to Exeter.'

Phyllida jerked her head up, only just managing to smother her gasp. Lucifer stood not two feet away. How had he got so close?

He raised one dark brow; reaching out, he took the flower basket from her nerveless fingers. She forced her gaze to a rosebush; cupping one bloom, she snipped it. As she laid it in the basket, she said, 'If you can wait until I put these in water, then yes. A drive would be pleasant, and there are a few people I should see in Exeter.'

Lucifer inclined his head. 'For the pleasure of your company, I'll wait.'

Twenty minutes later, he handed her into his curricle, then stepped up to the box seat, sat, picked up the reins, and gave his blacks the office. As he tooled the carriage down the drive, he knew relief.

Phyllida sat beside him, self-contained, a touch aloof – but she was there. After his performance last night, he hadn't been at all sure of his reception; he'd been prepared to kidnap her if she hadn't come of her own accord. But she had, thank heaven. She'd even come without a bonnet.

The blacks swept out of the Grange drive; he glanced at her – she had deployed a parasol to shade her fair skin from the summer sun, but he could see her face. He scanned her features, noted the line of her lips, the set of her chin, then gave his attention to his horses.

After last night, he would have to watch his every step.

They rattled on through the countryside in silence, a silence that became progressively more companionable as the miles fell beneath the blacks' hooves. The sunshine seemed to wilt her starchiness; when they reached Honiton, she spontaneously pointed out the sights.

He'd taken the more northerly route so they could check at the inns in Honiton, just in case a gentleman had hired a horse on the Sunday Horatio had been killed. Phyllida directed him to the appropriate establishments, then left him to make the inquiries. As they'd expected, there was no news to be had. Leaving Honiton, they bowled along the highway to Exeter.

The road was in good condition and the blacks were fresh. They leaned into the traces and the curricle flew. The wind of their passing whipped at Phyllida's hair. The speed was exhilarating, the warmth of the sun relaxing – she couldn't help but lift her face to the breeze and smile.

'Why are we going to Exeter?'

She waited, eyes half shut, lips curved; she felt Lucifer's gaze roam her face, then he answered. 'I need to call on Crabbs and, for completeness' sake, we should check the stables. Then I thought we could have lunch by the river before heading back along the coast road.'

Phyllida nodded. 'That sounds pleasant.'

'You mentioned there were some people you wished to see?'

'I'd like to call at the Customs House, a courtesy to preserve contact with Lieutenant Niles. And while you're consulting with Mr Crabbs, I'll have a word with Robert.' She glanced at Lucifer, but he merely nodded.

'If you like, we can go to the Customs House first.'

She shook her head. 'The livery stables first, then Mr Crabbs, then the Customs House, then lunch at the Mermaid.' She slanted Lucifer another glance – this time he caught it. She searched his eyes, then smiled and looked ahead. 'Jonas tells me they have the best ale in Exeter.

We can leave directly from there along the coast road.'

Lucifer grinned. 'Agreed.' He slowed the blacks as the first houses appeared. 'Now, my dear, which way?'

Phyllida directed him with an airy enthusiasm which warmed him as much as the sun. They called at the livery stables and received the same answer – no gentleman had hired a horse that Sunday. Continuing on to Mr Crabbs, Lucifer went with that venerable gentleman into the solicitor's private sanctum, leaving Phyllida to dally in the outer office, where Robert Collins worked at his desk. Fifteen minutes later, Lucifer emerged to find Phyllida smiling serenely and Robert looking less tense than before.

Exchanging bows with Crabbs, who punctiliously took his leave of Phyllida, they strolled out to the pavement, where an urchin held the blacks. Lucifer tossed the boy a coin, then handed Phyllida up. 'What did you say to Robert? Does he know I know about the letters?'

'Not precisely.' Phyllida gathered her skirts so he could sit beside her. 'I told him you were letting me search for the writing desk. He's been terribly worried over the whole business.'

'So I noticed.' Lucifer wondered about the letters, but let the matter slide. 'Where's the Customs House?'

It stood on the quay, a few minutes down a sloping cobbled road from the High Street. Lucifer eased the blacks down the steep slope. The quay lined the River Exe; boats were tied to it, bobbing on the tide. Lucifer drew up before the handsome, two-storied brick building Phyllida pointed out. A cabin boy was slouching nearby. His eyes lit at the sight of the blacks; Lucifer waved him over.

There was an inn farther along the quay, tucked into the hill behind it. The sign of a mermaid swung outside. Lucifer instructed the boy to walk the horses to the inn and hand them to the ostler.

'This won't take long,' Phyllida said as he helped her down to the cobbles.

She led the way into the building and walked directly to the counter along one wall. 'I'd like to speak with Lieutenant Niles, please. If you would tell him Miss Tallent is here?'

The man behind the counter eyed her as she stripped off her gloves. 'The Lieutenant's busy. He only handles business matters here.'

Phyllida lifted her head and fixed the man with a direct glance. 'This is business.'

Strolling up in her wake, Lucifer came to stand directly behind her. He looked at the clerk.

The clerk met his eyes, then swallowed and glanced at Phyllida. 'I'll tell him. Miss Tallent, you said?'

'Indeed.' Phyllida waited until the clerk had disappeared through a door before looking over her shoulder at Lucifer. 'What did you do to him?'

Lucifer opened his eyes wide. 'Nothing.' He smiled. 'Just me being me.'

Phyllida searched his face, then humphed. She turned back to the counter as the door beside it opened. A gentleman in the uniform of the Revenue Service came striding out, smiling, his hands outstretched.

'Miss Tallent.' He grasped her hand, then looked past her to Lucifer.

'Good morning, Lieutenant Niles.' Phyllida gestured at Lucifer. 'Allow me to present Mr Cynster. He's come to live in Colyton.'

'Oh?' All innocent inquiry, Niles shook Lucifer's hand. 'Does that mean you'll be taking an interest in the Colyton Import Company?'

'A benign interest,' Lucifer returned. 'Purely in an advisory capacity.'

He knew when Phyllida let out the breath she'd held. Niles turned back to her and she reclaimed his attention. 'I just wanted to check the overall totals with you, and whether we need to change any of our payments.'

'Indeed, indeed.' Niles waved them to the door. 'If you'll just come this way?'

He bowed them into his office, then he and Phyllida settled to a brisk discussion of the various goods the Company had brought in and expected to bring in in the near future, and the levels of the duties payable on the differing cargoes. Lucifer sat back and listened, intrigued by how, once she'd been given the opportunity – given the right to lead – Phyllida managed the interview, and Niles, so well. She was a business woman to her toes.

He was inwardly smiling by the time she'd finished with the Lieutenant. Tucking a list of the latest tariffs into her reticule, she stood, turned, and caught his eye. She waited until they'd taken their leave of Niles and were out on the quay before asking, 'Now, what so amuses you in that?'

'Nothing at all. I'm appreciative, not amused. It just occurred to me that, in the same way I could be of assistance to you with the Company, you, too, could to great effect assist me with my business.' Taking her arm, he turned her toward the Mermaid.

'Business?' She looked up at him. 'What sort of business do you engage in?'

It took all of lunchtime and more to tell her. By the time he'd finished and they were in the curricle heading east along the road that would eventually take them home along the coast, she was intrigued.

'I had no idea. I thought you were a London swell – that all you ever did was waltz around ballrooms and charm ladies.'

'I do that, too, but one has to have something to do to while away the days.'

'Humph.' She shot him a measuring glance. 'So this interest of yours in a cattle stud is quite genuine?'

'Given I've now got the land, it seems a pity not to use it, and establishing a stud seems the farming equivalent of being a collector.'

'I hadn't thought of it in quite those terms, but I suppose that's true.' Phyllida looked ahead. Then she gripped his arm. 'Stop!'

391

Drawing on the reins, Lucifer looked at her. 'What?'

She'd swiveled around on the seat, staring back along the road. Reins tight, Lucifer shifted and also looked back. A tinker was ambling along, heading into Exeter.

'The hat!' Phyllida swung to face him, eyes wide. 'That tinker's got *the hat*!'

He turned the horses and set them trotting back along the road. 'Quiet,' he warned Phyllida as they drew level with the tinker. She stared hard at the man – at his hat – but didn't argue. Lucifer drove a hundred yards farther on, then turned the curricle again. He drove back, almost to where the tinker slogged along, then drew rein.

'Good day.'

The tinker stopped and touched the brim of the hat – the hat that even the most cursory glance declared was not his.

'Good day to you, sir. Ma'am.'

'That hat,' Phyllida said. 'Have you had it long?'

A wary look passed through the tinker's eyes. 'I found it, fair and square. I didn't steal it.'

'I didn't think you had.' Phyllida smiled reassuringly. 'We were just wondering where you found it.'

'Along the coast a ways.'

'How far back? Before Sidmouth?'

'Aye – it was a ways before. I'd left Axmouth and decided to go inland a bit. There's a sleepy little village there, name of Colyton.'

'We know it,' Lucifer said.

'I sharpen knives.' The tinker gestured to the packs on his back. 'After I finished in the village, I headed on, west, then northwest – there's a path leads on to Honiton, which was my next port o'call. I found the hat along the way, a bit out of Colyton.'

Phyllida nodded. 'You must have gone up the lane, past the church and the forge – up the hill—'

'Aye, that's right.'

'And then there's a bit of a dip, a shallow valley, you eventually get to the next ridge – stop me when I get to where you found the hat – and then there's tall gateposts, and then the lane narrows, and winds down and around toward the sea—'

'That's it! That's where I found it. It was rolling along at the bottom of the hedge just short of where that seaward leg ends. I picked it up, dusted it off – wasn't no name in it. I looked around, but there was no house or hut for miles. Then I walked but a few yards on and the lane turned into a path and swung northwest for Honiton.'

The tinker beamed at Phyllida; she beamed back.

'Here.' Lucifer held out two guineas. 'One for the hat, one for your help. You'll be able to buy yourself a good cap, find a comfortable room, and have a good dinner and a few drinks on us.'

The tinker's eyes, fixed on the largesse, gleamed. 'My lucky day – the day I found that hat.' He handed it to Phyllida.

393

Lucifer handed over the coins. 'And which day was that – the day you found the hat?'

The tinker screwed up his face. 'I left Axmouth on a Monday, and spent a day between there and in and about Colyton. I slept in the lych-gate and set out for Honiton early the next morn – that was when I found the hat.'

'So you found it on Tuesday?'

'Aye, but not this Tuesday. 'Twould have been the one before that – I was nearly a week in Honiton, and then I went down to Sidmouth.'

'Tuesday before last.' Lucifer nodded. 'Our thanks.'

The tinker looked down at the coins in his hand. 'I'm thinking 'twas my pleasure entirely.'

They left him bemused by his good fortune; Lucifer set the blacks pacing smartly, then glanced at Phyllida.

She was holding the hat in her lap, staring down at it. 'No wonder we couldn't find it – never saw it. He must have got rid of it straightaway.'

Her tone was distant. Lucifer frowned. 'Those tall gateposts you mentioned – that's the entrance to Ballyclose Manor, I take it.'

Phyllida nodded.

'So what is at the end of the seaward leg of the lane?'

She exhaled. 'It's a rear entrance to Ballyclose. It's not even a gate, just a gap in the hedge, but it's been there forever. Everyone who rides at Ballyclose uses it to come and go unless they're riding directly into the village.'

'So if someone was out riding from Ballyclose and didn't want to return by riding through the village, they'd use that entrance?'

'Yes.'

The tone of the word had Lucifer glancing at Phyllida again. 'What are you thinking?' He couldn't tell from her face.

She drew in a breath. 'It must be Cedric after all.'

He looked to his horses. 'There are other possibilities.'

'Such as?'

'That it's not Cedric's hat, for a start.'

Phyllida held the hat up, turning it around. 'Just because I can't recall seeing him wearing it doesn't mean it isn't his. You saw how many hats he has. I didn't recognize half of them.'

'Equally, just because he has a hat fetish doesn't mean that one's his.' Lucifer looked at the hat again. 'I really don't think it is.'

'If I can't be sure, I can't see how you can be.' Lucifer swallowed his explanation of why he didn't think the hat was Cedric's – he was, after all, only guessing. After a moment, he said, 'Very well, consider this. The murderer, not Cedric, knows that the books in Horatio's library leave Cedric with a real motive for killing Horatio, which, I admit, is more than we've been able to uncover for anyone else. The murderer, however, has another motive – one we have no idea of. Needing to get rid of the hat, he plants it at a place where enough people come past, so that, at some time, it'll be discovered and all will point to Cedric, not him.'

Phyllida stared at him. 'That's tortuous reasoning. Do you really think anyone actually thinks like that?'

Lucifer shot her a glance. 'Our murderer has eluded us multiple times – he's ruthless, clever, and without compunction. He probably has the sort of mind that works like that all the time.'

'Hmm.' Phyllida looked down at the hat. 'Or he could simply be Cedric.'

Lucifer let out a long sigh. 'I have serious difficulty casting Cedric in the role. Not because I don't think he could do it, but because I don't think he *would*.'

'I can't imagine him as a murderer, either, but . . .' Phyllida looked up; her gaze fixed forward. 'I think we should go directly to Ballyclose.'

'Why?'

'Because of this.' She brandished the hat. 'I cannot bear to go on thinking Cedric might be the murderer, and just not knowing. I want to find out – with this – now.'

'What on earth do you plan to do? Barge in and ask him if the hat's his?'

Phyllida lifted her chin. 'Precisely.'

'Phyllida—'

Lucifer argued, reasonably, then not so reasonably; Phyllida held firm. She wanted the matter settled, one way or another, today. In the end,

Lucifer looked at the hat in her lap, then, lips compressed, shook his head and faced forward.

'Very well,' he growled after a tense minute had crawled by. 'We'll go to Ballyclose, and *you* can do the talking.'

Nose in the air, Phyllida inclined her head, accepting his terms.

They rolled onto the gravel circle before Ballyclose's front steps half an hour later. A groom came running; Lucifer handed over the reins. He handed Phyllida down; she preceded him up the steps.

The butler smiled and bowed them in. He showed them into the drawing room, then went to confer with his master. He returned a moment later. 'Sir Cedric's in the library, if you would care to join him there, miss. Sir.'

Lucifer gave Phyllida his hand; she rose from the chair she'd only just sunk into. Carrying the hat before her, she led the way to the library. The butler held the door wide; Phyllida swept through. Cedric was seated behind his desk; he smiled and rose. Phyllida swept straight to the desk and plunked the hat down in the middle of Cedric's blotter.

Cedric stared at it.

Standing poker-straight before the desk, Phyllida almost glared at him. 'Is this hat yours, Cedric?'

Startled, Cedric blinked at her. 'No.'

'How can you be sure?'

Cedric glanced at Lucifer, who had halted behind Phyllida, then, warily, looked at her again.

Moving slowly, he reached for the hat, lifted it, and placed it on his head.

It was Phyllida's turn to stare. 'Oh.'

The hat sat on Cedric's head, propped high, well above his ears. It was patently too small for him.

All the steel went out of Phyllida; groping for a nearby armchair, she sank into it. Then she covered her eyes with her hands. 'Thank God!'

Lucifer closed a hand on her shoulder briefly, then held out his hand to Cedric. 'There is a sane explanation.'

'Glad to hear it.' Cedric shook hands, then removed the hat and studied it. 'Not but what this does look familiar.'

Phyllida removed her hands from her face. 'Do you know whose it is?'

Cedric grimaced. 'Can't place it this minute, but it'll come back to me. I usually notice hats.'

Lucifer flicked Phyllida a glance; she met it, but only briefly.

She looked at Cedric. 'It's very important that we find out whose hat that is, Cedric.'

He looked at her, then at Lucifer. 'Why?'

They told him.

'The inscriptions,' Lucifer said, having tactfully explained their existence, 'did give you an apparent motive for wanting to remove books from Horatio's library and, potentially, to do away with Horatio.'

Cedric blinked. 'Because they might call my paternity into question?'

Phyllida nodded. 'And therefore, Pommeroy could claim Sir Bentley's estate.'

Cedric regarded her for a moment, then coughed and glanced down the room. He lowered his voice. 'Actually, that wouldn't work. Papa worded his will specifically, naming me his principal heir. And as for Pommeroy, while there might be a question over my paternity, there's absolutely none about his. He's not Papa's son.'

'He's not?' Phyllida looked horrified.

Cedric shook his head. 'Not common knowledge, of course. Mama wouldn't like that.'

'Indeed not.' Phyllida blinked, then dazedly shook her head.

'So, you see, laboring under that misapprehension as we were . . .' Lucifer continued their explanation, omitting nothing. The ridiculous sight of the hat perched on Cedric's head had effectively removed him from their list of suspects. Cedric took the information that he'd topped the list for some time relatively well. When, cheeks rosy, Phyllida apologized, he waved it aside.

'You had to suspect everyone who wasn't at church that Sunday. As it is, I can't account for my time—'

'Perhaps you can't, but I can.'

Both Lucifer and Phyllida turned. Jocasta Smollet rose from a wing chair facing the windows some way down the room. She'd been sitting, hidden from sight when they'd entered.

Cedric got to his feet. 'Jocasta—'

Jocasta smiled at him – it was the most natural expression Lucifer had yet seen on her face. 'Don't fret, Cedric, but I'm not going to stand by and see your reputation sullied even by suspicion purely on account of my brother's pride. If we're truly to break free of it, then we may as well start as we mean to go on.'

Coming to stand beside Cedric, Jocasta looked at Phyllida, and at Lucifer, who had also risen. 'Cedric,' she said, 'was with me that Sunday – the Sunday morning when Horatio was killed.'

The announcement was so unexpected, Phyllida simply stared. Cedric harrumphed, then pulled up a chair for Jocasta. 'Here – sit down.'

She did; Cedric and Lucifer resumed their seats.

Jocasta folded her hands in her lap and regarded Lucifer and Phyllida calmly. 'Cedric wished to speak with me about our future – Sunday morning, when both Mama and Basil were in church, was the only time that was possible. He rode up shortly after the carriage left for church. The stable lad who took his horse would remember. We met privately, but our housekeeper, Mrs Swithins, was in the next room and the door was ajar. She can confirm that Cedric was with me for more than an hour. He left just before the carriage returned from church.'

'My dear, if we're going to tell them that much, then we should tell them the rest.' Cedric turned to Lucifer and Phyllida. 'Jocasta and I were close – oh, for many years. But when I asked for her hand

400

eight years ago, Basil would have none of it. He and I have our differences.' Looking down, Cedric shrugged. 'Basil wouldn't hear of us marrying, and, well, I dug in my heels and words were exchanged. And then Mama heard of it and she wasn't in favor, either, and things fell into a heap. Jocasta and I stopped seeing each other – we've avoided each other for years. But then Mama started insisting that I marry' – he glanced at Phyllida – 'specifically, that I marry *you*, my dear. Yet the more time I spent with you, the more I thought of Jocasta. I realized she was the only woman I wanted for my wife.' He looked at Jocasta, then held out a hand; she took it and smiled.

Face alight, Jocasta said, 'Cedric tried to talk to Basil last night, but he's still very set against the marriage.' She glanced at Cedric and squeezed his hand. 'But we've decided not to waste any more years. Regardless of what Basil and Mama may say—' 'Or my mama, either,' Cedric put in.

Jocasta inclined her head. 'Regardless, we've decided to marry.'

Phyllida found she was smiling. She rose; Jocasta rose, too. Phyllida embraced the older woman, touching cheeks. 'I'm so pleased for you.'

Jocasta's smile was a little crooked, but she met Phyllida's eyes. 'Thank you. I know I haven't been the kindest of souls over the years, but I hope you understand.'

'Of course.' Beaming, Phyllida turned to hug Cedric. 'I wish you both joy.'

'Very kind of you, m'dear.' Cedric patted her shoulder. 'Well' – he blew out a breath – 'at least you'll know why, if Mama comes screaming to cry on your shoulder.'

Phyllida grinned.

Lucifer shook hands with Cedric and Jocasta, wishing them both well; then he and Phyllida took their leave.

'Well!' Phyllida said as he tooled the carriage down the drive. 'Jocasta and Cedric! Whoever would have thought it.'

Lucifer kept his mouth shut.

An instant later, Phyllida sighed. 'Basil is going to have an apoplectic fit.' She smiled and leaned back, the murderer's brown hat, temporarily forgotten, in her lap.

CHAPTER 17

The next day was Sunday. Lucifer strode briskly up the common. An onshore breeze flirted with fleecy clouds in the pale blue sky. The last stragglers were making their way into the church; Lucifer joined them, sliding into a pew at the rear.

Scanning the congregation, he searched for Phyllida. He'd driven her home the previous afternoon; they hadn't discussed their next meeting. Leaving Dodswell watching the Manor, he'd come to ask her to spend the day with him, looking at books, reading inscriptions, strolling the lawns . . . whatever she wished to do.

He located Sir Jasper. Lady Huddlesford and Frederick sat beside him. Miss Sweet was there, too. He couldn't see Phyllida. Or Jonas.

The organ swelled; the congregation rose as Mr Filing and the small band of choristers paraded in. Lucifer hesitated, then left his seat; he made his way as unobtrusively as he could down the aisle to Sir Jasper's side.

Sir Jasper smiled.

'Phyllida?' Lucifer mouthed.

Sir Jasper leaned close and whispered, 'Headache. She's resting at home.'

Headache. Lucifer drew breath, then nodded and retreated. At the rear of the church, he hovered by the last pew, then turned and quit the church.

Face setting, he strode back down the common even faster than he'd gone up. There was nothing – nothing – to suggest that Phyllida didn't have a headache. Women did get headaches; they also used the term to excuse other, less mentionable ailments. When he reached the Grange and discovered Phyllida laid down upon her bed, he'd be able to accept her indisposition as truth and the nagging worry rising like a tide in his mind would subside.

Until then, with a killer on the loose, focused on her, his imagination was primed and ready to bolt. Reaching the lane, he broke into a lope.

From the church, it was faster to reach the Grange via the lane. Within minutes, he was turning through the gateposts. Gaining the front porch, he rang the bell, then opened the door and walked in. 'Phyllida?'

A door opened; Jonas emerged from the library. He stared at Lucifer, consternation showing through his usual benign mask. 'She's not with you?'

Lucifer opened his mouth; Jonas stopped him with an upraised hand. 'I walked Phyllida to the Manor via the wood. I just got back. She said you don't normally go to church and that you'd be there.'

Lucifer grimaced. 'Normally, but today I walked up to the church to meet her.'

Jonas grinned. Lucifer turned back to the door. 'I left Dodswell at the Manor, so there's no harm done.' In the doorway, he paused and looked back. 'Did she give any particular reason for wanting to see me?'

Still grinning, Jonas shook his head. 'Nothing she wanted to share with me. But she was carrying that brown hat, and her reticule, too, and a parasol. I assumed she wanted you to take her somewhere.'

'Hmm. No doubt I'll learn where soon enough.' With a nod, Lucifer stepped back through the door and closed it behind him.

Take her somewhere. As he strode around the Grange and into the wood, he tried to imagine where Phyllida had in mind. He'd assumed they were at a temporary standstill with their investigations, that they'd need to consider the question of where next. Presumably Phyllida had already done so and had come up with an answer.

He knew where he would like to take her, but that didn't require either parasol or reticule. She didn't normally carry either when visiting the Manor.

He lengthened his stride. A few paces later, he started to jog. The path through the wood was too uneven to risk a flat-out run. The tide of impending panic hadn't receded in the least – it was welling even higher.

He did run through the kitchen garden, slowing

only once inside the house. Dodswell met him in the front hall.

One look at his face, and the tide rushed in.

'Thank Gawd.' Dodswell held out a note. 'Miss Phyllida was here looking for you.'

'I've been looking for *her*.' Lucifer unfolded the note. Another note contained within it fell into his hands. Phyllida had written:

L – our tweeny brought this up just before I was to leave for church – she said she answered a tap on the back door and found it on the step. As you will see from the note, it appears we might at last have found Horatio's murderer, or at least someone who knows to whom the brown hat belongs. Molly is Lady Fortemain 's seamstress. I intended asking you to accompany me to the rendezvous, however, that was not to be, and Jonas had already left before I realized you weren't here, and I didn't wish to take Dodswell and leave the Manor unguarded. If I haven't returned by the time you come back from church, perhaps you can meet me there, or on the way back. P.

A postscript containing a set of directions followed. Lucifer turned his attention to the other note, the one Phyllida had received. 'Miss Tallent' was inscribed on the front in an obviously feminine hand. He opened the note. It read:

Dear Miss Tallent,

As you know, I work at Ballyclose, and I heard as how you was asking after who owned a certain brown hat. I know of a gentleman who has lost a brown hat, but I am not sure as it would be right to say who he is, not unless I am sure it is his hat.

I dont want it known, not by anyone, especially not this gentleman, that I am talking to you. I dont get much time away, but I can slip away from the house on Sunday while they are all off at church. If you want me to look at the hat you have and see if it is the one I am thinking of, then if you meet me at the old Drayton cottage during Sunday service, I will try to help you.

Yrs respectfully, Molly

The note looked genuine. The words were carefully inked; it was easy to imagine a seamstress laboring over its composition.

Lucifer waited for his panic to recede. It didn't. Some primitive part of him was on full alert, prodding like some diabolical demon with a fiery prong for him to move – fast. His body was tensed, tight with the need to fly into action.

He swore and juggled the notes.

Was it intuition that urged that she wasn't safe, that she was, in fact, walking into danger? Or was it instinct, elemental, primal, that insisted she was not truly safe except when in his care?

Or was it simply panic, the black fear that, at any time she was out of his sight, she might be taken from him?

He thrust the questions aside and tried to make sense of Phyllida's directions. The old Drayton cottage stood some way north of the fields bordering the lane to Dottswood and Highgate. He'd heard it described as abandoned. While his logical mind reiterated that all would be well, that the murderer could not know that Phyllida was out walking alone that way, even his logical mind had to admit the Drayton cottage sounded an odd rendezvous for some woman walking from Ballyclose to suggest.

Who knew what went on in the minds of women?

His own words uttered earlier in relation to Phyllida. He thrust the notes into his pocket. 'I'll follow Miss Tallent.'

Dodswell nodded. 'Aye. I'll wait here and keep an eye out.'

The way was clear to the point where the narrow ridge lane met the village lane. Thereafter, Lucifer checked Phyllida's instructions frequently as he strode along walking paths, over fields, across stiles, past copses. The sun rode the sky and beat down on his shoulders. It would have been a pleasant walk if he hadn't been so tense, if he hadn't been striding so fast.

Rounding a copse, he paused to consult Phyllida's note. The breeze shifted – he smelled smoke.

Head up, he sniffed – and caught the scent again. He glanced at the note, then stuffed it into his pocket and started to run.

He had one more field to cross; the abandoned cottage supposedly lay in a clearing beyond. He broke through the hedge and ran full tilt through the knee-high crops. Trees screened what lay ahead, but the smoke was more definite on the breeze. He vaulted the gate and plunged into the trees. A greedy crackling reached his ears.

Bursting from the trees, he saw the cottage standing on a low crest above him, already well alight. The front door stood open; as he raced up the flags of an old garden path, he registered the fact that the door was propped open. Windows were open, too.

The roof was old thatch, brittle and dry; flames were already thrusting through it. The open windows and door fed the inferno.

Smoke billowed out at him as if trying to drive him from the door. He coughed, turned away, dragged in a breath, then dove in.

His eyes watered; even ignoring that, he could barely see. Smoke curled and eddied, a tangible shroud growing thicker by the minute. He felt walls to his right and left. A corridor. Head down, hand outstretched, his handkerchief held to his nose and mouth, he felt along it.

Wood – a doorframe. He went to turn into the room. His feet struck something; he lurched and fell to his knees.

Flames raced across the room's ceiling with a whooshing roar. They licked over the top of the door-frame, voraciously reaching for the sustaining air outside.

On his hands and knees, Lucifer coughed. He'd lost his handkerchief; he could barely breathe. His lungs already felt raw.

What had he tumbled over? He reached out blindly; he could have wept with relief when his hands closed over a leg – a female leg. Phyllida – or the seamstress? He reached further, going quicker and quicker, tracing the body, until he got to her head. Her hair.

Phyllida. The feel of the silken fall under his palm was a remembered delight. The shape of her skull cradled in his hand was imprinted on his brain.

Phyllida.

The relief was so great, for an instant he stopped, head down, and struggled to take it in. She lay face-down, still breathing, but barely.

He could barely breathe himself; he couldn't concentrate, could hardly think.

A long, groaning creak sounded overhead; a sharp crack like a pistol shot echoed. Another gout of whooshing flames seared the air above them, eating it up. The heat intensified, beating down on them, scorching, shriveling.

He could no longer expand his chest. Taking shallow little breaths, he staggered to his feet, not straightening. Bending over Phyllida, he grasped her waist, then struggled and shrugged and wrestled her over his shoulder.

A shower of cinders rained down as he turned to where he knew the door was. He staggered two steps and fetched up against the doorframe. Phyllida hung down behind him, her head bumping on his lower back. He kept his hold on her legs and shuffled into the corridor. Step by shuffling step, he headed for the front door. No point looking up – the ceiling glowed red behind the blanket of smoke that lay thick and heavy all about them.

He bounced off the corridor wall, then half tripped and fell. He put a hand out – and grasped the edge of the front door. His head was swimming. For an instant, he remained, dazed, sick, reeling. Above, something popped, then snapped. Burning wood rained down. A piece struck his hand; more bits hit Phyllida's skirts. He gasped, but caught no air, then frantically brushed the burning fragments from Phyllida. Her skirt was scorched, but hadn't caught alight.

A draft of cool air wafted to him. The flames above and behind them roared.

Lucifer dragged the taste of survival deep, held it in, and struggled to his feet.

He stumbled across the threshold and got three steps along the path before he collapsed again. They were out of the worst, but not free. They were still too close.

Coughing, almost retching, he looked back, blinking his stinging eyes. The front doorway was haloed in flame, bright and hungry. The open windows were belching smoke; behind their sills, flames danced.

If Molly the seamstress was in there, he could do nothing to save her.

He looked down at Phyllida. She'd slipped from his shoulder when he'd fallen and now lay unconsious beside him. He hauled in a breath and felt it score its way into his lungs. Gasping, he rose – to his knees. He couldn't manage his feet.

Head whirling, he wrapped an arm around Phyllida and locked her to his side, dragging her with him as he crawled off the path, onto the lawn, taking the most direct route away from the house. He reached a point where the lawn sloped down toward the trees. He lay down, pulled Phyllida's unconscious form to him, cradling her face into his chest, protecting her head and shoulders with his arms – then he rolled.

Their momentum carried them most of the way down; they fetched up on a shallow shelf of mossy grass, well away from the burning cottage.

Lucifer lifted his head and looked back at the cottage. Flames shot through every window, greedily licking up the outside walls. It was the ultimate death trap.

Phyllida lay unconscious, barely breathing beside him. Still alive.

He exhaled, closed his eyes, and flopped back on the grass.

★   ★   ★

The wind shifted, carrying the taint of smoke as far as the common. A fire in the country at this time of year triggered an immediate response. Men came running with pitchforks, sacks – anything they could lay their hands on.

The Thompson brothers were the first to come thundering up. Others arrived on foot, still others on horses, some saddled, some not. Grooms, stable lads, footmen, and their employers all turned out. Lucifer glimpsed Basil stalking the scene, shouting orders. Coat off, Cedric wielded a pitchfork, breaking up thatch as it fell away, dispersing it so those with sacks could beat the flames to death.

Focused on the cottage, no one saw them. Lucifer lay still, head pounding, too weak to move, and listened to the almost indiscernible huff of Phyllida's breathing. The sound held him to consciousness, to some degree of lucidity.

Then the flames started to falter, running out of fuel. The cottage had burned more or less to the ground. Thompson retreated into the garden to catch his breath, and saw them. He let out a surprised 'Oy!' and came lumbering down the slope.

Others turned, saw, and followed. Lucifer braced. He waved Thompson to him; with the big man's help, he managed to sit. The backs of his hands were scorched, as were the pads of his fingers. His hair had largely escaped, but his coat was ruined, shoulders and back pocked with burns and scorch marks. A crowd gathered about them – Oscar, Filing, Cedric, Basil, Henry Grisby, and more. Every face was shocked, deeply and utterly shocked. Clearing his throat, Lucifer managed to say, 'I found her unconscious in the cottage. It was already well alight.'

Filing pushed through and went to his knee beside Phyllida. She lay on her stomach, her face to the side. Gripping gently, Filing raised her shoulder just enough to confirm she still lived, still breathed. He eased her back to the cushioning moss. 'We'll have to get you both out of here – Phyllida needs to be back at the Grange.'

Lucifer closed his eyes. The world was still swaying. 'Sir Jasper?'

'The Grange household left the church before the alarm was raised.'

Lucifer wasn't sure if that was good or not. Sir Jasper would have been shaken, but he could still have counted on the older man to take charge. He himself was not up to it at present.

Basil hunkered down beside Phyllida. He stretched out a hand and lifted a fallen lock of her hair back from her face. His face was set, blank with shock. Phyllida's hair was scorched here and there; her blue gown had fared worse, even worse than Lucifer's coat. Thankfully, she'd worn a cambric walking dress, not one of her thin muslin gowns. With luck, she would escape any major burns. Basil's hand shook as he drew it back; he had paled.

So, too, had the others. Henry Grisby caught his breath and volunteered, 'Dottswood's closest. I've a farm cart I can bring up the old lane. It'll still be a way away, but . . .' His voice trailed away.

Filing nodded. 'Yes, Henry. That's the best suggestion. Go, now.'

Henry nodded. He drew back, his gaze on Phyllida. Then he turned and started climbing the slope, slowly, then more quickly. At the top, he broke into a run.

'Terrible, terrible.' As shaken as the rest, Cedric straightened; the effort he made to regain his composure was visible. He looked at Lucifer. 'Was it about that hat?'

Lucifer looked at him, then glanced at the smoldering cottage. 'I believe she had the hat with her.'

Phyllida regained consciousness on the journey back to the Grange. The gentle rocking of the cart, the freshening breeze, tugged her back to reality. She opened her eyes and was immediately beset by a paroxysm of coughing.

A large hand closed over hers.

'It's all right. You're safe.'

She looked up; through stinging tears, she saw the face that, in the moment she'd thought would be her last, had been the only face in her mind. Her last instant of lucidity had been filled with regret — regret for what they wouldn't have a chance to share. Closing her eyes, she let her head slump and gave silent thanks. Fate had been kind – they still had their chance.

Sliding her fingers in his, she clung. 'Who saved me?' His coat was burned, an unsalvageable wreck.

'Hush – don't talk.'

She heard a rustle on the cart's seat; then Henry Grisby's voice reached her.

'Lucifer saved you – thank God.'

His tone was fervent. Lucifer had, it seemed, been elevated from demon to god, at least in Henry's eyes.

Not only in Henry's eyes. Phyllida squeezed Lucifer's fingers, inexpressibly relieved to feel them firm and strong around hers.

The hours that followed were a confusion of sounds perceived through a haze – her lungs felt tight, dizziness threatened, she couldn't stand or speak, she could barely move, not even her head. Her eyes burned, but at least she could see – at least she was still alive.

Every time her mind touched on that, she wept – tears of joy, of relief, of emotion too overwhelming to contain.

Her father was shocked, shaken. She tried to reassure him but had no idea if what she said was even coherent. Jonas carried her upstairs, but it was Lucifer who lingered, leaning over her bed, stroking her hair back from her face. Behind him, Sweetie, Gladys, and her aunt rushed and fussed and spoke in whispers. Lucifer leaned close, his face sootstreaked, his expression softer than she'd ever known it.

He touched his lips to hers. 'Rest. I'll be here when you wake. Then we'll talk.'

Her lids drifted closed of their own accord. She thought she nodded.

Evening shadows were playing across her room when she awoke. For long minutes, she simply lay there, thrilled by the fact of being alive.

With the help of Sweetie and her aunt, she'd stripped off her ruined clothes, then bathed. She'd had Sweetie snip the scorched locks from her hair. Gladys had produced a salve. After annointing every minor burn and scorched spot, she'd donned a fine cotton robe and lain down on her bed.

They'd left her and she'd slept. It had been like falling into a deep well, black, soundless, undisturbed.

She felt a great deal better. Gingerly, she eased up to sit, then, encouraged, swung her legs over the side of the bed. Holding onto the bed, she stood. Her limbs seemed in working order. A twinge here and there, the scorches and bruises, too, but nothing incapacitating.

A cough caught her; rasping pain gripped her lungs. She clung to the bed, struggling to master her breathing. Her throat felt scorched; it hurt to breathe other than shallowly. If she drew a deeper breath, coughing threatened.

417

Once the paroxysm faded, she straightened and walked, carefully, to the bellpull.

Her little maid, Becky, came up. Twenty minutes later, Phyllida felt human again – resurrected. In a gown of soft lavender trimmed with a flounce and a narrow band of darker ribbon, with a gauzy scarf around her throat and perfume dabbed liberally, hair neat and sleek once more, she felt ready to face what lay beyond her door.

The maid opened it for her. Before she could cross the threshold, Lucifer was there.

He frowned. 'You should have rung. I would have—' He stopped, then grimaced. 'Got Jonas to carry you down.'

Phyllida smiled; with her heart and soul in her eyes, she smiled into his. Then she let her gaze roam, drinking in the fact that he, too, had rested and recovered. He was wearing a coat of that particular shade of dark blue that best set off his eyes and made his hair appear blacker than jet. The sight erased a lingering worry in her heart; only with its easing did she realize it had been there.

'You shouldn't be walking.'

His voice was rough and raspy. She studied his hard face, then calmly said, 'Why not? You are.'

He scowled, trying to read her eyes. 'I wasn't knocked unconscious.'

She raised her brows. 'Was I?'

'Yes.'

'Well, I'm conscious now. If you'll just give me your arm, I'm sure we'll manage.' He did.

He hovered solicitously down the stairs and all the way to the library, but, as she'd predicted, they managed perfectly well.

Pausing before the library door, she let her gaze linger on his face. Raising a finger, she traced his cheek, as she first had two weeks ago. 'When we work together we're invincible.'

She'd intended the comment to refer to their descent; hearing it, she realized it applied to much more.

She lifted her eyes and he met them, his blue gaze steady. He trapped her hand, pressed a kiss to her palm. 'So it would appear.'

He held her gaze for a moment longer, then reached past her and opened the library door.

Her father rose as they entered. So, too, did Cedric. Jonas was standing by the long windows.

'My dear!' Sir Jasper came forward, hands outstretched, concern very evident in his face.

Phyllida put her hands in his. 'Papa.' She returned his kiss. 'I'm feeling much better, and I really should tell you what happened.' Her voice was as raspy as Lucifer's.

'Humph'.' Sir Jasper looked at her, shaggy brows drawn down. 'You're quite sure you're up to it?'

'Quite sure.' Retaking Lucifer's arm, she allowed him to steer her to the *chaise*. She nodded to Cedric.

Handing her to the *chaise*, Lucifer murmured, 'I thought Cedric should be here – there are points he might be able to help us with.'

Phyllida nodded and settled back. Before she could blink, Lucifer lifted her ankles and swung her feet up. Previously, she'd have glared and swung them back down. Now she just wriggled into a more comfortable position.

'Well, then.' Clearing his throat, her father sat in a nearby chair. 'If you're determined to explain it tonight, we'd better start, heh?'

'Perhaps' – Lucifer took the chair beside the *chaise* – 'to save Phyllida's throat, I could fill in the background, then she need only describe the events only she knows.'

Sir Jasper turned his gaze expectantly to Lucifer. Cedric, in another armchair, did the same. Jonas held to his position by the windows, his attention fixed on Lucifer.

Lucifer settled back. 'To begin, there are some elements in our investigations which concern others not implicated in Horatio's murder or the subsequent attacks on Phyllida, but to whom we, Phyllida and I, owe a certain measure of confidentiality.' He looked at Sir Jasper. 'If you will accept some of our discoveries without detailed explanations of how we made them, then we can preserve those confidentialities without prejudicing our account.'

Every inch the magistrate, Sir Jasper nodded. 'Sometimes that's the way of things. If mentioning unnecessary details will trouble someone who has done no wrong, then there's no need for me to know.'

Lucifer nodded. 'On that basis, then. Phyllida saw a hat at the murder scene soon after the murder, but later that hat disappeared. Bristleford and the Hemmingses never saw it. It was not Horatio's. When the attacks on Phyllida became obvious and concerted, she concluded that the hat would identify the murderer – or so the murderer believes. There's nothing else Phyllida knows that could explain the murderer's interest in her.'

'Did Phyllida recognize the hat?' Sir Jasper asked.

Lucifer shook his head. 'She has no idea whose hat it is, but even though she has obviously not remembered – given she's raised no hue and cry – as evidenced by his continued attacks on her, the murderer's convinced she will, at some point, recall, and she's therefore a continuing threat to him.'

'How did the murderer know Phyl had seen the hat?'

The question came from Jonas; Lucifer turned to look at him. 'We don't know. We can only assume that, from hiding, he saw her take note of it.'

Turning back to Sir Jasper and Cedric, Lucifer continued. 'Phyllida kept her eyes open for the hat – a brown one. Simultaneously, I was pursuing the idea that something in Horatio's library was behind his death. For instance, some information hidden in a book that the murderer wished to hide. We found such information. Unexpectedly, we also found the brown hat.'

'Both the information and the brown hat led us to Cedric, but when we confronted him with both, it was quickly proved that he wasn't the murderer. The hat didn't fit, and the information wasn't as vital as it had seemed. Cedric also has a solid alibi for the time when Horatio was killed. We established all that yesterday, by which time it was evening.'

'This morning, before church, Phyllida received this note.' Lucifer drew the note from his pocket and handed it to Sir Jasper. Sir Jasper read it, then, his expression hardening, passed it to Cedric.

Sir Jasper looked at Phyllida. 'So you didn't have a headache?'

Phyllida colored and shook her head. 'Molly asked for no one to know. I got Jonas to take me to the Manor, intending to show only Lucifer and have him escort me to the cottage.'

'But I wasn't there – I'd gone to look for Phyllida.'

'I assumed,' Phyllida said, 'that the note was genuine, so when Lucifer wasn't at the Manor, I went on to the cottage alone, reasoning that I'd be safe, as the murderer could not know I was out, walking that way.'

Cedric handed the note back to Sir Jasper. 'Whoever wrote it, it wasn't Molly. She's in Truro visiting her family, and, on top of that, the girl doesn't read or write much above a few words. Mama's forever lamenting that she has to make the lists of stuffs to buy herself.'

'So,' Lucifer continued, 'someone wrote the note making sure it looked innocuous, unthreatening, but also believable. Phyllida knew Molly; we'd found the hat near the back of Ballyclose Manor. No one saw who left the note here – Jonas checked with the staff indoors and out.'

Sir Jasper humphed. 'Whoever he is, he's clever and very careful not to be seen.'

'Which suggests,' Jonas put in, 'that if he was seen, most people would know who he was.'

Lucifer nodded. 'My thoughts exactly. It's someone widely known in the village. That's inescapable.'

'So what happened next?' Sir Jasper addressed the question to Phyllida. All eyes swung to her.

She drew in a breath, careful not to make it too deep. 'I reached the cottage. The front door was open as if someone was waiting inside. I went in, calling for Molly, but there was no reply. I went into the parlor and stopped just inside the door. There was no one about . . .'

Phyllida had to stop to take another breath, to break the hold of the paralyzing fear, to remind herself she'd survived. Lucifer rose and came around the *chaise* to perch on the back. He reached down and took her hand, his fingers curling over hers. She glanced up – his expression was closed, but she drew strength from his touch.

She looked at her father. 'I was about to turn back to the door. A black cloth dropped over my head. Hands closed around my throat and squeezed – I struggled, but it was no good. He held on, but the cloth was too thick – he couldn't strangle me through it.'

Lucifer glanced down. There were bruises about her throat, just blossoming, largely hidden by the scarf she'd wound around her neck.

'He . . . I think he lost his temper. He swore and muttered about me leading a charmed life, but his voice was so . . . so *fraught*, through the material I couldn't recognize it.'

'But it was the same man who attacked you before?' Sir Jasper asked.

She nodded. 'The same man who attacked me in the graveyard.' She hesitated, then went on. 'He still held me, but he took away one hand. I heard a scrape . . . I jerked back.' She looked up at Lucifer. 'I think he hit me with something.'

With one finger, Lucifer touched the bump behind her ear. He'd discovered it while in the farm cart. 'Here.' An inch farther forward – where the murderer had been aiming – and he'd have killed her. As it was, the blow had been glancing.

Eyes too wide, Phyllida looked into his face. 'I don't remember anything more. Not until I woke up in the cart.'

Lucifer would have liked to smile, just a little, to reassure her. He couldn't. 'You were unconscious. He assumed that you'd die in the fire.'

'I nearly did.'

Lucifer tightened his hold on her hand. He looked at Sir Jasper. 'I was following Phyllida to the cottage – I smelled the smoke.' He briefly described how he'd found her. 'And then, thankfully, the others arrived.'

Head bowed to his steepled fingers, Sir Jasper pondered, then he regarded Phyllida and Lucifer. 'The brown hat?'

Phyllida glanced at Lucifer. 'I dropped it in the cottage.'

Lucifer shook his head. 'I didn't see it. The smoke was so thick I only found Phyllida by touch. I think we can assume the brown hat is now cinders.'

Sir Jasper addressed Phyllida. 'Any sense in making a list of all the local men who wear brown hats?'

'I already did that. Even with the hat in my hand, I couldn't remember it on any of them.'

Sir Jasper grimaced. 'In that case, I don't think there's any point raising a hue and cry for a man who wears a brown hat. That would cover half the county. Even *I* wear brown hats.'

'I agree.' Lucifer glanced at Phyllida, then at Sir Jasper. 'Much as I hate to say it, we're no nearer to identifying the murderer than we were when Horatio died. We had the brown hat – I was going to suggest that we take it around the village. While Phyllida couldn't place it, others might. Cedric even thought it was familiar. But the murderer acted. Whoever he is, he's clever and able to act decisively under pressure. If we'd started showing the hat around, he might well have been unmasked.

Instead, he struck boldly and removed the hat, and nearly removed Phyllida, too. He's ruthless and very dangerous. And we have no clue who he is.'

'Only,' Jonas said, 'that he probably still believes that, at some point, Phyl will remember who owned the hat.'

Phyllida sighed. 'The truth is, I never will. As far as I know, the first time I saw that hat was on Horatio's drawing room table after he'd been killed.'

That conclusion did not make anyone feel more comfortable. Lucifer eventually put their helplessness into words. 'All we can do is pray that the murderer realizes that Phyllida is no threat to him.'

CHAPTER 18

Cedric excused himself and returned to Ballyclose. At Sir Jasper's urging, Lucifer stayed to dine at the Grange.

The meal was a family affair. All present were subdued, reflecting on Phyllida's near escape. Even Lady Huddlesford spoke rarely, and then in a quiet tone quite different from her usual imperiousness. The only moment of interest arose when Percy declared he'd decided to leave the next day for 'the congenial company of some friends in Yorkshire.' The announcement was met with blank silence, then everyone returned to his meal.

When the ladies retreated to the drawing room and the port was set upon the table, Percy excused himself and retired to pack.

Frederick moved to a chair next to Jonas. 'I say, terrible business. Is there anything I can do?'

The question – surely the first intimation that Frederick thought of anything beyond himself – arrested the three other men. Then Sir Jasper harrumphed, but kindly. 'Nothing I can think of, m'boy. Nothing to be done – nothing we can do at present.'

Lucifer wasn't so sure. His gaze on Jonas, he spoke to Sir Jasper. 'I wonder, sir, if I might have a private word.'

Jonas rose. 'Come on, Frederick. Let's go pot some balls.'

Frederick murmured his farewells and followed Jonas out of the room.

His face tight with worry, Sir Jasper turned to Lucifer. 'Thought of something, have you?'

'In a way, yes. Lady Huddlesford mentioned earlier that you were expecting guests tomorrow.'

Sir Jasper looked blank, then consternation filled his face. 'Damn! Forgot. My sister, Eliza, her husband, and their brood arrive tomorrow. They come for a few weeks every summer.' He looked at Lucifer. 'Six children.'

'Although I'm sure she'll declare otherwise, I doubt Phyllida is up to coping with such an invasion at present.'

'Indeed, not – the four girls are a handful. Drive us insane. They tend to cling to Phyllida.'

'Not this time.'

'No. You're right. Although how to keep them from bothering her . . .' Sir Jasper shook his head. 'I won't hide it from you, m'boy – I'm deuced worried about Phyllida.'

'As am I. Which is why I'd like to suggest that Phyllida stay as a guest at the Manor for as long as this murderer is on the loose, for as long as we have reason to think her in danger. I realize the suggestion is somewhat unusual, but I've already made plain my intentions toward her and they haven't changed. For her part, Phyllida is aware of them.'

'She hasn't refused?'

'No, but she has yet to agree.' Lucifer sat back. 'However, in this, I'm thinking primarily of her safety. After the incident of our nighttime intruder, I ordered locks for all the doors and windows at the Manor. They've arrived – Thompson started installing them yesterday. He's completing the task as we speak. Once that's done, the Manor will be thoroughly secure. The Grange is not.' He shrugged. 'Most country houses aren't.'

'True. So little need, generally speaking.'

'Exactly, but this isn't a usual case. There's also the fact that my staff have no other guest to deal with, so they'll be on hand to ensure Phyllida is cared for and protected at all times. Of course, I would imagine Miss Sweet would accompany Phyllida; thus, the proprieties will be observed.'

Sir Jasper humphed. 'Very neat. For myself, given the seriousness of the situation, I'm grateful for the suggestion and to hell with the proprieties. But the ladies set such store by 'em, best to do what we can to preserve them.'

'My thoughts exactly.'

Sir Jasper looked at Lucifer, then nodded. 'As I said before, whatever permission you need, consider it given.' He paused, then asked, 'Do you think she'll agree?'

Lucifer's expression remained impassive. 'You may leave that to me.'

'Where are you taking me?' Phyllida looked up, into Lucifer's face, and waited for an answer. With her cradled in his arms, he was striding through the shrubbery. They'd set out for a moonlit stroll around the back lawn, but then he'd scooped her up into his arms and turned between the hedges.

Her throat was still sore; despite having slept for half the day, she was tiring. She'd only just remembered to give orders for rooms for her aunt and family to be prepared for their arrival tomorrow. While she'd been talking to Gladys, Lucifer had chatted to Sweetie, then strolled up and inveigled her into believing that a turn about the gardens in the cool of the night would help her still difficult breathing.

An image of Sweetie's face as, parting from Lucifer, she'd turned to go upstairs suddenly glowed in Phyllida's mind. She tightened her arms about Lucifer's neck. The end of the shrubbery was approaching. 'Stop.'

He didn't. He kept straight on through the gap in the hedges and onto the path through the wood.

Phyllida inwardly sighed. She relaxed her arms. 'You're taking me to the Manor. Why?'

For a moment, he didn't say anything; then he stopped in a spot where the moonlight beamed down. He could see her face bathed in silver; she could barely see his as he looked down at her.

'You're going to let me take care of you.'

She wasn't sure there was a question involved. She tried to think what her answer should be. She was the one who cared for everyone else – she couldn't remember the last time someone had set themselves to care for her.

He shifted her weight in his arms, gathering her closer, tightening his hold – not enough to make her feel trapped, just enough to make her feel totally secure. Totally safe.

'You have to let me protect you.'

Those words were softer, more like a plea.

She tried to read his eyes, but couldn't. There was, however, no one more capable of protecting her than he.

And she knew she needed protection.

She'd wondered how she was going to fall asleep, tired though she was. The fear and panic that had swamped her in the cottage hovered, a shadow at the edge of her mind. She would sleep much better knowing he was near.

Besides, if she wanted a marriage of sharing, of give and take, then perhaps this was one of those times she should give . . . and take. 'Very well.' An instant later, she added, 'If you wish to.'

His soft snort suggested, strongly, that her qualification was absurd. He started forward again.

'Sweetie's packing your things. She'll stay, too, so there'll be no scandal. She'll drive around in the carriage. We'll be safe through the wood – no one could know we'd be out here.'

431

Phyllida considered that. 'Our man – the murderer – has been like that, hasn't he? All his attacks have been carefully planned. Even that time at Ballyclose, it was almost as if he'd been watching. It was all too neat.'

Lucifer nodded. 'He knew we were looking for brown hats and that Cedric had a shelfful, and that you'd know Cedric wore brown hats. Everyone knew we'd both be at Ballyclose that night.'

'That suggests the murderer knows the Ballyclose household well. He knew where Cedric kept his hats.'

'True, but you mentioned that Sir Bentley was ill for some time. I take it he held court in his bedroom and that many of the local gentry attended.'

Phyllida grimaced. 'Yes, but the murderer also knew of Molly. He knew she existed and that I knew her, too.'

Lucifer frowned. 'You're right.'

Some minutes later, he stepped out from the trees. Ahead, the Manor stood pale and solid, a modern castle. Welcoming lights shone from the kitchen; one hung over the back door, which swung open as they neared. Mrs Hemmings looked out and beamed.

'Welcome, Miss Phyllida, and right glad we be to see you safe and sound.' She stood back and let Lucifer past, then followed hard on his heels. 'Now, you just let the master carry you on up to the old master's bedroom – it's the biggest and I've done my best to make it seem homey. The bed's nice and big. All you need do is lie back and let us all take care of you.'

The eager anticipation in Mrs Hemmings's voice was impossible to mistake. As Lucifer started up the stairs, Phyllida looked into his impassive countenance – and wondered just what she'd agreed to.

Three hours later, Phyllida lay in the big bed in Horatio's old room – the bed that, unbeknownst to Mrs Hemmings, she'd occupied once before – and listened to the deep bongs of the longcase clock on the landing send waves through the silence of the house.

Twelve resonating bongs, then silence returned, deeper, thicker than it had been before. Beyond the Manor, the village and its surrounding houses lay sleeping. Somewhere lay a murderer, asleep – or awake?

Wriggling onto her side, she closed her eyes and waited for sleep to reclaim her. Instead, black filled her mind – the black of the shroud – she could feel his hands on her throat! Her eyes flew open. She was breathing too fast, too shallowly. Her skin felt cold; all warmth had drained away.

She shivered and drew in a breath, then exhaled and threw back the covers.

She moved quietly but not silently along the corridor, eyes open to their widest extent, ready to speak – or squeak – if necessary. She remembered the sword Lucifer had carried the last time they'd met in the dark. She didn't know how good his night vision was.

His door stood open. She halted in the doorway; she hadn't been in this room before. All the curtains were open letting starlight stream in; the moon had waned. Shadows lay thick, but she could make out the chests that stood between the windows, with what she assumed were items from Horatio's collection arrayed on their tops. Tallboys and armoires lined the other walls. A long wall mirror hung opposite the bed – a huge four-poster with curtains cinched by tasseled cords at each post.

The rich covers were half turned down; white sheets and pillows filled the bed above. In their midst, Lucifer lay sprawled on his stomach, much as he'd been that first night at the Grange. The only difference was, this time he was wearing no nightshirt. Full knowledge of what wouldn't be covered blossomed in her mind. She hesitated, uncertain what to do next, but she had no intention of retreating.

She'd made up her mind, although she wasn't sure when. Perhaps when she'd woken in the cart and found him beside her, her savior, her protector who had faced death for her and rescued her from its vicious teeth. Perhaps later in the wood when she'd heard his plea, heard his heart speak without any social glamor to shield it. Or maybe it had been when she'd realized that it was the facet of his care she found most difficult to accept – his possessive protectiveness – that had given her a second chance at life and love. Whenever it had been, her decision was made.

Her time alone – managing alone, being alone, sleeping alone – had come to an end. She was here to let him know.

Whether he'd been asleep or not, she had no idea, but he slowly rose on one elbow and studied her.

'What is it?'

His voice was even, a little hoarse, but whether from the smoke or something else, she couldn't tell.

Barefoot, she padded over the threshold, then paused, turned back, and shut the door. Clutching her robe around her, she walked – heart in her mouth – to the side of the bed. She stopped a foot from it. The bed was a mass of shadows; she couldn't see his face.

She licked her dry lips, then drew breath and lifted her chin. 'I want to sleep with you.' She meant more than just sleep, but surely he'd understand.

For one instant, he just stared at her, then his smile flashed. 'Good.' He lifted the covers beside him. 'I want you to sleep with me, too.'

A sigh of relief escaped her, chased by a shivery, anticipatory tingle. She shrugged the robe off her shoulders. It fell to puddle at her feet.

Noting his suddenly arrested state – the locking of muscles throughout his large body at the sight of her naked limbs – she shyly slid into his bed.

He let go of the sheets. And reached for her.

'You've just made my favorite dream come true.'

She reached for him and drew him to her. 'Do you think you can return the favor?'

He looked into her face. 'I'll do my very best.' He lowered his head. 'You can count on it.'

That first kiss sealed that promise; she felt it in her bones. Warmth unfurled between them, driving out her chill. She sank into it, offering her mouth and more. Although he claimed her lips, tangled her tongue, mesmerized her wits with slow, tantalizing surges, with one hand framing her face, the other trapped next to her shoulder, he remained beside her, his body a hot line alongside hers, but not touching.

She wanted to touch, to feel, to explore. She wanted to give herself to him and take all he would give in return. There was something very liberating in the thought, a free exchange that, ultimately, would balance, with body, mind, heart, and soul all freely offered on the scales. She turned and pressed, stretched upward against him, matching her body to his.

He gave a wicked chuckle, one not entirely steady. Closing his arms around her, he shifted onto his back, urging her across him. She followed his lead, quite content to sprawl atop him. Much easier to explore from there.

She took his urging as invitation. Wriggling until she straddled his hips, knees bent, calves gripping lightly along his flanks, she braced her arms, palms flat on his chest, and lifted up – so she could survey her prize.

His chest had always fascinated her – the sharp contrasts of smooth, lightly tanned skin and crisp black hair, the palpable weight of muscle and the heavier, harder curves of bone. Fingers splayed, she pressed, glorying in the resilience of muscle, the solid resistance of bone. Then she softened her touch and went searching, caressing lightly, then lovingly, across the broad muscles, down over his ribs, across the ridges of his abdomen. Only her position stopped her from reaching further, but she had all night.

'None of your chest was burned.' Her sighing comment reeked with satisfaction.

'No real burns. Just the backs of my hands got scorched.'

She examined his hands as he held them up. 'Do they hurt?'

He skimmed his palms down her back. 'Not enough to stop me from touching you.'

She responded to the long, artful caress with a low, murmurous moan.

Of their own volition, her hands stroked upward again to cover his flat nipples. She let her fingers tease and draw, then circle, roll – until his nipples were as tight as hers.

That seemed fair. She smiled and leaned forward, remembering what else he liked to do to her. And how much she liked his doing it. Presumably the same actions worked in reverse.

The way he stiffened even before her tongue touched convinced her that was true. She licked, laved, then nipped lightly. That last made him jerk. His hands gripped her hips, fingers sinking in, but he made no effort to stop her.

So she played, fingers firm on one bud while she tortured the other with lips, tongue, and teeth. Then she switched hand and head, trailing wet, openmouthed kisses across his chest on the way. She settled to her task and thought she heard a low moan. He was burning up beneath her, his skin fire-hot everywhere she touched.

A wicked thought occurred. She pressed her body lower, so that her breasts caressed his lower chest and the backs of her thighs moved against his hips, the hot, wet, aching flesh at the juncture of her thighs a bare inch above his flat stomach. Just out of reach of the ultimate prize.

Then she moved. Sliding her body from side to side, she caressed him.

He sucked in a breath; his body tensed beneath her. She sensed his struggle to lie still. His fingers flexed on her hips, tightening before he forced them to relax . . . she felt their touch drift upward, over her shoulders. She suckled one nipple lightly, then tightly. He arched beneath her. His fingers tangled in her hair, clutched – then he drew her away, turning her face to his.

He swooped – his lips closed on hers in a searing kiss so full of heated passion it stole her breath. The kiss went on and on. He started to turn, to

438

roll her beneath him. She pulled away, hand on his shoulder pressing him back. She shook her head, then found her voice, a little hoarse, like his. 'Not yet.'

He was tempted to disobey – the tension in his body told her that – but after a fraught moment, he eased back to the bed. His eyes, dark in the night, watched her; his gaze held a heat all its own. His chest rose and fell beneath her hands. 'All right. For now.'

She smiled and made the gesture beautific, then ducked her head to lick first one aching nipple, then the other. Then she shuffled her legs, her hips, farther down his body, lifting slightly to accommodate the hard shaft of rampant flesh that thrust upward so aggressively from its thicket of black hair, then lowering again so she caressed it, too, sliding the slick, swollen flesh between her thighs down from its broad head all along its ridged length.

A heartfelt groan was her reward; his body bowed, head and shoulders pressing back in reaction. 'Dammit! You're an innocent – I know you are.'

'Hmm.' Innocent she might be, but she had a few ideas.

She put them into action. Her body and mouth moving on him, over him, slowly and in concert, seemed almost more than he could stand. His fingers gripped her shoulders, then tightened about her head – even then, he remembered and avoided the bump on one side. She'd started the evening with a mild but persistent headache. It had disappeared the instant their naked bodies had touched.

She wasn't about to let a few bruises stop her learning all she wanted to know. Only her breathing was still a restriction, and even that was easier now. Shallow little breaths. A little panting. All that she could manage.

Her hands continued their exploration; her mouth followed them down his body. She shifted lower, lower, until her swollen breasts brushed his rock-hard thighs.

The sheet was pushed behind her, leaving him fully exposed so she could worship by starlight. Resting her cheek on his hip, she traced, circled, then closed her hand around him. She'd done that before – it wasn't that which made him so tense. It was the anticipation that where her fingers went, her lips, her mouth, would follow. Lips curving, she let her fingers play.

Lucifer lay back and tried to think of England. The only part he could remember was a certain bed in Devon. His fingers sifted through Phyllida's hair, sliding through the sable silk, tracing her skull – tightening when he couldn't help himself. Her touch wasn't so much artful as wondering, naive, enthusiastically natural. His body reacted, helplessly in thrall.

She was a warm, supple, rounded weight lying across his thighs. Her head lay heavy to one side of his groin, her hand cupping, her fingers gliding over her current obsession. He felt possessed, as if in permitting it – letting her have her way – he'd somehow surrendered to her.

He had. He just hadn't told her so in words. Only groans.

Then she shifted and he felt her breath on him, an insubstantial warmth brushing him to even more painful erection. She was going to kill him, not with need, but through the violent clash of powerful emotions – the gut-wrenching desire to have her take him in her mouth, the fear she wouldn't, the suspicion she had no idea she could, and the nearly overwhelming, protective urge that insisted that she shouldn't. It was enough to drive a man insane.

Then she raised her head, not moving closer but over. Her fingers traced his throbbing head again, fascination very clear in her touch. Then she bent her head.

Every muscle in his body locked tight at the first touch of her lips; she trailed openmouthed kisses around, then down, then licked, gently, then more firmly, as if she liked his taste. Then her tongue went questing and he thought he might die. His chest hurt – he dragged in a quick breath—

Without warning she took him into her mouth, closed that hot, wet sweetness around him, taking just a little, then, deliberately, more. For a definable instant, he lost touch with the world and floated in a sensual heaven. He felt her tongue curl, around, then about. He slumped back, easing

441

muscles he hadn't known he'd tensed. He was breathing raggedly and they'd only just begun. He knew that for a fact; it made him feel light-headed. His hands sifted through her hair, caressing, tensing responsively as she tightened, sucked, kissed, then went back for more.

He was clinging to sanity by his fingernails, guiding her, just a little – it was too much, too precious, to break the moment, but . . . she was wearing him down.

Tightening his stomach, he half sat and reached down and around to grasp her hips. 'Enough.' He barely recognized his voice, so rough, so low. She looked up, releasing him; the loss of her wet heat was almost painful. She slid her palms to his chest, bracing to push him back down. He gathered her in his arms, lifted her to his chest, then rolled and trapped her beneath him.

One hand on his shoulder, she met his gaze. Her eyes were dark pools, wide and lustrous. That was all he could see in the starlight. But he could sense something else in that dark gaze, a weight of instinctive feminine knowledge, of innate womanly need.

'I haven't finished yet,' she murmured, and the sound was close to a purr. Her gaze lowered to his lips as she spoke. She licked hers.

The knowledge that she was responding instinctively didn't help at all. 'No,' he agreed, 'but it's my turn now.'

He bent his head and took her lips, and she

surrendered her mouth readily. Sliding her arms around his neck, she leaned back against the bank of pillows. Her body softened under his.

His turn. His turn to worship, to visit pleasure on her heated flesh. To lave and lick and suckle until she gasped and arched beneath him. When her breasts were swollen and aching, he moved lower, anointing the skin over her ribs, past her waist to her navel, then lower still, over the flickering tautness of her stomach to the thatch of dark curls at its base.

Her fingers sank into his shoulders at the first delicate probing of his tongue. Hands trailing down from her hips to grip her buttocks, he kneaded, then slid his palms even lower, over the backs of her thighs. Grasping gently, he urged them wider. She hesitated, then, with a gasp close to a sob, she parted them. Gripping her hips again, he bent his head. He licked, and her fingers clenched in his hair.

She was a delight – wanton in her passion, open and eager in her desire to be his. All his. He claimed every last slick inch, tasted every soft fold. Her essence swirled through his senses and sank deep.

He wound her tight, then tighter, calling on experience to further her horizons, ruthlessly sending her spinning, then reeling her back the instant before she went over the edge.

Some primal need drove him. She'd come to him, offered him all she was, knowing what his demands would be – not just of the flesh but of the soul. Her own actions made it clear she wanted to plunge head first into their new life; that was so much like her, so much a reflection of the directness he prized in her, that he was more than willing to teach her how to fly and extend himself to be her safety net, at least in this arena.

For the rest – the emotional adjustments, the more subtle changes – whether he would teach her or she him was moot. Perhaps they'd learn together. But for tonight, she'd chosen to open her arms to passion. His, and hers.

He stoked both and let her feel the power rise, the insatiable hunger, the greedy need, the hot urgency that poured like molten gold down their veins.

And then he joined with her. Bracing his arms, he held himself above her and filled her with long, steady strokes. Eyes closed, he concentrated on the rhythm, concentrated on the hot embrace of her body, on their pulsing, driving need. He felt her hands, fingers extended, trail down his chest. Cracking open his lids, he looked down. Eyes shut, head thrown back, pressed into the pillows, she was lost in their union. Caught in the sensual waves that rolled through him, through her, she surrendered and rode the tide. Every thrust lifted her, rocked her breasts, her hips, shifted her head against the pillows. Her dark hair rasped softly, silk against linen, again and again.

Her breath came in little pants. She lifted her

hips and met him, took him in, accepted him deep, then let him ease back so he could love her again.

They were drowning in each other, drowning in a sea of desire so intense it was close to rapture. Then that, too, swirled into the mix, into their bodies, into their blood. And took them.

He felt her shatter beneath him, felt her hands clutch, her body cling. Then she eased, her heated softness rippling about him in the ultimate caress. Head back, eyes shut, he clung to the moment; then his own release swept through him. He shuddered and filled her, then slowly collapsed, turning, taking her with him, holding her close, wrapping her limbs about him.

He would never let her go.

On the cusp of oblivion, Phyllida felt him within her, hot and liquid at her core. With her hands, her arms, her body, she held him tight. If she was his, then he was hers. And he'd definitely lived up to her dreams.

She woke to find herself high in the bed. His head against her breast, his arms wrapped around her waist, he was a warm, solid mass of muscle trapping her mostly beneath him.

She was curiously comfortable and not in the least sleepy – presumably the afternoon's rest had been enough. She felt relaxed. No specter of death could possibly haunt her, not in his bed. Raising one hand, she lifted a dark lock from his forehead, smoothing it back amid the rest.

He stirred, tensed for an instant, then, eyes still

closed, hugged her and placed a deliberate kiss on the nipple all but against his lips. 'Very nice.'

Phyllida laughed. He sounded like a very large human cat, purring with masculine satisfaction. Shifting, he freed a hand from beneath her, then settled back, head cradled on one breast, his hand on the other. He touched her gently, soothingly – not so much with desirous intent as for sensual comfort. She had no difficulty making the distinction.

Content, she lay back, luxuriating in the warm caresses, in the golden glow of the moment that still held them. Fingers stroking his hair, she set her mind free – free to feel, to think. To wonder. 'I think I love you.' It had to be that, this golden feeling.

The lazy drift of his fingers ceased. 'Why aren't you sure?'

She answered truthfully. 'I don't know what love is.' Lifting her head, she peered at his face. 'Do you?'

He met her gaze, eyes dark, mysterious. Then he looked at his fingers, lying on her breast, and started to gently stroke once more.

She smiled and leaned back on the pillows, her gaze lost in the shadows of the canopy above. She didn't press for an answer. If she didn't know, why would he?

Then again . . . 'Do you love me?' She didn't look down but she felt him look up.

After a moment, he said, 'Can't you tell?'

'No.'

She waited. He shifted, lifting his head, moving back just a little. She felt his gaze on her face; it lingered for some time, then swept down, over her breasts, over her waist, over her hips, down her long legs. It returned, but stopped at the top of her thighs. The hand at her breast firmed. His touch changed.

'I'll have to demonstrate, then.'

'Demonstrate?'

'Hmm. Cynsters are better with actions than words.'

He proved it. The night became a heated odyssey through realms of passion, desire, sensation, anticipation, hunger, and need. He drew from them both and created the landscape, then guided her through it, ever onward to peaks gilded with ecstasy.

Each touch became invested with more than just feeling, each joining with more than the physical fact. Sensations battered at them, emotions drove them, onward, upward, to impossible bliss.

At the last, she shattered and drank it in, and felt it sink into her bones. A heartbeat later, he joined her. They clung, and the wave washed over them, through them, then the tension slowly drained. Her lips curved. She leaned her forehead to his. He traced her face, then touched his lips to hers in a chaste, final kiss.

Their pact was sealed.

Giddy with release, relaxed beyond this world,

they slumped together, drew the sheets up, and slept in each other's arms.

At ten the next morning, Lucifer left the Manor and set off for the old Drayton cottage. The night had given him more than he'd thought he'd ever have, but it had also left him with much to think about. Possessing for such as he always entailed a certain responsibility – the obligation to take due care. How much did he care for Phyllida? There wasn't a word to encompass the reality.

He strode out, drawing the morning air deep, letting it clear his mind. He'd been up since dawn when he'd lifted Phyllida, still asleep, from the cocoon of his bed and carried her to her own. She'd clutched at him as he'd placed her between the cold sheets. He'd stayed with her, sharing his warmth, until the first sound of his awakening household had sent him back to his bed.

His extremely rumpled, storm-tossed bed. God only knew what Mrs Hemmings would make of it, but he was quite sure she wouldn't imagine the truth. Or, at least, nothing like the whole truth. That was hard enough for even him to believe.

Underneath her serenely decorous facade, Miss Phyllida Tallent was a wanton in disguise. He now knew that for a fact, and very comforting it was. He'd strolled into her room after breakfast, having been informed by Sweetie that her erstwhile charge had agreed to rest quietly for the morning but was suitably attired to permit of a visit. So he'd visited and with just one look, one wicked, suggestive grin, had sent a wave of heat rising to her cheeks.

She'd glared, then had to hide it as Sweetie bustled in. He'd stayed long enough to assure himself that Phyllida was indeed well; with carefully worded replies, she'd given him to understand that she was suffering more from sexually induced lethargy than from fire-induced trauma.

He'd been careful not to smile too triumphantly, or to show his relief. He'd explained where he was headed and why, then left her sewing on the buttons he'd sliced off the week before.

Striding along the tracks, he followed the acrid smell of burned thatch. The day was cool, so peaceful, when yesterday had held so much panic.

And resulted in so much being resolved.

In actions, at least – intentions declared but not stated. He understood what Phyllida had meant to tell him – at least, he thought he did. What he was far less sure about was why she'd made her decision.

Who knew what went on in the minds of women?

After all these years, he really ought to have a clue.

She'd asked whether he knew what love was. He knew what he felt for her – the compelling need to know she was well, safe, and happy, the joy he felt when she laughed, when she smiled. He knew how his gut knotted when she was in danger and how his nerves flickered when she was away from his side. He knew the pride that warmed him as he watched her going about her daily round, so competent, so caring, so giving in that managing yet selfless way that was so uniquely hers. Knew, too, the overwhelming impulse to cosset her, to protect her emotionally and physically, to care for her. To meet her every need, to give her all she could ever desire.

So, yes, he knew about love. He loved her and always would. She loved him, too, but didn't know it – couldn't see it – even though she wanted to see, to know.

Could he teach her what love was?

He could hear fate cackling in the wings, but he shut his ears and set his jaw. If that was what Phyllida wanted, someone to show her, to point out the truth in such a way that she could see it, too, then . . . if he wanted their marriage to be what it could be, it behooved him to do it.

Decision made – simple, easy. She wasn't the only one who could act decisively.

He emerged from the last copse and looked up; the blackened ruin of the cottage stood on the crest, still smoking, charred timbers listing crazily against the summer sky. He heard a grunt and saw Thompson grappling with a crowbar at one side of the shell. An instant later, Oscar joined him.

Lucifer strolled up the path and around to where they worked on the one wall still standing. They both stopped and nodded, leaning on their tools.

'Miss Phyllida?' Oscar asked.

'She's well. Still resting, but I doubt there'll be any lingering effects.'

'Best not be,' Thompson growled. 'But we've got to find this maniac. Doesn't look like he's about to stop.'

'I came up to take a look around.' Lucifer looked at the half-collapsed wall. 'Do you need a hand?'

'Nah.' Thompson turned back to the wall. 'We'll have this down soon enough. If we left it standing, sure as the sky is blue, some of the tykes would come up to play, and then we'd have an accident.'

He leaned on his crowbar and a burned log split.

Lucifer stepped back. 'I'll leave you to it.' He glanced around, then walked down the overgrown track toward Dottswood, the way most of the locals had come running yesterday. A little way down, he stopped and turned; eyes narrowed, he surveyed the cottage. If he'd been the murderer . . .

Two minutes later, he started back up the slope, then cut around, away from the front of the cottage, circling through the overgrown trees and shrubs at its rear.

He found what he'd been certain he would – and just a little more – in a small clearing tucked away behind a stand of rhododendrons run wild. He stared, then hunkered down and looked more closely, hardly daring to believe their luck. Then he stood and went to fetch Thompson.

Thompson came; Oscar followed. The three of them stood behind the rhododendrons and stared

451

down at the clear impression of a horse's hooves – all four of them.

'Ordinary-sized beast, but well set up.' Thompson knelt to inspect the indentations. He traced one with a broad fingertip. 'Better yet – it's my own work, that is.'

'You're sure?'

'I'm sure.' With a grunt, Thompson got to his feet. 'I'm the only one hereabouts who uses those particular nails. See the odd-shaped heads?'

Both Lucifer and Oscar looked, and nodded.

'And that left back shoe?' Lucifer asked.

'Gets better'n better, it does. I haven't seen this horse recently, but I'm going to soon, and then we'll have our man.' Thompson nodded at the left back hoofprint. 'That shoe's going to come off any day.'

Lucifer had to wait until later that evening when Sweetie retired and he and Phyllida were finally alone in the library before he could tell her the news.

'Don't mention it to anyone,' he warned. 'Thompson has customers from beyond Lyme Regis, so it's not possible to search for the horse. We have to wait for the shoe to fall and the animal to be brought in. Only you, me, Thompson, and Oscar know of it – we've agreed to say nothing, so there's no possibility the murderer will realize and take the horse somewhere else.'

Phyllida sat in the armchair by the desk, her

face, for once, awash with emotions. 'Soon, Thompson said?'

'It depends on how often the horse is ridden. If it's ridden every day, Thompson says in less than a week. Ridden less, and it'll be longer, but he doesn't expect that shoe to stay on much above a fortnight.'

She considered, then asked, 'And it's been the same horse every time?'

'I believe so.' Lucifer frowned. 'Just to be sure, I'll send Dodswell to look at the latest prints. The others would all have washed away by now.'

'I really don't believe we have more than one phantom horseman in the village,' Phyllida returned. 'He always hides his horse, too, doesn't he?'

'He makes sure it isn't somewhere where a chance passerby would see it. That suggests the horse, too, would identify him, which makes our prospects of catching him at last look good.' Lucifer met Phyllida's gaze. 'It's ironic. He tried to kill you and succeeded in destroying the one piece of hard evidence we had. But in doing so, he's given us another piece of even better evidence. We might never have traced the hat. It's unlikely we won't trace the horse.'

Phyllida blinked. 'I didn't think of that.'

Lucifer rose and circled the desk. 'I think we need to think of that.' Halting before Phyllida, he hunkered down so his face was level with hers. 'This murderer, whoever he is, has shown himself

453

capable of the most ruthless acts. Murdering Horatio. Trying to kill you.' Reaching out, he smoothed her hair, then cupped her face lightly. 'We can't take any chances for the next few weeks.'

Phyllida looked into his eyes, then smiled. She leaned forward and touched her lips to his. 'You're right.'

Lucifer blinked. His hand remained about her face, stopping her from retreating. He held her gaze. 'I'm not letting you out of my sight.'

Phyllida's smile softened. 'Is that a promise?'

Lucifer studied her eyes, then drew her nearer. 'A sworn oath.'

Five minutes later, distinctly breathless, she drew back, tried to frown at him, and lifted the book that had fallen, forgotten, in her lap. 'We haven't finished these yet.' She held the book like a shield between them.

Lucifer glanced at the pile of tomes with inscriptions that Covey had left stacked between the desk and the chair.

'We might have nearly identified Horatio's murderer, but we've yet to find any explanation for why he's so interested in Horatio's books.' Phyllida picked up the top volume and slapped it against Lucifer's chest.

He grimaced and took it. 'As you say.' He rose.

Phyllida looked up at him. 'Have you any idea what that item was that Horatio wanted you to look at?'

Lucifer shook his head. 'That, too, remains a

mystery. It's possible we'll never know what it was Horatio had found.'

'Don't give up hope.' Phyllida handed him two more books. 'Not when there's so many places still left to search for clues.'

Smiling, Lucifer returned to the desk. 'Speaking of searching, you still haven't discovered that writing desk and the oh-so-important letters.'

'I know.' Smiling, Phyllida shook her head. 'When Mary Anne visited this afternoon, she never mentioned the letters, even when Mrs Farthingale left us alone. All she could talk about was the fire, and me staying here with you.'

'Perspective,' Lucifer said, sitting down and opening a book. 'It comes to us all.'

Phyllida humphed, then settled to deciphering notations.

An hour later, they called a halt. The house was already secured for the night; Dodswell had stuck his head into the library and reported that fact. All they had to do was to turn out the lamps, collect their candles from the table in the hall, and climb the stairs.

They turned along the corridor. All about them was quiet and still. Sweetie had the other back corner room at the end of the other corridor. When they reached the point where they would part, each to their separate rooms, Phyllida halted. She glanced at Lucifer. 'You're the experienced one. Your room or mine?'

Lucifer looked into her dark eyes, lit by the

candle flame. It was on the tip of his tongue to inform her that in this particular arena, the one they were playing in, he was no more experienced than she.

Except, perhaps, that wasn't quite true.

He was a Cynster. He had generations of love matches behind him. These days, love matches abounded all around him. It was something in the blood, something not even he could resist. He'd grown up knowing of no other sort of marriage. It was the only sort that would do for him.

He bent his head and kissed her lightly. 'Are you sure?' He breathed the question over her lips, then eased back.

Her hand had fisted on his lapel; she held him near, her eyes locked on his. Then her gaze dropped to his lips. Hers, he noted, curved gently. 'Yes,' she whispered. 'I'm sure.'

'Your room, then, for now. We'll have the rest of our lives to enjoy mine.'

CHAPTER 19

Early the next morning, Lucifer stood at his bedchamber windows and looked out over Horatio's garden. The sight soothed him, helped clear his mind and focus his thinking.

He couldn't ask Phyllida to marry him – not yet. Not while the murderer was still loose, with her very much in his sights. The man had to be growing desperate; that gave him an overwhelmingly powerful reason for wanting Phyllida completely within his protective care. If he asked her to marry him now . . . no. He wasn't going to risk it. He would not give her even the flimsiest reason to imagine his proposal had any motive bar one.

She wanted to learn about love – so be it. He would make sure she saw it clearly, uncamouflaged, undisguised. Make sure she learned enough so she would recognize it instantly, so that no possibility of confusion would exist when he finally asked her to be his.

He took a determined breath, then exhaled. His gaze was drawn to the jeweled tapestry below, bedewed and glittering with the first touch of the

457

morning sun. A self-conscious smile tugged at his lips. Turning, he grabbed his coat, shrugged into it, and headed downstairs.

When Phyllida joined him at the breakfast table half an hour later, a spray of summer blooms lay beside her plate. She blinked at them; hesitantly, with one fingertip, she touched the velvet petal of a perfect white rose. Then she glanced up at him as, having held her chair for her, he moved back to his. 'I didn't know you'd been out.'

'Only for those. Only for you.' He sat. 'Through one impulsive act, I've shattered my suave London persona. I filched the shears from the garden room. When I came back in, the Hemmingses were turning the place upside down looking for them. I'd forgotten today is the day Mrs Hemmings does the church flowers.'

Phyllida raised the fragrant blooms to her face to hide her smile. As well as the white rose, there was rose lavender and honeysuckle, all set off with violets. 'Thank you,' she murmured. 'I appreciate the sacrifice.'

He reached for the coffeepot. 'Strange to tell, it didn't hurl: at all.'

That made her giggle. Laying aside the spray, making a mental note to set it in a vase by her bed – the bed they presently shared – she helped herself to toast. 'What now? We can't simply sit on our hands for the next two weeks and hope everything comes right in the end.'

Lucifer hesitated, then said, 'I sent a letter off

yesterday while you were busy with the Farthingales. The contents aren't important so much as any results it might bring.'

'Results?'

'I wrote to my cousin Devil. He'll be at Somersham at present – that's in Cambridgeshire. I gave him a brief outline of what's happened here, and the names of the gentlemen we've not yet eliminated.'

'What do you expect him – Devil – to do?'

'Ask questions. Or have other people ask them. That's something Devil does well. He'll be discreet, but if there's any useful information lying about the capital, you can rest assured Devil and his troops will find it.'

'His troops?'

'Whoever he calls on.'

Head tilted, Phyllida regarded him. 'What aren't you telling me?'

Lucifer grinned. 'Devil is the Duke of St Ives. If he wants something, he'll get it.'

'Ah.' Phyllida nodded. 'I take it he's a despot. Is he a close relation?'

'First cousin.'

Her face blanked. 'You're first cousin to a *duke*?'

Thankful that Sweetie was twittering about outside, helping the Hemmingses, Lucifer nodded. 'Don't let it bother you.'

It was obvious it did. 'If you're a near relative of a duke—'

'Near but a long way from the title, so I can

marry as I choose.' Brows rising, he added, 'Not that any of us ever do anything else.'

Frowning, Phyllida studied him. 'You're serious.'

'There's no reason to hold my birth against me.'

She glared, but let the point slide. 'So you've asked your cousin for help—'

'And I think, now matters have reached this pass, that it's time to inform Horatio's peers of his murder and appeal for their help.'

'Other collectors like Horatio?'

Lucifer nodded. 'I know most of them. Covey will have the addresses. I'll write and ask if they can shed any light on what might be in Horatio's collection that could have led to his murder, and also if they know of any special item he might have recently discovered.'

'Would you like me to help?'

'If you would, we'd get the letters out faster. There must be someone who knows something to the point.'

Phyllida looked at him, so large and darkly hand-some he dominated the room. 'I should help Mrs Hemmings with the church vases – I didn't clear them yesterday.'

'Mrs Hemmings can take Sweetie – they'll be delighted to relieve you of the burden.' Lucifer returned her gaze steadily; he reached out and closed his hand over hers. 'I don't want to keep you locked inside like some maiden in a tower, but until we have this man in keeping, you should not go out on your usual errands. No church flowers, no Colyton Import

460

Company. No visiting Mrs Dewbridge or any of your other old ducks. No excursion that anyone could predict or anticipate.'

She stared at him. 'What does that leave?'

Later that afternoon, she found herself on the box seat of his curricle with the blacks trotting smartly along the lane. Despite her position, she was surrounded by male – Jonas to one side, Lucifer on the other, and as Jonas was handling the ribbons, Lucifer had stretched one arm behind her along the seat. There was absolutely no doubt she was safe from the murderer. As she watched Jonas work to keep the blacks in line, she wasn't so certain she was safe from her twin landing them all in a ditch.

Lucifer seemed much more sanguine, issuing instructions and explanations in a relaxed tone. Phyllida watched and listened. When they reached the end of the lane and Lucifer took back the reins and wheeled his pair, she held out her gloved hand commandingly. 'My turn.'

They both looked at her. Their jaws set.

She ignored that and all other evidence of masculine disapproval, along with all their arguments. She drove the curricle back into Colyton and felt a great deal better for the outing.

The days that followed settled into a rhythm – an uneasy one. After penning missives to all Horatio's known associates, they refocused their attention on the large number of books not yet inspected.

'It's amazing how long it takes to do just one shelf.'

'Indeed,' Lucifer returned without looking up. 'I don't want to know how many shelves there are.'

The activity ate the hours; visits from others punctuated the sessions and, in some measure, relieved the tedium. Her father stopped in, bright and surprisingly sprightly – all for show, she could tell. Worry and deep concern lurked in his eyes, permanent residents; she wished she could send them away. All she could do was smile and squeeze his hand, and let him know she was happy. That, at least, seemed to honestly cheer him.

Jonas was frequently on hand, but she didn't count him a visitor. He was like a shadow, simply there; she didn't need to entertain or even consider him. Others, however, proved much more distracting.

Her aunt Eliza called with her brood, a noisy invasion. She was guiltily grateful when Lucifer, abetted by her aunt Huddlesford, shooed the children across the lane to the duck pond. Eliza remained to squeeze her hand, comment on Lucifer's handsomeness, and set her mind at rest; they were remaining at the Grange for only eight days.

Lady Fortemain was an early caller. While shocked by the attempt on Phyllida's life, she clearly believed fate had made some monumental mistake in having Lucifer, rather than Cedric, save her. Beyond that, however, she was cloyingly solicitous, insisting she would send a footman with some of Ballyclose's damson jam.

Cedric and Jocasta, Phyllida had expected; their newfound happiness radiated from them and made her smile. They were concerned, but not smotheringly so – their visit was a definite success.

Not so Basil's. He called when Lucifer had, at her insistence, gone to have a word with Thompson. Basil's concern for her health was clearly genuine, but he found her presence under Lucifer's roof difficult to comprehend. Luckily, Lucifer returned before she lost her temper; he clarified matters – Basil departed with no false illusions.

They were just the first. Mr Filing visited regularly, as did the Farthingales. Henry Grisby called twice, bringing daisies; he spoke reasonably and made no unwelcome protestations. Phyllida thought better of him than she previously had. Wednesday brought a deluge – all the older ladies and women Phyllida visited came to call, to hear how she was faring, to press their advice and cast measuring glances at Lucifer. All brought gifts, little tokens of affection – a crocheted pot warmer, a sprig of broom tied with ribbon, a pot of salve for her scorched skin. When old Mrs Grisby herself stumped up the front path, Phyllida felt overwhelmed.

The ladies fussed and fretted and clearly enjoyed it immensely; she could not find it in her to push them away. When they finally left, all pressing her hands and beaming their approval, she slumped back in an armchair and looked at Lucifer. 'What on earth has got into them?'

He smiled and sat on the chair's arm. 'You have.'

'Me? Nonsense! *I'm* the one who takes care of *them,* not the other way about.'

Lucifer put an arm around her and hugged, then dropped a kiss on her hair. 'True, but unless I miss my guess, this is the first time in recent memory that you've needed to be taken care of. They're seizing the opportunity to let you know how much they – to borrow Lady Fortemain's phrase – treasure you. They want to pay you back.'

Phyllida humphed. Beneath his arm, she wriggled. 'It was uncomfortable, being the object of their . . . care.'

Lucifer's arm tightened, then eased. 'For some, it is difficult – sometimes very difficult – to let someone take care of them. Yet sometimes that's precisely what the other person needs most. Caring for them means letting them care for you.'

Phyllida turned her head and looked up at him. His dark blue eyes met hers without guile. Then his lips curved, not teasing but inviting her to laugh with him – the joke, after all, was on them.

There was a bustle in the hall, Mrs Hemmings coming to clear the tea tray. Lucifer lifted one hand, tapped a finger to the tip of her nose, then rose and left her.

Day followed day. Despite the activities that filled their time, there was an inescapable sense of

464

waiting for something to happen – for that horse-shoe to fall. It was as if they were living through some hiatus, the dead calm before a storm. As the week lengthened, the tension grew.

On Friday, a packet arrived with 'St Ives' boldly scrawled across one corner. Seated at his desk behind a stack of tomes, Lucifer broke the seal. Phyllida watched as he spread out the sheets, many more than one.

He read the first, started on the second, then stopped. Refolding the second and subsequent sheets, he slipped them into his pocket, leaving the first sheet on the blotter. 'It's a progress report from Devil. He's got Montague following up the names I sent.' Lucifer glanced at Phyllida. 'Montague's the family's man of business. He's exceedingly thorough. If there's anything to be learned in the City, he'll find it.'

Lucifer looked back at the note. 'At first sounding, however, the names rang no bells. Devil has recruited one of my other cousins – Harry, better known as Demon. He was kicking his heels down in Kent with his older brother, so Devil sent him word and Demon's now in London, haunting the taverns off Whitehall, looking up all our ex-guardsmen friends.'

'Why the Guards?' Phyllida asked.

'Not the Guards. He wasn't a guardsman.'

'Who? Appleby?'

'He's one of the men we have to check on.'

'But—'

'But you decided he wasn't the murderer because he should have been in the ballroom doing his duty in Cedric's place while we were dodging the murderer upstairs?'

Phyllida grimaced. 'I suppose you're going to say that's an assumption, and as we don't *know* he was in the ballroom, then he might have been the villain?'

'There's also the fact that the note from Molly looked as if a female had written it. That it was supposed to be labored over helped, but not many men would have thought of it.'

'But someone who spent his life writing and reading letters might have thought of it.'

'Precisely.'

'Why were you so sure Appleby was in the army?'

'It's his stance, the stiffness in his shoulders, the way he bows. It's something learned, and the place you learn it is on the drill field. I'd wager he was in the infantry.'

'So, again: Why the Guards?'

'Ex-Guards. Plenty of those about who served with us at Waterloo. They're now secretaries and aides-de-camp to the generals and commanders. They're the ones with access to the records. Demon will find out which regiment Appleby served with, and who his immediate superior was, and have a chat with the man. If he says Appleby's straight as an arrow, we'll have at least learned that much.'

Phyllida studied Lucifer's face. 'You think it's him.'

Lucifer grimaced. 'I think the murderer has shown an odd combination of planning carefully, acting ruthlessly, but being so cautious, his caution has interfered with his success. When things go wrong, he doesn't lose his nerve. He acts, but he misses opportunities and doesn't quite succeed in his purpose.'

He swiveled to face her. 'That's a good description of the characteristics of a regimented foot soldier, one who's reasonably clever. They always have a plan; they don't like operating extemporaneously. They're cautious. And although they don't lose their nerve when things go wrong, their responses aren't always the most likely to succeed – because they haven't had time to plan.'

'You sound like you know a lot about soldiering.'

'I *saw* a lot of soldiering – a lot of infantry fighting – at Waterloo.'

She remembered the saber. 'You were in the cavalry.'

He nodded. 'We played by different rules – following plans was never our forte. Making it up as we went was much more our style.'

'Why couldn't it be Basil? He's cautious.'

'He was in church when Horatio was murdered, but I'm not taking any chances and assuming it's Appleby.' Lucifer caught Phyllida's gaze. 'With luck, we'll have proof of who it is soon enough.'

By Sunday night, she felt wound tight – waiting for that proof to arrive. Lucifer understood. In that peaceful hour after the sun had set but darkness had yet to descend, he drew her outside to stroll in the scented sweetness of Horatio's garden.

Her hand in his, she walked beside him down the gravel paths. Apart from the main ones from the gate and the side of the house to the front door, there were many others winding through the carefully tended beds.

'He might be out there.' Phyllida looked at the shadows deepening beyond the trees.

'He isn't. We don't make a habit of walking in the garden of an evening.'

'We don't make a habit of anything anymore—' Phyllida caught herself and amended, 'Not outside.'

Lucifer laughed; the sound was like a warm hand sliding comfortingly down her back, an invitation to relax. Phyllida breathed deeply – the scent of night stock wreathed around them. 'He hasn't gone away.'

'No.'

They knew that because, just that morning, Dodswell had reported that someone had tried to force the dining room window, the one that used to have a faulty latch. They'd all gone to look, even Sweetie. There'd been scrapes on the window frame and gouges in the earth where the man's heels had dug in, but no clear footprints.

Phyllida exhaled, long and slow. 'It's been a week.'

'Only a week – Thompson said it might take two.'

Lucifer drew her closer and turned down another path. 'Did you read Honoria's missive?'

The rest of the packet that had come from the duke had proved to be a long letter from the duchess to her. Lucifer had remembered to give it to her after they'd discovered the attempted break-in. Given what Honoria had written, she had to wonder if he would otherwise have 'remembered' it at all.

It had certainly distracted her. Honoria had opened by saying that she realized she might be a trifle precipitate in welcoming her to the family, but if they were so unwise as to live their lives according to their menfolk's whims . . . from there, the letter had got only more interesting. Phyllida smiled. 'You have a fascinating family.'

'A big one, certainly, especially if you add all the connections.'

'You mentioned a brother – Gabriel.'

'He's a year older than me.' Lucifer glanced at her as they strolled. 'He got married a few weeks ago – the day before I arrived here.'

'The day before?'

'Hmm. Gabriel and Alathea – we used to be a threesome when we were young. When they married and left London, I felt like they'd gone off on some adventure and left me behind. Instead, here I am, with you, neck-deep in adventure.' He glanced at her again. 'Heart-deep in something more.'

She wasn't yet ready to inquire into that last

statement. 'Do you have other brothers and sisters?'

'Three sisters – they're half my age. Heather, Eliza, and Angelica. Gabriel is harboring fond hopes that Alathea will succeed in teaching them not to giggle.'

Phyllida smiled. 'They'll grow out of it.'

'Hmm – that's not something we like to envisage. We don't, as a rule, deal well with our sisters growing up.'

Alerted by his tone, she studied his face. 'Now who are you thinking of?'

He looked at her, then grimaced. 'Two of our cousins – the twins. Due to a sad accident some years ago, they haven't any older brother to watch over them, so we all do. Did.'

'We?'

He slanted her a glance. 'Didn't Honoria mention the Bar Cynster?'

Phyllida smiled and looked ahead. 'She did, as a matter of fact. Very interesting, I found it.'

Lucifer snorted. 'Don't read too much into it – those days are gone.'

'Really?'

'Yes – really!' He frowned. 'Though I'm not at all happy about the twins.'

'According to Honoria, the twins are quite capable of managing their own lives, and if you mention interfering, I'm to remind you of that fact.'

'With all due respect, Honoria is a duchess, and

Devil's her duke. She's never set foot in the ton without him metaphorically if not physically at her elbow. Not quite the same as swanning through the ballrooms totally unprotected.'

'I'm to tell you your cousins are sensible young ladies and they'll manage perfectly well.'

'I know – but I don't have to like it.'

His disgusted tone very nearly had her laughing. She glanced at him. 'What are you going to be like with your own daughters?'

'I shudder to think.' He looked at her. 'Of course, I'll need to beget them first.'

He drew her nearer, one arm sliding around her waist, then his hand spread, warm and alive, over her hip, urging her back against him. The gravel path ended in an arbor framed by a bed of rioting peonies. They halted. Holding her before him, he bent his head; his lips touched, tracing lightly, laying a line of heat from temple to ear, then down the curve of her throat to where her pulse beat hotly.

'How many children would you like?' Her whisper was a little shaky.

'A dozen would be nice.' He murmured the words against her throat, then turned her and brushed her lips. 'But at least one boy and one girl, I think.'

Phyllida settled in his arms and lightly kissed him back. 'At least.'

He stood with his arms loosely about her, their bodies just touching. There was honeysuckle close;

the perfume drifted over them, subtly tempting. The same scent wreathed their bed. His palms moved, just a little, on her back. He looked into her face. 'Have I told you the story about this garden?'

Night was falling, slowly closing about them, gently creeping over the land.

'Story?' Enough light remained for them to see each other's face, and the expression in each other's eyes.

'When I first came here, the garden caught me.' He looked around. 'Even before I'd gone into the house, I stopped and stared. Then I realized it was Martha's garden.'

'Martha – Horatio's wife?'

'Yes. This is a copy of the garden she designed and grew beside their house overlooking Lake Windemere.'

'Horatio re-created it here?'

'Yes, and that truly puzzled me. That first day, before I went inside, I felt as if Martha was trying to tell me something. Later, I thought it must have been some presentiment that Horatio was dead. Later yet, I realized it wasn't that at all.'

Lucifer returned his gaze to Phyllida's face. 'It was Martha who always created things – as women do. She created the atmosphere that filled their house, created the garden that surrounded it. Horatio knew nothing about gardening – I can still see them walking arm in arm down the paths with Martha showing him this and that. The garden in many ways personified Martha and, even more, the love she bore Horatio. The garden was part of her expression of that love, a permanent and public declaration. That's what I felt – still feel – in this garden.

'I said I was puzzled to find it here. I knew Horatio left the house at Lake Windemere because he couldn't bear the memories of Martha all around him. It was too painful. Yet here was Martha's garden, now Horatio's garden. Why?

'It took a while to work it out, but there's only one explanation that fits.' His lips twisted wryly; he looked into Phyllida's eyes. 'And I now know what Martha was trying to metaphysically jog my elbow about that first day.'

'What?'

'You. Not just you, but the possibility of what we could share. Martha was trying to tell me to open my eyes so I wouldn't miss it.'

He glanced around again; his arms tightened as he brought his gaze back to her face. 'Horatio re-created Martha's garden because he realized, as I now do, that you can't turn aside from love. You can't choose to love – it doesn't work like that – but once you do love, you love forever. You can't move counties and leave it behind; it stays with you, in your heart, your mind – it becomes a part of your soul. Horatio recreated the garden for the same reason Martha created it in the first place – as an expression of his love for her and recognition of her love for him. Martha was still with Horatio when he died – I know that as definitely as I stand here with you. They're still here, both of them, memories living within this garden. Their love, shared love, created it; while it lives, their love lives, too.'

His lips twisted again, this time in self-deprecation. 'For all that we – the men in my family – try to avoid love, for the best and most logical of reasons, when it strikes, there's not one of us, not through all the generations, who has turned his back and walked away. For us, not walking away is harder, more frightening, than fighting any battle, but if there's one thing I've learned from my family, it's that surrendering to love, to the demands of love, is the only road to real happiness.

'While I've seen love in action in my family, I've learned a great deal from Horatio and Martha. Love simply is – it asks no permissions. Acceptance is all love asks, the only demand it makes, but it is an absolute one. You can either admit it to your heart or refuse it, but there's no other option.'

For a long moment, he studied her dark eyes, wide and lustrous. 'You wondered what love was, what it was like – it's surrounded you for the past week. Have you felt it?'

'Yes.' Her lips softened; her eyes searched his. 'It's a frightening, sometimes scarifying reality, but so wonderful and glowing, so vital.' She drew a shaky breath.

He bent his head and drew it from her. 'Have you made your decision – whether to accept love or not?'

He whispered the question against her lips. They curved gently. 'You know I have.'

He kissed her again, gentle and easy. 'When the time comes, I'll ask and you can tell me.'

'Why not now?'

'It's not the right time.'

When Phyllida surfaced from the next kiss, she managed to breathe, 'When will be the right time?'

'Soon.'

The next kiss made it clear that that was all the answer she would get that night. But he'd told her enough, shown her enough; she was content.

Content to let him awaken her, slowly, expertly, until she floated, languid, on a sea of anticipation. They drew back, turned; arms around each other, her head on his shoulder, they strolled through the garden – redolent with perfumes, burgeoning growth, and the never-ending promise of love – back to the house, to the bed, to the love they already shared.

Day followed day and the tension mounted. Jonas spent most of his time at the Manor; Sir Jasper called at least twice a day. Even Sweetie seemed more highly strung, although Lucifer wasn't sure how much she understood. She was the sweetest ditherer he'd ever met, and he knew quite a few;

the idea of introducing her to his great-aunt Clara grew to an obsession.

The only thing that, however transiently, broke the tedium and, temporarily, the escalating tension was the replies that arrived from other collectors. The responses distracted Phyllida, and for that Lucifer was grateful. Unfortunately, although all of them expressed horror over Horatio's demise, none had any light to shed on the twin mysteries surrounding Horatio's collection.

Doggedly, Lucifer and Phyllida plowed through it, searching for . . . something. Some hint as to why Horatio had been killed, some hint as to what he had wanted Lucifer to appraise. Although no one stated it aloud, they were aware they had no idea what they were looking for. That put a definite dampener on their enthusiasm.

By Wednesday afternoon, Lucifer started to wonder why he'd received no further communication from Devil. His cousin was never one to drag his boots. The answer to his question arrived late that evening, just as he, Phyllida, and Sweetie were rising from the dining table.

The rattle of wheels on the drive was followed by the heavy thud of stamping hooves. Lucifer looked at Phyllida. 'That, I believe, will be Devil's messenger.'

It was – but it was a vision with guinea-gold curls and a neat figure encased in cerulean blue that first reached the front door.

'Felicity!' Lucifer went forward, hands out-

476

stretched. He should, of course, have expected it, but he hadn't thought things through.

'Hello!' Demon's youthful wife took his hands and raised her face for a cousinly kiss, but her gaze had already traveled past him. 'And you must be Phyllida.' Releasing Lucifer, Felicity stepped past him and descended on Phyllida. 'Honoria wrote and told me. I'm Felicity. We've come to help.'

Phyllida smiled – impossible not to when faced with Felicity's charm. She could see no point in dissembling, so she touched cheeks and clasped hands as if they were already related.

'Good God! You're almost at Land's End.'

Phyllida looked up to see a tall, broad-shouldered, fair-haired Cynster shake Lucifer's hand.

'Not quite – it's a few miles farther on.' Lucifer grinned and clapped Demon's shoulder. 'It's good to see you.' He glanced at Felicity. 'Are you sure you can spare the time?'

Turning from greeting Sweetie, Felicity shot a warning glance at her husband, tilted her chin at Lucifer, and slipped her arm into Phyllida's. 'We were with Vane and Patience when Devil's and Honoria's letters arrived.'

Demon came forward. Taking the hand Phyllida held out, he calmly kissed her on both cheeks. 'Welcome to the family, my dear. We did tell him running into the country wouldn't help – and here he is, right enough. Captivated.'

Phyllida looked into a pair of blue eyes many shades lighter than Lucifer's. They did, however, contain a familiar devil-may-care gleam. She ignored it. 'Welcome to the Manor and to Colyton, too.'

'Perhaps . . . ?' Lucifer cocked an eyebrow at Phyllida.

He was asking her to act as his hostess – as his wife. With a calm smile, she gestured to the drawing room. 'Why don't we sit comfortably and you can tell us the family news. You must be parched. Have you dined?'

'At Yeovil,' Felicity replied. 'We weren't sure how much further Colyton was. Demon didn't want to take any chances.'

Lucifer blinked, but said nothing. He ushered Felicity and Demon into the drawing room. Phyllida gave orders to Bristleford to prepare rooms and bring the tea trolley in, then joined them.

'Well,' Felicity said as Phyllida joined her on the *chaise*, 'you two seem to be having all the excitement in the family at present, so we came to share. Honoria would have come, but in her condition Devil refuses to let her as far as the front door. And Vane's much the same – he seems to imagine Patience is made of bone china. Scandal was tempted, but Catriona agreed he could come if he brought her, so they're still at Somersham. And no one has any idea where Gabriel and Alathea are.' She smiled at Lucifer. 'So it's just us, I'm afraid.'

The ingenuous speech had made Lucifer blanch – its conclusion revived him. 'Thank God!' He glanced at Demon. 'I didn't expect the whole troop to descend.'

Demon shrugged. 'It's summer – what else have we to do?'

Bristleford entered with the tea trolley and plates of cakes. They broke off to partake; Phyllida and Felicity sipped and nibbled delicately while they chatted; Demon and Lucifer settled for brandy and demolishing the cakes.

'So,' Lucifer said as Demon finished the last cake. 'Cut line – what have you learned?'

Demon didn't glance his way; his gaze was fixed on the *chaise*. Following it, Lucifer was just in time to see Felicity try to smother, then hide, a yawn.

'On the other hand,' Lucifer said, 'it's getting late and you'll need to get settled. Is there anything that won't wait until morning?'

Demon threw him a grateful look. 'No.' He considered, then shook his head and stood. 'There's nothing that'll make any difference tonight, and I'd rather you told us what's been happening here before I fill you in on my discoveries, minor though they are. Knowing the details will help me set what I found in better perspective.'

Phyllida stood, drawing Felicity with her. She'd seen the yawn and caught the earlier, fleeting reference, too. 'Indeed. A good night's sleep all around, then we can start first thing in the morning.' She smiled at Felicity. 'Come, I'll introduce you to Mrs Hemmings and show you your room.'

They all met the next morning at the breakfast table. Rested and refreshed, Flick – she insisted everyone call her that – was agog to hear their tale. Demon, relieved of his own anxiety, was similiarly eager. Lucifer and Phyllida started their story over the teacups, then continued when they adjourned to the library. Concisely, they described incident after incident; Demon interrupted with a question here and there. Flick sat and simply stared.

'How atrocious!' she declared when they'd concluded their tale. 'That's monstrous – leaving you to die in a burning cottage!'

Phyllida agreed.

Lucifer looked at Demon. 'So what's the news from London?'

'First of all, your neighbors are exceedingly lawabiding souls – Montague gave them all a clean bill of health. No debts, no peculiar past histories, nothing. All he found on Appleby was that he's the illegitimate son of a minor peer – old Croxton, now deceased. His papa was not fond, but did educate him and pave the way into the army. Infantry – you were right about that.'

'So,' Lucifer concluded, 'Appleby is an impoverished ex-infantryman with an education sufficient to allow him to serve as a gentleman's amanuensis.'

'Yes, but there's more. Appleby was the only one on your list who'd served in any capacity, so I had a relatively easy time. I tracked down his regiment – he saw action at Waterloo.' Demon glanced at Lucifer. 'He was with the Ninth. I managed to locate his immediate superior, a Captain Hastings.

That's where things got interesting. I had to all but drink Hastings under the table to wring the nightmare from him, but it transpires that Hastings suspects that Appleby committed murder on the battlefield.'

'Murder during a battle?' Flick frowned. 'Can that happen?'

Lucifer nodded. 'If you shoot someone on your own side deliberately.'

Phyllida shivered. 'How horrible.'

'Indeed,' Demon concurred. 'During one particular cavalry charge —' He glanced at Phyllida and Flick. 'The cavalry often charge from the flank, across the infantry's line of sight – the infantry usually put up their pieces during the charge. Most would use the time to clean and reload. Well, during this one charge, Hastings was standing almost directly behind Appleby. He swears Appleby drew a line on one of our own. He believes he saw Appleby shoot and one of the guardsmen fall, but . . . it was midmorning, and that was a hellish day. By the end of it, so many were dead and we all had our own nightmares. Hastings wasn't sure enough to make any immediate charge, but he'd seen enough to check who the fallen man was.

'It turned out to be Appleby's best friend. They'd even shared a tent the previous night. Although wounded himself, Appleby had gone out and retrieved the body and was, to all appearances, deeply cut up. Hastings concluded that Appleby had merely been using his sight to keep a steadier eye on his friend through the charge. That's what he told himself. That's what he still tells himself, but when his tongue is loosened by good brandy, the truth tumbles out. Hastings still believes in his heart that he saw Appleby kill his best friend, Corporal Sherring.' Demon looked at Lucifer. 'Incidentally, Hastings said Appleby was an excellent shot with a musket.'

'So' – Lucifer looked at Phyllida – 'it *could* be Appleby.'

'But is it?' Demon asked. 'All we have is an unprovable possibility that Appleby has killed in cold blood before. We haven't anything to tie him to Horatio or his collection.'

'And that,' Lucifer acknowledged, 'is the rub.'

The entire matter hinged on the mysterious volume the murderer thought was buried in Horatio's collection. Demon and Flick joined the party searching through Horatio's tomes.

After an hour, Flick stepped back from the book case she was working through. 'Why are we doing this?' She turned to Lucifer. 'Whoever it is, they've presumably been searching every Sunday for months. But if they knew which book they were searching for, and presumably they must, then it wouldn't take that long to find it.'

'Unfortunately, it would.' Lucifer strolled along the shelves, then stopped and pulled out an innocuous looking volume. He showed it to Flick. 'Brent's *Roman Legions*. Nice binding, worth a few guineas, but nothing to get excited over.' Then he slid the entire cover free. 'In reality, however, this is a first edition of Cruickshank's *Treatise of the Powers*, worth a small fortune.'

'Oh.' Flick studied the cover and the book it had concealed. 'Are there many like that in here?'

'Every few shelves and sometimes more often.' Phyllida reached for the next book on her shelf.

'Many collectors use fake covers to hide their most precious works.' Lucifer returned the priceless volume to its protective cover. 'So in order to search Horatio's collection, every book would need to be checked.'

They went back to checking.

After lunch, Lucifer and Demon, at their ladies' behest, walked up to the forge to confer with Thompson. No horse with a loose shoe had yet been brought in. As they ambled back down the lane, Lucifer slid a glance at Demon. 'I have to say I'm surprised you agreed to bring Flick into this – I assume she's in an interesting condition?'

'Yes.' Demon's proud grin was exceedingly brief. 'But the damned woman wouldn't be left behind. She insists she's perfectly well and refuses to be cosseted. It's as much as a warm bed's worth to argue too hard. And, of course, Honoria supported her.'

'Honoria?'

'Honoria, who is so damned pregnant, Devil has all but lost his ducal authority. He bowed to her decree that Flick was perfectly well enough to travel down here – he even urged me to bring her! Not, of course, because he thought it was a good idea, but because he didn't want Honoria upset!'

'Good God! Is that what I've got to look forward to?'

'Unless you're thinking of a platonic relationship – and I can't believe you are – yes, and that's the least of what's in store. Judging by the state Vane's presently in, it only gets worse.'

Lucifer shook his head. 'Why do we do this?'

'God only knows.'

They exchanged glances, then smiled and lengthened their strides.

It was Flick who, late in the afternoon, put what they were all independently thinking into words. She waved her arms at the library's bookshelves. 'If the murderer's after something here, why don't we just let him come and get it?'

She faced the rest of the room. 'I don't mean let him get away with it, of course, but what if we organized a household picnic or some such affair, made sure the whole village heard of it so everyone would know there would be no one left at home, and then we'd go, but circle back and keep watch?' She looked at them. 'What do you think?'

Demon looked at Lucifer. 'I think there's some merit in the idea. We need to accept that there's a definite possibility that the murderer's taken care of that loose shoe in some way other than bringing the horse to Thompson.'

'The village fete is two days from now.'

They all looked at Phyllida.

'It's on Saturday,' she said. 'Everyone for miles around attends. It's virtually compulsory.' Standing, she crossed to the window; Flick joined her as she waved. 'It's held in the field just behind the church.'

Both Lucifer and Demon joined them at the window, looking up the slope of the common to the church. Demon narrowed his eyes. 'That's a very attractive proposition.'

'Easy enough to arrange for a watch to be kept on the house – and on the possible suspects, too.' Lucifer slowly nodded. 'And the doors here, while locked at night, are never locked during the day, even now.'

'On the morning of the fete, we'll all be coming and going, taking food and trestles up.' Phyllida faced the others. 'It should be easy for anyone to watch unobtrusively and note when we're all out of the house.'

They considered, exchanging glances, then Lucifer nodded. 'Right. Let's do it. But we'll need to work out all the details first.'

They spent the whole evening planning, and were still arguing over the details of who should watch whom, when and from where, the next morning when the mail arrived. Bristleford brought the letters into the library on a salver and placed them on the big desk by Lucifer's elbow.

When they paused in their deliberations to

consume tea and a plate of Mrs Hemmings's butter cakes, Lucifer sifted through the pile. He tossed some to Phyllida and started opening the rest. 'More replies from other collectors.'

He'd finished opening and perusing those he'd kept and laid them aside with a shake of his head when Phyllida sat bolt upright, staring at the sheet she was holding in her hand. '*Good gracious!* Listen to this! It's from a solicitor in Huddersfield. He writes that our recent letter to one of his late clients was brought to his attention. In the circumstances, he felt he should bring to our notice the fact that his late client, an associate of Horatio's, died at the hands of an unknown assailant some eighteen months ago.'

'*Heavens!*'

They all rose and went to read over Phyllida's shoulder. She held the letter out so they could see. 'It says the other collector was strangled late one night and his records were ransacked.'

Lucifer reached out to steady the sheet. 'Shelby. I wonder . . .' He returned to the desk and sat. From a bottom drawer, he retrieved a stack of cards. 'Horatio always noted on his name-cards what sort of items he'd most recently traded with each person. The notes refer back to his ledgers.' He flipped through the cards. 'Shelby, Shelby . . . *hullo!*'

The shock in his voice had the other three looking up at him. Lucifer sat, frozen, a card in his hand. 'Well, well.' He glanced at Demon. 'Sherring.'

'*Sherring?*' Demon came to look over his shoulder. 'The Sherring Corporal Hastings thinks Appleby shot?'

'More likely his father.' Lucifer laid the card down, then checked the stack further. 'There's entries for Shelby, but they're more than three years ago and it looks like they were only trading furniture.'

He restacked the other cards and put them back in the drawer, then returned his attention to the card for Sherring. 'Books. One buy, just over five years ago.'

'Almost immediately after Waterloo,' Demon added.

Lucifer nodded. 'Where are those ledgers?'

Demon laid a hand on his shoulder. 'Before you do that, write a letter to this solicitor. Give him Appleby's name – see if he recognizes it.'

Lucifer hesitated, then pulled out a sheet of paper. 'We won't hear in time, presuming that horseshoe falls, but if all else fails . . . I'll include a description of Appleby as well. If it was him, he might not have used his real name.'

The letter was quickly written. Dodswell was dispatched to race it into Chard to catch the night mail.

Then Lucifer unearthed Horatio's ledgers – this time, they had a date and quickly found the entry. It listed nine books. They wrote the list on four scraps of paper, then they each took one and started along the shelves.

487

Jonas arrived. Amazed at the news, he joined in the hunt. Covey did, too. He checked the inventory they'd made thus far, which cut down the bookshelves they needed to search.

Lucifer told them to scan the titles on the grounds that none of the books appeared valuable enough to warrant a false cover. Even with six of them scanning, it still took most of the day, but finally they located all nine books. Along the way, they found three fake covers of *Dr Johnson's Sermons*, six fake covers of *Gulliver's Travels*, and a staggering eight of *Aesop's Fables*.

'Enough to confuse anyone,' Demon remarked.

'No wonder the murderer has had to search so carefully.' Phyllida glanced along the ranks of bookshelves. 'And there's no telling if Horatio, for whatever reason, concealed one of the Sherring volumes.'

Lucifer shook his head. Carrying Horatio's card, he was checking the nine books. 'No – these are the Sherring volumes. Horatio noted all the details, and he never doubled up on specific volumes.'

'Only to use for fake covers,' Demon replied.

At Lucifer's instructions, they'd pulled the books forward in the shelves, but left them where they found them.

At five o'clock, Lucifer went around the nine books for the third time, paying special attention to the *Sermons*, the *Travels*, and the *Fables*. He noted the location of each book on his list, then pushed them back to stand unobtrusively with their fellows.

He, Phyllida, Flick, Demon, Jonas, and Covey had all studied each book. There was absolutely nothing to explain why anyone would commit murder for any of them.

Demon sank onto the *chaise* beside Flick. 'We must be missing something.'

'Presumably.' Lucifer settled into an armchair and considered the list. 'Let's assume our man started searching in the library.'

'Why?' Jonas asked.

'Because if I'd wanted to search for a valuable book in this house, I'd assume Horatio would keep it in his inner sanctum,' Demon supplied.

Lucifer nodded. 'So he finished in the library, tripping over heaps of fake covers in the process, and had started in here' – he paused to glance at the bookcases covering almost every foot of wall space in the drawing room – 'when Horatio disturbed him. The night Phyllida and I saw him, he was still trying to search in here.'

'Most of the Sherring books are in the library or in here,' Phyllida said. 'Only the real *Travels* and *Fables* are in the dining room.' She looked at Lucifer. 'Is that why you studied the books here and those two books especially?'

He nodded. 'Four books, and while it's not my area of expertise, I would happily swear there's not a thing that makes any of them valuable. The *Aesop's Fables* has been used to hide something – the front

489

cover's been hollowed out, but that's not unusual. The front of such books was a popular place to hide wills and such at one time. There's nothing there now except some canvas padding – I peeled away a corner of the covering paper and checked.'

They all sat, digesting the information. In the end, Demon sighed. 'This could, of course, all be some remarkable coincidence and the murderer is in fact someone else.'

Lucifer grimaced. 'Very true, which is why we need to give even more thought to how we approach tomorrow.'

They returned to their plans, to the arguments, the suggestions – the possibilities of how to trap a murderer.

CHAPTER 20

The day of the fete dawned still and clear. Throughout the morning, men and boys lugged boards and trestles up the common and over the rise. Thompson and Oscar helped Juggs roll two heavy barrels slowly up from the lych-gate, then down the slope behind the church. By nine o'clock a steady stream of women, gaily dressed in bright gowns and aprons, were ferrying all manner of foods up in baskets.

By eleven o'clock, when the Manor household climbed the common, a heat haze had formed – there was not a breath of wind to blow it away. The air lay heavy against the skin, almost cloying. Pausing beside the church on the highest point of the rise, Phyllida looked toward the horizon. 'We'll have a storm tonight.'

Lucifer followed her gaze. The horizon was smudged charcoal gray. 'Looks like a big one.'

Jonas nodded. 'Our storms are something to experience. They sweep in from the Channel with a magnificent rush.'

In the dip behind the church, the villagers and all the surrounding families were gathering. The

491

Manor folk descended, exchanging greetings, introducing Demon and Flick; they merged with the throng and, as they naturally would, parted. They each had their roles to play.

Only those involved were privy to their plans. The more people who knew, the more likely someone would inadvertently do or say something to tip the murderer the wink. They'd agreed not to assume that Appleby was the murderer; their net was designed to cover all eventualities.

They'd decided on a simple scheme. Phyllida would be safe while surrounded by the entire village, yet Lucifer and Demon had been adamant that she and Flick should at all times stay together, and that both should wear their wide-brimmed villager hats, one tied with a lavender scarf, the other with a blue one – easy to spot in the crowd.

Lucifer and Demon shared the watch on their ladies and on Appleby. In the latter case, they were careful to do nothing overt. Lucifer introduced Demon and left him chatting. Subsequently, they passed Appleby in the crowd, exchanged a word if appropriate, but gave no indication that he remained always under observation. They were the only ones they trusted to do the job right.

Jonas had been assigned to idly wander about, keeping his eyes peeled for any unusual behavior in any of the other men, however unlikely. He conscripted a number of young ladies to aid him in disguising his intent, but behind his easygoing facade, he remained watchful and alert.

The others had the hardest task. Dodswell, Demon's groom Gillies, Covey, and Hemmings rotated the watch on the house, two of them watching at all times, one at the back, one at the front. They lay concealed in the shrubbery and the wood, but they had to change the guard frequently so that each appeared often among the crowds at the fete.

As the day wore on, the heat became oppressive. Phyllida introduced Flick to the local ladies; moving about the field, they chatted easily. Again and again, by a look, a veiled reference, the thoughts behind a pleased smile, it was borne in on Phyllida that the change Lucifer had wrought was complete.

She might not have answered any question or spoken any vow, yet she was, by her actions and her thoughts – her very desires – already his wife. The little changes in her station, the adjustments in the ways the other ladies related to her, were already made. The consensus seemed to be that her recent brush with death, combined with the lingering presence of her would-be murderer, more than excused a period of waiting before any banns were read. None doubted the wedding would come shortly.

Yet what had changed most was herself. She felt it inside her as she smiled and listened to the continuation of stories she'd heard developing all her life. She'd drawn back from them, not shutting them out, but they were no longer the central focus of her life; they'd moved to the periphery, where they rightly belonged. Her life was no longer an accumulation of theirs – their joys and sorrows, their problems, their needs. She'd started making a new life, one for herself and Lucifer at the Manor.

For the first time in her twenty-four years, she felt truly at one with the role that was hers to play – no regrets, no unfulfilled wishes, no nebulous yearnings.

After lunching on delicate sandwiches washed down, courtesy of Ballyclose Manor, with glasses of champagne, she and Flick helped Mr Filing with the children's races, then, nothing loath, they supervised some games.

'I'm melting.' Flick tipped her hat back from her face. 'Even though I know why they wanted us to wear these hats, I'm quite glad we did.'

'Easier to manage than a parasol.' Phyllida saw Jonas cruising past with one of the local misses hanging on his arm. She caught his eye and raised a brow – he returned her look with his usual benign expression.

'What's the word?' Flick asked, looking the other way.

'Jonas knows nothing.' Phyllida turned to look in the same direction and sighed. Heavily. Through clenched teeth. 'If nothing happens today, I swear I'll scream. At the very least, I'll have hysterics.'

Flick chuckled. 'You'll shock everyone to their toes if you do.'

Phyllida humphed. She saw Mary Anne and

Robert through the crowd. They'd stopped and spoken with her earlier. Although they'd inquired about the letters, they'd accepted her lack of progress without panic. It was almost as if they'd finally realized that the letters were only a minor matter – nothing to get hysterical about.

Nothing to compare with a possibly multiple murderer.

The day wore on.

Then Appleby stopped beside the Ballyclose butler, said a few words, then strode off, openly making for Ballyclose Manor. Lucifer and Demon watched him go.

'To circle around, perhaps?' Demon suggested.

Lucifer nodded. 'Most likely.'

They parted and moved through the crowd. They visually checked their respective ladies but didn't approach. They worked steadily back through the throng, heading to where, standing by the church's side and concealed in its shadow, they could look down on the Manor.

That was their aim, but before they gained the graveyard, Oscar pushed through the crowd and caught Lucifer's sleeve. 'Some' at you need to know.'

Lucifer collected Demon with a glance and stepped back, a little away from all the others. 'What is it?'

'Wel—' Oscar stopped as Demon joined them.

'My cousin,' Lucifer said. 'You can speak freely.'

Having taken stock of Demon, Oscar nodded.

'Right. Well, I've just received this message, and it's left me in a quandary, like. I don't know as whether Miss Phyllida has explained about the gang that works out of Beer?'

'She said they were all but legendary in the annals of local smuggling.'

'Aye, well, they're the real thing, no doubt whatsoever. Hardnosed lot, but we've always rubbed along well enough, and now they've sent me a message. Says a person contacted 'em about a passage 'cross the Channel – 'parently it *has* to be tonight. Beer hasn't got a cargo lined up for tonight, but they knew we generally would, so they told this cargo where to meet up with us on the cliffs. All straight enough, but as you know, the vessel we'll be meeting is a legitimate trader, not a smuggler's boat. The Cap'n won't want no truck with any suspicious passenger.'

Oscar glanced to where Phyllida and Flick stood talking to three young girls. 'Didn't rightly want to bother Miss Phyllida with such a matter, and I don't know as how Mr Filing would be much help, neither.'

Lucifer frowned. 'Quite. Are you running a cargo tonight?'

'We should've been.' Oscar looked at the ever-darkening horizon. 'But I'm doubting we will. That bugger's going to sweep right over us. Ain't none of us going to be putting out in the teeth of that.'

'In that case, let's see what happens –' Lucifer

broke off as Thompson pushed through and joined them.

Winded, Thompson struggled for breath. Excitement rippled through him. 'Got 'im! M'boy just told me a horse was brought in with a loose rear left shoe this morning. The lad forgot, what with the fair. I just ducked back to check – it's the same horse. I'll take my oath on it.'

'Who owns it?'

'Ballyclose Manor. Not one of Sir Cedric's – one of the general hacks. I collared the groom who brought it in. He says no one's been riding this one much that he knew of. Just Mr Appleby now and then.'

Demon glanced at Lucifer. 'Is that enough?'

Lucifer's smile was all teeth. 'I think so. Let's find Sir Jasper—'

'*Cynster*! Where the devil are you, man?'

Both Lucifer and Demon turned. Cedric came barreling through the crowd. He saw them, waved, and plowed toward them. Jocasta Smollet hurried after him. Others, anticipating some sensation, quickly gathered.

'It's Appleby, man – *Appleby!*' Cedric halted, puffing, before them. 'Just got the word from Burton, m'butler. Appleby told him he's off home – touch of the sun. Silly blighter came with no hat. *That's* when I remembered. The hat! The hat Phyllida said was the murderer's hat. It's *Appleby's*. Seen it in his hands times without number, but I rarely saw it on his head. Just put

497

it together. He hasn't been wearing a hat since Horatio was killed.'

'That's correct, sir,' Burton, the Ballyclose butler, stated. 'While I cannot vouch for the particular hat in question, Mr Appleby has not worn a hat for some time.'

'I'm fairly certain Cedric's right,' Jocasta put in. 'I didn't get a good look at the hat that day, but I do know Appleby was forever doffing his – quite the gentleman in his way. He hasn't worn a hat for the past several weeks.'

'We're going after him.' Cedric straightened and looked around. 'Hue and cry – that's what we need! We'll round him up and haul him back here to Sir Jasper.'

'Excellent idea!' Basil surprised everyone with his vehement agreement. 'We've plenty of men here – he won't escape this time.'

Cedric blinked, but nodded. 'Right, then! Finn, Mullens – come along, lads.'

Basil was already collecting his workers. Grisby, too, was gathering his forces to join the swelling throng. The crowd was awash with exclamations and gabbling.

Sir Jasper strode through. 'Cedric! What's this? There's to be no summary justice, you hear?'

'I know, I know – we'll truss him up and bring him back to you, and then we can hang him.'

A rousing cheer rose. Before anything more could be said, the assembled congregation was off, streaming like a tide after Cedric, Basil, and

Grisby, cresting the lip of the field, then pouring over, heading for Ballyclose Manor.

'He won't be there,' Demon muttered.

'Assuredly not.' Lucifer turned as Phyllida and Flick, having been deserted by the children, came up. Other than their small group and the older ladies and village women, the fete field was bare.

Sir Jasper eyed Lucifer, shrewd suspicion and certainty in his gaze. 'Now, what's afoot?'

'We believe,' Lucifer said, waving their group toward the church, farther from the remaining ladies, 'that Appleby, if, as now seems likely, he's our murderer, will make another attempt to get at Horatio's books. That's what he's been after all along. To that end, we've purposely left the Manor vacant and the doors unlocked.'

'A trap, heh?'

'Oh, *no!*'

They all turned. Mrs Hemmings was staring round-eyed at Lucifer. 'What is it?' he asked.

'Did you say that that murdering Mr Appleby will be going to the Manor?'

'So we believe. But it's empty—'

Mrs Hemmings was shaking her head. ''Tisn't. Amelia went back a while ago – too hot for her, it was.'

Lucifer frowned. 'Amelia?'

'Oh, God!' Phyllida grabbed his arm. 'Sweetie!'

Lucifer looked at Phyllida. 'She went back?'

'Apparently. I had no idea.'

'She left nearly an hour ago,' Lady Huddlesford

put in. 'Quite wilting, she was, but she didn't want to cause any fuss, so she just slipped away.'

Lucifer cursed beneath his breath. Grim-faced, Demon waved them up the rise. 'We'd better get a move on.'

They started up the slope. Before they reached the church, Jonas came pelting around it. He skidded to a halt. 'Filing. He just went into the Manor. I saw him come up this way, then I realized he hadn't come back, so I went to check – I just glimpsed him going through the front door.'

'*Filing?*' Demon said. 'Where the hell does he fit in?'

'God knows, I'm sure,' Lucifer muttered, 'but I suggest we'd better go and find out. In case you haven't noticed, our simple plan has got holes shot through it.'

'Never did trust plans.' Demon locked his fingers about Flick's elbow as they rounded the church.

'Oi!'

They halted again. Dodswell came lumbering up from the Rectory. 'Where're you off to?' He scrambled up the path to join them. 'I just came to tell you that Appleby arrived and went in the back. He came through the wood. He's been inside for a good fifteen minutes or more. I had to come round by the shrubbery to stay out of sight.'

Lucifer and Demon exchanged glances. 'Right.' Lucifer looked down the slope. 'Only one thing for it – we go in and invent as we go.'

He considered their assembled company. As well

as himself, Phyllida, Demon and Flick, Jonas, Sir Jasper, and Dodswell, they had Lady Huddlesford, Frederick, and the Hemmingses.

'All of us go in – there's enough of us to make him feel too pressured to try anything clever, but not enough, if we all keep calm, to make him panic.' He looked at Frederick and Lady Huddlesford, then at Jonas and Sir Jasper. 'One thing – if you're coming down there with us, you must do nothing except what I tell you to do. At this stage, we just want to get Appleby out of the Manor and get Sweetie back without her, or anyone else, being harmed. No heroics. Agreed?'

Everyone nodded.

At the last, Lucifer met Phyllida's gaze.

'I'd never do anything to risk Sweetie.'

Lucifer grasped her hand. 'Naturally not.' He looked at the others. 'Let's go.'

They reached the duck pond and saw Covey dodging through the trees. Dodswell waved him over.

'Miss Sweet came home,' Covey gasped. 'Before I could come to warn you, I saw Mr Filing up by the church looking down. Then he came down, and I couldn't get out. He's gone in, too.'

Lucifer nodded. 'Join the crowd. We're going in to sort this out.'

It wasn't quite the same as leading a charge, but with Demon at his shoulder and Phyllida and Flick at their backs, it had much the same momentum. Lucifer pushed open the Manor gate, uncaring of its squeak. He strode up the main path and rounded the fountain—

'Stop right there!'

He halted. All the others formed up behind him.

The figure of Lucius Appleby was just visible in the shadows of the front hall. Locked before him, held captive in one arm, Sweetie in her pale gown was more easily seen. Light glinted off the blade of a knife.

'Can you see it?' Appleby asked.

'Yes.' Lucifer didn't need to say anything else; his tone was enough.

'If you do exactly as I say, she won't be harmed.'

'We're prepared to do that.' Lucifer spoke calmly. 'What do you want us to do?'

'File in, single file, slowly.'

Phyllida grabbed the back of Lucifer's coat and refused to let go; Demon shot her a scowl and stepped behind her. They all followed Lucifer over the front step and into the cool of the Manor's front hall.

'Stop.'

They did, blinking as their eyes adjusted. Phyllida focused on Sweetie. Her old governess's eyes were so wide she looked goggle-eyed, her face so pale it was the same bone-ivory hue as her fussy, frilly summer gown. Appleby had one arm about Sweetie's shoulders, trapping her against him; as he pulled her back down the hall, she moved stiffly. In his other hand, Appleby held a wicked-looking knife.

A groan drew all eyes deeper into the hall. By the stairs, Mr Filing lay prone; as they watched, he struggled onto one elbow. A trickle of blood ran down his chin.

Some of them started forward—

'Stop!'

They all froze at Appleby's shout. He looked down the line. 'You. Covey. Help the meddling curate.'

Covey hurried down the hall; he bent and struggled to help Mr Filing to his feet. Jonas snorted. With an unimpressed glance at Appleby, he strolled out of the line toward Filing. 'Covey can't manage alone.'

Appleby glared at him. Jonas returned the glare with his best blank expression. Appleby's lips tightened. 'Very well. Just get him to his feet and keep up with the rest.'

Appleby pulled back to stand almost against the wall to the right of the drawing room door. 'Inside.' He gestured with his head. 'But stay in line and move slowly.' He raised the knife and laid it against Sweetie's exposed throat. 'You don't want to make me nervous.'

'No,' Lucifer said. 'We don't.'

Appleby looked into his face. 'Line up along the wall of bookshelves opposite the windows.'

They did. Jonas and Covey helped Mr Filing into the room. Appleby followed with Sweetie. 'Perfect.' He scanned their number. 'There's two of you to a bookcase. I want you to search for a particular book – *Aesop's Fables.* You'll need to pull out each book and look inside the cover – some of the covers are fakes. Look at every book.'

They all stared at him.

'Get to it,' he ordered. 'Now! I haven't got all day – Miss Sweet hasn't got all day.'

They all turned to the bookshelves. Phyllida lifted a hand to a tome and caught Lucifer's eye. She raised a brow – they, Demon and Flick, Jonas and Covey, all knew *Aesop's Fables* was in the dining room. With a nod, Lucifer indicated the books. He pulled out the first volume on the top shelf.

Phyllida started on the middle shelf. Beside her, Flick and Demon also started pulling tomes.

After a few minutes of silence, Lucifer glanced over his shoulder. 'Why don't you let Miss Sweet sit down?' He waved at a straight-backed chair closer to the windows. 'You're far enough away from us to still use her as your shield. And if she doesn't sit down soon, she might faint, which none of us would want.' His gaze had fastened on Sweetie's wide eyes; he'd emphasized the word 'none'.

Appleby heard it. 'Indeed. That wouldn't be at all helpful – not to any of us.' He gauged the distance to the chair, then shuffled Miss Sweet to it. Before he released her, he looked at them. 'Keep searching!'

They all turned back to the shelves.

Lucifer continued to pull books out and study them, then return them to the shelf. Phyllida pulled books out and shoved them in; her gaze lingered on Lucifer's face. She saw him exchange glances with Demon. She followed the exchange back and forth. It was as if they were communicating without words – as if their thoughts in such a situation were obvious, at least to each other.

Phyllida looked at Flick. She, too, had noted the silent communion. She met Phyllida's gaze and gave a helpless shrug – she didn't know what they were thinking, either. Flick went back to removing books; Phyllida did the same.

A minute later, Lucifer murmured, 'Was this volume of *Aesop's Fables* the reason you killed Corporal Sherring?'

Despite the fact that he'd murmured, his voice carried through the room. He turned to glance at Appleby; Phyllida did the same.

Appleby's face was a mask of blank astonishment. His mouth opened, then shut, then opened again. 'How did—' He broke off. 'It hardly matters now.' He paused, but couldn't stop himself. 'How did you learn of it?'

'Hastings saw you do it.' Demon glanced around, then looked back at the shelves.

'He never said anything.'

'Hastings is a decent man.' Again Demon glanced at Appleby. 'He couldn't conceive of the sort of man who would kill his closest friend.'

Appleby stiffened. 'Sherring was a *fool*. A provincial nobody with a father rich from trade. They'd bought their way into a title and an estate – and all the luxuries that went with it. I was born better than him, but I would never have had half of what would have been his.'

'So you arranged to even the score?' Like Demon, Lucifer continued to methodically search. The others glanced at them and followed suit.

Having everyone so steadily occupied calmed Appleby. 'Yes, in a way. But they showed me how – he and his father. The night before the last battle, letters were brought around. I never had any, of course, so, thinking to be kind, Jerry Sherring read his aloud. His father had filled his library with expensive books and his gallery with valuable paintings.

'His heir, Jerry's older brother, cared not a fig for anything but hard coin. The old man was in failing health, but, almost on his deathbed, he'd made a fantastic discovery. He'd stumbled on a miniature by an old master. He was sure it was genuine, but wasn't strong enough to follow it up. He didn't want his heir to know of it and sell it off cheaply, so he hid it until Jerry, who felt as he did, could return from the war and help him.'

'So he hid the painting in the book?' Lucifer glanced around briefly.

'Yes.' Appleby stood directly behind Sweetie. Although clearly swept back into the past, he was too close to the chair for Lucifer to attempt to overpower him. 'It was all there in the letter. The old man even warned Jerry to tell no one of it. Jerry didn't consider that he'd read the letter to me.'

'He trusted you.'

'He was a fool – he trusted everyone.'

'So he died.'

'On the battlefield. He would most likely have died there anyway. I just made sure of it.'

'And then you accompanied his body back to his family, playing the grieving friend.' Lucifer glanced along the shelves. The others remained facing the books, but their searching had slowed; all were following the tale. 'So what went wrong?'

'*Everything* – everything that could.' Appleby's tone turned bitter. 'It took two weeks to get free of the army and across the Channel, then all the way up to Scunthorpe. The Sherrings lived beyond that. I arrived to discover the father dead and the brother already in possession.'

'I'm surprised that was a problem.'

'It wasn't in itself, but the brother's wife was an unexpected complication.'

'Women often are.'

'Not in that way.' Appleby's tone was contemptuous. 'The damned female was a tightfist, just like the brother. They'd known Jerry would kick up a fuss over selling the father's collections, so they'd had the dealers around before the old man was cold in his grave. They'd sold the *Aesop's Fables*.'

Lucifer looked at Appleby. 'You're not going to tell me you've been searching through all the collections in England?'

Appleby laughed, but the sound wasn't humorous. 'If necessary, I might even have done that.

Nevertheless, as has happened repeatedly in my search for this treasure, hope gleamed in the darkest hour. The brother's wife had a list of those she'd invited to the sale of the library. Fifteen collectors and dealers. I spun her a tale of wanting to buy some book of Jerry's as a memento and she gave me the list.' He laughed again, bitterly. 'Like everything in my life, that list was a boon and a burden rolled into one.'

Lucifer turned back to the shelves. 'The list was alphabetical?'

'Yes!' Appleby's temper exploded in a threatening hiss. 'If I'd started working on it in reverse, I would be a hugely wealthy man today. Instead, I followed the list.'

'That, I assume, accounts for the unexpected demise of Mr Shelby of Swanscote, near Huddersfield.'

Silence held sway for a long moment, then Appleby said, 'You have been busy.' Lucifer said nothing, nor did he turn around. Eventually Appleby continued. 'Shelby would have lived if he hadn't been such a suspicious old coot. He caught me in his library one night. If he'd simply walked in, I'd have been able to slide away – I had an excuse ready. But he stood there and watched me search for some time. After that, I had to kill him.

'I could never let any of them suspect I was searching for anything – that's why it's taken me five long years to reach Welham's library. In every one of the fourteen other cases, I had to find a job, sometimes with the collector, which made life easier, but often in the neighborhood, then learn enough about the collector's household to know when I could search. I've become an expert on reading dealers' disposal ledgers. That was always the first thing I checked. But none of them has sold that book and the painting hidden in it has never surfaced – you may be sure I kept my ear to the ground over that. I know the book's here, and the painting's still inside. You're going to find it for me – I'm going to have it in my hands tonight.'

There was a feverish intensity in Appleby's last words that had everyone exchanging glances. With a sigh, Lucifer turned. 'If that's the way it is, then . . . we've already finished cataloguing this room. And the library. There's no copy of *Aesop's Fables* in either room. False covers, yes, but not the book.'

Appleby considered him through narrowed eyes.

Lucifer waved toward the library. 'If you'd like to look at the inventory . . .'

'No, that won't be necessary, will it?' Appleby's eyes were slits, but his tone was more confident. 'You just want me out of here, don't you? You're so damned rich you don't give a damn about any painting, old master or not.'

'I wouldn't go quite that far, but the painting certainly doesn't rate against Miss Sweet's life, which brings us to much the same point.'

Appleby studied Lucifer's face, then nodded.

'Very well. Which room do you suggest we search next?'

'I'd take the dining room next. The back parlor seems to run more to garden, household, and recipe books.'

They'd all stopped searching and turned; Appleby ran his eye along the line. He drew a tight breath. 'We'll move in reverse. I'm going to back out of the door, then I'll wait in the front hall. I want you to file out, single file still, cross the hall, and go into the dining room.'

Pulling Miss Sweet to her feet, he held her to him and backed out of the door. Everyone followed, trooping silently along. Toward the rear of the line, Phyllida stared at the door, then glanced at the shadowy space behind it and the huge halberd standing there.

'No,' Lucifer whispered. 'We don't need it – all we need to get Sweetie free is that volume of *Aesop's Fables.*'

Phyllida frowned, but shuffled past the halberd and out of the room.

As they filed into the dining room with the big table in the center and bookcases all around, Appleby waved the ladies to one side and the men to the other. Phyllida hesitated; Lucifer squeezed her fingers, then let her go. His last words ringing in her mind, she made for the bookcase by the corner window. Ironic that in this house of bookcases, the one that housed the vital volume was the one Appleby had passed most often, the one by the window with the faulty latch. Phyllida started searching along the shelves; Flick searched the bookcase beside her.

Appleby retreated to a corner of the room, pulling a chair from the table and pushing Sweetie onto it. He had a wall of bookcases at his back, the door at some distance, and Mrs Hemmings was the closest person – no threat.

Once they were all settled, Lucifer asked, in a mildly conversational tone, 'How did Horatio die?'

'It was an accident. I never meant to kill him. I didn't even know he was in the house. I didn't hear him come downstairs and along the hall – his feet were bare, so there was no sound. He was suddenly there, in the doorway, asking what the devil I was doing. He'd seen me searching. I rose and walked toward him. He was a fair size and in reasonable health – I didn't think I could strangle him. He stood there and watched me come. Then I saw the letter knife on the table.' He paused, then said, 'It's surprisingly easy if you know how.'

'Why did you try to kill Phyllida?' Sir Jasper turned, frowning, then forced himself to continue searching.

'Miss Tallent?' There was laughter in Appleby's voice. 'That was such a farce, with her stumbling on the body and then Cynster coming in and the halberd falling. I was so strung up I nearly laughed aloud. I saw her notice the hat, but then she bolted. When I left the house, hat and identity still concealed, I knew that no matter what happened, no matter what hurdles appeared, I was meant, in the end, to have that painting. I'd be able to live like I was meant to live – in reasonable comfort, like a gentleman.'

'So why go after Phyllida?' Jonas asked.

'She came back for the hat.'

Phyllida turned to stare at Appleby. He smiled, tightly. 'I was in the hall when you asked Bristleford about the hat. You hadn't forgotten it – you weren't going to forget it.'

'But I didn't know whose it was.'

'I could hardly rely on your faulty memory continuing faulty. You'd seen me often enough wearing the wretched thing – it was the only hat I had. Of course, with Cynster here to fill your eyes and your mind, you were distracted enough not to remember, but you might have at any time.'

Lucifer caught Phyllida's eye and frowned – she shut her lips on the information that she'd never noticed Appleby enough to remember his hat. She turned back to the bookshelves.

'I'd got rid of the hat immediately, of course. I stuffed it in a hedge at the back of Ballyclose. Later, I got to thinking, so I went back to find it and burn it, but it was gone. I assumed some tramp had taken it. I thought I was safe, or would be once I ensured Miss Tallent didn't remember whose hat it was.'

'So you tried to shoot her.'

'Yes.' Appleby's voice tensed. 'Then I tried to strangle her. All that did was make Cynster keep a closer watch on her, but I hoped it was also frightening her enough to keep her from remembering me. I tried to get at her again during the Ballyclose ball – I suspected she might search Cedric's hats. My plan didn't work, but then . . . she got me to walk out onto the terrace and around the corner with her, asking after Cedric . . . I could hardly believe my luck. I almost strangled her and hid the body in the bushes, but people might have seen us leave the ballroom together. Then Cynster arrived. I had to watch her walk away again.'

Phyllida glanced, briefly, at Lucifer.

'Then she found the hat. Worse, she took it to Cedric. If I didn't act immediately, I'd be found out. So I wrote the note from Molly, knocked Phyllida out, and set the fire.

'The hat burned, Phyllida didn't.' Appleby's tone was terse. 'I gave up trying to kill her. At least the hat was gone – she had no proof to connect me with anything. But you'd put locks on this house, and there was still the possibility that suspicion would turn my way. I obviously had to act boldly and decisively to bring my search to a rapid and successful conclusion. The fete gave me the perfect opportunity. So here we are.'

After a moment, Lucifer said, 'You meant to take a hostage.'

'Of course. It was the only way to get the job done – too risky to search a shelf or two at a time. I want that volume of *Aesop's Fables* in my hands before nightfall.'

Phyllida's tongue burned with the need to ask why. She glanced at Flick, and saw the identical thought in her eyes. They both drew breath, then turned their attention back to the shelves and continued pretending to search.

Silence fell, broken only by the steady shuffle and thump as books were hauled out, then returned to their places. After some minutes, Phyllida glanced across the room. Lucifer caught her eye; he nodded.

Phyllida moved across the bookcase as if starting on the next shelf, and slid out the brown, buckramcovered tome whose spine bore the title *Aesop's Fables* in simple gold lettering. She weighed the book in her hand, then opened the cover — she could see where Lucifer had lifted a corner of the front cover paper. She pressed her fingers into the thick cover; there was a softness behind the paper. Lucifer had said he'd checked; she trusted he'd known what he'd been doing.

Shutting the book, she marveled that such an innocent-looking thing could be responsible for three deaths. For depriving Lucius Appleby of his sanity. Certainly his humanity. It had nearly accounted for her, too.

Straightening her shoulders, she lifted her head and looked across the room at Appleby. 'I believe this' – she held out the book – 'is the volume you seek.'

Appleby nearly stepped forward, nearly stepped away from Sweetie, but at the last he pulled back.

He couldn't read the title. He stared at the book hungrily, then licked his lips. He flicked a glance at Lucifer and Demon. 'Everyone stay still.' Appleby tugged Sweetie to her feet, then locked his arm about her shoulders as before, the knife in his right hand. He nodded at Phyllida. 'Hand the book to Mrs Hemmings, then retreat to where you are now. Everyone else, stay where you are.'

Phyllida did as he asked. Mrs Hemmings turned to Appleby. He beckoned her forward with the knife. 'Give the book to Miss Sweet.'

Mrs Hemmings approached cautiously, then pressed the book into her old friend's trembling hands. 'There, now.'

Mrs Hemmings stepped back.

'Good.' Appleby glanced briefly down at the book. He was shaking. 'Open the front cover.'

Sweetie fumbled but did so. His gaze on Lucifer, Demon, and the other men, Appleby grasped the cover, not looking but pressing his fingertips into the concealed pocket. A fleeting expression of unutterable relief, of flaring victory, traversed his face, then his expression blanked.

He closed the book. 'I want all of you to move to the end of the room, up against the bookcases.'

Lucifer hesitated, then moved down the room. The others followed. All except Lady Huddlesford. She stood her ground.

'Miss Sweet is nearly done in.' Lady Huddlesford lifted her chin; she had never looked so imperious. 'If you want a hostage, take me.'

Miss Sweet blinked. Trapped against Appleby like some poor, innocent bird, she peered at Lady Huddlesford and visibly rallied. 'Why, thank you, Margaret. That's a very kind offer, but . . .' Despite Appleby's arm, Sweetie straightened her spine. 'I believe I'll manage. It's quite all right, really.'

Lady Huddlesford considered, then inclined her head. 'If you're sure, Amelia.' With that, she swung majestically around and joined the others.

'If that's settled' – Appleby's voice sounded strained, wild excitement mingling with something closer to panic – 'we'll leave you. I'll take Miss Sweet as far as the wood. I'll hear any footsteps long before you reach us. If I do, things will not go well for Miss Sweet. However, if you remain precisely where you are until she returns to you, you have my word she will not be harmed.' He paused, his gaze flicking over Lucifer, Demon, Jonas, Sir Jasper – if he was searching for understanding, there was none to be had. 'I never meant to kill anyone, not even Jerry. If there'd been some other way . . .' He blinked, then straightened. Pulling Sweetie with him, he shuffled sideways to the door. 'I will kill anyone who gets in my way.'

'We'll wait here.' Lucifer kept his voice calm and steady, as he had throughout.

Appleby nodded. 'In that case, I'll bid you farewell.'

Under his breath, Lucifer murmured, *'Au revoir.'*

★　★　★

They waited. With a raised hand, Lucifer stopped anyone from moving. 'He's on the edge – we're not going to give him any reason to panic.'

Minutes crawled past. They heard the scrunch of gravel, the sound dying away as Appleby dragged Sweetie through the kitchen garden toward the wood. They exchanged glances but no words. They were all thinking of Sweetie.

Then came a patter on the gravel, drawing closer to the house. It was so light a sound, they were too afraid to imagine it was footsteps. Then the baize door at the back of the hall banged the wall; in a rush of pitter-patter steps, Sweetie appeared in the dining room doorway.

'He's gone!' She fluttered her hands furiously. 'Away through the woods he ran!' She flung out an arm in the general direction of the wood – then fainted.

Lucifer caught her before she hit the floor. He carried her into the drawing room and laid her on the *chaise*.

Later, when she recovered and told her story to the assembled ladies of the village, Miss Sweet was, for the first time in her life, the heroine of the hour.

CHAPTER 21

As afternoon edged into evening, Lucifer, Phyllida, Demon, and Flick, with Jonas, Sir Jasper, Mr Filing, and Cedric, gathered in the library to make a new plan.

'I've sent Dodswell to fetch Thompson and Oscar,' Lucifer told them.

'Aha!' Demon said. 'So *that's* what you meant by "*au revoir.*"'

Phyllida and Flick and everyone else looked their silent question; Lucifer explained. 'Someone approached the Beer smuggling gang to arrange passage to France. It had to be tonight. The Beer gang told the man to meet with Oscar's band, who would normally run a cargo tonight.'

Jonas looked out the window. The wind had come up as the sun had gone down; the storm was moving steadily in. 'No one will be running anything tonight.'

'I know that, you know that, most of us know that. The question is, will Appleby know that?'

'He was born and raised and lived most of his life in Stafford,' Demon put in. 'Stafford's about as far from the coast as it's possible to get, so chances are he won't immediately recognize the implications of the weather.'

'Then he'll go to the meeting place expecting to meet smugglers.' Phyllida was sitting beside Lucifer's desk.

'Men who have as much to hide as he does,' Lucifer observed. 'That's the only sort he'll feel safe approaching. He intended today to be a last and successful effort. He came to the Manor with his plans made, his arrangements in place – he never intended to return to Ballyclose.'

Cedric snorted. 'The horse he rode here came back a few hours ago. No other horses are missing.'

Lucifer glanced at Demon. 'With us here, both with strong teams, escaping on horseback would have been risky.'

'He's a cautious sort, yet . . .' Demon shook his head. 'Fancy spending five years searching for something you'd only heard of from someone else's letter. And then it turns out the thing's not even still there to be found.'

'He didn't know that. He's obsessed.' Phyllida hugged herself. 'That's the only explanation. He's mad.'

'This picture that Appleby thought was in the book – he said it hadn't surfaced.' Sir Jasper glanced at Lucifer. 'That seem reasonable to you?'

Lucifer nodded. 'The fanfare surrounding the discovery of a lost miniature by an old master would not be easy to miss. He's correct on that. I haven't heard anything.'

'But if it's not in the book and hasn't been rediscovered, where is it?'

Lucifer looked at Phyllida. 'You remember the item Horatio asked me to appraise – the item that brought me here?'

Phyllida stared. 'You think it might be that?'

'It's the sort of thing Horatio would ask my opinion on. I'm familiar with the private collections of old masters held by various members of the aristocracy as well as the Crown. Even more to the point, it's an item he would guard very closely and tell no one else about.'

'So where is it?'

'Hidden.' Lucifer looked up at the sound of the front-door knocker. 'We'll have to turn the house inside out, but first we must deal with Appleby.'

Bristleford ushered Thompson and Oscar in, then approached Lucifer. As the others pulled up chairs to join the council, Bristleford murmured, 'With your permission, sir, Covey, Hemmings, and I would respectfully ask to be included in any little excursion you might be planning.'

Lucifer glanced into Bristleford's earnest face, then nodded. 'Yes, of course. In fact, if Mrs Hemmings can manage out there, perhaps you, Covey, and Hemmings could join us.'

'Thank you, sir. I'll fetch Covey and Hemmings.'

Bristleford retreated. Phyllida caught Lucifer's eye; she closed her hand over his on the desk. 'They haven't yet gotten over the fact that they let someone kill Horatio.'

Lucifer nodded, then turned to the others. Briskly, he outlined the situation. Oscar described the area where the smugglers met, the knoll to which the Beer gang had directed the impatient human cargo. They made their plans quickly, then they rose.

'Remember,' Sir Jasper warned, 'no heroics and no unnecessary violence. I don't want to have to take anyone else up for murder.'

'There should be no need for any real action. There's too many of us for him to escape, and other than that knife, he'll be unarmed.' Lucifer scanned the men's faces. 'We'll meet at the knoll as soon as darkness falls – no one be late.'

With the words 'Aye' and 'We'll be there—' the men departed.

Following them into the hall, Flick caught Phyllida's eye. 'I wonder if I could have a word.' Linking her arm in Phyllida's, Flick turned to the stairs.

Lucifer and Demon, reaching the library door, saw the loves of their lives, heads together, disappear upstairs.

'That doesn't look good,' Demon said.

Lucifer grimaced. 'I suppose we'd better face this like men.'

His expression hardening, Demon headed for the stairs. 'We can but try.'

Twenty minutes later, Lucifer and Demon met at the head of the stairs. Their ladies were with them. Lucifer stared at Flick. Demon stared, equally surprised, at Phyllida. Then the cousins looked at each other.

'I won't ask if you don't,' Demon offered.

Grim-faced, Lucifer nodded. 'Agreed.'

Neither Flick nor Phyllida appeared to hear; they led the way down the stairs, stepping easily in breeches and boots.

With Lucifer, Demon followed, his gaze shifting from his beloved's neat rear to Phyllida's shapely thighs. As they descended the last flight, he shook his head. 'I'll be damned if any of our forebears ever had to deal with this.'

Dodswell and Gillies were waiting, mounted, at the side of the house, both holding a pair of horses saddled – no sidesaddles, Lucifer noted. There was quite a little party gathered in the twilight, none of whom seemed to find anything remarkable in Flick's or Phyllida's attire. As they lifted their respective ladies to their saddles, then mounted alongside them, both Cynsters' hackles subsided – a little.

They set out. Lucifer kept a close eye on Phyllida; she sent him a sidelong glance. After she soared over the first fence and left him pushing to regain his position beside her, he stopped watching her and paid attention to their direction.

Crossing field after field, they headed south to the coast. Phyllida led the way – she was the only one who knew where they were going. The breeze strengthened, the salty tang increasing. A cottage appeared through the gloom, dwarfed by the huge barn behind it. Phyllida turned up the rutted track; she led them to the barn. They'd agreed to leave the horses there so as not to risk alerting Appleby.

The old farmer and his wife greeted Phyllida, clearly old friends. Dodswell returned from tethering their mounts. 'Quite a few already in there – looks like Thompson with Sir Jasper and the others.'

'Good.' Lucifer looked around. 'Oscar will walk in with the gang and ponies as usual.'

Demon, too, had been scanning the woods. 'How do you want to do this?'

'Strung out, single file, slowly. The meeting's not until full dark – we have time to be careful.'

They were. With Phyllida in the lead, Lucifer at her shoulder, they walked quietly through the woods, silently skirted two fields, then entered the last stand of stunted trees close by the cliff's edge.

The others were there, waiting. Without words, the party from the Manor spread out, clinging to the deepening shadows under the trees almost encircling the grassy knoll. The land sloped up from the tree line to the cliff's edge and up from either side; beyond the knoll, the cliff fell away.

They settled, crouching in the shadows, the sounds of their shuffling subsumed beneath the relentless pounding of the surf on the rocks far below. The wind was strong, blowing cold in their faces. No ship would dare approach this treacherous coast with such a wind behind it.

An hour later, the storm had taken possession of the skies; darkness had fallen like a shroud across the land. Muscles had stiffened, joints were aching, yet still they waited patiently.

Then the tramp of feet reached them. Minutes later, the night shift of the Colyton Import Company arrived on the scene. They were all there – Oscar, Hugey, Marsh, and the rest. They milled about on the lower slope of the knoll, huddling against the wind.

'How long do we have to wait for this blighter?' Hugey asked for them all.

'He'd better make it soon,' Oscar growled. 'We got better things to do.'

'I'm here, said a voice. 'If it's me you're waiting for.'

They all turned, peering through the darkness. Lucius Appleby staggered up from a hollow off to the side of the knoll. His clothes were disheveled. He clutched the volume of *Aesop's Fables* to his chest. His hair ruffled wildly in the wind. For a moment he appeared drunk, uncoordinated, then, with a visible effort, he pulled himself together. 'About time you got here. I want nothing more than to leave this wretched place.'

Every word stung, bitter as gall. He swayed, his gaze fixed on the supposed smugglers. He spared not a glance toward the trees. 'Well?' he grumbled, voice rising. 'What're we waiting for? Let's go.'

He took an unsteady step toward them.

The smugglers, all except Oscar, backed away. They fanned out as they went, eyes never leaving Appleby. Then they joined with those moving forward, out from under the trees.

Appleby's eyes widened. Even in the poor light, the shock on his face as he took in the solid cordon and realized its meaning was evident. '*No!*'

Whirling, he scrambled up the knoll.

'Here!' Oscar remained on the knoll's lower slope. 'Don't go near the edge.'

Sir Jasper stepped forward. He regarded Appleby sternly. 'In my capacity as magistrate, I charge you, Lucius Appleby, with three counts of murder and three of attempted murder, to all of which you stand self-confessed.' He waited for a moment, then beckoned. 'Come down, man – you can see there's no escape. No sense making it worse.'

Book clutched to his chest, Appleby stared at him, then threw back his head and laughed maniacally. '*Make it worse?*' He caught his breath on a gasp and stared at Sir Jasper. 'You have no idea.'

'You see this?' Appleby thrust out the book, staggering back as he did so. 'I killed three men to get my hands on this. Bartered my immortal soul and worse. Five long years I patiently searched, and for what? What do you think my life, my soul, would be worth?'

He wrenched open the front cover, holding it for all to see. The cover paper had been ripped away, the padding, too, exposing the blank board of the inner face. 'Nothing.' Appleby's voice dropped to a sobbing whisper, then abruptly rose to a shriek. *'There's nothing there!'* He yelled it to the skies. 'Some bastard got there before me!'

Eyes wild, he flung the book at Sir Jasper, then whirled and raced onto the knoll.

'No! Don't – !' Oscar scrabbled up the slope. Thompson moved up behind his brother; Lucifer and Demon stepped forward.

Lips drawn back, Appleby turned on them. 'Come and get me, then.' He brandished his knife. 'Who'll be first?'

He staggered wildly as he backed, grotesquely outlined against the roiling sky.

Thompson reached forward and locked a huge hand on Oscar's shoulder. 'You don't understand—'

'It's *you* who don't understand. I'm not going to pay – not when there's *nothing there.*' Appleby laughed wildly. 'I've already paid with the last five years of my life.'

'You took the lives of three others.' Lucifer pitched his voice over the rising wind.

'They got in my way!' Appleby yelled. He edged back, eyes darting this way, then that. 'If they hadn't, they'd still be alive – it was *their fault.*'

The last word was swallowed by a thunderous, murmurous *shusssh.*

Everyone froze.

Then Thompson pulled Oscar back. In the trees, Phyllida clutched Flick's arm. 'Oh, no.'

Appleby didn't understand. He stood on the cliff's edge, staring wildly from one shocked face to the next.

'What?' he asked. *'Wha—'*

The ground beneath him disappeared; one instant he was there, then he was gone.

Lightning flashed, but it was tons of earth hitting rocks, crashing into the sea, that provided the thunder. The wind gusted hard, forcing them to hide their faces until the buffeting eased.

They looked up the slope. The new cliff edge cut through the middle of the knoll's top.

Both Lucifer and Demon turned and walked back into the trees. Phyllida went wordlessly into Lucifer's arms, hugging him tight, inexpressibly thankful for his warmth, for the solidity of the arms that locked about her, for the feel of his jaw against her hair. 'Will he be dead?' she finally whispered.

'That cliff's at least six hundred feet high. I don't think there's any alternative.'

Others wanted to be certain. They started off through the trees, Sir Jasper and Oscar bringing up the rear.

'The cliff path Oscar's band uses is safe,' Phyllida explained. Together with Flick and Demon, she and Lucifer trailed the band. They reached the windswept outcrop where the path started. Most of the group were strung out below, heading down.

A series of lightning flashes out over the Channel provided sudden illumination. Everyone stopped and searched. Then there were shouts of 'There!' Arms pointed. From within the protection of Lucifer's arms, Phyllida looked down. The body of Lucius Appleby lay spread-eagled, facedown on the black water. There was no sign of movement, of life. Distance hid the damage undoubtedly inflicted by the rocks and the waves. As they watched, the body lifted on the swell, then whirled and was drawn out, toward the dark sea.

The light faded. Night closed in, blacker than before.

Lucifer's arms tightened around her. He bent his head and pressed a kiss to her temple. 'It's over,' he murmured. 'Come, let's go home.'

To her surprise, he took her back to the Grange. Demon and Flick didn't come in; at Lucifer's request, they took his and Phyllida's horses with them when they rode on to the Manor.

Everyone gathered in the drawing room. Phyllida, still in breeches, organized drinks and sustenance to chase away the lingering chills, both of the elements and of the evil that had been Lucius Appleby.

There were many exclamations and much shaking of heads, but a sense of ending, of relief, of rightness, prevailed. The threat that had disturbed the peace of Colyton was gone.

In the instant Phyllida fully realized that truth, she sought Lucifer's eye and smiled; she was no longer surprised they were here. At last she had her peaceful life back – the serenity and security of the village were restored. She was safe again. The only thing they'd lost was Horatio. And in his place, they had Lucifer.

Her eyes followed him as he moved through the room, exchanging words – the right words, she was sure – with Oscar, Thompson, and the other men. Life turned, changed, and moved on. Fate sometimes moved in mysterious ways.

Gradually, the crowd departed, at peace again. By tomorrow morning, the tidings would be spread throughout the village, the great houses, the farms and cottages.

Phyllida stopped beside Lucifer. Gazing out at the darkness of the back lawn, he drained his glass, then looked down at her. His gaze roved her face, then returned to her eyes. 'There's a question I've been wanting to ask you, but it can wait until tomorrow.' He hesitated, then handed her his glass. 'I'll call in the morning.'

Phyllida opened her eyes wide. 'Does that mean you're going to leave me to walk back through the wood alone in the dark?' When he frowned at her, she smiled and patted his arm. 'I'm coming home – to the Manor.'

He blinked, then cast a glance at Sir Jasper, shaking hands with Cedric, the last of the others to leave. 'Much as I might wish that—'

'It's got nothing to do with your wishes,' she informed him. 'You forget – all my things are there.'

'All?'

'When you told Sweetie to pack my things, she

did – all of them. She's an incurable romantic, so, for better or for worse, I'm afraid *all* my things are at the Manor.'

Lucifer looked down at her, his dark eyes very blue. Then he brushed a thumb over her lower lip. 'For better or for worse?'

Phyllida smiled; she pushed him toward the French doors. 'Wait for me on the terrace – I must speak with Papa.'

Lucifer glanced back at Sir Jasper, but Phyllida shook her head and pushed, so he went. She watched as he stepped over the threshold, drank in the broad shoulders, the strength cloaked in that effortless grace, then she smiled serenely and returned to her father.

Sir Jasper met her in the middle of the room. He took her hands in his. 'Well, m'dear – a great relief, having this settled. Can't say I'm sorry Appleby's gone – a bad egg he was, no doubt of that.'

'Indeed, Papa.'

'Well, then.' Sir Jasper stole a glance at Lucifer, waiting on the terrace looking out at the night. 'I suppose, now there's no more danger, you'll be moving back, heh?'

His tone was neither insistent nor expectant; it was curious. He peered at her from under his shaggy brows, a light very like hope in his eyes.

'No, Papa.' Smiling, Phyllida stretched up and placed a kiss on his cheek. 'My place now is elsewhere.'

'Oh?' Sir Jasper brightened; he all but grinned and rubbed his hands in delight. 'Right, then – well, I daresay I'll see you tomorrow . . . ?'

Phyllida chuckled and patted his arm. 'I daresay. And now I'll bid you a good night.'

Leaving her father, she walked to the French doors. Stepping outside, she slid a hand into Lucifer's arm. Just as he had been doing, she looked up at the sky, at the racing clouds streaming, fleeing before the thunderheads.

Lucifer glanced back, then she felt his gaze on her face. After a moment, she met his eyes. In the poor light, she couldn't see their expression, but possessiveness, protectiveness, fell about her like a cloak.

He closed his hand over hers. 'Let's go home.'

She let him lead her there, through the wood, now a-flurry with the storm. As the wind rose and the branches lashed more furiously, they walked faster and faster; eventually, he pulled her along at a run. She was laughing when he dragged her from the trees, down the drive, and around the house. She imagined he was heading for the front door, but once they gained the front of the house, she realized that wasn't his goal.

He tugged her across Horatio's garden – it was screened from the wind by the wood, the house, the village, and its own stand of trees. In the dark of the humid night, it was a paradise of evocative scents, of lush growth and mysterious shapes. Lucifer hurried her to the honeysuckle-draped, peony-backed arbor where they'd once before paused of an evening and discussed the realities of love.

Halting, he faced her. His dark hair was tousled, as if she'd already run her fingers through it; his face was hard-edged, his mobile lips straight. He studied her as she was studying him, then, her hands in his, he went down on one knee.

'Phyllida Tallent, will you marry me? Will you help me tend this garden over all the years to come?'

He'd pitched his voice above the roar of the wind, above the wild threshing of the leaves.

Phyllida looked down, into his face. He'd spun her world around, then steadied it; he'd taught her so much, answered so many questions. She had only one left. 'This garden needs constant love to keep it blooming. Do you love me that much?'

He held her gaze. 'More.' He kissed the backs of her hands, first one, then the other. 'I'll love you forever.'

Phyllida pulled him to his feet. 'Just as well, for I'll love you for even longer.' She went into his arms, forever safe where she belonged. 'I'll love you for longer than forever.'

His arms closed around her. Their lips met, melded; their bodies eased against each other, seeking remembered delights.

Lucifer broke the kiss to ask, 'When can we marry?'

Phyllida drew back. 'It's Saturday. If we speak to Mr Filing tonight, he could read the banns tomorrow. Then we could marry in just over two weeks.'

They looked up the common at the Rectory. The small house lay in darkness. 'I really don't think,' Lucifer said, 'that Filing will mind being woken – not for this.'

He didn't; the curate was delighted when he heard their reason for hauling him from his bed. He assured them that the banns would be called in the morning. Declining his offer of a celebratory sherry on the grounds of the imminent downpour, they left the Rectory and raced down the common – anticipating a celebration of a different sort.

They reached the duck pond and the skies opened. They were soaked, dripping and bedraggled by the time they reached the Manor's front porch. The smell of rain-washed greenery and the ever-present perfume of the garden – their garden now – swept over them as they stood catching their breath while Lucifer hunted for his key.

He unlocked the door and swung it wide. Phyllida entered; Lucifer followed and reset the lock. Turning, he saw Phyllida standing just outside the open drawing room. He joined her as she stepped into the doorway. Slipping an arm around her waist, he held her back against him.

Phyllida crossed her arms over his and leaned back to whisper, 'It's peaceful here now – can you sense it?'

He could. He rubbed his chin over the wet silk

of her hair. 'Horatio's gone to talk to Martha about her pansies.'

Phyllida turned her head and smiled. Sliding around in his arms, she touched his cheek. 'You're the most fanciful man.'

He kissed her, then murmured, 'I know what I fancy at the moment.'

So did she. Her sigh was just a little skittery, just a touch breathless. 'We'd better get upstairs.'

'If you insist.'

Phyllida led the way with him padding at her heels like some obedient jungle cat. She detoured via the linen press to fetch two large towels, then led him, not to her room, but to his. He made no demur but went past her to light the lamp that sat atop one tallboy.

It was pouring outside. Lightning still flickered and thunder rolled, but the storm front had already swept past. Rubbing her hair with the towel, Phyllida pushed the door shut, then turned – just as Lucifer adjusted the wick so the lamp shed a golden glow through the room.

'Great heavens!' She stared. 'That's *it!*'

She walked toward Lucifer, her gaze fixed beyond him. He glanced around to see what had so excited her. 'It, what?' Then the penny dropped and he stared, too.

'Don't tell me it's always been here.' Phyllida reached up to lift the traveling writing desk from its perch on the corner of the tallboy.

'All right, I won't tell you,' Lucifer replied. 'But

you didn't say *traveling* writing desk – I've been looking for something with four legs.'

With the polished wooden box in her hands, Phyllida turned. 'I *must* have said . . .' She caught his eye and grimaced. 'Well, maybe I didn't. But I *meant* a traveling writing desk – *I* knew what I was looking for.'

'Anyway, I thought you'd searched the whole house.'

'I didn't search in here. I didn't imagine you'd miss a traveling writing desk if it was sitting in your room. The only other time I've been in here was at night in the dark.'

'I didn't miss it – I knew it was there. It just never occurred to me that *that's* the sort of desk you meant.' He studied the box. 'Where's this secret drawer? It doesn't look big enough to have one.'

'That's why it's such a good hiding place.' Phyllida sat on the bed and placed the desk on her thighs; Lucifer sat beside her. 'It's here – see?' Running her fingers along one of the back side panels, she found the catch and pressed it. The panel swung outward. Sliding her fingers in, she felt around, then gripped and pulled a sheaf of papers into the light.

She stared at them. 'Good Lord!' She dropped the bundle between them on the bedspread.

They both sat, transfixed, not by the bundle of letters predictably tied with a pink ribbon, but by the small rolled canvas that had been tucked in with them.

535

It had unrolled just a little. Just enough to show the deep browns and rich reds of oils, and part of a hand.

Lucifer recovered first. 'Careful – we're both dripping.'

Phyllida wriggled off the bed. Lucifer stood and grabbed the second towel. While he rubbed at his hair and mopped his face, Phyllida shut the secret drawer and put the writing desk back on the tallboy. Returning to the bed, she swiped up her towel and dried her hands and reblotted her face, then twisted her hair up in the towel. Then she gingerly picked up Mary Anne's and Robert's letters and deposited them beside the writing desk. 'Don't want to get them wet and have the ink run, not after all this.'

Lucifer humphed. He joined her as she went back to the bed.

Phyllida eyed the rolled painting, then gestured. 'You do it.'

Lucifer picked up the canvas; touching only the unpainted edges, he unrolled it.

Even in the lamplight, the jeweled tones glowed. A woman – a lady by the richness of her dress – sat smiling at the painter. Her gown of wine-dark velvet had a square, heavily embroidered neckline; her headdress was a form of wimple, artfully folded. Her forehead was high, plucked, as had been the fashion centuries before.

Phyllida drew in a breath. 'This is what was in *Aesop's Fables*, isn't it? This is the item Horatio

536

invited you down here to appraise. The miniature – the old masterpiece – that Appleby killed three men for.'

Lucifer nodded. 'I wouldn't be surprised if he wasn't the first to have killed for this lady.'

Phyllida looked from the miniature to his face, then back again. 'It's genuine?'

'It's too perfect not to be. Too much like his other works.'

'Whose work? Who painted it?'

'Holbein the Younger, court-portraitist for Henry the Eighth.'

They spent the next hour talking, speculating, deciding that the miniature belonged in a museum. That resolved, Lucifer returned the painting to the secret drawer, then fetched the lamp and placed it on the table beside the bed.

He'd pulled off his wet boots and stripped off his coat and shirt long before; Phyllida was still in her damp shirt and breeches. She regarded him speculatively, fascinated by the way the flickering lamplight played over the muscles of his chest. She let her gaze drift downward, to where the wet fabric of his breeches molded lovingly to his form, then languidly brought her gaze back to his face – to his eyes, smoldering blue.

She raised a haughty brow.

He smiled. Intently. His fingers closed on the buttons on his waistband. He held her gaze as if daring her to watch as he peeled the wet breeches from him. Phyllida raised her brow higher – and did. His breeches hit the floor with a splat. He came onto the bed in a prowling crawl. With an ease that still shocked her – tantalized her and left her breath stuck in her throat – he picked her up and rearranged her so she was kneeling, sitting back on her ankles, her back to him as he knelt behind her, his naked thighs outside hers. She was facing the end of the four-poster bed. With the curtains tied back, she looked out at her reflection in the long, wide mirror hanging on the opposite wall.

The sight was mesmerizing. His shoulders showed above and beyond hers; she looked fragile and vulnerable all but surrounded by him. Female and male, one dressed, one naked; the contrasts were dramatic. His hands looked very large clamped about her waist. He checked the vision he was creating, then glanced down. Phyllida watched as his hands rose and his fingers busied themselves with the buttons of her shirt. At least, this time she wouldn't have to sew them back on.

'I'm going to strip these wet clothes from you, then I'm going to dry you, then warm you up – we wouldn't want you to catch a chill.'

Phyllida had no wish to argue. She leaned her turbaned head back on his shoulder and, watching from under half closed lids, let him get on with it.

Let him peel the wet shirt from her, then unwind her sodden bands. Watched him grab a towel and apply it to her breasts in a slow, circular motion

538

When her breasts were not only dry but swollen and warm, peaked and firm, he dropped the towel and started on her breeches. Removing them required a little more cooperation; giggling at the curses and inventive suggestions he murmured between laying kisses along the back of her bare shoulders and licking errant drops from her skin, she helped him ease the cold, clinging fabric from her hips and down her thighs.

Without warning, he lifted her, whisking the wet garment over her knees and calves; it went flying to join the pile on the floor. He picked up the towel as he set her down before him, still on her knees, still facing the mirror. Fragile, vulnerable, and naked, surrounded by his strength.

He wielded the towel to telling effect, using the lightly abrasive pile to tease and tantalize until all of her body was flushed and heated, until every inch of her skin was sensitized and aching, until she was awash with a wanton desire that only he could slake.

Then he dropped the towel.

She was dry. He set his clever fingers, strong hands, wicked lips, and even wickeder tongue to the task of warming her up. Until she was gasping, heated to the point where her skin felt afire and molten need had spread through every vein. Through her lashes she saw her body flushed with desire, a glow unlike any other. She needed him, wanted him – she arched in his arms, sank her fingers into his thighs, and dropped her head back to his shoulder.

He shifted her, urging her on, molding her as he wished, showing her how to be as wanton as she dared.

Then he joined with her. So easily, so perfectly, so completely. He closed his arms around her and rocked her, rocked into her; she closed her eyes and savored the feel of him buried so deep within her.

He was as hot as the sun, burning up all around her, muscles flexing like hot steel all about her. He showed her what could be, then let her choose, let her turn and clasp her long legs about his hips and take him deep, let her wrap her arms about him and find his lips with hers, let her take him with her into oblivion.

Together. Forever.

They were married on a Monday, the day after Mr Filing read the banns for the third time. Mr Filing officiated before a church packed to the rafters. Everyone from the village, everyone from the surrounding farms and houses, was there, as were numerous Cynsters who had moved heaven and earth to be present.

Gabriel stood beside his brother and happily handed him the ring. Flick and Mary Anne were bridesmaids. Demon was the second groomsman.

In the body of the church sat Gabriel's wife, Alathea, smiling fondly, and Celia Cynster, Lucifer's mother, who cried happily throughout the short service. Beside her, Martin, Lucifer's father, looked smugly satisfied as he handed clean hand-kerchiefs to his spouse. Lucifer's three sisters, Heather, Eliza, and Angelica, all beamed.

Then it was done, and the last member of the Bar Cynster was wed.

Lucifer bent to kiss Phyllida; the sun broke from the wispy clouds to pour through the oriel window, enclosing the bride and groom in a nimbus of jeweled light. Then they smiled and turned, man and wife, to greet their family and friends.

At the bride and groom's insistence, the wedding breakfast was held at the Manor. The guests spread through the house, spilled onto the lawns, and strolled the wonderful garden. Standing at one side of the lawn with his father, Gabriel, and Demon, Lucifer watched as Celia all but paraded her new daughter-in-law, her delight in her second son's choice plain to see. Phyllida had, to the last, remained nervous of her reception into the ducal dynasty; it had taken Celia only three minutes to lay such trepidations to rest. In doing so, she'd earned her second son's enduring gratitude, but that wasn't something he intended to tell her. As a Cynster wife, Celia had weapons enough.

Beside him, Martin chuckled, the sound fond but wary. Lucifer, Demon, and Gabriel glanced at him, then followed his gaze to where Celia and Phyllida had met up with Alathea and Flick. They had their heads together.

Lucifer straightened. Demon sighed. Gabriel shook his head. It was left to Martin to put their thoughts into words. 'Why we bother fighting it, the Lord only knows. Inevitability, thy name is woman.'

Lucifer's lips lifted. 'Actually, for us, I believe that should go: Inevitability, thy name is *wife.*'

'Too true,' Gabriel murmured.

'Indeed.' Demon watched as their four ladies broke from their huddle and headed their way. 'What now?'

'Whatever it is, we can't escape,' Martin replied. 'Take my advice – surrender with good grace.' He strolled forward to intercept Celia.

Gabriel grimaced. 'I wish he hadn't used that word.'

'"Surrender"?' Demon asked.

'Hmm. It might be the truth, but I don't want to hear it.' So saying, Gabriel gracefully deflected Alathea, turning her toward the shrubbery.

'There's a secluded little folly down by the lake,' Lucifer murmured to Demon.

'Where are you headed?' Demon murmured back.

'There's this arbor in the garden I'm working on filling with pleasant memories.'

Demon grinned. 'Good luck.'

Lucifer saluted as they parted, each to his own special lady. 'Good luck to us all.'

And with that, the Bar Cynster surrendered gladly, each to his own, very special, fate.

EPILOGUE

August 1820
Somersham, Cambridgeshire

It was nearly two years to the day that she'd first sighted this house, first strolled the wide lawns. Honoria, Duchess of St Ives, stood on the front porch of her home, Somersham Place, and looked about her, marveling at the changes, and at how much, despite all, remained the same.

The side lawn was filled with family and connections, the froth of summer gowns scattered like confetti over the green. Many had taken advantage of the shade offered by the ancient trees to lounge at ease; others strolled, stopping by the various groups to chat, to learn the latest news, and, most of all, to greet the new family members.

There were many of those. That fact infused the gathering with an untempered joy, an effervescent sense of burgeoning life that was tangible.

Two years ago, many of those present had gathered here to mourn. Although Tolly, and even Charles, had not been forgotten, the family, like all great families, had moved on. They'd prospered,

543

they'd conquered – now they were enjoying the fruits of their labors.

Cradling one such apple in one arm, Honoria raised her skirts and descended to the lawn. Before she'd taken three steps, her husband detached himself from one group and strode, fiendishly handsome and arrogantly confident as ever, to join her.

'How is he?' Devil bent his dark head to peek at his second son.

Michael blinked, yawned, then grabbed his sire's finger.

'He's fed and dry and therefore content. And I believe it's your turn to play nursemaid.' Honoria divested herself of the shawl-wrapped bundle. Devil accepted the charge with alacrity. Honoria hid her grin; she knew he'd been waiting to play the proud father. It never ceased to amaze her that he – indeed, all the males of his family – while so strong and powerful and so arrogantly assured, so totally dominant, could and would, at the wave of a tiny hand, readily devote himself so completely to his offspring.

'Where's Sebastian?' She scanned the lawns for sign of their firstborn. He'd recently started to walk; running could not be far behind.

'He's with the twins.' Devil lifted his head and located the girls. 'They're on the steps of the summerhouse.'

There was a frown in his eyes; Honoria knew it wasn't because he doubted the twins' ability to watch over Sebastian. She patted his arm; when

544

he transfered his pale green gaze to her face, she smiled up at him. 'Consider this. Better they dream of having children of their own, therefore accepting all the steps that come before, than that they don't.'

It took him a moment to follow her reasoning, then his eyes hardened. 'I'd rather they didn't think about any of that at all.'

'You've as much chance of achieving that as of holding back the sun.' She squeezed his arm, then waved imperiously toward the guests. 'Now go and play host and show off our son, while I go and admire the others.'

Majestically established in a wrought-iron seat placed at the center of the lawn, the Dowager and Horatia held court. Between them, they lovingly juggled three tiny, shawl-wrapped bundles, exclaiming fondly, displaying their grandchildren for the edification of the surrounding crowd that, for the past thirty minutes, had constantly changed but not diminished in the least.

In a lounger to one side of the seat, Catriona, Lady of the Vale, lay resting, still pale, her hair a fiery halo around her head. The glow in her face as she watched Helena cradle her babies rendered her nothing less than radiant. She looked precisely what she was, a madonna who'd been blessed.

Richard stood beside the lounger, his fingers entwined with hers. His gaze constantly switched from his wife to his children and back again.

545

The expression in his dark eyes, on his lean, harsh-featured face, spoke louder than words of his pride and his joy.

Twins – one boy, one girl. If Catriona had guessed, she hadn't said a word, knowing how important it had been for Richard to travel south for this summer gathering of his clan. But twins rarely obeyed the typical schedules; they'd arrived a month early, small but hale and whole. So the next Lady of the Vale, Lucilla, had been the first ever born outside that mystical Scottish valley. She'd been born here, at Somersham Place, the ancestral home of her Sassenach forebears. Catriona had accepted that without a blink – she'd merely smiled and reminded Richard that the Lady knew what she was about.

And to keep him busy, there was Marcus – a son to train in all the complex management of the Vale lands and the people they supported. That was no longer a job that could be done by just one, so now they had two.

While much attention centered on the twins' red heads, there was just as much lavished on the fairhaired bundle Horatia rocked and jiggled. Christopher Reginald Cynster, Patience and Vane's son, had been born four weeks before, two weeks after Michael had made his orderly appearance. Thus, in common with Michael, Christopher was now an old hand at family gatherings; he yawned hugely, then batted aside his blankets, trying to latch onto a trailing lock of his grandmother's hair.

Everyone watching cooed and smiled delightedly; Christopher took it as nothing more than his due.

Noting his detachment, Lady Osbaldestone snorted. 'A Cynster to his toes – already! Always knew it was inherited. Looks to have passed on undiluted.' She shook her head, then paused, then she cackled as she turned away. 'Heaven help the ladies of 1850.'

Honoria checked that Helena and Horatia weren't tiring, exchanged a soft word and an understanding smile with Catriona, pressed Richard's hand, then moved on, looking over the throng, checking all was as it should be.

Having been delivered four weeks before, Patience was fully recovered, up and about. However, since it was his first time, Vane had yet to reconcile himself to allowing his wife out of his sight, indeed, very far from the protective circle of his arm. Honoria found them chatting with the General, Flick's erstwhile guardian, and his son, Dillon; they'd driven across for the day from Newmarket. In that circle, horses reigned supreme. Honoria exchanged speaking glances with Patience, then strolled on.

Flick and Demon were standing with a group surrounding Great-aunt Clara and little Miss Sweet, whom Lucifer and Phyllida had brought with them from Devon. Clara had already asked Miss Sweet to visit her in Cheshire; arrangements were being discussed and plans made.

Elsewhere, Gabriel and Alathea, and Lucifer and

Phyllida, like Flick and Demon, were making the rounds, ensuring they met and spoke with all the relatives, all the connections and close acquaintances, who had eagerly traveled to Cambridgeshire for the express purpose of meeting the new wives, and welcoming them and the latest crop of infants into the wider family.

Satisfied that all was well, Honoria spent a few minutes quietly slipping through the shade, noting, as a matriarch should, just where and with whom, and in what manner, the younger members of the family were employed.

Simon was there, growing taller by the hour, or so it seemed. His fair hair shone guinea-gold in the sun, as bright as Flick's. His face was finer boned than those of his older cousins, not as overtly aggressive. But the same strength was there, behind a countenance that was so like an angel's that it would undoubtedly, in time, make women weep. He was not of the Bar Cynster, but he was a Cynster nonetheless – the one who would bridge the gap between Honoria's sons' generation and their fathers'.

In the same group, spread upon the grass like so many tulips, so many blossoms just waiting to fully flower, were Heather, Eliza, Angelica, Henrietta, and Mary. Some younger, some older, but all with the same eagerness for life, an enthusiasm for living, in their faces.

Honoria smiled and strolled on. She turned her steps toward the summerhouse.

The twins greeted her with joy in their faces; the cause of their happiness was not far to seek.

'We're free!' Amanda flung her arms wide, just missing Sebastian as he clambered into Honoria's lap as she sat on the steps in the sun.

Settling him, Honoria leaned back against the archway and smiled at the girls. 'True, but now Lucifer's fixed in Devon, and between you and me, I can't see either him or Gabriel or even Demon back in town next Season – I rather think they'll have other things on their minds, if you take my meaning – then what, my dears, are your plans?'

'We're going to go through the ton's gentlemen,' Amelia answered.

'Systematically and methodically,' Amanda qualified

'We're not going to rush, and we're not going to be rushed.'

'We'll be nineteen next Season, so we have years yet, if we chose to be picky.'

'And there's no reason we shouldn't be – picky, I mean. After all, we are talking about the rest of our lives.'

'Indeed.' Honoria inclined her head in approval. There was so much she wanted to tell them, to warn them of, to guide them, but how could she explain when, for all that they had had two Seasons, they were still so inexperienced, so unaware? 'One thing,' she said, and knew she had their complete attention. 'If you seek love, don't expect it to be simple, don't expect it to be easy. If one thing is certain, it's that it'll be neither.

'If you want love, then by all means seek it out – search for it high and low. You know you'll always have us – all of us – here to help you, but when it comes down to it, love is a matter for each individual heart. No one can tell you, no one can warn you, no one can prepare you for what it will be like. When it comes, if it comes, you'll know it – and then you'll have to decide just how much you want it, how much you're willing to give to let it live.'

They heard her in silence; in silence, they digested her wisdom. Honoria looked across the lawn to where her disgustingly handsome husband, he who now stood at the very center of her life, cradled their younger son. Their elder son lay, a warm, heavy weight in her lap.

'Is it worth it?'

She couldn't be sure which of them had voiced the question – Amanda or Amelia; it didn't matter. The answer was the same, now and forever.

'Yes. Many times over, it's worth it, but only if you have the courage to give, and let it live.'

After a moment, Honoria stirred. Gathering sleepy Sebastian in her arms, she hefted him and stood, then strolled across the lawn to where she belonged, at his sire's side.

Devil had been watching her; one part of his mind and most of his soul was always with her. Who could have known? Who would have guessed?

Not even the joys of twitting his archenemy, not an enemy at all but they so enjoyed butting horns, was enough to interfere with that ephemeral connection between himself and his wife.

'Just whose idea was it,' Chillingworth asked, 'to elect me an honorary Cynster?'

At the accusatory tone, Devil turned a mild smile his way. 'Gabriel suggested it, and as you've been so remarkably helpful in assisting us in securing our futures, I seconded the motion, as did Demon, and the others were happy to support it. That's all it took. You are now, by election, a member of the clan.'

Chillingworth met his gaze. 'In *ceremonial* name only.'

Devil grinned. 'That will do.'

'It won't. I can assure you with absolutely no risk of contradiction that *electing* me to the clan will not make me susceptible to your particular curse.' After a moment of consideration, Chillingworth snorted. 'Anyway, what sort of thanks is that to bestow, even on your worst enemy?'

'In your case, it's the most useful of all – consider it as giving you a secret map to some treasure. Follow the instructions and you, too, could be rich. Take it from us – we did, and see where it's got us.'

What Chillingworth said in reply made Devil's lips twitch. 'Anyway,' he returned, 'you can't escape, so why not take the bull by the horns and make a virtue of necessity? You do, after all, need an heir, or that vacuous cousin of yours from Hampstead will inherit the title. Have I got that right?'

'You have, damn you – don't remind me. My mother's actually started holding you up as a pattern card of virtue. I'm tempted to invite you and Honoria to the Castle simply so experience can set her straight.'

'Do invite us down,' Devil murmured. 'We'll bring the family.'

'That's precisely why I haven't – I'm not that daft.' Chillingworth nodded at Michael, asleep in Devil's arm. 'Deposit that in my mother's lap and my life will be hell.'

'You're going to need one someday.'

'Ah, but I'm altogether adamant on the price I'm willing to pay.' Chillingworth watched as Honoria, Devil's heir asleep on her shoulder, stepped away from a group of guests and continued on her way toward them. One glance at Devil's face and Chillingworth shook his head. 'A simple marriage will achieve the necessary result. I see absolutely no reason to indulge in the extremes you Cynsters seem to find so unavoidable.'

Devil chuckled. 'I'm going to seriously enjoy dancing at your wedding.'

'The pertinent question is' – Chillingworth lowered his voice as Honoria neared – 'will I?' He smiled and sketched a bow to Honoria. 'I you'll excuse me, my dear, I must get back to

London tonight. I'll leave your husband to your tender mercies.'

He nodded at Devil, a smug glint in his eye.

Devil grinned back, unrepentant, undeterred.

'What was that about?' Honoria asked as Chillingworth strolled off.

'Vain hope.' Devil watched his old friend stride away, then he looked at his wife. He jiggled the sleeping baby. 'He's getting heavy. And Sebastian's sound asleep. Perhaps we should take them up to the nursery.'

Honoria was too busy checking Sebastian's sleeping face to notice the unreliable gleam that had appeared in her husband's green eyes. 'I'll find their nannies and have them take them up.'

'Let the nannies enjoy the last of the afternoon. We can take them up. There's plenty of people indoors to keep an ear open for them.'

'Well . . .' The motherly need to tuck her darlings in herself warred with Honoria's hostessly instincts. 'All right. We'll take them up, and I'll send the nannies up when we come down.'

They strolled into the house and up the stairs, the sleeping children their obvious excuse. No one thought anything of their departure.

No one noticed when they didn't immediately reappear.

Indeed, only those with sharp eyes and suspicious minds noticed that when the duke and duchess eventually rejoined their guests, the duchess's ivory skin was delicately flushed and her eyes held the dreamy look of a woman well loved, and that a certain male pride – a wholly Cynster expression – glowed in her husband's green eyes.

Times may change; Cynsters never do.